Lost PROPHECY

REALM OF SECRETS

C.C. RAE

iUniverse

LOST PROPHECY
REALM OF SECRETS

iUniverse books may be ordered through booksellers or by contacting:

iUniverse
1663 Liberty Drive
Bloomington, IN 47403
www.iuniverse.com
1-800-Authors (1-800-288-4677)

ISBN: 978-1-5320-3181-6 (sc)
ISBN: 978-1-5320-3180-9 (hc)
ISBN: 978-1-5320-3182-3 (e)

Library of Congress Control Number: 2017913834

Print information available on the last page

iUniverse rev. date: 09/26/2017

To my niece Jennah,
Growing up does not mean you have to stop believing in magic or chasing dreams. Be different, be silly, be you, no matter what others say.

1. Depart

Nicole sat in the middle of her bedroom floor with a nearly full camping backpack. It was the largest bag she had. There was still some space to spare. She glanced around her room, looking for her old school backpack with Raiden's books. She spotted it slouched against the wall below the window. As she stood, she could still feel the faintest ache in every muscle, a whisper of pain lingering from her encounter with Moira. With a sigh she leaned down, grabbed the strap of the bag, and brought it over to her pack.

On top was the book she had been reading, *Spell Casting: The Advanced Art*. She dropped it into the camping pack. Next she grabbed two more books, glanced at their spines—*Everyday Incantations, Charms & Curses* and *Magical Concepts and Theory*—and placed them with the first book.

At the bottom of the backpack there was one last book with a soft and pliable leather binding. There was no title on its cover or spine—a journal. As she turned the journal over in her hands, she couldn't believe it was only a week ago that all this had started. The night in Veil when they'd gone for the books and she'd learned about the Council had also been the night she'd met Gordan and set him free.

"Hey." Raiden's voice came from the hall outside her room. She jumped, ripped away from her thoughts, clutching the journal to her chest.

"Sorry," he said with a smile.

"It's okay," she replied, looking up at him framed by the doorway. He wore

1

a thin sweater. The bottom half was dark gray with horizontal white pinstripes, and the top half from neck to elbows was the same color as his turquoise eyes. He was still the most unbelievable part of all this to her. Not because his Caribbean-ocean eyes stood out in striking contrast to his brown skin and deep auburn hair, not even because he had come into her life through a portal from another realm, but because she'd never thought she would be drawn to someone as she was to him—she'd never wanted to be.

His gaze fell to the bags lying before her. "You're packing."

"We slept a whole day away," she said. "You're the one who said we needed to leave before another portal could open. It's already been twenty-four hours."

"Given everything that happened yesterday, I think it's acceptable to sleep," he said with a chuckle. "Even Gordan was exhausted. He's probably still asleep outside your window."

"I am not," Gordan said, his smug voice coming in through the open window.

Nicole let herself smile. At least she would have them while she lived on the run. What worried her was time. Every hour that passed meant a portal might open, and that meant a doorway that would lead her enemies right to her.

"Are you packed?" she asked Raiden. "We should at least be ready to leave by now."

He laughed. "I don't have anything to pack."

"Yes you do," she said. "The clothes I gave you."

"Your brother's clothes," he said.

"Just pack them. Mitch won't miss them."

"All right, if I go pack, will you feel better?"

"No," she admitted. Yesterday morning he had been prepared to run off to Veil to spy on the Council. She was worried he hadn't let that plan go. "Leaving will make me feel better."

He sighed. "Okay. Packing—right now," he said, backing out of the doorway with his hands up in surrender.

Nicole groaned as she hung her head forward and leaned on her bag. She still had the journal pressed to her chest like a teddy bear.

"So where will we be going?" Gordan asked from the window.

Nicole sighed, then sat up. "Tucson. We're going back with Mitchell. From there, I don't know—maybe Ventura. We still don't know how long I can stay someplace before opening a portal."

"As long as there is no portal between this realm and Veil, no one there can touch you. May I suggest you do yourself a favor and don't worry over what hasn't happened yet. You have enemies, Nicole, and they will find fearful prey easy to catch. Don't make it easy for them. Don't let them into your head. You do that, and they have already won—it just comes down to who finds you first."

Nicole dropped the journal to her lap as she listened. He was right but not in the way he supposed. She wasn't scared of the Council; she was scared of herself. Since that moment she'd lost herself in her own powers on the bridge, she'd wondered if she deserved to be in a cage somewhere—for everyone's safety. The force inside her seemed to tremble, coiled and humming, ready to burst out of her. No, it wasn't the Council or this Venarius person that frightened her.

She couldn't stop worrying that someone close to her might get hurt—her father, her brothers, Raiden, or Gordan. What if she couldn't control herself when she faced her enemies again, like on the bridge with Moira? What if someone she loved got in the way and ended up like the kelpie in the stream? The sooner she left, the sooner her dad would be safe. She'd agreed to go to Tucson with her brother for their dad's sake, but she was already anxious to leave Tucson to avoid putting Mitch at risk. Just thinking about it churned her magic into a frenzy.

"Nicole." Gordan's voice seized her attention. She looked up and saw the loose objects of her room floating and spinning and rattling. With a deep breath she managed to quell the sinking anxiety in her chest. Right on cue everything in her room went quiet and still.

"Maybe you should take a break from packing," he said. "Take some time to enjoy the peace and quiet." Gordan turned away from the window and disappeared.

Nicole sighed. She unfolded her legs and straightened herself upright. After dropping the journal into her bag, she shuffled out of her room and down the carpeted hall. Mitchell came up the stairs hidden behind a mound of clean clothes in a laundry basket. She stopped, letting him pass as he reached the landing. He spotted her before he turned down the hall toward his room.

"And where are you going?" he asked, his teasing voice muffled by jeans and sweatshirts.

She laughed. "Where do you think?"

As he turned into his room, he stopped and gave her a look over his shoulder that said, *Just remember I'm in the room next door.*

With an exaggerated roll of her eyes, she stepped into Raiden's room and closed the door emphatically.

"I'll have you know I'm packed," Raiden declared, presenting his bag beside the door.

"Really?" She looked down at it in disbelief. He'd only left her room two minutes ago. She crossed her arms. "And what spell did you use to accomplish that?"

"You tell me," he said, declaring his challenge with a lifted brow and a curl at the corner of his mouth.

She racked her brain for spells, determined not to fail this pop quiz. She preferred spells even though she didn't need them. They brought order to the chaotic force pinging around inside her. "Could it be … *imperium*?"

Raiden's lips strained against a smile, and she knew she'd won. "All right," he said, tossing his hands up. "Claim your prize, then."

Nicole took a moment to look around, as if she wasn't sure what she wanted, but she knew. She took a step closer and grabbed his shirt to pull his lips to hers. She lingered there a long moment, allowing herself a silly, giddy moment in light of all that was closing in on her. She lost herself for a few heartbeats in the warmth of his mouth, the rush of heat through her body, the scent of eucalyptus on his skin. Then she released his shirt and leaned back.

"I was hoping that's what you'd choose."

A laugh crept up from her lungs as she leaned into him, and they toppled back onto the bed.

"I can hear you!" came Mitchell's warning, muffled through the wall.

Their mouths merged, and their laughter mingled, filling the quiet room. Raiden's arms closed around her back, clamping her against him, and still she didn't feel close enough. Her head was spinning. Fire pulsed beneath her skin, and suddenly she was burning up in her clothes.

A shout and a piercing shriek from Mitchell's room startled them apart, and they looked at each other with mirrored expressions of confusion. Nicole jumped off the bed. She lunged for the door and wrenched it open to see a white-beige blur rush out of her brother's room and down the hall. She took a step into the hallway and peered into Mitchell's room.

"What was that?" she asked.

"Hell if I know," Mitch said, standing in his room with his clean clothes scattered everywhere.

There came a sharp bark and a great screech from downstairs. Nicole lurched down the hall and ran for the stairs just as Raiden came out of the room behind her.

"You all right, Mitch?" she heard Raiden ask as she thudded down the stairs on quick feet.

Downstairs she saw the beige form of fur and wings again as their shaggy black Labrador chased it out of the living room.

"Bandit," she cried, running after him. She could hear the sound of claws and nails scrambling over the tile floors, moving through the entryway and around toward the kitchen. Immediately, she turned around and ran into the kitchen from the living room just as Bandit and his quarry came in from the other side.

The creature charged directly toward her. It was no bigger than Bandit, with large paws on its forelegs and talons on the rear. A pair of wings flapped frantically, and a pair of wide eagle eyes peered at her over a sharp beak. Despite the disbelief in her brain, she crouched down and scooped up the frightened mass of fur and feathers. As she stood, she was surprised by how light it was in her arms. It was about the same size as Bandit but only half as heavy—large but gangly.

"Bandit," she warned, raising her foot to halt his pursuit. "No." At the sound of her stern voice, the dog stopped. "Go," she commanded. Bandit shuffled backward out of the kitchen and stopped just beyond the doorway, watching anxiously. The creature in her arms trembled furiously.

"Nicole?" Raiden called as he came down the stairs.

She couldn't find her voice. All she could do was turn to face him, holding the fearful animal against her chest. As her adrenaline waned and her stunned arms tightened protectively, its trembling ceased, and it pressed its head into her shoulder.

"Oh no." Raiden's voice sank but then gave way to a soft chuckle.

"Am I"—she knew she had the words somewhere—"holding a griffin?"

Raiden took a deep breath. "That you are."

"Hey," Mitchell called from upstairs, "I think we got a problem."

Nicole stepped out of the kitchen just as her brother appeared on the landing.

"You mean the griffin in the house?" she asked with a smile, watching with satisfaction as Mitchell's eyes went wide at the clear view of the creature in her arms.

Mitch shook his head. "No. I mean the portal in my room."

Nicole shifted her gaze to Raiden, who looked at her with the same fearful, nauseated expression. In the commotion she hadn't even stopped to think where their visitor had come from. Apparently Raiden hadn't either.

"That's a problem," Nicole agreed.

"We better return your new friend and close that portal before we have any other unexpected visitors," Raiden said, raising his hand toward the stairs.

"What's going on in here?" Gordan appeared on the landing.

Mitchell gave him a dumbfounded stare before turning a questioning scowl down at his sister. It occurred to her that he had heard about Gordan but never actually seen him.

When Mitchell turned his scrutiny back to the dragon, Gordan acknowledged Mitchell's confusion with a nod and introduced himself. "Gordan. We haven't met."

"Right." Mitchell bobbed his head. "The dragon."

"Okay, there will be time for this later," Raiden said, his tone tight.

Nicole made her feet move, and her muscle memory found each step easily despite not seeing them. Everyone filed into Mitchell's room, where clothes were still strewn about—the chaotic aftermath of a laundry detonation.

By the time Nicole stepped through the doorway into Mitch's room, the warm griffin bundle in her arms had begun to purr, nestling deeper into her embrace. The soothing vibration permeated her chest and made her heart ache.

"Aww," she groaned.

"Don't even go there, Nikki," her brother warned with a chastising glare.

"But just listen," she insisted. "It's purring."

The griffin let out a tiny sound halfway between a chirp and a mew.

"Here we go again," Raiden muttered.

When Nicole saw the distorted swirl of the portal in the air across the room just in front of the closet door, her heart sank for too many reasons. She couldn't keep herself from dropping her face into the griffin's silky, feathery neck.

"Nicole, we don't know how closely the Council or Venarius might be monitoring Cantis. They could already have someone there searching," he said with a gentle voice that told her he felt the weight in her heart.

"Nikki, it's a griffin for Christ's sake, not a defenseless kitten. Throw it back," Mitchell said with an exasperated huff.

She glanced at Gordan, who stood there watching her silently with sympathy in his eyes. She gave him a tiny smile, surrendering to the reality that she couldn't keep every creature she rescued. Not to mention her dad might have a stroke if she asked him to let a griffin stay in the house.

"All right," she said on the tail of a sigh. "Time to go home, you."

The griffin pulled its head out of her shoulder and looked up at her, blinking its big gold eyes. Her heart broke a little. With confidence in her step, she moved forward. She was used to crossing portals now, and she could almost laugh at that realization. The instant she stepped through, she pitched forward. There was no earth underfoot. She fell, and her startled cry cut through the cold silence.

The griffin dropped from her grasp as she flailed, and a spark of fear ignited the magic within her, slowing her descent to a halt for a brief moment before she could hit the ground. Her new friend landed lightly on its feet, and she flopped face-first into a bed of snow. Heart racing, she jumped up, brushing the snow from her clothes as her body shuddered from the cold. She struck her palm to her forehead and looked over her shoulder at the portal above her. *Duh, we were on the second floor!*

At least someone wandering around looking for a portal wouldn't find it down on the ground. She scanned her surroundings with cautious eyes. The forest was sparse, and the trees naked, most of them blackened from fire. The thick blanket of snow on the ground was fresh. Cantis seemed like an entirely different place than it had been yesterday. Then she noticed the griffin standing beside her, regarding her with those great gold saucer eyes.

"Go on; go home," she said, forcing cheer into her voice.

It cocked its head at her before prancing off into the trees. She wondered for a moment where home was for the griffin and whether she would ever have a real home again—a place where she didn't have to worry, where she could always feel safe and welcome, where her loved ones weren't at risk because of her.

With a shiver and a sigh she turned and looked up at the portal.

Gordan studied the portal, feeling the pull toward Nicole like a tether knotted deep in his chest. What was just a subtle tug when they were in the same realm became a relentless tension when they were in different realms. If he did not lean back against it, the force might yank him off his feet.

"What has you in such a good mood?" Raiden asked with stiff words, and Gordan realized there was a small smile on his lips.

"Her, I suppose," he confessed, "just being … her. She looked at me the same way."

"I remember," Raiden said.

"She can't seem to help herself, can she? She wants to rescue anyone or anything that crosses her path."

Mitchell laughed. "That's Nicole. In the third grade she hit a boy twice her size for making fun of her friend. The kid never bothered them again."

Gordan's brow pinched. Where was that Nicole now, and who was this anxious girl so prepared to run from her problems?

"Hello?" Nicole's voice called, warbling and faint with distance as it came through the portal. "I need a hand here, guys."

Raiden was the first one to the portal, and Gordan was fairly sure he saw a smug hike at the corner of his mouth. As Raiden leaned into the portal, half his torso disappeared, and his balance wavered. Gordan decided not to let him tumble after Nicole this time and caught him by the arm while indulging in a satisfied chuckle. In a strange way his contact with Raiden, who was now far closer to Nicole than Gordan was, eased the ceaseless tension in his chest.

He waited patiently, listening to their voices quiver through the portal.

"I am never going to get used to that," Nicole said as half of Raiden appeared overhead, some victim of a magic show gone wrong.

"Come on; we should get back and close this portal before we draw any unwanted attention," he said with a laugh, reaching his hand out to her.

"Gladly," she shivered. Her toes were numb now, the socks on her feet dampened with snow. She took a steadying breath, attempting to set aside her uncertainty just long enough to defy gravity. Reluctantly, she tapped into the humming force lurking deep in her core. It spread through her, igniting every nerve, spreading its heat down into her toes and all the way up into her hair.

She jumped, gliding upward like a swimmer surfacing from the depth of a pool. Just as she came face-to-face with Raiden, her stomach flipped in that weightless moment between rising and falling. He hooked his arm around her before she could sink back into gravity's pull. Her heart gave a hard punch against her ribs as he pulled her back through the portal into Mitchell's room.

Her weight nearly knocked him over, but Gordan was standing behind him and propped him up while they steadied themselves on their feet. Raiden's arm remained cinched around her waist.

"There, that was simple enough. Do you remember the spell to close the portal?" he asked softly, as though he was saying something the others shouldn't hear.

"No, I should go get the book," she said as a bloom of heat filled her cheeks.

Then Raiden's face changed. His subtly curled lips turned into a stiff line, and his eyes went wide, his brow crumpling with distress.

"What?" she asked, concern weighing her voice down.

Then Raiden was yanked toward the portal. His grip on her slipped away. Nicole only managed to catch his arm before he could disappear. Her wet socks slipped against the carpet as she leaned back, desperately clinging to him. Gordan clamped his arms around her, anchoring her down.

"Raiden!" Nicole's voice was strained with her effort to hang on to him.

"What's happening?" Mitchell raised his voice behind them.

"The Council," Raiden replied, barely able to speak.

"They've cast a summoning," Gordan said. "The only reason Raiden isn't in Atrium this very moment is probably because he was on this side of the portal."

"Then we'll close it," Nicole said. "Mitch, the book on portals is downstairs in the living room."

"On it," he said, running from the room.

"Nicole, we don't know what the force of the spell will do to him if we close the portal. There's a chance the portal might not close at all," Gordan warned.

"What are we supposed to do, then?" Her question became a sad cry.

"Let … go," Raiden said, straining to speak, cringing against the spell.

"No," Nicole snapped, aghast at the idea.

"Let … me go, Nicole." He forced the words out and gasped for a breath.

All she could do was shake her head at him.

"Gordan?" Raiden choked out.

"I've got her," he answered.

"Don't," she warned, but Raiden reached for her hands and pried them open just enough. "No!"

He slipped from her grasp, and the portal swallowed him up.

2. Welcome

Raiden flew backward through the portal. The summoning spell held him like a crushing fist, dragging him across hundreds of miles in seconds. He felt immaterial for that time, like he was just a haze of vertigo and nausea until he was spit out onto a cold marble floor. Unbelievably, he landed on his feet but promptly fell onto his hands and knees, queasy from the leap to Atrium. For a moment he stayed there, unsure if his stomach was about to turn itself out onto his reflection in the mossy-green marble or not.

"Welcome, Raiden," a cold female voice greeted him, bouncing around the polished floor and high ceiling. It was dim, but he could make out the column-lined walls on either side of him. His head was still spinning, but he picked himself up, wobbling on unsteady legs.

"We apologize for the aftereffects of the summoning." A man's low, grating voice spoke this time.

Raiden fought back one last wave of nausea, and as it ebbed, his mind finally caught up with him. Every ounce of hate and sorrow hit him like a battering ram, but he kept his face composed. If any distaste showed in his expression, he was sure it would only seem like vertigo from his unpleasantly abrupt journey. What else could he do now but what he had been planning to do only days ago? He hadn't been greeted by armed guards or summoned into a jail cell. *This will work*, he told himself. *It has to.* Otherwise, what chance did they have?

"We grew concerned about your well-being when we could not contact or summon Sinnrick. We did not expect any casualties, circumstances being what they are with this girl."

Raiden's jaw clenched. *You mean you expected this to be easy.* He looked up at them sitting atop their high, crescent-shaped bench in identical robes. In fact, they almost all looked identical at first glance because they were all bald, their heads shaven.

"Can you tell us anything about the fera?" The question pushed his thoughts back on track.

"It's only been a week," Raiden said, to remind himself just as much as them. "How close did you expect me to get in just seven days?" He hoped they felt like fools; he did. He almost couldn't believe how close he and Nicole had become in that time. Not even ten minutes ago he'd had her in his arms as close as he could hold her. He closed his eyes longer than he wanted. *Keep talking. Tell as much truth as you can,* he thought. *Don't let them know how much time you've spent with her.*

"My search for the portal led me into some trouble with the resident murderer of Cantis." This was true, and he was glad for the opportunity to point out their failure in Cantis. "It's a long story, but I ended up in over my head. I guess Sinnrick did too. Moira found out about the fera and took an interest in what we knew." Sinnrick had died in the castle that night, so Raiden could safely incorporate him into the fabricated parts of his story. "I only encountered the fera briefly the night before last. Moira managed to get her into the castle," he added.

"Yes, Moira. We've kept an eye on her since the decimation. She had well known ties to many prominent members of Dawn, and so we were suspicious of her activities in Cantis."

Raiden crushed his jaws together until his ears rang. They decided to pay attention *after* thousands of people had been killed senselessly. For a moment he thought the rage in his chest might asphyxiate him.

"What have you been doing since you encountered the fera?" The indignant tone carried through the hall.

"I managed to find the portal. I was in the process of getting closer to her," he said, and their most recent embrace flashed before his eyes. "I found myself some clothes to blend in and noticed that she seemed to be packing to leave, but that's when you summoned me. As I understand it, a portal depends mostly on there being a source of magic on the other side to contact. If she leaves, we won't know where to open another portal." It was easy to sound like he cared about their efforts thanks to all the thought he had put into evading them.

"That's no matter. We have ways of detecting portals throughout the realm. Since they are so seldom an occurrence these days, she should prove easy enough to track down. She'll compromise the barrier between the realms eventually, and when she does, we will locate her." The man who spoke had a careful, steady cadence to his words.

"Since you had an encounter with her and she knows your face, we think it best to assign a new agent to this matter, one she will not recognize. We would like you to share what you know with him, anything that might help him get close to the fera. He should be waiting for you outside this chamber."

Raiden took a deep breath to maintain his composure. He should have expected this, but he had hoped they would keep him on the mission. At least then he could see her, let her get away, keep the Council from getting too close. He had no way to warn her about another agent, what he would look like. She wouldn't see him coming. Raiden knew he needed to trust in Gordan, and the only reason he could was because he trusted Nicole and she trusted the dragon. Raiden had faith in Nicole, in her determination and her instinct. He could trust even a dragon, but he couldn't trust the Council or anyone who served them.

"We do have another assignment for you. There has been a lingering rebel movement within the city, and it has been more difficult than anticipated to locate their whereabouts and infiltrate their ranks in the last year or so. We have need of a new face, one they won't recognize as one of our own. You have experience, albeit rather informal, which we need. You'll be housed in the fifth district of the city. An assistant will bring the locator key to your home, and a messenger will arrive with all the information we have on the rebel faction."

The Council's trust in him was hard to believe. He knew he should have been pleased, but all he could wonder was how he was supposed to help Nicole while he was chasing down a group of rebels. Then it occurred to him that he should respond.

"Yes … thank you." He fought back the bile rising in his throat. It hit his wisdom teeth with a biting twinge as he uttered, "It's an honor."

"You are dismissed until two days hence. Get some rest, Raiden," one of the women said. Hers was the first warm voice he'd heard since arriving, but somehow her kindness rolled through him like cold water.

He responded with a stiff nod and looked around, unsure where they'd hidden the door to escape the Council's lifeless hall. It was directly behind him, and he turned and crossed the glassy floor with long, grateful strides. Somehow the great double doors seemed to sense him before he could touch the massive iron handle, and they opened of their own accord, shutting behind him with a heavy boom that startled him.

A cloud of sound enveloped him, and he sagged with relief to hear the clatter of feet crossing the wide corridor before him. Voices murmured to each other. Papers shuffled. Raiden hadn't realized how dark it had been in the Council's hall until now. White crystal clusters on the ceiling high above lit the corridor, at the other end of which was another pair of large double doors. On either side of the doors there were tall, narrow windows. Through the panes he could see the darkness outside and the lights of Atrium glittering in the distance.

It occurred to him that the sun had been rising around this time yesterday. It had to be early, before dawn, and the courts were already bustling with people who served the Council.

"Raiden?"

Raiden pried his eyes away from the doors at the other end of the corridor to see the face of the man who would be hunting Nicole. At first he only saw a man of his same height, perhaps slightly shorter, with wavy black hair hanging around his face. Then his eyes focused, and he saw the blue eyes like lapis stones and registered the look of disbelief on the man's face. Raiden knew this man; rather, he had known him as a boy.

"Caeruleus?"

The familiar stranger stepped forward without hesitation and clapped his arms around Raiden before pushing him away again to study him. "Look at you. You're alive. I thought I'd never see you again. They said everyone was gone—that Cantis was gone. I can't believe this." Words tumbled from Caeruleus's mouth just like Raiden remembered, only his boyish voice was gone, replaced by deeper tones.

Raiden was strangely disoriented by the thoughts and feelings clashing in his mind. His childhood friend was the agent assigned to find Nicole. Raiden's heart was joyous and pained. He had hated this man before he'd seen his face, and now he suddenly felt as much concern for him as for Nicole.

Nicole struggled against Gordan's arms locked around her torso, kicking at the air. "Let go," she snapped with venom in her voice.

He released her, and she lurched forward, through the portal, prepared for the drop this time. Her heart fluttered as she fell, seething. Her magic swelled in her chest, making her body lighter. She landed on steady legs as though she had hopped only a couple of feet, followed immediately by the sound of crunching snow under Gordan's feet behind her.

"He's already gone, Nicole. He's in Atrium by now," he said.

"We could have figured something out," she said, whirling around and shoving Gordan hard. An angry pulse of magic moved through her hands, forcing him back, but he maintained his balance.

"He will be fine," he said, his expression unfazed by her outburst.

"You don't know that. They could be arresting him right now." Her frantic voice disturbed the silence.

"Better him than you."

"I can't believe you just said that," she said softly, her volume dropping out of shock. "He's supposed to be the jerk, not you. If they execute him for treason, it will be my fault."

"That was his choice, Nicole. He, at least, has some chance of talking himself out of trouble. You, on the other hand … you are on their execution list no matter what. So, yes, better him than you."

"He shouldn't have to pay the consequences for my problem, for—"

"For you existing?" Gordan snapped, startling her with anger that had to come from somewhere deep. "You're not running from a crime. They're hunting you, Nicole. Perhaps it has been easy to pay little regard to that fact until now because you've not yet seen how far they will go. This is just beginning. They thought Raiden was doing their dirty work. They will send others. They will chase you until you can't run anymore." His voice trembled, and Nicole looked at him with wide eyes, astonished by the emotion in his words.

Gordan shook his head, took a careful breath, and steadied his voice, speaking softly this time. "Raiden made his choice. To be quite honest, I think when he met you, there *was* no other choice for him, not unlike how I had no choice. He may not be here, but he's on your side. I'm on your side. We're going to fight with you whether you like it or not. You don't get to blame yourself for our choices. Understand?"

His quiet words were far more potent than his anger, and they stole the wind from her sails, leaving her deflated.

"Fine. Then tell me why we shouldn't be there too."

"We can't just go charging into the courts where the Council has hundreds of men ready to fight. This isn't a battle for three people. Even if one of them is a fera. Maybe it's time to consider that this one is better fought from the inside." The silence grew warm, and waves of heat radiated from Nicole. She was burning with hate and magic, and she just needed to get away from it. Gordan was right about one thing at least: her enemies would soon come.

She looked up and saw the glimmer of light like a mirage—the portal. The snow around her feet turned to slush. She let her magic build in her legs until they burned, and then she jumped. As she passed through the portal, the barrier prickled her skin. The air on the other side was thick and stale after the crisp, cool air of Cantis.

Mitchell stood there in the doorway with the book in his hand. "What happened? Where's Raiden?" he asked.

"Gone," Nicole answered as she stormed past him.

"Wait! There's still the matter of the portal in my room!" Mitch raised his voice after her. "Do you know how to close that thing?"

As she stomped into her room, she heard Gordan answer, "I'll need the book." His voice was level and calm, which only infuriated her more.

With her sights set on her packed bag, she bent down and yanked the long cord to cinch it closed and flipped the top flap over so she could buckle it down. Then she swung the bulky bag over one shoulder. She took long, angry strides out of her room and down the stairs. Her feet thumped heavily against each step with her frustration and the extra weight on her back.

She knew she couldn't be angry with Raiden. The summoning spell had taken choice out of the equation. That look of pain on his face lingered in her mind, and she imagined the crushing force of that magic pulling him away from her. She knew that Gordan couldn't do anything about it either. But all she wanted right now was to be angry, at both of them, at the Council, at anything and everything.

It killed her that her enemies had so many ways to hurt her, using each person she cared for, and yet there was no way she could hit them back. She yanked the front door open and slammed it closed behind her.

She marched with purpose across the front of the house to where the family's 1986 Toyota pickup sat parked on the far side of the driveway in front of the side gate. It had been her dad's first business truck, long since retired. It had blown a head gasket nearly two years ago. Her dad had his larger, newer truck to drive, and Mitchell had the family Corolla away at school. Everyone was too busy for the project, so here the old truck sat waiting to be fixed.

Now it was urgent. Nicole needed to get out. This wasn't some weekend visit to her brother's or even a relaxing weeklong vacation to let some little problem blow over. She needed to move and keep moving. Her own home had become a twenty-four-hour pit stop now. The driver-side door was unlocked. She opened the door and tossed her bag into the cab before pulling the latch that popped the hood. With a clang the hood released, and she circled around the cab to heave it open and secure the prop.

The engine was filthy, dust and grime everywhere. She felt as if she'd just opened the chest of a centuries-old corpse, expecting to revive him. All she could hope was that a few different spells to make everything clean and to mend what was broken would be enough.

It was a gusty day, and the wind slithered through the fabric of her clothes. She shuddered, and the heat of her magic moved eagerly to the surface. The prickling energy radiated from her, slipping from her grasp, like too much sand in a clenched fist, whisked away on the wind.

The green palo brea tree beside the driveway rustled and shook, its thin branches dancing with life. In seconds its swaying canopy turned from green to bright yellow with blossoms that shouldn't be there until May. A tiny spark of delight went off in her brain at the sight of her favorite thing about Arizona— the desert in bloom. In that moment she realized she didn't care anymore if the world saw her magic. As dangerous and unpredictable as it might be, she could love the spontaneous beauty that sprang forth from it.

A sigh of acceptance escaped her, swallowed up by the vigorous breeze. She focused on the silent engine. Her thoughts rushed through the pages of spells she had read. The word for the cleaning spell was on the tip of her tongue— cleaning and repairing were probably the first spells she'd made a conscious note to remember.

"*Purgandum,*" she said. The spell took form on her lips, tingling with warm electricity that arched unseen through the air. The whole truck shuddered as though the engine were turning over, but it made no sound. Then a cloud of filth rolled off the vehicle and wheezed out from under the hood. The wind carried it away while Nicole blinked in astonishment.

She wondered if there would ever come a time when magic didn't amaze her. Absently, she touched her fingers to her lips, which were still tingling from the spell. The engine looked remarkable. She'd never thought it could be so clean. The last time it had looked like this had to have been when it was brand new. She leaned closer to inspect her spell's work. Every bolt, every tube, every vent was pristine, but there was one last thing. Although everything was clean, she needed to fix the head gasket. She couldn't help doubting the success of a spell on a part she couldn't see without taking the cylinder head off the engine block.

"Worth a try," she muttered with a shrug. She closed her eyes and deconstructed the engine in her mind, picturing the thin head gasket and keeping it secure in her mind. "*Novo,*" she intoned with as much confidence as she could muster. She opened her eyes to see white light leaking out from the car as if the engine might burst. Then the light dissipated.

With an anxious sigh she removed the prop from the hood. She lowered it back down and let it drop closed the last few inches. It shut with a loud metal bang. She climbed into the cab and shut the door before she realized she didn't have the key. *Of course,* she thought with a huff and held out her hand. "Keys," she demanded through her teeth.

Her magic raced through her veins and filled her hand with heat. A green spark in her palm grew into a flash, and suddenly the keys were there. For a brief moment she wondered where they had been hiding, somewhere in the chaos of her room no doubt. She closed her prickling hand around the keys. Her fingers cried out from the pressure as if her hand had fallen asleep. She ignored the discomfort and inserted the key into the ignition. Her heart pounded. *Moment of truth.* She gave the key a twist. The engine turned, grumbling like a beast waking unwillingly from its slumber. The truck gave a shake and then settled into a steady vibration, idling.

"Yes!" she cried, throwing her hands against the wheel.

"Where might you be going?" Gordan's calm voice was almost lost in the engine noise and yet still managed to startle her.

"Does it matter? You can get in or hop in the back." She hitched her thumb over her shoulder. "You can even fly if you want to. I don't care, as long as we get away from here."

"Not that I mind this nomadic vision of yours, but there are some people here who deserve to know where you're going." His voice softened to the point where she barely heard him over the engine. She wanted to smile at his concern for her dad and her brother. It would be easier to leave and apologize later over the phone, but Gordan was right.

A flustered groan escaped her lungs, and she turned the key. The engine went quiet again. "Fine."

3. Gone

The polite sound of someone clearing their throat shifted Raiden's attention to a rather short man with a tiny pair of spectacles perched on the bridge of his nose.

"Pardon me, are you Raiden Aldor Cael?"

Raiden flinched. He wished people didn't know his full name—Cael was his father's name. "Yes," he answered.

The short man presented an envelope, holding it out with a straight, rigid arm.

Raiden took the parcel. "Thank you."

"Good day to you," the man said with a quick nod before turning on his heel and hustling away.

Caeruleus clapped Raiden on the back and pulled him forward into a stroll down the wide corridor, leaving the great double doors of the Council behind them.

"Let's go see this place of yours," Caeruleus said.

Raiden still couldn't find words. Talking to Nicole the first time—after the shock of accidentally running through a portal and crashing into a stranger in another realm—had been easier than thinking of something to say to his oldest friend. After all those years alone, wondering what his friend's life was like, safe and hopefully happy, wishing he could speak to Caeruleus again, Raiden had nothing to say.

From the corner of his eye, he saw the grin fade from Caeruleus's face. The years and tragedy that had separated them seemed to creep into the air between them. Caeruleus might have been spared from witnessing that day, safe on the mainland, but he had to have been affected by what had happened on the island in his absence.

"You've been in Cantis this whole time," Caeruleus said.

"Yes."

"They said everyone was gone, but I guess there must have been plenty of survivors they didn't know about."

"No. Only me and maybe a couple others." The weight of Raiden's answer said everything that he couldn't bring himself to speak.

"I'm sorry, Ray. You know she was a mother to me too." Caeruleus's murmur was nearly inaudible.

"I know. Where have you been? How did you end up in the courts?" Raiden struggled to keep the distaste out of his last question.

Marble pillars lined the hall, slipping slowly past them as they walked. Their footsteps were lost in the cacophony of feet clattering around them. Dozens of people passed by, but no one seemed to see them.

"My father moved us to Nol, where he had some old friends whose family used to be nobility before the Dragon Wars. Everyone always talked about how the Council was spread too thin, how there were barely enough men and women to keep order across the mainland. Father kept what had happened in Cantis a secret from me. I guess it wasn't hard. There was enough to talk about on the mainland; Cantis never made any news in Nol. I overheard him and his colleagues talking about it one night when I was sixteen. I was so angry with him for never telling me that I left. I figured maybe if the Council had had more agents back then, they might have been able to stop what had happened. I decided that if there was a chance to help the Council fix this bloody realm, I would take it."

"You can't make up for their failure," Raiden said and immediately regretted his cold words. His friend had shouldered guilt that wasn't his to carry. "But I'm sure you've done a lot of good, Ruleus."

Caeruleus chuckled. "I haven't heard that name in—"

"Ten years?" Raiden guessed. Caeruleus's father never shortened his son's name. Raiden and his mother had been the only ones who called him that.

"Has it been that long? What did you do with yourself for all that time?"

"A lot of reading," Raiden answered with a shrug.

They came to the towering archway of the double doors leading outside, and a stout man pushed one of the doors open for them. Raiden looked at the sea of mostly dark buildings in the city and the lit streets that spread like arteries from the courts out to the city wall.

"This is the first clear night we've had in a few weeks," Caeruleus said with a laugh.

Raiden looked up at the deep blue sky. The lights of the city drowned out the stars above. This was a completely different sky than the one in Cantis for the past nine years, where not a single light competed with the sea of stars.

They came to a halt at the top of the steps that descended to the street below. The court building was built upon a large hill in the center of the city. There were wide thoroughfares leading away from the court building and out through the city, eight spokes of a wheel with a wall as its rim. There were few vehicles on the streets at this time. Around the courts the buildings were all nearly identical in height and architecture.

"Well, this is Atrium," Caeruleus said.

"We used to think Cantis was a big place," Raiden said as the memory bubbled up in his mind.

Caeruleus chuckled. "We were boys then, Ray."

"You're right," he said. "We aren't those boys anymore."

"Mitchell," Nicole said as she materialized in the hall. As her body unfurled from thin air, she steadied herself against the doorframe.

He jumped. "Jeez, don't do that!"

She glanced to her left, into the empty room beside her brother's. Her compulsion to leave swelled inside her, but she would not let her thoughts travel any further down that avenue.

"Gordan and I are hitting the road. It's time for me to get out of here," she explained.

He laughed and continued folding his laundry. "Oh? How you gonna do that? You two gonna take a flying carpet?"

"I fixed the truck," she said.

"Wait—what?" He dropped the shirt in his hands and looked at her. "How?"

"It's cute that you still ask that question," she said, shaking her head as she crossed his room and planted a swift kiss on his cheek. "I'll give you a heads-up when we're headed toward Tucson, okay?"

"Uh, yeah, okay."

"Love you." She said it fast enough that she didn't have to feel it. If she lingered to see those words reach his eyes, she might have to bear the weight of them and acknowledge the possibility that this was the last time she would say those words to her brother. Her magic flared. She let it unravel her and pull her through the air.

Gordan waited, leaning against the truck. He seemed completely unfazed by her sudden formation before him, as if he'd felt her coming.

"All right, time to go," she announced.

"What about your father?"

"He's at work. We'll stop to say goodbye on the way. Satisfied?"

He didn't answer, only gave her a subtle smile and eased away from the driver-side door. His long legs made his gait look more like gliding. The strides were slow, yet he covered a distance that made him faster than his movements seemed. When he reached the passenger door, he paused a moment, studying the handle. She wondered if he was considering the truck bed instead, but he pulled the handle up and opened the door. He ducked inside and climbed in, folding himself up to fit in the small cab. She wished she could give him more room. Unfortunately, with the bench seat and her only slightly above average height, she couldn't put the seat back for him and still reach the pedals.

The smell of sawdust and desert sand rekindled an ember of joy from years ago. She remembered going everywhere with her dad in this truck. He'd taught her how to drive it when she was twelve.

"Ready?" she asked Gordan.

"For anything," Gordan replied with a solemn smile.

She tried not to hear the note of severity in his words. Instead, she smiled back and turned the key in the ignition. The engine rumbled to life, and she couldn't be sure if it was the vibration of the truck or her own anticipation that sent a tremble through her body and down into her core.

They walked under the streetlamps, Raiden holding the key to his apartment in his open hand. Another set of soft footsteps shuffled along ahead of them, but he kept his eyes on the key, leading them to the door it would unlock.

"At least they put you in a decent neighborhood," Caeruleus said, bobbing his head in approval of their surroundings. "Pretty much as far as you can be from the barracks where they house the rest of us." There was a little disappointment in his voice.

Raiden had the feeling the Council had their way of keeping a close eye on him nonetheless. Despite Caeruleus's attempts at conversation, Raiden's mind raced through plans. He needed to find some means of communicating with Nicole and Gordan. There had to be some way he could warn them about the Council's movements. But he certainly couldn't go off on his own little mission without first knowing the extent of the Council's eyes and ears around him.

Dawn was finally emerging from below the wall at the edge of the city. People stepped out of their homes, opened shop doors, and set up their carts. The day in Atrium was beginning around him. Two days—that was how much time he had to figure out what to do.

"Ray?"

"What?"

"Did you hear me?"

"No, sorry. I'm a little lost in my thoughts. It's been a chaotic week," Raiden confessed easily.

"I said, 'We're close,'" he said, pointing down at the key.

Raiden blinked, astonished that he'd been staring at the key but hadn't even registered the fact that it was buzzing brightly in his palm.

He looked around, familiarizing himself with the area. These streets and the people who frequented them were a part of his new home, even if he didn't like it. He could nod in greeting to the shop owner sweeping dust out his front door. He could smile at the old woman sitting at her street cart stringing beads for sale. He could inhale deep into his lungs the smell of hot bread coming out of ovens as they passed by a bakery, even if he'd rather have the smell of morning coffee and the citrus scent of Nicole's hair instead.

The key nearly leaped from Raiden's hand.

"Well, that must be it," Caeruleus said, turning to look up at the building across the street.

The narrow red brick building was two units wide and six stories tall. Black metal staircases stood as spiral columns at both sides of the building.

"Welcome home," Caeruleus said, nudging Raiden with his elbow.

"Yeah," Raiden replied halfheartedly.

Nicole killed the engine in front of a house with cream stucco and a coffee-brown tile roof. Her dad was inside with his crew working on a bathroom remodel. She pulled her phone out of her pocket and texted him, "I'm out front. Need to talk to you." Her heart tightened as she sent the message and waited.

"What are you going to tell him?" Gordan asked.

"Everything, which is why this is so hard."

The front door of the house opened, and Michael stepped outside.

Nicole inhaled and let out a trembling breath before getting out of the truck. She left the door open as her dad caught her in his arms for a brief hug.

"Hey, babycakes," he said with a confused smile on his face. "How did you—?" He stopped himself, shook his head, and chuckled. She saw the realization in his eyes. "Never mind."

"Well, you got it faster than Mitch," she said, forcing out a little laugh.

"What's going on?" He looked past her and had to lean down slightly to identify the passenger in the truck. "Gordan," he said with a nod. Then he straightened up and said, holding back a laugh, "That's a sight, I must say."

"We're heading out," Nicole said.

"Why so soon? I thought you weren't going to Tucson with Mitch until Sunday."

"We, um, had to change our plans."

Michael cocked his head in thought. "Where's Raiden?"

"He's gone. A portal opened in Mitchell's room and …" She had to pause to swallow back a lump in her throat.

"Already?" His voice betrayed his concern.

"Raiden was summoned by the Council. It just pulled him through the portal, and he was gone."

Michael's forehead furrowed. "The people who are looking for you?"

"Yes."

"Honey, I'm so sorry."

She shook her head. "There's nothing we could do. I had less time than I thought. It's better if I leave. If someone comes looking, they shouldn't be able to open a portal without me here to provide a link. I think I've spent too much time here. Maybe in a new place I'll have more time before a portal opens."

"I don't like the thought of you living your life on the run."

"What else can I do, Dad? Someone *will* come sooner or later. They know where the last few portals have been. I don't want to bring them right into our backyard. They tried the gentle approach eliciting Raiden to find me, but there's no telling what their tactics will be the longer I elude them."

"Where are you planning to go?"

"Well, I was thinking Ventura." She smiled.

He nodded. "That makes me feel a little better."

Her father's calm finally broke Nicole's composure. For all his acceptance and understanding in the face of this new chaos in their lives, it occurred to her that he was only capable of rolling with the punches because he still thought it was all some strange dream. Her eyes burned with approaching tears because she realized this could be goodbye but he did not. She shut her eyes to hold the stinging moisture back, pressing her lips together in a grimace, but it was too late. To hide the hot fear seeping from her eyes, she stepped back into her dad's arms and pressed her face into his shirt.

"Everything is going to be okay," he said.

"You don't know that. Not even Raiden knew," she mumbled, keeping her knowledge of Raiden's horrible visions of the future locked in her heart. Her dad didn't need to hear what the Sight had shown Raiden.

"No, but it's my job to say it."

Nicole tightened her arms around her dad, reluctant to let go. The moment she did it would be time to leave.

"Just come home for a day every other week or so. All right?"

"I will," she said, her words muffled against him.

4. Unknown

*T*he inside of Raiden's apartment was pitch black at first and then suddenly filled with light. He took in the layout. The front room was mostly bare save for a short couch and a single upholstered chair. The wood floor was a rich brown, the light shining off its glossy surface. The walls were the color of book pages that had turned yellow with age. The couch was a burnt gold and the chair a deep blood red.

He looked back at Caeruleus, who was standing at the light switch and nodding in approval. "Not bad. At least it's not empty," he said with a chuckle.

"It's great," Raiden said, hoping he sounded convincing as he turned to venture farther into his home.

A partition wall extended halfway across the space and separated the sitting room from the kitchen. There was a small round dining table with two chairs.

Caeruleus crossed the apartment, his footsteps quiet knocks against the floor. "Raiden," he began, as if requesting entrance to Raiden's thoughts.

"What?" Raiden asked, facing his friend.

"Can I ask you something?"

"Sure."

"What happened that day?"

Raiden knew Caeruleus must have been carrying that question around in his chest for years, and no one but Raiden had the answer. The need to know was screaming in Caeruleus's stony blue eyes. For a moment Raiden could see the friend he had known in that gaze.

"It was the middle of the day," Raiden recalled, reluctant to go back, but standing in this unfamiliar place seemed almost like protection. Perhaps the ghosts would remain in Cantis. "Mother was brewing afternoon tea. I'm fairly certain she knew. I just don't know for how long. She had prepared for it, and yet she was capable of going about the day like she always did.

"It seemed strange to me then, but she asked me to go get my father's sword from the downstairs closet. We never took it out. Do you remember how mad she was that day I brought it out to show you?"

Caeruleus laughed through a nostalgic smile. "I remember."

"Well, I went to get it, and she locked me in."

Caeruleus's smile died.

"She had that door enforced with one hell of a spell. I couldn't get out and nothing could get in for thirteen hours. It seemed like an eternity. I heard the mayhem through the house, outside on the streets, people screaming, trying to fight them off. I heard the golems crash through the windows into the house. Then there was just silence.

"When I finally got out of that bloody closet, it was all over. I caught a few glimpses of the golems, stumbling and crawling through the streets as their spell died. There was nothing but soot and bodies left."

"And you've been alone, this whole time," Caeruleus said, shaking his head.

Raiden wanted to say, *No, not this whole time.* He'd had Nicole, even if only for a week. He had found a dear friend and something more. That single week far outweighed the years of solitude.

"Now I'm here." Raiden hoped he sounded glad. He turned and crossed his kitchen/dining room to the closed door. Beyond the doorway he found a washroom and the bedroom. The light from the living room spilled into the back of the apartment, and he cast a terrible black shadow across the narrow bed and single chest of drawers. Straight back through his room was a window in the back wall.

"Forget how to turn lights on?" Caeruleus laughed behind him, and the light in the room blinked on.

Raiden almost smiled. He pulled open the top drawer of the dresser, surprised to find it wasn't empty. His hand was drawn to the odd mask sitting within looking up at him.

"What's this?"

"Looks like your uniform," Caeruleus said, crossing the room.

"A mask?" Raiden held it up with an uncertain grimace.

"It's your shield. With the rebellion we've had a lot of attacks on our agents, so they had to issue the face shields. It repels virtually any magical attack, although its protective spells will need maintenance every so often. It also allows us to see through glamours, spells of any kind really. Probably most important is the vox link—it allows us to talk to the nearest agents should we need backup and even communicate with the courts. There is even more to it, I know. But I've never been the best with spells."

"I remember," Raiden said. As he pulled the drawer out farther, he spotted the short sword and handgun at the back. The sword was slightly too long for the drawer and lay at a diagonal, while the gun was not quite the length of his forearm.

"It might take some getting used to. I'll be around, though. And there is mandatory training every week, so you'll pick it all up in no time."

Raiden bobbed his head absently as he placed the mask back in the drawer and closed it. He opened the next drawer down. Clothes. *Why would the Council provide all this?* he wondered.

"So about the fera …"

Raiden tensed.

"The Council assigned me to it. I know Sinnrick didn't come back, but can you tell me anything specific? How dangerous is this thing?"

"I hate to break this to you, Caeruleus." Raiden faced him, holding back his hostility and disappointment. "But you're going to find out sooner or later that the fera is a person. It's not so easy to think of the fera as some monster when you're looking at a girl your age. The Council is doing you no favors by ignoring that fact. Prepare yourself for it, because she doesn't look like an enemy."

"Neither do the rebels, Raiden. But they are the enemy."

Raiden smiled—the Council's enemy, maybe, but they didn't have to be his. "Nevertheless, it might be harder than you think."

Caeruleus sighed. "I'm sorry. You're probably right. You're the one who has experience with the fera, after all. If I'm being honest, I'm worried about going back to Cantis."

"Don't worry, then. She's gone. Before the Council summoned me, she was leaving town. There probably won't be any portals in Cantis anymore now that she's on the move."

"That does complicate things. But she'll slip up. The Council has their way of tracking portals down. They have been doing it since the Dragon Wars ended. Keeping portals closed keeps Veil safe."

Raiden looked down at the drawer of clothing. "Would you mind if I took a minute to change?"

"Not at all." Caeruleus stepped into the kitchen.

Raiden's mind was a storm of thoughts. Caeruleus was so deep in the Council's camp he couldn't possibly understand a reality where the fera might not be a threat, let alone that she was someone Raiden cared about. Raiden wanted to believe that Caeruleus might reconsider everything he thought he knew if Raiden told him about Nicole. But hearing all he had now from Caeruleus, Raiden couldn't risk revealing his betrayal. This man had once been his childhood friend, but now Caeruleus belonged to the Council; he believed in them and their agendas. Raiden pulled off his warm sweater and held the soft, weighty garment in his hands, hoping to absorb every second of contact it had had with her that day. That had been less than an hour ago, and yet it already felt as if days had slipped by, pushing him and Nicole further apart.

In the lifeless silence of the Cantis castle, a man walked past the cold body of Sinnrick Stultus without interest. There was nothing to find here. His associate Moira was not in her chamber. The dragon she had been charged to watch was not in the tower, or anywhere in the castle.

He slid his hand into the pocket of his heavy leather overcoat, which was weighty with his hunting tools lining the inside, and retrieved a small oval mirror that fit in the palm of his hand. After he pressed two fingers against the glass, the reflection shuddered and twisted into darkness.

"This is Vinderek. There's nothing here," he said into the darkness. "The dragon is gone."

A voice answered, "New information has come in. She is on the move. You must open a portal before the link to the other realm grows too faint. Hurry."

He pressed two fingers to the glass once more, and the darkness melted away. The face of the mirror was a reflection once again.

Nicole shut the door of the truck and pulled her seat belt around her.

"Drive safe, baby," Michael said, leaning down to speak through the window.

"I will," she said. She turned the key. The engine rumbled.

"Call me when you get there," he said.

"I will."

"I love you."

"Love you too."

The truck pulled away from the house, and they were on the road.

Nicole took a long, deep breath, and Gordan could feel the air in the cab tremble with her anxiety. He could hear her heart pounding even over the roar of the truck's engine. They sat in noisy silence while Nicole navigated out of the neighborhood and through the city streets. Very few of the buildings they passed were any more than two floors. It had been centuries since Gordan had called this realm home. This was nothing like the old world he knew, but it had a sense of the familiar in the way a place can surround you and yet still feel inaccessible, a place where you did not belong. Then the buildings were no more, and they drove across a wide bridge over a lazy green river, the shores choked with tall, grassy vegetation. Nicole turned left and took them onto a two-lane road that stretched out ahead until it disappeared in the distance.

Gordan almost had to shout over the endless mechanical roar of the vehicle and the familiar drone of wind. "What's in Ventura?" he asked.

"My brother Anthony," she answered.

"You have another brother," Gordan said, trying to remember if he had heard that before now or not. Part of him wondered if the noise filling his head was the problem.

Nicole nodded, in answer and in time with the music coming through the circular speakers in the doors by their feet. At last she cranked a small handle attached to her door, and her window crept up one slow inch at a time. Gordan looked at his door and saw no such lever, just a metal knob in the door where the lever should have been. When he turned back to Nicole to say something, she held out the little brown lever. He studied the knob at one end and the grooved hole at the other.

Gordan took the object, fit the grooved hole onto the ridged metal stub on his door, and cranked. First, the half-closed window responded by lowering. He cranked the other direction, and, at last, the window closed. The cab went quiet—at least relative to before. The wind wasn't as enjoyable from inside the vehicle as the peaceful roar he enjoyed over the sea. That used to be the only time he came close to feeling happy. But this, sitting beside Nicole in this tiny space, was new and oddly pleasant to him.

He settled into the scents around him, the dusty upholstery, the smell of sand and sunlight and wood shavings. Beside him Nicole grew calm, and the air eased into a steady, gentle pulse of relief and exhilaration.

Gordan glanced at her and saw a smile creeping across her face. She laughed.

"What?"

"I've been dreaming about leaving Yuma for years." Her voice broke into laughter again. "This is not how I imagined it."

"You mean on the run in the company of a dragon?"

Another laugh burst past her smile. "Yeah, I didn't see this one coming," she said, shaking her head. "But I got what I wanted, didn't I? I guess that's why people say to be careful what you wish for."

"So what do you wish for now?" Gordan asked. His unique sense provided insight into the wordless depths of the heart, not the sea of thoughts within the mind.

She thought for a long time. So long he couldn't be sure whether she was searching for words or refusing to answer.

"I want to stop my heart from being used against me," she said. "If I'd stayed at home, they would have come for me there. It was an invitation for them to hurt my family."

"And Raiden?"

"I'm afraid of a lot of things these days. When Raiden wanted to go to Atrium yesterday, I was scared of seeing him go. But when he decided to stay, I realized I was even more scared of what it meant to stay together."

"You're saying you're glad the Council abducted him?" Gordan could hardly believe it.

"In a way, yeah, I'm relieved. Feeling like I need him around … scares me. But he got what he wanted, right? The chance to play the hero by himself," she scoffed.

"What?" he asked, prying deeper.

"I was so angry about that stupid plan because I didn't want to be treated like some damsel who needed to be left behind and protected. And now, here we are—he's facing *my* enemies, and I'm running."

"Can you blame him?" Gordan challenged.

Nicole glowered out the windshield.

"After all he's lost, what he went through? He couldn't stop what happened in Cantis; he couldn't protect the ones he loved. I don't believe he thinks you need to be saved, Nicole. I think *he* needs to believe that he can do something this time."

She remained quiet, but Gordan felt the churning annoyance in the cab go still and sad. He understood. The desire to preserve another life was entirely new to him, and Nicole was experiencing this dreadful need for the first time as well. But their dear Raiden had lived the horror of that failure for almost as long as Gordan had lived in his tower prison.

"Trust me," he added. "I'm something of an authority in the matter of human emotions." In a way Gordan too was glad Raiden was gone. The weight of his psyche had been particularly difficult to bear, even more so than the strange depths of Nicole's. "Don't punish him for loving you."

Gordan immediately felt Nicole recoil. Her warm hum in the air spasmed with a clash of emotions—embarrassment, anxiety, joy, guilt.

"Maybe he's safer there with them than with me. With me he would be deemed a traitor on sight."

"As good as being a dragon," Gordan said.

"But with the Council he has some chance of hiding in plain sight … until he gets caught."

"He might not get caught," Gordan said.

"Either way, I can't do anything about it now. All I can do is worry about the people I *can* protect. Once I say goodbye to my other brother, that leaves only one." She looked at him.

"Why worry about me?" His stomach twisted, and his heart pounded. He couldn't remember the last time he'd experienced this sensation, the heat spreading through his chest.

Nicole smiled, and for a moment he thought she would leave him without an answer.

"I thought I was setting you free when I removed those chains. But the way I see it, I didn't really accomplish that goal. I will never forgive myself if I don't."

Gordan leaned back into the seat and looked out at the road unfurling into the desert. In the distance lay a sea of rolling sand dunes. Beyond that were the faint purple silhouettes of far-off mountains. If he had the choice to be back home in the Wastelands among his own kind in the safety of exile and surrounded by the illusion of freedom, he'd still rather be beside Nicole, going wherever this road would lead them.

5. Ready

Raiden fastened his shirt with deft fingers working their way up the buttons. He folded the clothes he had been wearing and placed them in the back of the empty bottom drawer before murmuring, "*Ungesewen*."

The clothes disappeared beneath a cloak of magic, and he closed the drawer. The muffled voice of Caeruleus caught Raiden's ear. It sounded as if he was talking to someone, speaking and pausing. Raiden stepped out of his room just as Caeruleus slipped a small object back into his pocket.

"Were you talking to someone?" Raiden asked.

"Just checking in. Someone else had to pick up my patrol since they called me in for the fera assignment. She's still getting to know the regulars."

"How much has the Council told you about this assignment, Caeruleus?" Raiden wasn't just concerned for Nicole.

"They aren't keeping secrets, Raiden," he said with a confident laugh.

"Really? You didn't know I was alive until I walked out of that hall today. One man is already dead because of the Council's mission to find the fera."

"Yes, because of the *fera*," Caeruleus corrected. "Sinnrick was inexperienced, and the Council underestimated the danger. From what I know, this fera is new to her powers. They thought that meant she would be easy to handle, but it seems to me she's as dangerous as the rest, having that kind of power and not knowing how to control it. That's only one reason why this is so urgent."

Raiden clenched his jaw, holding back his urge to argue with Caeruleus over something he wasn't supposed to have much knowledge about. He shouldn't be angry that Caeruleus was so convinced of Nicole's threat. After learning what had happened in Cantis, Caeruleus needed to believe the Council had been unable to intervene rather than unwilling. Raiden knew the corrosive nature of that knowledge all too well, and it dragged him down to the dank depths of hate, while Caeruleus enjoyed the hard-earned hope for a better future by trusting in the Council.

"Maybe you should consider the possibility that she's only dangerous because she's being targeted," Raiden said.

"Even if that's true, it doesn't change the fact that her presence in the other realm puts the barrier between Veil and the old world at risk. She could unravel it, Raiden, and we don't know what that means for the people of Veil should that happen."

"And what was the reason for hunting down the fera before Nicole, the ones in Veil?"

"The Council does what they must to keep Veil safe. The other fera proved they couldn't live in peace. They were threatening too many lives. Their powers were too volatile. Did you have the chance to see her capabilities?"

"I did."

"Can she control herself?"

"When she isn't provoked, when her life isn't being threatened—yes. I worry that the Council is creating their own problem and they're sending you in to confront it."

"You don't need to worry about me, Raiden. Besides, you know the most about her, and I'll have your guidance."

"What will the Council do if a portal doesn't open? What if she stays on the move and preserves the barrier's integrity?" He tried to conceal the hope in his challenge.

"That's just the simplest way to find her. We can open portals too, you know. It's difficult these days, but it can be done. It's a mere matter of making attempts to open a portal until you find someplace with just enough of a link. We'll find her eventually."

"Well, in that case, all I can do is help you prepare," Raiden said, his heart sinking in his chest.

Nicole and Gordan sat listening to a new species of silence, without words yet filled with the rumble of the truck. The landscape around them was all brown earth and parched blue sky.

"I feel oddly at home here," Gordan remarked as he studied the bare mountains out Nicole's window to the west, her profile set against them providing a soft contrast to the harsh, rocky backdrop as it scrolled past. "Of course, the Wastelands are lacking in roads, let alone anyone to travel them." His eyes shifted to a strange vehicle coming toward them. Its front end was much like Nicole's truck but much taller, and behind it stretched a massive rectangular box on wheels. It roared past, charging in the opposite direction, toward what he and Nicole were leaving behind them.

"No big rigs delivering goods to you guys out in the Wastelands?" A wry smile pulled the corner of her mouth upward.

"I don't think there has even been a single letter delivered to the Wastelands," Gordan said frankly. "There was a time we believed someone might come. We thought maybe one day the hostility would ebb. We actually started a road that was meant to cross the Wastelands, but it was abandoned. Given enough time, we let even our strongest of hopes die." His words were heavy.

"I think you're lying," she said, looking at the road ahead. "You think it's easier to be disappointed than to keep hoping. It hurts to hope for something that isn't coming, and the longer you wait, the more it hurts to hope. The dragons maybe gave up on the road, but I suspect you haven't stopped hoping."

Gordan looked at her, dumbfounded by her accuracy. For a brief moment he wondered whether his voice or words had betrayed his buried yearnings or whether Nicole's raw magic and his debt connected them in a way that let her tap into his own unique senses. He was the empath, yet she had peered deeper into his own heart than he ever took care to look.

"And what will you do? Give up hope or keep it?" he asked.

"I have more important things to worry about," Nicole said with a shrug. "What good does it do me to break my heart hoping for something I might never get? I'm better off focusing on what I have to do today; otherwise I'll defeat myself."

"You *will* see Raiden again." He was guessing—all he *could* do was guess. He could feel her longing, but he did not know what her mind was picturing, what her heart wanted.

She pressed her lips together and peered harder through the windshield, confirming his assumption. Gordan had to trust that Raiden wouldn't get caught. Gordan didn't care much for lying to Nicole. *Don't make me a liar, Raiden.*

In the backyard of Nicole's home, gleaming green and crowded with blooms, the plants no longer trembled. Their quivering growth in Nicole's presence had ceased, and the air was oddly still. Then the lingering traces of Nicole's magic in the ground and the blossoms of the rosebushes drained away, and the blue of the sky over the house rippled. The clovers shriveled into a brown shroud over the earth, and the flowers withered into crumbling husks as the portal above opened just long enough for a man to slip through.

Vinderek dropped onto the slope of the tile roof. The sole of his boot slipped down the red tile roof, and he crouched to steady himself. The portal was already closed, but that didn't matter. He wasn't going to return without the fera, and once he found her, he could open another. He stood, carefully this time, and made his way down the east side of the roof. When he reached the edge, he dropped down to the ground between the house and the wall.

With a confident stride, he rounded the corner of the house and walked across the patio, surveying the dry brown yard as he went. So this was where the fera had been all this time, living some mundane life without magic. Well, her fate had found her nonetheless. The last remaining fera must have thought she was escaping her destiny by coming to this realm. His chest shook with a silent laugh.

He approached the door into the house. It was dim inside, and he could hardly see through the window without pressing his face against the glass. He closed his hand around the knob, and to his surprise it turned. Vinderek stepped into the house. It was quiet. He scanned the living room with calculating eyes before heading for the stairs.

As he made his way toward the second floor, he slowed to study the photographs on the wall. Several frames contained a set of three children, two boys and a girl. That had to be her. As he went, the children in the photos grew older. At last he reached the landing. His eyes locked on a picture of three adults, two men and a young woman. He had just seen their lives unfold in candid moments and posed embraces. These were the same three children. This young woman was undoubtedly the fera.

He plucked the frame off the wall. Then he heard the low flap of fabric and a huff come from the room to the left of the landing. He moved carefully to the right, passing a washroom on his way to the door at the end of the hall, his heavy boots silent on the plush carpet. With the toe of his boot, he nudged the door open and peered inside. At first he couldn't be sure this was her room, but then he spotted a photograph sitting atop the dresser of the fera and another girl with long yellow hair embracing, their smiling faces pressed together.

He stepped through the doorway into her room and approached the dresser, leaning in close to study this picture. The fera and her friend were similar and yet opposite. The fera's long curls were dark brown and her friend's pale gold. The fera's skin was a tanned brown, and her friend's was fair. Vinderek committed the face to memory.

Wherever the fera had gone, he could wait. Now he had time to study her. He picked up an intricately carved wooden box that fit in the palm of his hand. It was covered in tiny five-petal flowers. When she returned, and he knew she would eventually, then he would be ready.

Caeruleus said farewell and left to meet with the agent who needed to be briefed on his patrol district. Raiden was both relieved and anxious. He didn't want to be in this apartment, but he was grateful to be alone again after his friend had insisted on questioning him about Nicole. He maintained that he hadn't interacted with her much beyond a brief encounter during the unfortunate events that night in the castle.

He paced the apartment, studying the blank walls, the cleanliness of its emptiness. He sat down in the red chair and let himself sink back in it. As a precaution, he kept his mind off Nicole. Instead he listened, watched, felt. The chair did not hum or grow slightly warm at all, no hint of magic. He stood, scanning the room with slow scrutiny as he moved toward the couch.

The walls did not shimmer or wiggle in the slightest as he combed them top to bottom with an untrusting gaze. Next he sat on the couch, the springs inside giving a little whine. He turned and lay across it, setting his eyes on the ceiling and the light. Everything was still. All was silent. At least as far as he could tell, there were no charms or spells spying on him in this room.

Raiden sat up, stood, and returned to the bedroom. After studying the room for several minutes and lying on the bed, which felt like any other bed yet didn't feel like he belonged in it, he determined that there was no magic left here either. He lay there, letting himself sink into the silence.

He didn't want to like it here. He had never set foot in this place before, and yet it was all too familiar. This room felt the same as the one in Cantis, and the solitude was unsurprisingly soothing to him. But he didn't want to return to that place, to slip back into that numb void again.

Raiden jerked upright and removed himself from the bed with haste. The Council had given him two days to settle in. He couldn't afford to waste that time. With the key to the apartment in his pocket, he turned the knob and yanked the door open. If the Council was watching him, he certainly couldn't be blamed for anything more than getting to know the city.

Outside the door, he pulled the key from his pocket and eyed it carefully, noticing the slightest wobble of light like a mirage, a telltale sign of magic embedded in the object. It could be innocent enough, just a key with a seeking spell to lead him back to the keyhole. He wasn't about to risk it, though.

He dropped the key back into the pocket of his trousers and waved his hand in front of the doorknob, locking it with a spell of his own. To be safe, he had to find someone who could erase the memories from the clothes Nicole had given him. As much as Raiden had learned from his room full of books, there was little he had actually put into practice over the years. He had focused on spells to survive—keeping his home safe, growing foods in the summer where the rocky island terrain permitted, fishing on the sagging, dilapidated docks—and to prepare for confronting Moira, nothing like what he needed now. Knowing magic in theory and putting it into practice were two totally different things. With a huff he turned away from the door and surveyed the street.

There had to be someone in this city, a master spell worker who wouldn't report him to the Council, someone who could help him. He wandered the dark and quiet streets as the sky above grew lighter. This place was vastly different from Cantis. There was life here. The lamps that lit the streets were fading as daylight arrived. The occasional pedestrian ventured out into the early morning, starting his or her day.

He knew it was unlikely that shops would be open before sunup. So he walked, taking in the city while it stirred from its slumber. As time went on, shop owners started to arrive at their shops, unlocking their doors and uncovering their windows. Vendors pushed their carts onto the street and began placing wares out for display. More and more people joined the morning bustle, until Raiden could not walk half a block without bumping at least three people.

He tried to insist that he could get used to crowds again, that the gradual increase in pedestrians was perfectly tolerable. He told himself he was fine surrounded by the citizens of Atrium. But against reason his heart rate increased, and the noise of the city stirred dark memories. Before he knew it, he came upon a side street that was virtually empty, and he escaped the throng of people.

Raiden kept to the quieter streets, trying to find the least crowded routes. So long as the foot traffic wasn't too great, he could keep the sounds of his past silent and his heart at ease. He focused on memorizing the streets and each turn he took, keeping in mind which way he was going.

He followed the key back to his apartment, committing the way to memory. His desire to avoid crowds seemed to bring him mostly through streets without shops. The buildings around him were residential. It was inevitable that he would have to traverse the busier streets sooner or later if he hoped to find a spell worker. Glancing at his apartment building as he passed, he set out to take a different route than he had before. He needed to know this city and these streets as much as he needed to find help.

The sun climbed higher, peeking over the tops of buildings. He scanned the shop fronts as he walked, peering into the windows in search for the right contents, not the merchandise but someone within who might benefit him. He came to a bookshop, dim and crowded with full shelves.

A memory flashed through his mind, of a moment in another room filled with books where Nicole stood with a bright and eager gaze observing the piles and stacks of books around her. The memory struck his heart with a pang, and he pushed it away in frustration. Lamenting over their unexpected separation would not help him, nor would it help her. If he wanted a future with her in it again, he would have to stop lingering in the past. Realizing he had paused outside the bookshop, his gaze lost among the countless spines of likely friends, he huffed and forced himself forward once more.

His eyes trailed along more doors and windows as he walked. A looking glass shop was filled with mirrors of every shape and size imaginable, all facing the window, throwing his passing scowl back at him.

He passed a small confectionery establishment, its door and window propped open to the street. Beneath the open window a man worked at a large cooking table filled with cylindrical depressions. A wave of heat rolled off the surface of his workplace. As Raiden passed, he watched the man ladle a sweet-smelling batter into the depressions, where they hissed and fizzled.

The scent of pancakes struck his brain with the intensity of the Sight—a morning spent in the kitchen with Nicole's family. Only now it occurred to him just how much he had lost, and he felt foolish for it, for letting himself think they had all become *his* family in a week.

With a quickened pace he pressed on. He passed a shoe shop, then a potions supply shop, its windows filled with bottles and vials, the shelves around the walls within packed with odd ingredients: pickled pieces of unknown things and withered, dry husks of what could have once been living creatures. He frowned, not at the vast and unappealing array of ingredients, but because he had never had the resources to teach himself this particular art. The contents of the potion shops in Cantis had been rifled through and ruined in people's futile attempts to find something, anything that would save them from the onslaught of golems flooding the city. The survival rate of that day revealed their success.

Annoyed by the plague of unpleasant memories, he scolded himself. He used to be so practiced at not feeling, and for a naive moment he wondered what had happened to him—Nicole had happened.

Just ahead the scraping sound of stiff bristles against the stone drew his eyes up from their unfocused stare. A middle-aged man stood in the door of his shop sweeping salt from the floor of his establishment, over the threshold, and out into the street gutter. As often as the mineral was used to flavor food, it was also used to clean out homes and scour away traces of residual magic, left behind from the many household spells and charms all working within.

Given enough time, a place could become so caked with the unseen grime of old magic that it could wreak havoc, interfering with other charms or spells and causing spontaneous upsets to nearby things—not unlike the way Nicole's magic would escape her and act randomly on the nearest objects. He recalled her room filled with hovering and spinning possessions while she slept.

Raiden refocused on the present. With each thrust of the broom, the tiny granules of salt leaped into the air, not white but every color, thousands of tiny sponges defiled with old magic. Some bits of salt glimmered in the daylight, and others jumped and even popped, giving off a tiny spark as the shopkeeper chased them out his door and into the gutter.

The man finished brushing the walkway clean and turned back to his store. He glanced at Raiden and gave a cordial nod in passing. A bell jingled as the door closed behind the shop owner, and Raiden read the words painted on the glass: TOVAR'S CHARMS & TRINKETS.

Raiden continued down the street until he reached the corner. The corner shop just off his left shoulder housed an elaborate display of wooden figurines—faceless and without clothes—sitting on carpets, riding astride broomsticks, or hanging from umbrellas, all charmed to fly about like a little circus. One figurine stepped through a small, glossy green door on one side of the display and appeared through another identical door on the other side. Gold letters upon the window gleamed at him: WORLDWIDE WANDERERS EMPORIUM—No Distance Too Great.

A smug snort escaped Raiden, and he turned to look across the street. On the opposite corner another store beckoned. The windowpane was enchanted to spell out words as if written by an invisible hand: *Larburrak's Spell Craft. Charms for every need. Spells for every deed. Enduring magic, guaranteed.* Raiden's eyes followed the glimmering letters as they looped and curled across the glass.

Entranced for a moment, he realized the cross street he had come to was far busier than the one behind him. He supposed he might as well see what this Larburrak had to offer. With a sigh he shrugged and pressed onward into the little stream of people making their way to the other side of the street.

In his attempt to not notice the people around him, Raiden concentrated on the shop ahead of him. Then the foul musk of someone's body odor mixed with what seemed to be burnt hair and a hint of fish disrupted his focus. Just a couple of steps in front of him a large wooden crate bobbed, strapped to a sweaty man's back. The painted words on the crate read E. TURNETTY GLUE. The man adjusted his load with a grunt and, to the relief of Raiden's nose, veered right down the cross street as Raiden went left toward the door into Larburrak's.

The golden knob turned before Raiden could touch it, and the door swung open for him just as the thick presence of all the people on the street began to press on him. He stepped into a rich, dark wood-paneled room lit by orange-tasseled lamps on the walls. Across the floor were three pairs of work desks, each pair sitting side by side facing the entrance. A long, ornate carpet bisected the room from back to front, separating the three desks on the left from the three on the right.

At each table sat a spell worker. Nearest him a freckle-skinned woman with sandy-brown hair pulled back to the nape of her neck sat bent over a compact mirror, two palm-sized silver disks hinged together. She examined her reflection in the glass, and a tiny ringing voice said, "Don't you look lowly today!" The woman frowned at the slight mistake in her spell work.

"Good man, good man. Welcome. I see you have never visited Larburrak's before." The boisterous voice crashed through the silence of the room. Several of the workers jumped in their seats.

At first Raiden could not be sure where the voice had come from, until he spotted a man's head bobbing along behind the long, high table at the back of the room. A short, round man came around the table and crossed the room with unexpected speed given his plumpness and short legs.

"Sorriso Larburrak," he said, taking Raiden's hand and giving it a vigorous shake.

Larburrak beamed a broad smile that pulled Raiden's eyes down from the lacquered black hair atop his head. "What brings you in? Come to commission a coat? Our impenetrable charms are the best for keeping you dry. If it's not rain, it's that incessant mist and fog, I tell you. Or perhaps you need an everlasting enchantment on a bouquet for some lucky young lady? We don't supply the flowers of course. I *just* sent a man out with the most secure wallet you will find. The expanded interior can hold more coins than a man could hope to carry, *and* an infallible security spell prevents anyone else access to the money—everyone else just finds an empty wallet."

Raiden was slightly amazed the man had managed all that in a single breath. "No," he answered, "no, I don't need anything like that, I'm afraid."

"Well then, come in, come in." Larburrak extended his arm toward the back of the room, inviting Raiden to follow the long, narrow carpet to the high table. "Let's discuss your needs more comfortably."

Raiden glanced up at the gaudy orange lampshades again as he took an uncertain step along the carpet.

"Electricity, my good man. We do not risk the slightest interference with our spell working," Larburrak chattered on.

As he passed the second pair of desks, Raiden couldn't help but notice a man turn his face and glare at his boss, who obviously didn't suppose his blaring sales pitch might disrupt his workers' concentration.

"You'll see there are no shelves here. No sir. We work every spell fresh. None of our products sit around losing their luster."

They reached the back table. Larburrak bustled around to the other side and stepped up three short steps so that, at last, he could look Raiden in the eye.

"Now then." Larburrak closed his hands together. He finally lowered his voice, having seemingly secured some kind of service from Raiden. "I can assure you I employ only the very best. There is no magic too difficult ..."

Raiden held back a smile. He highly doubted that. If they were the very best, the Council would most likely have them working magic for the courts, just as they'd rounded up every seer in the realm in order to rescue the noble Sight from its frivolous reputation of palm reading and fortune-telling. His mother's words rang in his ear. *Oh, they are paid well, the court's seers, but what does pay matter when you're a prisoner of your work?*

As a child he had been horrified, imagining the Council coming to take his mother and him away in chains to lock them away in some basement with all the other seers of the realm. *They are not prisoners of the courts, dear one; they are prisoners of the Sight. It does not have to be that way. I escaped it and ran as far as one can from such things. I am safe, and you are safe. Your father made sure of that.*

Raiden pulled himself out of his past in time to hear Larburrak's speech about excellence come to a conclusion.

"How are they with erasing objects' memories?" Raiden asked, but Larburrak didn't seem to listen and continued his sales pitch.

"We work from scratch here, but we provide repair work as well. Sometimes a spell starts to fail, you know, and people need it mended. Well, the best solution is to remove the spell work altogether and start from scratch. Of course, people never bring us our own work to mend, usually that of subpar workers whose spells won't last you a month, if that." Larburrak's volume crept back upward as he prattled praise over his business like a doting mother over a sour-faced brat.

"No." Raiden had to force his way back into the conversation. "I just need someone who can wipe objects of their memories. Can your people do that?"

Larburrak was stumped into silence for a moment before bursting with assurance. "We pride ourselves on excellence here. Only the very best."

Raiden's eyes drifted around as Larburrak fumbled. His long-winded boasts were now short, broken bits of everything he'd already said.

"Of course, even the best must encounter a task for the first time, but I assure you my team can solve any problem you have." His voice was louder than ever.

Just then, movement behind Larburrak caught Raiden's eye. On the back wall four of the wood panels swung open, revealing a narrow door. A young man with copper hair sidled through the door carrying a vase, spotted Raiden and Larburrak, and immediately looked frightened. Behind him Raiden could see a room that seemed to be endless, filled with shelves laden with things of all sorts: hats, dishes, jewelry boxes, lamps ...

"The bell, the bell, I told you," Larburrak growled through his teeth, and the boy jumped backward through the hidden door and slammed it shut.

Raiden mashed his lips together, attempting to suppress a grin. Larburrak whirled back around and attempted to continue as though Raiden were still completely oblivious to the door and the infinite storeroom behind it.

"We can schedule a consultation and have our most experienced spell workers assess your ... what was it you said you were having trouble with?" He was losing momentum, and consequently his volume diminished as well.

"I didn't," Raiden said. "I'm afraid I have somewhere to be."

"We'll schedule an appointment for you then," Larburrak persisted, pulling a thick logbook over to him and opening it hastily.

"That won't be necessary," Raiden said, a single chuckle breaking through his words as he took a step back. "Thank you for your time," he added as he turned toward the door.

While he crossed the long carpet again, he could have sworn he heard the spell workers snickering at their desks. Raiden strode out of the shop and halted before being nearly run over by a gaggle of women hurrying past the door discussing where the best prices for produce could be found.

"Apples for only five coppers per pound, just down the street."

"Oh, but heard it was only four over on McNabb."

Stalling, he glanced up at the street sign standing beside him. He stood on the corner of Rood and Hout Streets. His gaze shifted back to the Worldwide Wanderers Emporium on the opposite corner, tempting him to return to the quiet of Rood Street. Resisting the urge to double back, he wrestled his discomfort to the back of his mind. There had to be countless spell workers in this city and a genuine master of their craft somewhere among them.

Raiden stepped into the shuffling current of people moving along down Hout Street. He stayed on the right side of the street with the flood of people between him and the quiet stretch of Rood Street he already knew. He quickened his pace, as though he could escape his unsettling thoughts by leaving behind the slower pedestrians.

Busying himself with the task of searching the storefronts for another spell-working business, he moved at such a brisk pace that it was all his mind could do to analyze the potential of each sign and service he would find inside.

A hat shop, a grocer, a wand shop—wand makers were especially gifted but usually only with wands. He raked his gaze along the doors and windows of the shops across the street—a florist, a glamour shop, an inn, a shoe shop. On he walked, until he came to the next cross street, Mat Street. A warm, spicy mix of scents wafted down the street—food.

He turned right onto Mat Street before he could think better of it. With no money in his pockets and nothing but food vendors and restaurants before him, it would only be a waste of time. But still, his grumbling belly pulled him. As he passed a vendor of cured meats, a boy wearing an identical apron to the vendor was pushing tiny samples into the hands of passersby. Raiden took the little hunk of salty meat and chewed it slowly, careful not to let it disappear too quickly. It tasted a little too strongly of pepper, but at least it was something.

Mat Street was wide for a pedestrian-only street, and much of the street was crowded with tables, chairs, benches, and people enjoying their food, leaving a center walkway that could comfortably fit people walking five abreast.

As he went, he was bombarded by conversation from all sides.

"—and someone keeps charming the flowers in my window box to turn red!"

"Sounds like some harmless kid who's learned a new—"

"Grandfather actually suggested I get a wand. Can you believe that?"

"I practice with one. They *do* help with accuracy—"

"But they're so old-fashioned—"

"—missed the time of the next gathering. I couldn't hear a thing."

"It's going to be—"

"—Dolus can fix that. His work is affordable."

"Affordable always means poor workmanship."

"Trust me—he's *good* at what he does."

Raiden slowed to listen.

"Why so affordable, then?" The skeptical reply came from a large man hunched over a potpie. He shoveled a mouthful past his mustache. The big man's companion was half his size.

"Because he doesn't have a shop. Too many licenses and taxes—doesn't want to pay the fees and deal with all the regulatory paperwork the courts insist on these days."

In his attempt to hear more, Raiden turned toward the pie shop called Meat Pies & Sweet Pies. He was so focused on the strangers' conversation that his gaze remained fixed slightly over his shoulder.

"Can I get you anything?" The woman's voice came from behind the counter, stealing Raiden's attention from the discussion of Dolus.

He looked up and met the pale-blue eyes of a young woman with a long plait of hair the same pale blue as her gaze. Under the sun it shined silver. Raiden's spine went rigid. He knew this woman—or, rather, he would know her—from a glimpse of his future. The sight of her nearly stopped his heart. At his silence she smiled, her eyes maintaining her question.

"No." He took a step back and bumped into someone behind him. "I'm sorry," he said to them both as he turned toward the street.

"No harm done. Hello, Gwyn. Can I get a family meat pie? It's going to be a busy day," said the woman he had bumped into as she stepped up to the counter.

As he passed the two men, he listened closely but refused to slow his retreat from the silver-haired woman.

"—usually over on Black Street, sometimes on—" The man's voice was swallowed by the distance and the surrounding din of patrons.

Raiden could hear no more, so he continued down Mat Street. He couldn't even be sure the two men were still talking about that Dolus person anymore, but it was more information than he'd had before now, and the more space he put between himself and the woman with silver hair the better.

6. Lost

When the first salty whiff of the sea blustered through Nicole's open window, she inhaled it deeply. She let out a sigh and felt calmer, sinking back against the seat of the truck as it rumbled and rattled down the California 101 toward Ventura. The exit sign for Seaward Avenue prompted a bittersweet smile to stir her lips, which had been set in a firm line for the better part of the six-hour drive.

The exit ramp came to a T at Seaward. When she stopped the truck at the red light, the slight lurch made Gordan suddenly sit upright.

"Manage to fall asleep?" she asked, surprised that he could with the noise of the old vehicle at interstate speeds. Not to mention his tall, lanky frame seemed uncomfortably folded and hunched in his corner of the cab.

The light ahead turned green, and she put the truck into first gear and turned left onto Seaward, her heart accelerating as the truck did. Had she been this nervous about telling her dad or showing Mitchell what she had become? That had been only a week ago, and yet she couldn't remember. She couldn't think of anything except what she was going to say to Anthony.

Seaward took them over the 101 and past a grocery store. Straight ahead of them at the end of Seaward was the vast blue ocean. She turned left onto Pierpont Boulevard, and suddenly they were surrounded by a neighborhood of seaside homes. At the end of Pierpont the street led to a green park, and she turned right on the last street of the neighborhood, where the houses looked across the lane at a park.

They passed more than fifteen houses before they reached the end of the road. She turned around in the cul-de-sac that looked out over the beach and parked the truck along the park side of the street. For several minutes all she could do was sit there in the silent truck as the low whisper of surf rushed in around them.

As glad as she was to see her brother, she felt heavy with grief. She couldn't deny that this visit was a precautionary farewell. Her eyes stung again. Part of her hoped he might take her news badly, fear for his family, ask her to leave. But she knew Anthony. Nothing scared him.

After what seemed like ages wringing the steering wheel in her hands and inhaling the scent of the ocean mingling with the smell of desert dust in the cab of the truck, Nicole opened the door and climbed out. Gordan followed.

"Which one?" Gordan asked, looking across the street at the houses facing them.

Nicole pointed toward a house in the middle of the street several houses down, but she did not head that direction. She bent over, pulled off her red Chucks, and dropped them into the back of the truck.

It was a relief to refocus her senses—the grit of the sandy asphalt under her feet, the smell of washed-up seaweed with the slight, sharp rot of marine life trapped within it, the salty air in her lungs, the breeze pulling at her loose curls. She raked her hair back. Longer and wilder than ever, it seemed to have grown several months' worth in the short week since her life had ... changed.

"I thought we were going to your brother's house," Gordan said.

"He won't be home from work for another hour or so," Nicole said with a shrug as she stepped over the low wall at the end of the street.

Walking through the sand was cathartic. Even the sharp jabs from broken shells were welcome. They crossed the beach in just a minute, arriving at the cold, compact sand near the water. Nicole stood there and waited as a coming wave rushed toward her across the sand and tumbled over her feet. The wave slid back, and she sank a little, her feet half buried.

Like the waves, Raiden would slip from her mind but then rush back in after a time. Her heart felt confined, like her rib cage was just too crowded, churning with too many feelings. She worried; she hoped. She steeled herself against his absence. She wished he was there, and she was glad that he wasn't. She wanted to take this on alone and spare everyone she loved, but she was frightened. She cherished her independence but feared the utter solitude creeping in around her.

"If you keep that up, you will attract mermaids," Gordan said in a flat, matter-of-fact tone, his cool gaze moving across the water.

"I've always wanted to meet one." Her voice mirrored his.

"You don't. Trust me."

Nicole let out an amused sigh. "Right, we're talking about the sailor-drowning kind, not the animated kind."

"True, they kill men without discrimination. But they are perhaps more dangerous to women with broken hearts." Gordan's voice was grave.

Nicole almost protested the implication that her heart was broken, but she couldn't kid an empath, let alone herself. She knew it had been broken in ten different ways by now, especially after today, losing a friend, leaving home, saying goodbye to her family, not knowing if she would ever get to live again.

She looked out across the ocean, past the oil rig in the distance. She would be happy to know there were mermaids in those waters, even if they were dark, murderous creatures. But there was no magic in this world, save for her and Gordan now. Her hair whipped around her face, and the waves filled her ears. She would feel sorry for even vindictive creatures like mermaids if they had to live in these filthy oceans.

It seemed to her that the inhabitants of Veil were better off where they were, but was this realm better off without them, without magic? She wondered what Gordan thought and thought to break their silence, but an unknown pair of arms suddenly closed around her, lifting her easily.

Her heart lurched. A flare of terror and magic rushed through her. She heard his laugh just before her magic swallowed her up. She scattered, every molecule of her being burned, and she tumbled through the air on the breeze. Then the next instant she fell, solid and heavy again, into the salty, shallow waters.

The cold Pacific shocked her. Her thoughts were jumbled and confused. For a moment she thought she was elsewhere, in another body of cold water. Her racing heart brought her back, face-to-face with the kelpie. But then her mind reclaimed reality. The sun was shining overhead. She wasn't in a dark forest beneath dark waters peering into black eyes.

She heaved herself onto her feet, unsteady as the waves moved around her legs, still wobbly with disorientation. Throwing her wet hair from her face, she staggered under the weight of her sodden clothes toward the beach, where her oldest brother stood beside Gordan. There was a mask of complete shock on Anthony's face and a look of discreet amusement on Gordan's.

Nicole didn't know whether to laugh at Anthony's expression or curse at Gordan for letting him sneak up on her like that. She knew damn well that dragon had heard Anthony coming. She found a happy medium by throwing Gordan a fierce glare before releasing a bashful smile as she marched the short way up the beach.

Nicole stood before her brother and waited. He looked at her dripping form for a moment before speaking.

"Er ... sorry," he said with an attempted smile that came across as a cringe.

She broke down and laughed, her heart laden with affection, relief, and anxiety all together. For a second she felt as if her laughter might turn into sobs, but she kept them back and silenced herself.

"I thought you would be at work still" was all she could think to say.

"Dad called and said you were coming. I saw the truck on the street. I can't believe you drove that thing from Yuma."

"Yeah."

Anthony nodded. He was almost a carbon copy of their father; his eyes were the same grayish blue, only his hair was dirty blond, like Mitchell's.

"So I'm guessing this is the 'recent development' Dad was talking about." He sounded dazed.

"Yeah, the last week has been a little crazy." She twisted her anxiety into a smile.

"Mitch told me you found yourself a boyfriend. I was worried you were pregnant or something," Anthony teased.

Nicole scowled, remembering Mitchell's insistence that she torment Anthony with her magic. Her eyes narrowed, and with a quick pulse of magic her brother sank neck-deep into the sand in a blink.

He let out a startled cry. "Okay! All right! I'm sorry," he insisted, squirming and loosening the wet, compact sand around him. He heaved an arm free, then the other, and dragged himself out, completely coated in sand.

"Oh, it's too late for 'sorry,' Tony," she said with a devious grin. "You're looking at over a decade's worth of payback."

Anthony tried his best to brush the sand off his clothes, only partly succeeding. He laughed. "They say karma's a bitch. All joking aside, though"— he looked at her for a moment, then caught her in a real hug this time—"I'm glad you're here."

"Me too," she murmured into his sandy shirt.

When he released her, she looked down at herself, now partially covered in sand. As real as Anthony's affection was, she understood his ulterior motive.

"Thanks for that," she said with a sweet grimace.

"Anytime," he answered, throwing an arm around her shoulders to hold her to his side. "So who's your friend?" His question dripped with that same suggestive tone Mitchell had used the first time he'd seen Raiden.

Gordan stood by watching them with a twist of amusement on his mouth.

"This is Gordan," Nicole said, smiling at the memory of his natural form when she looked at him.

"I thought Mitch said it was … something with an *R*," Anthony said, scratching his head.

"Raiden …" Nicole trailed off.

"… is no longer with us," Gordan continued for her. "He had business elsewhere."

"Oh, all right. Well, should we head to the house, then?" Anthony looked down at his much-shorter sister, still clamped close to his side by his grip.

"Sure," she said. "Are the girls home?"

"They should be home soon."

"Um … should I keep this a secret?" Nicole asked. She didn't like secrets, but she felt it was her brother's decision.

"They're five, Nikki. Who's going to believe them when they say their aunt's a … what would you say?"

"You really want to know?" She let out a bitter laugh as they trekked through the deep, dry sand toward the neighborhood.

"What difference does it make?" He shrugged. "Like I said, no one will believe five-year-olds."

Nicole's heart nearly burst, and her eyes burned. She almost cursed out loud. She wanted to yell at him, at all of them, Mitch and her dad too. Why did they have to be so damn understanding, so accepting? It would be easier to keep them safe, to say goodbye and leave them behind, if they were afraid of her. For a moment she would have preferred they push her away so that she didn't have to do it herself.

She glanced at Gordan, who gave her a scrutinizing look. He was trying to decipher her; she could tell that much from his piercing violet eyes. Again her chest swelled with that painfully perfect warmth. At least she had Gordan. She watched his expression change from suspicion to surprise, and she knew he'd detected her sudden shift from distress to gratitude. Love, she admitted easily to herself. From the moment she'd first laid eyes on Gordan, she'd loved him, and it *still* confused him. A tiny snicker broke past her smile.

"So how did you and Gordan meet?" Anthony asked.

Nicole let out an audible laugh, impressed that her brother had managed to pinpoint the exact subject of the silence between her and Gordan. To her surprise, Gordan was the one to answer.

"Your sister saved my life," Gordan said matter-of-factly.

She choked, surprised by his blunt explanation and unusual talkativeness.

"Well ..." Anthony said, and Nicole pitied his search for a response. "I guess that's not altogether surprising. Nikki always had a habit of rescuing stray animals whenever the opportunity presented itself. Isn't that right?" He chuckled as they stepped over the low wall and into the cul-de-sac.

Nicole pressed her lips together as tight as she could to hold back her laughter, but when she looked at Gordan and saw his reaction to the word *stray*, she failed miserably.

"I'm guessing there's more to the story," Anthony said with a smile.

"I don't know," Nicole said, bending over the truck bed to grab her shoes. "You seem pretty spot on there."

Anthony only looked confused.

"Why don't I explain the last week of chaos from the beginning?" Nicole said.

"It will have to wait until after we get cleaned up," he said, giving his shirt a shake. Sand fell free from the damp material.

"That will take too long," Nicole said. As much as she would love the comfort of a warm shower after being dunked in the Pacific, there was a much-faster way.

She released a tiny burst of power from her core. The magic rolled through her, filling her up and moving outward like a wave. It warmed her, left her clothes dry, and carried away with it every last grain of sand. Her magic washed over her brother with enough force that he had to lean against it. A cloud of sand leaped away from him and dropped to the ground.

"There," she said.

7. Ally

It took Raiden the next couple of hours to find Black Street. He was leery of the potential that the Council might be monitoring him, and any indication that he was doing anything but wandering might seem odd. He hoped that the Council was more concerned with the seers looking for Nicole than what he might be up to in the city. The person he'd overheard those two men talking about ended up being easy to find, once he made it to Black Street. Raiden wandered down an alley where there was nothing to be found but a door that shouldn't have been there. He looked around once more before he knocked.

"One moment," a voice called.

After a few minutes the door opened, and a woman came out looking rather satisfied with an umbrella in her hands, followed by an average man. Everything about him was average. His hair was a shade of brown right between light and dark, and he was not as tall as Raiden but not short either.

"And you're sure my son will *have* to walk straight home when using it?" the woman verified, speaking over her shoulder as she walked through the door.

"That's right. Won't even know it. Should solve his troublemaking, at least on days that it might rain." The man's voice was a comfortable middle octave, its tone halfway between silky and gravely.

They both laughed. From what Raiden gathered, a clear, sunny day really was a rarity in this city. He glanced up at the blue sky.

"Thank you, Dolus. Are you *sure* the payment is enough? This is worth so much more."

"Now, now. I've told you: what's more valuable to me is you telling your friends and sending me business. Don't you worry."

They both noticed Raiden. The woman gave him a polite nod before hurrying down the alley and back to the street.

"Here for some spell work?" Dolus asked Raiden.

"That depends," Raiden answered.

"Well, if you don't mind taking a short walk with me, we can discuss what you need."

Dolus closed the door and then pulled it off the wall entirely. Behind it there was only a brick wall. He muttered something, and the door folded itself down to the size of a handbag, though it was rigid and square. Grasping it by the brass door handle, Dolus inclined his head toward the street. "Shall we?"

They walked out of the alley, turned onto Black Street, and walked a short way to the next street, Thorn. They turned, walked a ways, and crossed the street toward another alley. As they went, Raiden struggled to pinpoint the quality Dolus possessed that seemed odd to him. For such an unremarkable man, who would hardly stand out in one's memory without effort, to be so puzzling had Raiden at a loss for explanation.

"Here we are," Dolus said. He snapped his fingers, and the door leaped from his other hand, unfolded itself, and hung before him. Then he took the door, pushed it firmly against the solid wall in front of them, and opened it. Inside was a small but comfortable room with a worktable and a lamp.

"Company first," Dolus said, inviting Raiden to enter with a sweep of his hand.

Raiden stepped inside, and Dolus followed and closed the door.

"Impressive," Raiden admitted, looking around the room with a subtle bob of his head.

The room behind the door dripped with the presence of magic in that every object seemed to buzz around the edges and the air had a thickness to it, like humidity.

"It's better for business to move around throughout the day. Although, I do frequent the same streets so my customers can find me. Bad for business to be *too* elusive," he said with a chuckle. The sound seemed to waver between octaves, between harshness and softness, like his voice wasn't sure of itself.

"I've heard your prices are exceptionally affordable," Raiden said, still searching for the answer to what was odd about Dolus.

"True. I make up for it in the money I don't pay the city for a registered shop and spell certifications, blah, blah, blah. It costs enough to *live* in this city, let alone adding the cost to make money." Dolus walked around his table, pulled the wooden chair back, and took a seat.

There was another chair, but Raiden was not inclined to sit. This didn't quite add up to him. If Dolus's business depended on word of mouth and he received enough business to counteract his cheap prices, it seemed highly unlikely *no one* would let his business method slip to the authorities. The Council or someone working under them had to know of this.

The fact that Dolus could continue to do what he did had to mean someone in the courts was being bribed or otherwise compensated for turning a blind eye. If Dolus was so affordable, he likely wouldn't be *paying* someone in the courts to look the other way. But secrets could be worth more than money. With his business model he surely came across many who wished to keep their requests a secret from the courts as much as he supposedly kept his business concealed. Dolus seemed remarkably comfortable dealing in public and meeting a new stranger face-to-face, though. How could someone be so at ease doing business as a court informant—unless Dolus wasn't real?

When Raiden looked at Dolus, the man seemed to have the same barely noticeable quiver as the rest of the room. Then Raiden remembered Dolus's voice wavering between octaves. Not he—she. Dolus was a woman, smart enough to deal in precarious matters without putting herself at risk of retaliation. This traveling room was not to conceal her business but to camouflage the layers of magic altering her appearance and voice. In this room where everything had that minute tremble of magic, making things almost imperceptibly fuzzy, the magical disguise didn't stand out in the least. Dolus fit into this environment.

Though Raiden could see the truth, he supposed Dolus wouldn't still be in business if many others noticed her secret. Raiden perhaps wouldn't have either had he not spent nine years in a desolate city where there was no bustle of life to distract him from the subtle clues of the magic left behind after everyone was gone. In the total stillness and silence of Cantis he had honed an ability to detect spells without hardly realizing it.

A smile broke Raiden's stony concentration. Dolus's business was not providing spell work for people who couldn't otherwise afford it. She was selling information to the Council. A woman who needed an umbrella to guide an unruly son home was nothing special. But surely many people came to Dolus because their requests were unlawful.

"So then, is this call a matter of limited funds or a need for ... discretion?"

Something about Raiden apparently made Dolus suspect that money wasn't his reason for seeking the elusive spell worker. Perhaps it was his clothes, a clean-pressed shirt, not a single patch. Raiden glanced down at them, then across at Dolus, whose clothes were clean but considerably worn out. Raiden supposed he looked like someone of comfortable means. Or maybe this cunning woman had seen enough desperate men to spot Raiden a mile away. Either way, he had his answer. Dolus was not a prudent choice for an ally.

"I'm afraid I just realized I've left my wallet at home." Raiden managed a convincing look of displeasure, at the thought of "home" he was sure. "This will have to wait for another time."

"You know where to find me." Dolus sounded unbothered. "If you hear anyone needs a job done, send them my way."

"Of course," Raiden said with a nod before letting himself out.

The sky overhead was blushing that soft hue between pink and orange. The sun was setting. The day was mostly gone now. All Raiden had to show for all his wandering was a decent knowledge of the area's streets and two people he couldn't turn to to solve his problem.

He made his way back home, realizing he should have checked the cupboards for food—a sneer disturbed his mouth at the thought of the Council providing for him. Retracing his course back to where he'd started, he glowered to himself. Today he'd found nothing. What had the Council found? Did they already know where Nicole was hiding in the other realm? Had they managed to search his apartment while he was away, discover his clothes and their memories? Perhaps he shouldn't have taken them off ... but then he would have been recognized for his old-world attire, and the last thing he needed was to draw attention while he was on a mission to defy the Council.

He didn't pay much attention, but he knew he was almost there, back on the quiet streets again. It was not dark yet, but the street was entirely draped in the shade of the buildings around it.

A woman down the street spoke, her voice ringing clear in the almost silence. "Dear, take this to Tovar and see if he can't find out what is wrong with it. I will be here in the potions shop, all right?"

A young girl turned away from the woman and ran toward Raiden. The object she carried was concealed, clutched tightly to her chest. She didn't seem to see him at all, even when she veered toward the shop door right in front of him and ducked inside, narrowly avoiding a collision with him. As the door swung shut, Raiden recognized the wording from when he'd passed by earlier: Tovar's Charms & Trinkets.

His hunger had turned into a vague ache hours ago. All he had waiting for him back at his new place was solitude. He supposed he could waste fifteen more minutes in a little charm shop.

Raiden opened the door. A bell chimed overhead. He stepped inside and spotted the girl at the back of the shop holding out the object her mother had given her to the middle-aged shop owner, who was kneeling down to her level.

"It used to tell us the time and when everyone should be leaving the house or doing their chores, but Mum said it won't speak anymore, and Papa was late this morning," The words tumbled out of the girl's breathless lungs.

"I see. This can happen sometimes. Where in your house does your mother keep this clock?"

"On a shelf in the kitchen," she said.

Raiden listened, walking at a lazy pace around the shop but not paying much attention to the charmed objects on the shelves.

"And does your mother have a noise-dulling charm in your kitchen? Has she ever asked you to take something outside and empty the noise?"

"Yes! Great-Granny's yellow teapot," the girl said.

"Has Granny's teapot been talking recently when you take it outside?"

The girl's face pinched with thought and then lit up. She nodded.

"Well then, tell your mother she must find a new place for your clock. Its voice seems to be getting lost in the teapot. If you have a moment, I can check that its magic is all in working order before you leave. While you're waiting, there are some new singing daisies over on the shelf."

The girl smiled, whirled around, and crossed the shop at an eager skip to a shelf where several kinds of single-stem flowers waited in small, slender vases.

The shop was silent now, save for the slow, steady knock of Raiden's footsteps and the tiny, cheery voices of flowers singing to their admirer. From the corner of his eye, Raiden noticed the owner glance at him before going about his inspection of the miniature grandfather clock.

Then Raiden thought he heard something through the miniscule voices of the singing flowers. It was a barely audible hum that lasted only a moment. He paused, no longer pretending to look at the contents of the shelves, and listened. After two minutes there came the low hum again, like some invisible bug passing by his ear.

"What time is it?" the shop owner asked the face of the clock.

"Precisely an hour and a half until dinnertime," the clock replied in a polite voice.

The owner nodded in satisfaction and crossed the shop, carrying the clock back to the young girl. "Everything seems to be in working order. The magic is all still well laid. Now, what are you going to tell your mother?" he asked, smiling as he presented the clock.

"That we need to find a new place for it—not in the kitchen," she said, straightening up with pride and taking the clock back into her arms.

"Good girl," he said. He then looked down at the shelf of flowers, where one was just finishing its song. He plucked the white daisy out of the vase and tucked it into the little pocket on the front of the girl's coat. "Go on, then. I'm told it's close to dinnertime," he added with a wink.

The girl beamed at receiving the singing daisy and left the store crying, "Thank you!"

Raiden returned to listening to the shop, waiting for the hum again. The third time it came as more than a sound. It produced the faintest pressure in his head. A sudden realization sent his heart racing. This shop was more than what it seemed. The sound, the pressure, which seemed to repeat every couple of minutes—Raiden felt certain this was an extremely well-crafted shield to conceal something. Even concealment spells could give off the slightest trace of magic to those keen enough to detect it.

"Have you found what you're looking for?" the owner asked, returning to his seat behind the counter at the back of the shop.

"I think so," Raiden answered. "I wonder if you can do more than simple charms."

The owner's eyes narrowed. His gaze shifted past Raiden to the door of the shop that stood propped open. Without a word he stood up, crossed the shop once more, closed the door, and locked it.

"I've met few people who could detect that concealment," he confessed with a troubled wrinkle on his forehead.

Raiden felt an anxious heat spread through him. "I don't mean to accuse, only to ask for your help ... if you can."

"My help?" The man paced back toward Raiden. "And what do you need help with? Certainly not detecting cloaking spells," he said with a chuckle.

"No, I ..." Raiden hesitated. He had to make a decision and fast. Was he going to trust this man, tell him about Nicole, about the Council? In this moment he could end up helping Nicole or betraying her to her enemies. He began, not yet knowing how much he would explain, "I was ... brought to Atrium against my wishes to serve the Council."

The shop owner did not seem shocked at all by this fact, and Raiden should have expected his placid reaction. It was well known throughout the realm that the Council conscripted many of the men and women in their ranks, though most people seemed to esteem the Council's employ enough to consider it an honor even in those situations when the individuals had no initial desire to serve in the courts. As Raiden continued, however, the man's face betrayed a hint of surprise.

"They're looking for someone I care about. While I am here, I must learn what I can, confound their efforts, but I cannot do that without protecting my secret first, and I need help to do that." Raiden felt suddenly lighter having heaved those words from his chest.

"Meddling with the Council's affairs—that is a dangerous game you are asking me to play." The owner's voice was grave.

Raiden's heart thundered. Just confessing his disloyalty and his intent to betray the Council was enough to be condemned for treason. This man now had the power to destroy Raiden and perhaps Nicole too. He could either keep Raiden's secret or turn him in to the Council. Then again, this man was hiding something in his shop. That knowledge was enough to expose him. So they both knew each other's secret, to some extent at least.

"More dangerous than what you have worked so hard to conceal here?" Raiden was genuinely curious, but he wasn't above threatening this man to keep himself safe. He expected a frown in response but was surprised to see the man smile.

"Probably not," he said.

Raiden's rib cage seemed to shrink around his heart and lungs. "So you'll help me?"

"I've got nothing to lose—I will try," he said, extending his hand to Raiden. "Tovar," he introduced himself.

"Raiden," he replied, taking Tovar's hand as gratitude swept away his anxiety.

"Where do we start?" Tovar asked.

Raiden felt almost dizzy with relief, even momentarily nauseated by the risk he had just taken. "How are you with wiping objects' memories?"

Tovar answered with a smile.

8. Enemies

icole was oddly relieved to tell her brother about the portal, Raiden, her powers, and how she'd met Gordan—even as surreal as it was to talk about magic and dragons the way they usually talked about their favorite movies. Anthony listened to it all with a tiny smile and the slightest air of awestruck disbelief. Having to explain the complications that came with her newfound identity was much less amusing to Nicole. That part of it all, who—what—she was now was the most difficult to explain. She still didn't quite understand what being a fera meant. What were they, and was she like the rest of them?

"Unfortunately, there's a problem … a couple problems actually," she said. The confession stifled the otherwise pleasant atmosphere in the living room. "The guys in charge of the other realm want to find me. Raiden was supposed to be doing that for them, but, well, he doesn't like them. They claim to have a problem with my being here and opening portals. On top of that, there's apparently some other group of people looking for me …"

"The same man who held me captive for almost a decade. It is less clear why *he* is interested in Nicole," Gordan added. His voice was quiet, but there was a grumble of hate in his words.

"So I had to get out of Yuma. If I stay anywhere too long, I could open a portal, and that's basically a neon sign saying 'Here I am!'"

Her brother's jaw clenched, and his expression pinched with concern. It didn't matter what she was capable of—opening portals, killing kelpies—to Anthony she remained his baby sister, and he was clearly at a loss for how he could protect her from this.

"How long does it usually take," he asked, "for portals to start opening?"

Nicole couldn't stop the tiny smile that came at hearing him speak of portals so easily, no wincing, without hesitation. For a moment she was a kid again, discussing comics with her brother, musing about villains and life-threatening challenges safely contained within glossy colored pages.

"I guess a little more than twenty-four hours."

Gordan said, "I believe you can count on more time. Your home has been saturated with your magic for far longer than you think, well before your powers emerged I would wager."

Nicole considered this. The backyard had been a veritable oasis for months before the first portal had shown up and everything had gone crazy. Raiden *had* told her that her magic had most likely always been there. Her whole life living in that house, her powers had been developing inside her, slipping out here and there and building up in the world around her. So maybe she would have more time to stay in new places. Maybe she didn't have to worry so much.

"Okay, a few days maybe," she amended.

"Great. You'll stay here awhile," Anthony said with his indisputable brotherly authority.

"I should warn you, I don't have this whole magic thing *completely* figured out." She thought that sounded less dangerous than *I can't always control it.*

Anthony's stern expression softened into his previous smile. "We can handle twin five-year-olds, can't we? I think we'll be fine," he said.

Nicole looked at Gordan. Her lips twitched in an attempt to smile, and he looked her right in the eye as one side of his mouth moved upward.

"We'll stay as long as we can," she said, avoiding precise promises. "Then I think we'll head toward Tucson and stay with Mitch."

Nicole knew that Anthony bobbed his head in acceptance of this plan only because she was leaving his brotherly protection and going directly to the safety of Mitchell's. It was sweet the way they felt their fraternal guard was any match for what she was up against now.

In the courts of Atrium, Caeruleus walked at a brisk pace toward the Council's hall. He was one of very few who received orders directly from them. Almost a year ago the Council had introduced him to the more-pressing matters of the states. Three months ago, when the Council's seers had first glimpsed the foggy visions of danger emerging through a portal, they'd confided in him that there was a fera out there still, one that had eluded them all those years ago. Her future, like the others', was filled with dark destruction. Yet, with only one brief encounter with the fera, Raiden had more valuable information than all the intelligence from the Council's repeated encounters with the others of her kind. He had seen her, witnessed her abilities firsthand.

The gilded doors to the Council's hall opened and then closed with a heavy thud behind him as he strode down the length of the chamber to where they sat waiting for him. Their high table was curved like a sliver of the moon so that, when Caeruleus stood before them, their gazes half surrounded him.

"Welcome, Caeruleus. We have something to ask of you," one of the councilwomen said. He didn't know her name—he didn't know *any* of their names. The Council proved adept at preserving their collective identity by shedding their individuality and assuming an image of oneness, accentuated by their shaved heads and identical robes.

"Of course," he replied. Why else did he ever come here? His sole mission being the fera, he assumed there might be some development. "Has the fera been located already?" he asked, uncertain how prepared he was to face this task knowing all they had told him about the fera and what Raiden had encountered firsthand.

"No," the central councilman answered in a deep voice.

The answer immediately eased Caeruleus's anxiety. There was still more he would like to ask of Raiden to prepare himself for that encounter.

"We seek your insight in regard to Raiden. We have reason to believe he might be enthralled by this fera and could, perhaps, be an unwilling traitor."

Caeruleus frowned, baffled how they could get that idea. They didn't know Raiden like he did. The boy he remembered was as loyal as someone could be, but enthralled by the fera? Sure, Raiden was a little different after a decade, more somber than Caeruleus remembered, but he did not behave like a man gripped by some spellbound attraction.

A councilwoman said, "In the time you spent with him today, did he give you any reason to believe his agenda here might favor the fera and not *our* efforts?"

Caeruleus couldn't deny that Raiden had defended the fera, but he'd also seemed genuine in his desire to help him with the assignment. The Raiden he had known as a boy had always been incurably honest, save for one matter: he'd kept the Sight a secret from everyone—except Caeruleus. Caeruleus could not believe that a decade alone would have changed that. What influences could have prompted such a change when he'd had no one to interact with, when his life had been nine years of books and solitude?

But Caeruleus wondered whether he was really so sure or whether he merely wanted Raiden to be the same as he'd once been. He was convinced that Raiden's doubts concerning the Council and this matter with the fera were merely in his nature. Raiden did not know the Council and their past troubles with the fera like Caeruleus did. He did not think Raiden was enthralled by the fera, only unsure of everything after all the stars had been given and taken from him. Caeruleus could not blame his friend for that.

"No," he answered in a clear voice.

There was silence for a few moments. He wondered whether they had expected a different answer, or perhaps they had not agreed who would respond.

Finally a nasally man said, "Very well. We trust you will learn as much as you can from Raiden's encounter and be ready when the fera surfaces."

"I will."

Vinderek passed the time in the fera's bedroom. To get into her head, he picked up this and that, pondering her personality and musing about her behavior. He memorized her face from the picture, reclined for some time on the short couch beneath the loft bed, and examined her collection of books before getting back up in a restless need to move about the room once again. As a hunter, patience was easily one of his stronger traits. Getting to know his quarry was like a game.

It was late afternoon now. The rich golden light of day sinking into sunset fell through the window. Vinderek had already passed several hours in the confines of the fera's house. The brother had left a couple of hours ago, leaving Vinderek free to inspect the home in its entirety. But when he'd come across the large black dog asleep by the front door downstairs, he hadn't dared inspect any further and had returned to the fera's room.

The sound of the front door lock opening erupted into an exuberant commotion of whining and barking from the dog greeting someone whose voice was nearly lost in the dog's tumult of joy. "All right, buddy, okay. I missed you too."

After a few minutes, silence settled through the home. When footsteps on the stairs met his ears, Vinderek moved calmly into the closet and mostly closed the door, surrounding himself in shadow but leaving enough of an opening to observe the room.

A middle-aged man stepped into the room, looking around with tired eyes. Vinderek knew this man's face from the pictures he had seen, and even without the pictures basic reasoning would have sufficed to realize that this was the fera's father. The man lingered in the room for a few minutes, as if he too wanted to capture the fera's presence there. Then he turned and left the room with a sigh.

Vinderek watched and waited for another minute in case the man returned. Once he was sure the father was gone, he stepped out into the room. There was nothing he could do but wait here in this house, except maybe have a look around the area and see what he could find. There could be more that he might learn about his quarry, some weakness he might yet uncover.

He strolled out to the landing with a lazy pace and scanned the first floor below before descending. Halfway down the stairs two bell chimes rang through the house. Vinderek froze, watching the archway between the living room below him and the entranceway for the father. Instead he heard a door open.

"Roxanne—" The father sounded out of sorts.

"Hi, Mr. Jamison. Is Nicole here?" a young female voice asked in a rush.

"No, I'm sorry, she's not."

"Is she okay? She hasn't been at school. She hasn't been answering her phone—maybe it's dead. Do you know where she is?"

Vinderek moved silently down the rest of the stairs.

"She's out of town visiting her brother." The father's answer came so easily it sounded like the truth to Vinderek.

"When is she coming back?" the female voice pressed.

Vinderek leaned just enough to see beyond the edge of the archway to get a glimpse of the front door. The father had the door mostly closed and stood blocking the opening, so Vinderek could not see the girl. Vinderek took the opportunity to cross the archway and positioned himself by the back door.

"I'm not really sure," the father finally answered, and Vinderek turned the doorknob carefully under the cover of their conversation.

"Well, can you please let her know I came by? I brought the last week of work she missed too." The girl's disappointed voice hid the sound of Vinderek opening the door.

"I will, Roxanne. Take care," the father said, and Vinderek stepped outside.

As the fera's father shut the front door, Vinderek closed the back door. He ran lightly across the patio to the side of the house and scaled the wall easily. Hurrying along the wall, he made his way to the front of the house and managed get a clear view of the girl Roxanne as she lowered herself into her vehicle. A long curtain of yellow waves concealed her face until she tossed her hair back with a turn of her head. Her disappointment showed in her firmly pressed lips and troubled brow. He could barely see her through the dark window of her metallic-blue vessel. Vinderek watched as the vehicle backed onto the street and pulled away, crawling slowly down the street as the girl held up something like his own small looking glass for a moment.

After waiting until she was down the street a way, he hopped down from the wall and hurried along to keep her blue vehicle in sight. He had run down prey before, and this girl might prove to be useful to him.

Raiden returned to Tovar's shop with the bundle of his clothes under his arm. There was a CLOSED sign hanging in the window now, but he found the door unlocked for him and went inside.

"That was fast," Tovar remarked from behind his counter.

"I don't live far," Raiden answered, turning the metal knob that locked the door.

"Well, let's get started, shall we?" Tovar stood and motioned Raiden to join him at the back of the shop.

Tovar pulled a box of old doorknobs and handles from behind the counter and rummaged through it. When he found a tarnished brass doorknob that looked like several others, he replaced the box and turned to the back wall. He placed the knob against the wall where there appeared to be no recess of any kind. It clicked into place. He gave it a turn, and a line of light cut through the wall, outlining the shape of a door. The door opened inward.

"After you," Tovar said.

Raiden stepped through the doorway into a small room with no windows. He turned to see Tovar remove the knob and drop it into his pocket before entering the room and closing the door.

"Want to get back out, don't we?" He patted the knob in his pocket with a smile. There appeared to be no door from the inside of the room either.

A smile spread across Raiden's face at the thought of some poor fool who managed to find his way into the room only to get locked inside.

"So what is this room?"

"My private workroom. It's heavily protected. Magic can't get in or out, so whatever I'm working on won't be detected. Not to mention it's sound-and-smellproof, in case any projects go wrong," Tovar said with a chuckle.

Raiden looked around. Bookcases lined the walls, and, nodding toward them, he asked, "Trade secrets?"

"Criminal knowledge," Tovar answered. "Historical accounts the Council doesn't like, banned magical arts, the usual. There are enough books here for the courts to condemn me. Helping you keep a secret wouldn't hurt me any more."

The books compelled Raiden to cross the room. Perhaps he would have the chance to delve into those forbidden pages, but for now he had a more important task.

"Shall we add to your list of crimes, then?" Raiden dropped the armful of clothes onto the table.

Tovar smiled.

"We only have the one guest room," Anthony said to Nicole and Gordan.

Gordan could only blink at the notion that he would even sleep inside. He had to remind himself that Nicole's brother knew nothing about him yet.

"Gordan will probably sleep on the roof," Nicole said from the couch where she sat, her legs folded up and ankles crossed in front of her. Gordan, who was standing against the wall beside her, nodded in agreement.

"Uh, by all means, have at it," Anthony said with a shrug.

Nicole said, "What about time—"

The sound of a door opening somewhere beyond the kitchen and two children's voice disrupted their conversation.

"—no it's not."

"Is too."

"Nuh-uh! Papa's truck doesn't work. Daddy said so."

Two five-year-old girls trotted through the kitchen and into the living room. They were not identical, one having light-brown hair and the other pitch-black hair. But they were dressed alike and wore their hair at the same jaw length. They spotted Nicole and stopped. Anthony smiled, then cringed. Gordan could tell he was bracing himself. Nicole beamed at the children as they launched themselves across the living room, shrieking in delight. Nicole slid off the couch and onto her knees to catch them in her arms.

She glanced up at Gordan. Complete and utter joy shone in her eyes, and for a moment he could not sense even the faintest trace of her troubles.

The girls could not be contained by Nicole's embrace for long and broke free, jumping up and down.

"I told you it was Papa's truck!"

"Auntie Nikki! Auntie Nikki!"

"What's going on in here?" a much-calmer voice asked over the chanting, and a woman with dark hair and matching eyes appeared from the kitchen. "Nicole," she sang when she spotted her.

Nicole stood up to hug the woman. "Frances!"

"When did you get here? Did you know she was coming?" Frances looked at Anthony.

"Dad warned me," Anthony answered.

"Who's your friend?" Frances asked, spotting Gordan.

The two girls, still oblivious to Gordan, were chanting "Auntie Nikki" together in the middle of the living room. Gordan found he could not concentrate on anything but them. He couldn't recall ever being near humans at this age.

"This is my friend Gordan." Nicole's voice caught his attention.

Frances raised her eyebrows, and Gordan saw a question in her dark, almond-shaped eyes.

"Not that kind of friend," Nicole answered.

Before he could begin to fathom what kind of friend he wasn't, Frances addressed him with a smile. "Nice to meet you, Gordan." Her words were warm and welcoming, but he detected disappointment in the beats of her heart.

At last the girls seemed to pick up on the conversation being had over their heads and ceased dancing to look around the room. When they spotted Gordan, they shied toward Frances.

"Ryleigh, Ashley, say hello to Gordan," Frances said.

"Hi," they responded, their quiet voices barely audible.

"What have you been up to? Ditching school today?" Frances asked Nicole.

Nicole laughed. "Yeah, I just needed to get away."

Gordan found Nicole's ability to both tell the truth and conceal it at the same time quite remarkable.

"Girls, why don't you go get changed for karate," Anthony said.

Ryleigh and Ashley, who had not taken their suspicious eyes off Gordan since spotting him, turned and hurried down the hall.

Once the girls were out of the room, Anthony said, "Might as well tell her now."

"Tell me what?" Frances looked between Anthony and Nicole.

"Recent developments have … complicated my life just a tad," Nicole said. Gordan didn't blame her for stalling.

"Oh God, you're not pregnant, are you?" Frances looked to Anthony for affirmation.

"No! Why does everyone—?" She shook her head and sighed. "There is no good way to explain this," she muttered, and it occurred to Gordan that she was about to demonstrate.

Nicole placed her hand out before her, palm up, and with no more than a blink she summoned an apricot-sized orb of light. Then she turned her hand over to hold the light between both hands. She pulled her hands apart, and the bright sphere grew to the size of a melon, until at last it burst into a cloud of marble-sized suns, which filled the living room. When she dropped her hands, the lights shrank away.

Frances looked at Nicole with a slack mouth. She closed her eyes slowly and opened them. Then they glazed over, and she tipped back. Gordan was behind her before Anthony could jump up. Frances sagged against him for a moment before jerking herself upright. Startled by Gordan's sudden proximity, Frances jumped toward Anthony with a little yelp. Gordan moved away since Frances was once again stable on her feet.

"Surprise," Nicole said.

Frances sputtered, "Was that …? How did …?"

Gordan could hear Nicole's heart pounding. As lighthearted as she tried to sound, this moment terrified her every time. Then he spotted the twins standing in the hall with mouths and eyes open as wide as could be.

"How long?" Frances asked.

"Figured it out a week ago," Nicole answered.

Gordan cleared his throat, and the three adults looked at him. He nodded toward the hallway where Ryleigh and Ashley stood.

Everyone realized what the girls had seen as their awe gave way to excitement.

"Magic!"

"Do it again!"

"Please tell me this doesn't run in the family," Frances said to Nicole with a look of terror in her eyes as her daughters carried on.

Gordan entertained the thought. Most people were capable of some magic, after all. What people in this realm lacked was the right environment—the belief in such possibilities and the presence of magic, which Nicole carried in abundance, more than enough to share with the world around her. Perhaps given enough time around Nicole, the girls might discover some talent for magic themselves. But with Nicole on the move, she'd be here only a few days, and Gordan doubted that would be enough time.

"I don't think so," Nicole said. "As I understand it, this is a reincarnation thing, not a genetic trait."

Frances sagged with relief.

The girls each had Nicole by a leg now.

"Are you a genie?"

"Are you a witch?"

"Girls, please," Nicole said through her laughter.

They went silent, looking up at her with two wide pairs of dark-brown eyes like their mother's.

"I am not a genie *or* a witch," Nicole said.

Gordan could see them hanging on her every word.

"I am your fairy godmother, and Gordan is my dragon in disguise," she said.

Gordan's mouth twitched, caught between a smile and a scowl. The girls opened their mouths into wide Os of shock as they looked first at each other and then at him. They burst into squeals and shrieks of delight. Gordan grimaced as their tiny, shrill voices cut through his thoughts, scattering them like a startled flock of birds.

"Thanks for that," Anthony said, shaking his head.

"You're welcome." Nicole smiled.

It took a full fifteen minutes to convince the girls to calm down and get ready for their karate class. Nicole had to promise to show them more magic later, but only if they did exactly what their parents told them. Although Ryleigh and Ashley quieted down and obeyed with determined seriousness, elation radiated from them, and Gordan found himself almost dizzy with their excitement. If he hadn't been so sure the children weren't likely to display any magical ability in so short a time, he might have believed they were about to start flying.

The girls' mood proved to be contagious for Nicole at least. Gordan was relieved to feel *her* joy in the room too.

"All right, we're off to class," Frances said once the girls were wearing their proper attire.

"How many classes tonight?" Anthony asked.

"I'm coaching the Muay Thai class during kids' karate, so we'll be done at six thirty. Dominick has got the last two classes."

A sudden spasm of excitement from Nicole gave Gordan a start. She jumped up from the couch.

"Spencer Makenzie's for dinner?" Nicole asked.

Anthony and Frances laughed while the girls bounced up and down chanting, "Yeah, yeah, yeah!"

"Can't argue with that," Anthony said with a grin.

"Fine with me," Frances answered, laughing.

Anthony walked by and discreetly held his fist out to Nicole, who bumped it with her own. Gordan was puzzled by this gesture but sensed camaraderie.

Frances shook her head. "See you later." She and the girls left through the kitchen.

"Oh, I better call Dad," Nicole said.

"I sent him a text when I saw the truck out front," Anthony said.

"Thanks." Nicole's voice was heavy again, her spirits sinking back into their previous gloom. Gordan saw her brother frown.

"I've got a few emails to write, so I'll be back in the office if you need me. Cool?"

"Yeah, cool," she answered, nodding.

Anthony left her and Gordan alone in the living room. As Nicole looked around their peaceful surroundings, Gordan could feel her discomfort. This was her world, closed in by comfortable walls and windows. He was supposed to be the one who felt out of place on plush carpet and stuffed upholstered furniture, not her.

She huffed. "Now what?"

"What do you mean 'now what'?"

She looked him dead in the eye. "What am I supposed to do here? What does anyone do when they're on the run?"

"You enjoy time with your family. You relax. You allow yourself more than a few more minutes of happiness," he insisted, surprising himself with the fervor in his voice. "For the time being you're safe. Don't ruin it by thinking of its demise."

Her expression did not change, but a wave of relief rolled through the room. He watched her curiously as she moved toward him with her gaze on the floor. Before he realized what she was about to do, she had her arms around him. She held on tight, and he recalled the way she had clung to her father before they'd left. Unsure what else he was supposed to do, he lifted his arms and placed them around her.

The last time they had been this close he'd been pulling her and Raiden back through the closing portal. It had been necessity, duty. But this time, he could feel the pounding of her heart against his chest so distinctly that it might have been his own.

"You know, the safest way to ensure they don't find out what transpired between you two is to destroy these," Tovar said, looking down at the clothing, now folded and without any trace of precious moments with Nicole.

Raiden kept his gaze on the garments on the table. He had considered that option earlier when it had seemed he had no other choice, but he had a plan for these clothes.

"For that matter, why not remove the memories altogether?" Tovar added.

Raiden lifted his eyes to meet Tovar's. "What?" There was disgust in his voice.

"I don't mean destroy them entirely. But you can lock memories away where even you cannot reach them so that the Council can't either. You can have a strong enough will to prevent psychic intrusion, but they will know you're hiding something, and that is condemnation enough. Should they feel the need to cross that line, they can keep probing until you break."

"How can I accomplish anything that might help her if I can't remember her, remember why I'm here?" His words were indignant.

"Raiden, I'm not suggesting you wipe every memory of her. I'm saying you can be selective—leave the encounters that do not condemn you, enough to fit the story you told them. You can't deny that as much good as you can do here for her sake, you can do an equal amount of damage. How much do you know about her that could help them if they managed to obtain those memories?"

"I ... That's true, but ..."

"She is only safe as long as your secrets remain so too—you said that yourself."

Raiden could not bring himself to speak, because his response would prove Tovar right.

"It would be entirely your choice what to keep and what to hide. However, you must fill the holes with something. Most people go searching for the missing pieces when there are gaps in their memory."

"And how does one retrieve hidden memories?"

"By coming in contact with something physical from the memory. Since you are in no danger of returning to the places where these memories happened or coming into contact with some object that was present at the time, the only way to trigger those memories would be by coming in contact with her."

"That's a bit of a risk, isn't it?" Raiden said. "If she were to be found and brought in, it's unlikely I would have any chance of seeing her, let alone knowing I need to help her. You're suggesting I help her by condemning her to face this all on her own."

"I'm no seer, Raiden. I can't tell you how it will play out, but if you want to conceal your secrets *now*, I've given you my opinion on the best way to do it." Tovar placed the folded clothes on a large piece of brown paper.

Raiden shook his head, not willing to risk it. It felt like a plan to save himself, not her. "If I do that, my ability to help her is crippled, and I might as well be no help at all."

Tovar said while folding the paper around the garments, "If your secrets are discovered, you'll be charged with treason, and you'll be even less help to her."

Raiden hung his head and laughed.

"What?"

He sighed. "She was right," he said. "This was a stupid plan. We would have been better off together—the three of us."

"Three?"

"The less you know the better."

Tovar handed Raiden the parcel containing his clothing from the other realm. "What are you going to do, then?"

"I'll let you know tomorrow," Raiden answered.

Tovar nodded. "Tomorrow then."

9. Past

icole searched, arm deep in her bag, for her cell phone. Books and clothes spilled onto the bed as she pulled it out. The screen was black and unresponsive, so she turned it on. Five voice mails and seventeen text messages awaited her when the screen lit up. She knew she couldn't keep ignoring Roxanne's attempts to contact her, but right now she needed to check in with her dad.

"Sorry, Rox," she muttered and called her dad's cell.

The drone of the outgoing call rang in her ear twice before she turned on speakerphone and dropped the phone onto the bed. Another two rings filled the silence. Then her dad answered.

"Hey, baby girl," he said.

"Hi, Daddy," Nicole answered while she gathered up the clothes and stuffed them back into her bag.

"How'd he take it?"

"Pretty well," Nicole said, nodding. "Frances nearly fainted, and the girls went nuts."

"You showed the girls?"

"They're five, Dad. Would you believe a five-year-old who told you her aunt could do magic?"

He laughed, although there was still a hint of anxiety in the sound. "Good point. Hey, did you take that picture of you and your brother that was at the top of the stairs?"

Nicole knew the picture. It had been taken just a couple of months ago in November when her brothers had visited for her eighteenth birthday.

"No, I didn't take it," she said. "Maybe Mitch took it."

"Huh, maybe he did. Oh, Roxanne stopped by the house today."

"Oh," Nicole said, cringing.

"She brought over all your schoolwork from the last week," he said. "Didn't you withdraw?"

"I may have forgotten to bring the paperwork back," she confessed.

Her dad took a deep breath. "Are you sure you can't finish? We can always tell the school you've been sick." His voice was calm. "You might wish you had that diploma after all this blows over."

She couldn't help but smile at his optimistic delusion.

"I guess I can pick that schoolwork up on my next stop back home."

"Good," he answered, sounding relieved.

She felt guilty for letting him believe there was a chance things would go back to normal—homework and graduation photos, the cap and gown, going off to college after the summer. Was it cruel to let him keep that hope when it was an impossible one?

"So what are you up to over there? Any plans?" he asked.

"Oh, you know, I thought I might find the local cemetery and raise the dead before dinner. Reunite people with their loved ones, you know—do some good."

He laughed. "Are you all going to Spencer Makenzie's?" There was jealousy in his voice.

"I'll send you an order of fish tacos if you want," Nicole offered with a laugh.

"No, that's fine. No magic. Enjoy some time with your brother," he said, and she could hear the smile in his words.

"Okay, talk to you later, Dad."

"Give everyone a hug for me."

"I will. Love you."

"Love you too."

She tossed the phone onto the bed and turned to her bag. The idea of homework made her think she ought to be studying something useful. She pulled out her books, looking at their titles indecisively. What she needed was a book about the fera. She needed to know what Veil's literature said about her—her kind.

She had only a vague idea of what she was in the Council's eyes—a threat to the realm. But what was the whole story? She wanted to know what had happened to the other fera, what the people of Veil thought. Better yet, she needed to know where the fera came from, what they really were, and why this Venarius guy was so interested in her.

The uncertainty made her shudder. In a realm full of magic, she could not fathom what one man would want with a dragon and a fera. She spotted the small leather journal she had found gathering dust beneath the bed of Raiden's home. Lost or condemned to be forgotten, she didn't know which, but it had compelled her to grab it then as it did now. She picked it up to occupy her hands while she pondered. Pacing the room, she tried to piece together *something*.

A dragon and a fera—both apparently feared by the people of Veil. Did Venarius want to intimidate Veil to some end? No, that couldn't be. There were hundreds of dragons, thousands surely, and yet he had taken only Gordan.

If he had meant to use Gordan somehow, why lock him up and hide him in Cantis for nearly ten years? So then maybe it was not Gordan himself Venarius was after but something Gordan knew. She realized how little she actually knew about Gordan. She felt like an idiot trying to solve a puzzle with only a handful of pieces.

In her exasperation she flopped onto the bed and opened the journal. She flipped quickly through the pages and then looked at one page at a time. The pages were impossibly filled with writing. Whomever this journal had belonged to had first written in neat, spaced lines and then turned the journal upside down and scribbled cramped words *between* those lines. On many pages even more writing had been scrawled diagonally over the top. The jumble of writing almost made Nicole dizzy.

She turned to the next page and spotted some lines of neatly written text that she could make out: "I had a breathtaking vision today ..."

Nicole's heart fluttered, and she brought the journal closer to her face to pick through the tangle of words. "I saw a little boy. He had my family's eyes, those crystal clear blue-green pools, and my auburn hair and my brown complexion. I heard him laugh. My son. I am going to have a son. I saw him, and my heart aches when I picture his face."

An image flickered in Nicole's mind—Raiden as a boy. She could almost see him. Her heart hammered against her chest. "She's talking about Raiden," she muttered to herself.

"Everything all right?" Gordan's voice came from the doorway.

"Yeah," she answered and looked up at him with a smile. "This journal belonged to Raiden's mother."

Gordan crossed the room, eyeing the journal with a curious gaze. "I wonder, how did you come by that?"

"The night we found you in the tower," she said, watching his expression grow more interested. "We were in Cantis to get books—well, you know."

Gordan nodded.

"I ended up finding this under the bed, and because of it I happened upon this thing—what is it called?"

Gordan guessed, "A jump token?"

"Yes! This old building stone that Raiden tried to use to get into the castle."

"But it was from the wrong building; it took him to the tower instead," Gordan said softly. "I remember."

At first she was confused. Gordan remembered? "That's right," Nicole said, thinking back to that night. "He knew you were there. He didn't want me to go down there."

"Maybe a year before you arrived, the token brought him to the tower. I heard him cursing from the floor above me. I could feel his anger—it was the first time I had felt something in years. He spent a short time looking around. When he found me, he became unsettled and left."

Nicole closed the journal and gripped it so fiercely in her hands that her nails dug into the leather. "I can't believe he would—"

"Sure you can. You know what happened in Veil. You understand why people feel the way they do about dragons. Besides, things would have been very different if he had released me a year ago."

Nicole considered it for a moment. Freeing Gordan would have alerted Moira. Raiden's confrontation with her would have happened a year sooner. His death or victory would have meant he probably wouldn't have been in Cantis when the portal had opened. The Council would have sent someone else. She never would have met Gordan. She might be standing before the Council that very moment had Raiden made the choice to free Gordan a year ago.

"Fine. You're right," she said and opened the journal again, but it was impossible to find the page she had been reading. "I hope Raiden's mom didn't foresee what a jerk he turned out to be," she muttered as she flipped through page after page of visions.

Then she heard a soft, breathy sound and looked up to see Gordan chuckling. Her annoyance gave way to disbelief. "Are you laughing?" She put the book down and jumped up. "I didn't know you could laugh," she cried, mocking astonishment.

"Oh, shut up," he said, fighting back a smile.

There was a large envelope sitting outside his door when Raiden returned to his apartment. He stooped to pick it up before removing his spell and unlocking the door. He wondered whether the messenger had expected to let himself in and leave the parcel inside. He had no way of knowing. That small defiance alone could complicate his relationship with the Council. This was going to be a difficult dance to learn in the middle of the number. *Act trustworthy while you deceive; seem trusting while you chase your suspicions.* He was stumbling along already, and the tempo was picking up.

He heaved a sigh from his chest. He couldn't allow himself to be fooled by what seemed like trust. If he was going to keep the advantage, he had to assume the Council didn't trust him, even if they appeared to. He dropped the envelope and parcel of clothes onto his dining table and let out a groan of self-pity and loathing. Pushing the clothes aside, Raiden opened the envelope and dumped its contents onto the table.

There were images of known rebels that had evaded arrest, reports on incidents, articles filled with anti-rebel propaganda, and pamphlets and flyers expressing rebellious sentiments. He wondered how much of this was real information. For now he supposed his best course of action was to go about the assignment the Council had given him, follow orders, and quell any suspicion. He couldn't go snooping around the courts after two days, and he certainly couldn't take down the Council on his own, but maybe the rebels could.

The Council was basically pointing him in the direction of the allies he and Nicole needed. He did already have information to share with the rebels. Surely they wouldn't pass up the opportunity to have someone in the courts to be their eyes and ears. Maybe he didn't have to risk looking for the Council's weaknesses and secrets. He might be able to take them down from the outside by helping the rebels.

It seemed stupidly easy. He could effortlessly be a double agent—the Council had provided him with his alibi for seeking the rebels out. But there was still one problem: the Council could decide they needed more information about Nicole tomorrow. How aggressive would they be in their quest to learn anything and everything they could about her? Everything he knew about

Nicole—her family in the other realm, her being allied with a dragon—could be used against her.

As much as he hated to admit it, Tovar was absolutely right about his memories putting Nicole in danger. Even without remembering everything that had happened or how he felt about Nicole, Raiden still had motives to seek the Council's downfall considering the Council claimed to guard the people of Veil and yet had left Cantis utterly unprotected nine years ago. That would fuel his mission without him even knowing that helping Nicole was the real reason.

His heart dropped, a stone disappearing into the mouth of a well. He sighed. He had one more day to himself. One day to find a way to get a message to her. But what would he even say? If something went wrong, if he got caught … Well, the dread of never seeing her again would only torture him for one day longer.

He was fairly certain he could get a message to her if he could get back to Cantis. Going there without drawing suspicion from the Council was the trick.

All Gordan knew was that he, Nicole, and her brother were walking to some place to eat called Spencer Makenzie's. They led the way. He followed. Anthony asked Nicole about magic and what she was doing about school now that she was a fugitive in another realm. It was a strange conversation to listen to as Anthony had the jovial air of someone discussing trivial things rather than adversaries threatening his sister. This left Gordan rather confused as to whether Anthony was being facetiously chipper in light of the darker topics or didn't believe one bit of Nicole's strange new life but was amusing himself by playing along.

Gordan listened, growing more familiar with the currents and tides of Nicole's emotions. Her lack of distress and even slight hint of mirth convinced him that Anthony was indeed attempting to lighten the mood while prying the disheartening details out of Nicole. Eventually they turned inland, and not far from the water they arrived at a small building on a corner. It was white with aqua-green trim and was surrounded by outdoor benches and tables where people were eating.

Gordan looked up at the glowing sign that read World-Famous Fish Tacos in red. Outside there were people waiting at a window ordering and receiving their food, but Nicole and Anthony walked up to the door to the right of the serving window and went inside. Gordan followed Nicole's tall shadow. They walked past a long bar where several stools were taken. Past the narrow entranceway along the bar, the space opened up to a room with several tables. The walls were aqua green, and the floor was a black-and-white checkerboard. They paused a moment to survey the room. Nicole's presence flashed with exuberance when a group got up and vacated their table, which she and Anthony swooped in on before a waiter could even clear away the plates. The waiter, a young man with blond hair and a tanned face, greeted them with a friendly white smile as he gathered up the plates from the previous diners and gave the tabletop a swift wipe-down with a towel.

"Can I get you three some water to start?" the waiter asked.

"Six waters actually, two in kids' cups—my wife will be here shortly," Anthony answered.

"You got it." The waiter offered one more smile, and Gordan detected a flutter of interest from him as he glanced at Nicole before departing with his stack of dirty dishes.

"So, Gordan," Anthony said as he sat down, "you look, what, twenty-four, twenty-five?"

"Hundred, actually," Gordan said. Nicole slid across the bench seat, and Gordan lowered himself to sit beside her. He tried to block out the collective haze of delight, humor, and contentment from everyone in the room enjoying food and company.

Anthony's surprise broke through his casual composure. "You're one hundred years old?"

"No, twenty-five hundred years old," he said. "Well, to be exact, twenty-four hundred fifty-one, I believe. To be quite honest, I may have lost track of a year or two somewhere in the last few centuries."

"Holy shit," Anthony said, laughing.

Nicole looked at Gordan with a spark of wonder in her eyes. "Were you alive before the world divided? Before Veil?"

"That's right," Gordan said.

"Well, I think even in twenty-five hundred years you probably haven't eaten anything as good as what they have here … You can eat human food, right?" Anthony lowered his voice, which was easily unheard beyond their table with the low roar of combined conversations and kitchen noise in the relatively small space.

"Yes," Gordan said.

Nicole snickered.

"Oh good," Anthony said as he forced out a laugh.

"Do the years become hard to remember, living that long?" Nicole asked.

"Dragons have incredibly keen memories. We do not forget easily," Gordan answered.

"They say the same thing about elephants," Anthony said.

Nicole laughed, but Gordan wasn't quite sure why that was funny.

"You must be a walking history book," she said as she pulled a menu out from a stack held up by several bottles of substances unknown to Gordan.

"Aren't we all? Everything before this moment is history. My life just happens to be a little longer than yours."

Anthony scoffed. "A little? A life that long, you must have a pretty clear view of humanity by now."

The waiter returned with a tray of waters, four tall, open cups and two shorter cups with lids and straws. He looked again at Nicole, whose attention was fixed on the menu in front of her. Gordan waited for the waiter to smile and wander away again before answering.

"I have always tried not to concern myself with humans, until recently." He smiled. "Dragons usually live apart. Even before the divide and the Dragon Wars, we tended to live separately, not just from humans but other creatures of magic too."

"Wait, back up," Anthony said. "Dragon Wars?" There was a tone of intrigue and even amusement in his voice that Gordan found off-putting for a moment before he remembered that to Anthony this all sounded more like fiction. Anthony didn't know how real and horrifying the Dragon Wars had been.

"It was a dark time in Veil's history," Gordan said, hoping the severity of his words would deliver a whiff of reality to Anthony.

"Must've been pretty bad if you're being that vague," Anthony said with a chuckle. "Or your memory isn't as good as you say."

Nicole jerked almost imperceptibly, and he could taste her venomous annoyance. Gordan heard her foot strike Anthony's shin beneath the table, and her brother jumped in his seat. Gordan smirked.

"Ow, jeez, Nick," he hissed.

"My memory is as good as yours," Gordan continued as if nothing had transpired. "Even for me certain things slip away, and others I cannot forget. The moments that mold us always remain, whether we recognize their significance or not, whether we *want* them to or not. I did not say I do not remember the wars. I said I know little about them."

"Weren't you there?" Nicole asked.

"I was in Veil, but I took no part in the wars," he said, his heart sinking into the depth of the lie. Lying had once been so easy. He would have wondered what had changed, but the feeling of Nicole's relief washing over him, a soft, warm wave of trust, provided the answer. Her emotions beside him rang out loud and clear in the psyche-crowded noise of Spencer Makenzie's. He could hide his past from Nicole, shielding her heart from disappointment. As much as he despised that saga of his past, he would not change it even if he could.

"Just sat back and watched the fight, huh?" Anthony said with a cynical smile.

Gordan was willing to acknowledge that truth. "You could say that."

Anthony's wife, Frances, arrived, ushering Ashley and Ryleigh past the bar and to the table where Gordan, Nicole, and Anthony sat.

"Hi, Daddy," the girls chimed together.

"Perfect timing," Anthony said.

"Ever wish you had done it differently? Picked a side?" Nicole asked quietly for Gordan's ears only.

"Our pasts make us who we are, and mine got me here. I would not change a single moment."

10. Warning

The next morning Nicole ran alone along the beach, listening to the sound of her own breath and the low roar of the churning waves to her left. She ran at the water's edge, where the sand was firm underfoot. As a wave rushed across the sand, she skirted around it before setting her sights back on the Ventura Pier ahead of her.

It was an hour past dawn, but the misty marine layer cloaked the coast in a veil of gray. The sky was choked by clouds, replacing golden sunshine with hazy silver light. A vigorous breeze swept the salty spray across Nicole's face and the scent of seaweed into her nose. Her ponytail swung behind her in time with her stride, a pendulum of curls growing curlier and frizzy in the humid morning air.

Each time the sea slid up the sand, she kept her shoes just beyond its reach, and as the water slipped back out, it seemed to pull her gaze with it. The ocean kept drawing her eyes out into the surf, and she kept prying them away. A sheet of water nearly caught her, rushing higher than she expected. She sprinted sideways to keep away and couldn't help watching the wave slink back to its origin. Her stride shortened, and she slowed to a halt, feeling compelled to turn toward the sea that seemed desperate for her attention.

For several minutes all she could do was watch the water crash and churn, tumble, foam and roar, reach out to her, and rush back into the frenzy. She felt spellbound, drawn in as though it was pulling at her heart. It wasn't as though she had not seen the ocean before or sat at its shore for hours captivated by its perpetual, beautiful chaos. But now, in the gray morning light, she felt puzzled by it.

As she studied the deep blue-gray swells and how they heaved and turned green as they curled into white spray, she suddenly understood. The pull, the strange fascination, the need to observe it—it was a feeling of looking into a mirror. It was that instant when she saw her reflection—though she'd seen it a hundred thousand times before—and searched her features for some comprehension of herself. This, standing here, she saw the reflection of what lay deeper.

She felt a strange relief in suddenly comprehending this new part of herself. Since discovering the magic within her, she had been trying to control something she didn't even understand. Looking out at the sea, she could finally understand there was no controlling such a force, no taming it. All she could do was embrace its ebb and flow, know its tides like she knew the features of her own face.

There was beauty in that terrible force. There were as many wonders as dangers lurking within its depths. Her gaze traveled down the shore to where the waves turned vicious, crashing around the posts holding the pier high above the water. While the waves seemed deadly beneath the pier, it was the obstruction of the posts that made those currents dangerous.

It was strangely calming, to see a reflection of the fiery force inside her. Part of her supposed she should be frightened by this clarity, the understanding that this was her new nature, but she was relieved.

She lifted her gaze past the crashing waves to the flat blue horizon. It occurred to her that she feared herself now like she feared the ocean; she did not fear the water itself or her magic, but the unseen depths of it, what might be hiding there, its simultaneous beauty and potential to overpower her.

Then something strange caught her eye out on the water. For a moment she thought she saw land, a distinct, not-so-distant shore. Then she was positive she saw land, a new continent in the Pacific. The image wavered, as if she were looking through a gossamer curtain being moved by the breeze. The landmass was clear and then hazy. It would fade away and then return.

Nicole rubbed her eyes and looked again. Still she could see a thin brown coast across the water.

"I confess, there are times I wish I could hear your thoughts instead of your heart." Gordan's voice barely reached her ear over the sound of the waves.

"I was wondering where you might be," she said, smiling to herself.

"And what might you be running from this morning?"

81

"Dreams," she answered, still studying the sight of land before her.

He came to stand at her side, looking out to the ocean as she did. "What kind of dream?"

"There was fire all around me."

"A nightmare," he said.

"No. It wasn't a nightmare. I wasn't afraid. The fire didn't burn me. Actually, I felt ... safe surrounded by it."

"I see. So why are you running from something that made you feel safe?"

"I don't know."

They stood engulfed in the sound of the ocean.

"Do you ever see through the barrier?"

Gordan turned his eyes to her face. "No. Do you?"

"I get glimpses of Veil sometimes. It's happened before. The barrier somehow becomes transparent. I just thought you might notice it too."

"Well, we know that the presence of magic in this realm acts as a bridge to Veil, and your prolonged presence eventually opens a doorway through the barrier between realms. Perhaps since the magic comes from you, it gives you a unique lens that can peer through that divide. What do you see?"

"There's land out there. There shouldn't be, but I see it. So it has to be in Veil."

"You must be seeing the Wastelands. Cantis is the westernmost outpost of Veil. It is more secluded now than it once was. Continue west, and you will reach the Wastelands. Hence Cantis was the first to fall in the Dragon Wars."

"You mean the dragons lived out in the Wastelands before the wars? I thought they were only exiled there afterward," Nicole said.

"It's true that we live in exile there now. Before the wars dragons were free to live anywhere they desired; however, our kind does prefer isolation. History has proven to us time and again that we are better off when we keep to ourselves. The Dragon King made that viciously clear to everyone else when he set out to conquer all of Veil."

"How did the Dragon King convince a populace that prefers isolation to wage war on the rest of the realm?"

"By convincing them that all he wanted was to unite them, that dragons should stand together. Once he gained their trust and loyalty, he was able to convince them to do anything," Gordan answered. "The dragons did not know their king wanted more. You see, while our kind tends to value solitude, some of us have the propensity toward greed."

"You mean like dragons hoarding treasure?" She gazed back out toward the Wastelands, across two oceans and a barrier.

Gordan chuckled. "Indeed, although not all of us crave things that glisten. Dragons each have their own weakness. The Dragon King's weakness was power. Our kind never had a king before him. We lived in small clans, and many preferred our seclusion. He was the leader of his clan, and he seduced the rest with ideas that had never tempted us before. He claimed every dragon as his people and the vast Wastelands as *our* kingdom, but it was never enough. All of Veil would not have been enough."

Nicole took a deep breath. "Armies. Always armies. How are three people supposed to fight against two enemies with their own legions behind them?"

"A single person can end a war if they know their enemy. Imagine what the three of us can do," Gordan said with a smile.

"Oh yeah, we'll just dismantle the governing structure of the entire realm and weed out Venarius and all his followers," Nicole said with a laugh.

"If you play the game right," Gordan said with an affirmative nod.

Nicole let out a forceful laugh. But before she could dispute Gordan's optimism, he spoke again. "I used to do what you are doing," he said. "To get away from it all. I used to fly over the oceans just to get a glimpse of the mainland. I could ride the ocean winds for days without sleeping. But you run to accomplish this."

"Yeah, not fast enough some days. Hard to escape thoughts in your head."

"What do you do, then?" Gordan looked her in the eye.

"Frances lent me the key to the gym. I'll show you."

Nicole turned her back to the beach and hopped into the air to glide over the deep, dry sand, touching down every five feet or so in a slow kind of run until she reached the paved trail. Gordan followed, running barefoot beside her.

Back in Yuma in the dark hour before dawn, Vinderek slipped silently back into the house. His mouth was twisted with a smug smile. The simple lock of the door was a joke, but then, there was no magic here, so he supposed this was enough for protection. He listened for the sounds of the fera's father as he made his way up the stairs with swift strides.

When he reached the landing, he glanced right toward the fera's room at the end of the hall. Then he considered the two doors to the left. The fera's brother had been in the first room yesterday, and so Vinderek had not ventured beyond it. He had not been prepared enough to take advantage of that leverage before the brother had left. But he had yet to ever regret one of his choices on a mission. He was the best hunter for hire in Veil for a reason. Besides, families were strange, and there wasn't always love in them. They didn't always make the best leverage. The fera's friend, on the other hand ... there was undeniable value there.

The first door he came to was halfway open. The room was a mess. Even in the dim light Vinderek could see that there wasn't anything valuable to learn about the fera from the brother's room. He turned to the other door, half open, on his left.

The door whined as it swung. In the silent house the sound was like a scream. He halted for a moment and listened, but no sounds of stirring seemed to come from the other side of the house, so he proceeded. Compared to the other two, this room was tidy. It seemed to him that this room wasn't even lived in. Still, he stepped inside to investigate.

A packed bag sat on the floor just inside the room, and he wondered who had occupied this room—the other brother from the picture? The father had said the fera had gone to visit her brother somewhere. If the other brother didn't live here, then someone else had inhabited this room and left behind their packed bag.

The mattress was wrapped snugly, its sheets and blankets tucked under neatly at the bottom corners. There was nothing in this room to study—no picture frames on the dresser. He huffed, digging in his pack for his gloves. At last he drew out one of his most useful tools, a pair of black leather gloves laced with a *lembrar* enchantment. The gloves would allow him to see moments from the past associated with any object. He tugged the gloves onto his calloused hands. He couldn't be sure they would even work with so little magic left here, but it was worth trying.

With the gloves on, he touched the doorknob and got a faded glimpse of passing moments, hands clutching and turning the knob. He could barely make the images out, and part of him wondered if his imagination wasn't filling in the gaps.

He placed a hand on the packed bag by the door. The images were clearer; these memories were fresh. This bag had been packed magically, with garments folding themselves and dropping inside. He caught no glimpse of hands. Vinderek was intrigued. The person who had been in this room was well practiced with common spells.

Someone from Veil had been here with the fera. Perhaps this mission would be more troublesome than they anticipated. He had been told that she was raw and inexperienced, a young woman with no knowledge of Veil or magic, that her powers would hinder her more than help her. If she had more control over her powers than they expected, her retrieval would prove to be more difficult, but not impossible.

Vinderek stood up, leaving the bag where it lay, and looked at the bed, the blankets smooth and undisturbed. He sat down, sliding his gloved hands over the bed. The memories here started as hazy blurs of some human form sitting hunched over on the edge of the bed, but the more recent images became clearer. He could make out the faint shapes of two people sleeping. Last came a glimpse of two shadowy forms pressed together on the surface of the bed.

A chuckle escaped him. Now that was the kind of leverage he needed.

He next leaned toward the bedside table and placed a hand on the surface. A barrage of moments flashed by. The drawer of this table had been opened so many times that the images were the clearest he had seen thus far. He opened the drawer, and more brief, blurry memories filled his mind—the drawer being opened and closed. He had to take his hand off the handle for a moment to reclaim his thoughts. There was only one thing in the drawer, a letter. Behind him through the window, the sky was growing lighter. When he pulled the letter from the drawer, he saw a pair of hands gripping the edges, crumpling the paper. The sheet of parchment was worn from so much handling, and it looked as though it had been crushed at least once.

He could not focus on the words while the dim, shaky memories crowded into his head, so he set the letter down and removed the gloves. It was a relief, and not that surprising really, that there was enough magic here still that the gloves worked. The fera had lived her life in this house. Even if her abilities had been unknown to her most of her life, there would probably always be faint vestiges of magic in this place.

With the gloves stuffed back into his pack, he returned his attention to the letter. In the dim room he could not make out the words on the page, so he turned on the small lamp that sat atop the bedside table.

Vinderek read swiftly, taking in the contents of the letter with equal parts disbelief and relish. The man in this room had been Raiden Aldor Cael, one of the Council's own. He contained the urge to laugh. The Council's means of procuring the fera had been helping her instead.

The sound of feet shuffling through the house met his ears, and he flicked off the lamp. He stood and hurried to close the door. This time he moved it swiftly, and it did not whine. Turning the knob, he closed the door gently just as he heard light thumps upon the stairs. From out in the hallway, the soft sniffs of an animal investigating came under the door.

Vinderek listened to the low growl without concern. The door was shut. Then came a bark.

"Bandit?" the father called.

Vinderek sighed and reached into his pack for a knife. He had a decision to make and fast if he was discovered. His first choice was to fight his way out of the house without killing the father—that would be easy, but his presence would be exposed. He didn't want to risk the father warning the fera to stay away. Tracking her down in this realm was far less desirable than waiting for her to return home. His other option was to conceal his presence here by removing the father from the chessboard. He didn't want to give up that leverage, but if he had to, then so be it. At least he already had one piece of leverage that could lure the fera back to Veil.

The dog continued to growl and barked again. Vinderek could hear footsteps on the stairs.

"Bandit," the father said. "Come on—what's gotten into you?"

The dog barked. The footsteps drew nearer to the door. Vinderek stepped back against the wall behind the door and waited. The door opened. Through the gap at the hinges he could see the father peer into the room, a frown on his tanned, lined face. The black dog sniffed at Vinderek through the gap in the doorframe. Its hackles raised, but the father closed the door before it could get in.

"All right, you senile old man," the father said. "Let's go; come on."

The dog gave another woof, but then the sound of footsteps and the little metal clicks from the dog's collar moved away from the door and down the stairs.

Gordan kept up with Nicole as she ran several blocks inland from the beach. They came to a stop at a quiet building, its large windows dark. The sign on the glass door was red: BROOD 9.

"What are we doing here?" he asked through deep breaths. Running in human form was more taxing than he had expected. Perhaps his heart was only pounding because Nicole's was. His ability to detect the feelings of others seemed to grow more visceral every day. He wondered if his gift was developing with more exposure to others.

Nicole was panting and took several breaths before answering. When she finally spoke, her words were interrupted by her deep breathing. "Running is great … when you want to be alone … with your thoughts … not so much … when you want … to get away from them." She dug a key out of a tiny pocket in the waistband of her leggings.

"What is this place?"

"Brood Nine, Frances's martial arts gym. There is a weight area to train their competitive fighters," she answered as she unlocked the door. "Frances said I could come work out."

He followed her inside. She walked through the shadowy entryway and into a much larger and darker room. The lights flickered on. Gordan saw metal framework, bars, and large metal disks but couldn't make much sense of it.

"What is all this?"

"Weights," Nicole answered. "You use them to make basic movements more challenging, to get stronger." She beamed as she lifted the large silver bar from the rack and set it on the floor. Then she pulled a large black disk off its peg and heaved it over to the bar, where she maneuvered them together, metal bar through the hole in the center of the plate. She did the same on the other side.

"My brothers started lifting weights when they were in high school. I decided if they could do it, I could too, and I loved it," she said as she bent over a box of strange objects Gordan couldn't name and dug out a pair of long leather straps.

Gordan wasn't quite sure what he was expecting to see as she crouched down and strapped her hands to the bar, at slightly wider than shoulder-width apart. She situated herself, feet directly under the bar, and altered her crouch until her arms were straight and her back flat. Then she stood up, pulling the bar from the ground easily. Once she was erect, she lowered the bar back down. Her movement was fluid and controlled; her straight spine never broke into an arch. He counted—ten times she performed this motion.

"Why?"

Nicole looked at him as though puzzled for a moment. "Why do I love this?"

He nodded.

She went to retrieve another black plate.

"I wanted to see what I was capable of, if I could do what my brothers could do," she said as she pushed the plate onto the bar. "I realized how weak I was, and I wanted to be strong. I wanted to *feel* strong and capable."

An angry heat radiated from Nicole as she shoved another plate onto the other side. She took a deep breath. Gordan was baffled by this sudden flare of anger. He wondered if she still felt weak, if that weakness was lurking somewhere deeper than her muscles.

Although not quite as strong as his natural form, his altered shape remained much stronger than a human's. Out of curiosity he bent over the bar, took a firm grasp on the cold iron, and gave a tug. He stood up with relatively little effort, but he knew it was a significant weight, easily the weight of his own tail perhaps.

He placed the bar back down. "I am impressed. I imagine that is heavy to a human," he said as he backed away.

Nicole offered him half a smile—which to him validated his suspicion that she was trying to chase away a deeper feeling of weakness with this physical ritual—before resuming her position under the bar once more to strap her hands to the iron. He watched. Her hips hinged, her body straightened upright, and then she set the heavy bar back down. She repeated the process five times. Then she let the bar down, freed her hands, and stood up, her chest heaving.

"Ever since the change a week ago"—she paused to take several breaths—"everything about me feels different, like I'm buzzing all the time, every bit of me. Like when I'm lying in bed, I can feel the charge in my scalp, in my eyelids. Running, weight lifting … it makes your muscles burn, but it's nothing like this new sensation. Now my body knows a different kind of fire, and this is nothing in comparison." She tapped the bar with the bottom of her shoe.

"Your magic is a part of you," he said. "It may seem new and different, but it's always been there. Just like your body was always capable of this strength." He lifted his hand toward the weight bar. "You had to discover the desire for that strength, to dig it out and forge something out of it. The power in any of us is the same."

She was silent a moment, bobbing her head in the slightest of nods.

"You know what I learned by doing this?" she asked as she broke out of her silence and went for another plate. "How to focus on something no matter what chaos might be rattling around in my head."

"How is that?"

"If you're going to lift like this, you can't be distracted by anything. You have to focus—on your body, your movement and form, counting the reps, breathing—or else you can really hurt yourself. It's not a hypnotic repetition like running. I don't have to think about running, which gives me time alone with my thoughts, but lifting lets me step away from them, even if it's just for a few moments at a time."

"I'll confess I wish I had been able to escape my thoughts for a few moments for the last ten years," Gordan said. "I had nothing to do in that tower *but* think."

"What about?"

"Mostly about the mistakes I've made. When you've lived as long as I have, you'll find you make quite a lot."

"You must have good memories too," she said.

Gordan considered this, but somehow the brighter moments of his life before his stay in the tower no longer seemed as luminous standing here with Nicole as they had back in his dark cell.

"I suppose," he answered.

She gave him a scrutinizing look, pressing her lips together into a scowl. "You're determined to keep your life a secret, aren't you?" She turned back to the bar.

"I don't feel it matters all that much. What matters is what's happening now."

"Yeah, like a new one-rep max," Nicole declared.

Gordan observed as she repeated her ritual—plates, straps, fidget, then pull. A sound like a growl came from her throat as she straightened her body entirely before quickly crouching back down to return the bar to the ground. She sank to her knees and remained there as she let out a groan that seemed to be a strange mix of misery and triumph. Once her hands were free, she sat upright and raised her arms in silent victory. Finally, after a few deep breaths, she cheered, "Two thirty-five!"

Gordan chuckled. Then beneath his feet the ground trembled.

"Did you feel that?" he asked.

"What?"

"The earth shook."

"All I can feel is my heart pounding in my head," she said, standing up with concern in her eyes.

"It could have been nothing," Gordan said.

"It's never nothing anymore," she muttered.

Vinderek watched the father leave the house, the dog at his heels as he walked away from the front door and out of sight.

He nodded in satisfaction, having privacy once again to make his preparations.

Nicole worried, her forehead pinched as she chewed a bite of apple furiously. She and Gordan were walking at a brisk pace back to her brother's house. She tried to concentrate on her connection with the earth, waiting for another rumble, but as ravenous as she was, she couldn't be sure her grumbling stomach and the rhythm of her stride weren't fooling her. Hoping to fill the pit in her, she hurried down her apple and tore off a chunk of a protein bar from her other hand.

"What, dare I ask, are you so troubled by now?" Gordan asked.

Nicole swallowed her mouthful. "I think we need to get out of here, head to Tucson to see Mitch," she said.

"Already? We haven't even been here a full day."

"I know. I'm just worried about fault lines," she answered with a huff and took another bite of apple.

"About what now?"

"Fault lines ... in the earth, meaning there is a lot of earthquake activity in the area. The night before my magic made its grand entrance we had tremors in Yuma. It never occurred to me that I could have a negative effect on them. I mean, I know I tend to make plants grow and turn a drizzle into a rainstorm, but earthquakes didn't even cross my mind."

"Plants, rain, earthquakes, these are all natural occurrences. Why worry if the ground trembles?" Gordan asked.

"It's not a few tremors that I'm worried about but a massive seismic event. All the science says we're due for a big one, and I don't want to be the cause of it." Her pace quickened as she spoke.

"And what does it matter if, as you say, you are 'due for a big one'? Who is to say if you caused it, encouraged it, or had anything to do with it?"

She sighed. "Come on, Gordan."

"Come on, what? You're just looking for a reason to run. You aren't even running from your enemies this time; you're running from yourself."

Nicole's heart thundered, flushing her body with defiant heat and angry magic. "What else am I supposed to do, Gordan? Just tear the world apart around me because that's what I am? Just ignore the chaos I cause and not give a fuck?"

"Why should you have to run from who you are for everyone else's sake? The world isn't meant to stay the same. The earth shakes, storms come and go, with or without you. Did you ever stop to think maybe the world needs this kind of change?"

She hadn't realized they'd come to a stop, standing at a quiet intersection. The cloudy sky overhead seemed to be listening, waiting for her answer.

"I ..." She wasn't sure what she thought. The earth gave a slight tremble. "Oh no," she murmured. A base rumble raised the hair on her arms and neck. "Gordan, right now it doesn't matter whether or not I think this world could use a little more magic and a lot less self-destruction. I won't be the cause of a natural disaster. Not today anyway."

She looked him in the eye, and he frowned back at her. The emotions churning in her heart were turbulent. What was she scared of? Who was she so angry at? Where would she ever find peace? Her distress softened his expression.

"I go where you go," he said.

"You're sure you have to leave?" Frances asked for the second time.

"Yes," Nicole said, repressing a frustrated sigh as she swung her full bag into the back of the truck, where it landed with a thud. She turned around, flinging her clean, wet hair with the movement. She and Gordan had gotten back to the house while everyone was still asleep, and she'd even managed to shower before Frances had been the first to rise.

"But you said you could stay for a while," Anthony said, folding his arms.

"The brother voice isn't going to work today, Tony." Nicole's severe tone rivaled her brother's as she turned to look him in the eye. Gordan watched from the other side of the truck, standing outside the passenger door.

"How do you even know you caused the tremors? It's California, Nikki; they happen."

Nicole huffed. "You're right. I don't know. But I do know that when it rained back home last week, I made it worse. It turned into a downpour of record-breaking proportions, Tony. I don't particularly want to experiment with the effect of magic on a run-of-the-mill earthquake when my family is at the epicenter."

Anthony's forehead creased, and Frances pressed her lips together in a straight line of concern.

"I'll be back," Nicole said with a softer voice. "I just want to stay away for a bit, let the fault lines let off a little steam. Okay?"

"You going to Tucson, then?" Anthony asked.

"Yeah," Nicole said, opening the door of the truck.

"Well, drive safe," Frances said. "And let us know when you get there, all right?"

"I will," she answered with her most convincing smile before climbing into the cab. Gordan did the same.

A few minutes later they were parked at the gas station. The tank was full, and they were inside walking the aisles in search of snacks.

"None of this even looks like food," Gordan muttered, picking up a candy bar.

Nicole laughed. "This might be more to your taste," she said, tossing him a pouch of beef jerky. In her pocket her phone buzzed, and she pulled it out with a cringe. But it wasn't a text from Roxanne as she expected. She felt some short-lived relief at the thought that her friend might have given up. It wasn't that she didn't want to tell Roxanne; it was just that it got harder and harder every day that passed. With every day the story got longer and more complicated. It wasn't something she could explain in a text message or even over the phone.

This message, however, was from her dad. It was a picture of Bandit in the back of her dad's work truck. The image rescued her from her anxiety for a happy moment. The caption made her smile: "Bring your dog to work day."

Nicole typed out a reply: "Hitting the road to Tucson. Tremors in CA. Don't wanna risk it."

She tapped "send" and went back to scanning the aisle for the most food-like items she could find—a pouch of jerky, a bag of cashews, and a container of dried mango.

Her phone buzzed with a reply from her dad: "Had a tiny tremble here. I wondered. Drive safe."

Nicole retrieved two huge water bottles from the refrigerators at the back of the store. At the counter she grabbed a banana and a couple of apples from the usually ignored basket by the cash register, and the attendant rang up their supplies.

In five minutes the old white truck was back on the interstate. Nicole felt oddly at ease to have the roar of the engine and the rattling of the truck filling her ears. The wind whirled through the open windows, rustling the plastic bag of their snacks sitting between them.

"Feeling better, I see," Gordan said, gazing out the passenger-side window.

"Yeah," she admitted, her voice virtually lost in the low roar. She waited for Gordan to continue his admonishment, but he remained silent, so she did too. Her mind slipped back to Roxanne, and she filled the time cruising down the 101 with how she might explain everything to her best friend if she ever got the chance.

Nicole's imagination conjured every potential outcome like a computer running simulations. She'd come up with the just-right words, and then Roxie would laugh at her, or Roxie would get angry over such a ridiculous joke when she had been worried sick, or she might remember that last day Nicole had been at school and suddenly see all those strange events in a new light.

"Would you stop that?" Gordan asked with a force of annoyance that must have built up over time. "Whatever you're thinking about, your angst is driving me mad."

Nicole forced an uneasy laugh. "Sorry," she said and took a deep breath. "Can't you—I don't know—block it out?"

"I'm finding that rather difficult these days," he muttered.

"I'll try to think of something that doesn't send me spiraling into a pit of anxiety," she said with lackluster enthusiasm. There didn't seem to be much in the way of happy subjects to think about lately.

Resolutely, she forced her mind back to the beginning, reliving the moments when she hadn't known about the terrible truth of what she was, about her enemies out there looking for her. She had been talking to Roxanne that morning when it had happened—she glanced at Gordan with a guilty cringe on her face, but his eyes were closed.

Nicole marveled at how long ago it seemed now, just over a week ago. She recalled Bandit getting freaked out by the portal before anyone had known it was there. Poor dog, his life had gone crazy—people appearing out of nowhere, strange things happening every day, griffins crashing through portals into the house. She laughed. She missed that dog. At least her dad had taken him to work today, so Bandit wasn't home alone.

She drove. Gordan slept, or just kept his eyes closed, she couldn't be sure. When she made pit stops, he kept his eyes shut.

"Don't you have a human-sized bladder now? How do you not have to go after four hours?" she asked when she stopped the truck the second time. They were on Interstate 10, which would take them all the way to Tucson.

"I haven't been drinking water endlessly like you," he said, his eyes still shut.

"Well, you should be; we're crossing a desert," she said, tossing one of the water bottles toward his belly. He snatched it from the air before it could land on his gut.

"I'll be right back," she said, shutting the door.

On her way back from the bathroom, she dried her wet hands on her pants and pulled out her phone to call her dad. He answered after three rings.

"Hey, baby girl. How's the drive going?"

"It's going," she answered with a laugh. "Just wanted to touch base. We got on the Ten about twenty minutes ago."

"Well, it's a good thing you left early. I've got Bandit here with me. Say hi, buddy."

She could hear Bandit panting and her dad drumming the dog's side with his hand.

"I bet he's having a blast with the guys today."

"Yeah, it's been a while since I brought him along with me. He was acting strange this morning, probably since he is so used to the morning routine with you. I figured I'd get him out of the house for a change of pace."

The idea that her absence might be upsetting Bandit sent a pang of guilt ringing through her ribs. She finished making her way toward the truck and paused outside the driver-side door. "Strange? What was he doing?"

"He was upstairs wanting into Raiden's room—Anthony's room, you know—growling at the door," he said.

"Oh," she said. Her keys jangled as she pulled them from her waistband. "Maybe he still thinks that griffin is somewhere in the house, huh?" The door whined as it opened.

"That's what I thought too. Anyway, sounds like you're getting back in the truck."

"Yep." She dropped down into the seat and scooted in before shutting the door.

"I'll let you go. Drive safe. Let me know when you get to Mitch's place."

"Okay, Dad. Talk to you later."

"Love you."

"Love you too," she said and ended the call. "Ready?" she asked Gordan.

"As ever," he said, eyes shut.

Nicole had the distinct feeling that he was trying to annoy her, but that only made her smile and suppress a laugh.

"If you stay human for too long, will you get stuck that way?"

His eyes opened. "Of course not," he said.

She chuckled and turned the key in the ignition. In a matter of minutes they were cruising down the interstate at seventy miles per hour.

Gordan closed his eyes once more, which gave her the chance to steal glances at him without being scrutinized for it. It was funny how quickly they'd seemed to get attached to each other, Raiden to her, her to Raiden, her to Gordan, and him to her. Was it their personalities, or were their remarkable circumstances enough to bring any group of people together?

A thought crossed her mind, and she picked up her phone from the seat beside her. Quickly, she opened her phone's camera and snapped a picture of Gordan. A massive grin possessed her face as she put the phone back down. Then she realized she didn't have a picture of Raiden, and she wondered how soon she would forget the features of his face.

Then for some reason her mind took her back to something her father had said yesterday, about the photo of her and her brothers. Mitch wouldn't have taken that picture, because he had his own copy of it. She had been the one to hang it in his apartment. She wrung her hands on the steering wheel.

Then she remembered what her dad had said, that Bandit had wanted into Raiden's room. The door must have been closed then. She knew she hadn't closed it before she'd left, though, and Mitchell wouldn't have. Her dad must have shut it then, obviously. She shook her head against these silly, incoherent suspicions.

Still, she heard her dad saying, *He was upstairs wanting into Raiden's room— Anthony's room, you know—growling at the door.* Nicole's heart thudded a little harder in her chest as she recalled Bandit growling at the portal that morning this all started a week ago. A portrait of her and her brothers was missing from the wall, and Bandit had been growling outside Raiden's room this morning.

Her heart thundered against her ribs.

Gordan jerked upright. "What is it? What's wrong?"

"Oh no …" Her words were lost in the noise of the truck. "I think there's someone in the house."

"What?"

She didn't know if he hadn't heard her or couldn't believe her. She thought her heart might combust. She thought her hands might crush the steering wheel.

"Oh my God," she muttered, fumbling to grab her phone again. It took only three taps on the screen to call her dad. She held the phone to her ear, unsure if the severe shaking was from her hand or the vibrations of the truck.

"Hey," he answered.

"Dad," she said, raising her voice above the noise.

"Honey, are you—"

"Dad, I need you to stay away from the house. *Don't* take Bandit home."

"Why?"

"Just don't go back home for lunch or anything." She felt like she was yelling. Then she realized the roar of the engine was getting louder. She glanced at the speedometer—eighty-five—and pulled her heavy foot off the accelerator. "Wait for me to get there, okay?"

"You're coming back to Yuma? Now? What's going on?"

"I don't know yet. Gotta go. I love you." She hung up.

"What are you going to do?" Gordan asked.

"Hold on to something," she said, dropping her phone onto the seat and gripping the steering wheel with both hands.

"Nicole," Gordan said, persisting for an answer, as he latched his hands under the bench seat.

"We're taking a shortcut," she said while deciding which Yuma road had the lowest chance of having any vehicles on it on a Saturday afternoon. Her heart was a battering ram against her ribs. The adrenaline racing in her veins stoked that familiar fire deep inside her.

She didn't hold anything back. The tingling surge of magic prickled her skin. It seeped out her pores and saturated the turbulent air in the cabin. The steering wheel in her hands, the seat beneath her, the entire truck radiated with heat pregnant with energy, as though the truck had become an extension of her. All she could do was focus on the chosen dirt road in her mind, hope with every fiber of her being that the truck would make it in one piece, and hold on tight.

Like striking a match in a gas-filled room, the truck around her seemed to combust into white light, drowning out the sight of the interstate unfurling before them. She shut her eyes against the harsh brightness.

The truck lurched and shook furiously, accompanied by the dings and clangs of rocks against the undercarriage. Nicole forced her eyes open and screamed, delighted and disbelieving to see the dirt road before her.

"It worked," she cried, allowing the truck to coast and slow to a bumpy crawl. "It actually worked!"

Then she looked to her right. Gordan was gone. His seat belt was still buckled, but the seat was empty.

"Gordan!" She stomped the brake pedal, locking up the tires and throwing herself against her seat belt as the truck skidded to a halt. She pulled the shifter out of gear, freed herself from her restraint, and threw the door open.

"Gordan," she yelled as she jumped out of the truck, searching the fields and dirt roads around her for any sign of him. Her voice shrank to a whisper. "Where are you?"

Gordan picked himself up and brushed the sand from his clothes. Aside from his head spinning, his body seemed to be intact.

"Nicole," he called, and his voice drifted away across the rolling hills of the sand dunes.

He focused his eyes and looked around to see nothing but golden dunes all around. If Nicole had been aiming for Yuma, then he had to be in the same dunes he had seen on their way out of town yesterday.

The road was nowhere in sight. He did not know if Nicole had made it back to Yuma, but he knew he could find her. All he had to do was give in to that invisible tether, his debt to her, like a cord rooted deep in his chest, reeling him toward her.

He just hoped that connection to Nicole would also allow him to transform despite the distance from her—the only well of magic around. The pull turned his stumble into a run. He was about to find out how difficult it was, or whether it was even possible, to transform in this realm with just his debt to link him to the only source of magic there was.

11. Hunter

Nicole's panic twisted into dread as she remembered why she was back in Yuma. As much as it pained her to not know where Gordan was or what had happened, she couldn't waste another moment if her suspicions were correct. She got back into the truck, threw it into gear, and charged down the dirt road, heading toward home. The roar of the engine couldn't drown out the thrum of her racing heart.

It was a struggle to abide by traffic laws and speed limits once she was back on paved roads. The grid of long straight roads through the vegetable fields tempted her to floor the gas pedal, but she kept her anxious foot from stomping down as she passed islands of suburban home developments out in the flat sea of romaine, iceberg, and broccoli and made her way back into town. The lazy traffic of a Saturday morning through Yuma was a strange setting for her racing heart. By the time she pulled up to the house, she thought her heart was going to burst under the pressure.

The neighborhood was quiet as usual. The sky was clear as usual. She climbed out of the truck and felt foolish for approaching her front door with so much apprehension when all seemed so peaceful. She fumbled with her keys, her hands trembling as she searched for the one that opened the door.

The deadbolt slid aside with a clack. Then she unlocked the handle and opened the door quietly. The house was silent.

"Dad," she called, trying to keep her voice steady and convincing. "I'm home," she announced, even though she knew he wasn't there. If someone *was* there, she didn't want them to know she was looking for them, that she was on her guard.

She scanned the house discreetly, trying to act natural. If she weren't looking for an intruder, she would go right upstairs to her room. So she did. The living room, the kitchen, both were empty. At the top of the stairs, her eyes locked onto the nail in the wall marking the missing photograph. She paused for just a moment to listen. Not the slightest creak from the floor to be heard.

It took everything she had to not run down the hall into her room and turn frantic in her search behind every door. Her room was empty. No one in the closet, up on her bed, or even cramped in her antique wardrobe. On her way back down the hall, she stopped in the bathroom. No one was behind the shower curtain. With every empty hiding spot she checked, she grew more anxious to check the place she suspected this person had been hiding. Raiden's room.

This stranger—her enemy, she had to remind herself, make the distinction clear—had been behind the door when her father had been up here. The thought made her stomach turn and a shudder roll down her spine. The moment she turned the doorknob, her enemy would be prepared. She opened the door with one swift push. But the room was empty. Silent. Unaltered from the last time she'd seen it.

Her heart sank, but not with relief. She checked behind the door. No one. Then she opened the closet door. Nothing. She checked Mitchell's room. Nothing. At last she gave up her ruse of nonchalance and hurried down the stairs. After clearing her dad's room, she sat on the edge of the bed to think.

There was no one in the house right now, but they could be coming and going. She got up and walked to the back door. It was unlocked. She stepped outside, surveying the yard. For a moment she stopped, stunned at the withered brown scene. It had been lush and green when she'd left just yesterday. She wore her troubled tension on her brow as she crossed the yard. The dead, dried clovers revived under her red-and-white running shoes, leaving a brilliant green path behind her.

The shop was closed up as always, the garage door down and the entrance shut. When she reached for the knob, she desperately hoped it wouldn't turn, but it did. The door opened. Her heart rate accelerated, winding up again. But there was nothing to be found, except, of course, everything that was supposed to be there. The couch, the workout equipment, her dad's workbench and table saw, his tool chests and air compressor.

This time Nicole let out a huff of annoyance. She crossed the shop to open the door to the bathroom—a tiny closet just big enough for a toilet and a basin sink. She opened it without hesitation, having already decided she was being stupid. But as the door swung open, a tall, blonde-haired girl threw her head back and looked at Nicole with terrified blue eyes.

"Roxanne?" Nicole couldn't believe her eyes as she lurched toward her friend. Roxanne's wrists were tied behind her, her ankles bound and anchored to the base of the toilet.

"Nicole!" she cried.

Nicole jumped from the bathroom, ran to the tool chest, and retrieved a box cutter. "What are you doing in here? What happened?" She sliced through the duct tape binding Roxanne's ankles to the toilet.

"Some psycho … he …" Roxanne was shaking. "He jumped into my car with a knife—made me drive somewhere to hide it. Then … I don't know. I woke up, and he had me over his shoulder. Before I could think straight, he shoved me in here. I …" She looked out into the shop while Nicole cut the tape from her wrists with care. He had wrapped them at least five times, tightly. "I wasn't even sure I was in your shop until now."

"Shit, I am so sorry, Roxie. I never imagined you would get pulled in like this," Nicole said, pulling the tape off her friend's sleeves.

"'Pulled in'? What the hell does that mean? You know what this is about?"

"It's about me. He's looking for me."

"Why?"

"That's—well—I," she stammered. Her well-planned explanation was nowhere to be found now. "For the same reason I haven't been at school, why all those weird things happened—the picnic tables, the power outages, the freak storm. This past week I've been dealing with some changes—some new abilities."

"Could you make sense, please?" Roxanne asked, rubbing her wrists.

"Can we get out of here now, and I'll explain things later? I think this guy is in the house somewhere—"

"You'd be wrong," a man's voice said.

Roxanne jumped back, falling onto the toilet once again as Nicole whirled around. His hair was white and cut close to his scalp, his skin so suntanned it looked like leather. There was a cold grin on his face and determination in his dark eyes. He was standing there in the shop as if he had been there the whole time.

"You're the fera, I presume." He held up the picture frame containing the photograph of her and her brothers.

"And you are?" Nicole didn't know what else to do but talk while she tried to think, her magic building in the back of her throat like bile.

"Vinderek. Hunter," he said with a little bow.

"The Council send you?"

He laughed with genuine gusto, suggesting the answer was no.

Nicole shouted the first spell she could think of. "*Ilumina!*" She turned her head and threw her arm up against her eyes as a tremendous flash of light erupted between them. His shout was the only thing Nicole heard through the pounding of her heart in her ears. She leaned into the bathroom, grabbed Roxanne's hand, and pulled her forward. "Run!"

Vinderek was still rubbing his eyes and shaking his head, stumbling to get around the table as Nicole and Roxanne ran past him, out the door, and around the shop toward the gate at the back wall. She could not think of spells now. All she could do was let her magic out and hope for the best. As they charged for the gate, she thought, *Open, open, open!*

Power came off her in a hot wave, breaking the lock and throwing the gate open with a bang.

"Come on," she cried, turning to Roxanne and shepherding her through the gate. She could hear cursing and a clang from inside the shop.

"Where do we go?!"

Nicole fell in behind Roxanne, sprinting on adrenaline-charged legs. Her frantic eyes could only look ahead. They ran across the street, their high school campus directly in front of them—Nicole could think of nowhere else. The chain-link fence enclosing the parking lot and practice fields behind the school whined and broke open. "He doesn't know the school," Nicole said breathlessly.

She stole a glance over her shoulder as they jumped through the mangled fence. Vinderek appeared through the gate, agitated.

"Go—go!" she cried with a burst of panic that radiated from her and brought the fence to life. She looked back. The metal quivered and twisted back together, closing before Vinderek could get through. He struck the fence with his palms, making the links ring with anger, but he hoisted himself up easily.

Nicole summoned up every ounce of speed she could and gained on Roxanne, running beside her as they passed the fine arts building. They ran beneath the great, shaded breezeway, across the courtyard, and past the main gate. As they passed the school statue of the Cibola Raider holding his shield, the rosebushes on either side of it trembled and grew. Branches and thorns swelled, drinking in Nicole's frightened magic from the air. In seconds the statue was engulfed in the twisting, biting branches.

"What the hell is going on?" Roxanne gasped as she slowed her pace and skirted around the growing bushes that were curling and reaching for Nicole.

"Hide first. Talk after," Nicole said, pulling her friend back into a run while the monstrous rosebushes filled the courtyard.

Vinderek halted before a veritable wall of thorns. He sighed and turned his head toward his shoulder, popping the vertebrae of his neck. Determined to salvage this mission, he knew first he would need his portal ready and waiting. Then he just needed to draw out his quarry and his leverage. This mission was far from lost.

He looked to his left at one of the long red brick buildings surrounding the courtyard choked with thorns. The building appeared to extend well past the other side of the tangle of rose branches and thus provided a simple way to get to the other side of this obstacle. Unlocking doors would be far less trouble than fighting a living, growing nest of teeth.

Vinderek smiled as he backed away from the thorns and headed for the entrance at the end of the building near him.

Raiden walked at an anxious pace toward the court building at the center of the city. There was a blanket of clouds overhead, and as the sun rose, the darkness reluctantly shifted into a dim gray light. The light of the streetlamps shrank away.

He was hoping to find Caeruleus. This was his last day to work uninterrupted by the Council, and he hoped he would be able to steal Caeruleus away for what he had planned. As he walked, he let himself remember the days when they had been boys together, but it felt more like a history review from school than fond reminiscing.

The din of the traffic rose up around him, and cold anxiety stirred in his chest. As children he and Caeruleus had spent their time racing through the crowded streets of Cantis. Those memories shuddered in his mind. The bustling market around him melded with boyhood memories and twisted into a frenzy of panic and screams. Instead of two boys dodging and pushing through the bodies of their neighbors, golems lunged and tore through fleeing people turned to prey.

Raiden shook the broken memory from his mind and took a deep breath. He didn't have Nicole to pull him out of that place now. This Caeruleus was not the friend he'd had all those years ago. This man did not know who Raiden had become. Raiden had no allies in the courts, and he needed to remember that.

Raiden went over his plan meticulously in his head to keep his mind off the crowds as he made his way to the courts. Down the street, over the heads of early marketgoers, he could see the marble building standing tall on its small hill. He wasn't quite sure which of the surrounding buildings were the barracks, where most of the Council's agents were housed. He hoped to catch Caeruleus before his old friend could get involved with the Council and the mission of finding Nicole for the day. Raiden was counting on Caeruleus accompanying him to Cantis. Going by himself would seem suspicious. Going with Caeruleus would look precisely like Raiden was helping Caeruleus learn what he could about Nicole—and perhaps two men finally saying farewell to their past.

Raiden trudged up the daunting flight of white steps he suspected were meant to intimidate visitors. He was not the only one ascending from the lowly streets to the Council's lofty perch. In the cold, misty morning it was a wonder to him that the stone steps did not seem quite as cold as they should, like the cobblestones and pavements of the streets he had just walked on below. He slowed, paying close attention to the white stone beneath his feet. A faint hum of magic seemed to be coming off the steps, and it was only for fear of the attention he'd draw that he did not stop to lower an ear closer to verify his suspicion.

He had to force himself to resume his brisk pace while he wondered what magic might be at work—honesty hexes perhaps or even charms to inspire loyalty or maybe fear. He tried not to let mistrust show on his face as he maintained a vigilant self-awareness, just in case he found himself suddenly sympathizing with the Council.

The great doors of the hall were open, and golden light spilled out from the court entrance. Raiden wasn't all that surprised to see Caeruleus crossing the massive threshold on his way outside.

"Ruleus," Raiden said out of habit.

"Ray," Caeruleus answered just as naturally.

"I was hoping I could borrow you today."

"For what?"

"To go back to Cantis," Raiden said clearly, even as people passed by.

If the thought of returning to Cantis made Caeruleus apprehensive, his face did not show it. A silent moment passed, long enough for Caeruleus to blink once.

"Right. Let me file a temporary departure," he said with a smile.

"You can leave, just like that, then?" Raiden had expected more of a hassle.

Caeruleus motioned for Raiden to follow as he turned back into the well-lit hall. "I have a decent rank," he said with a chuckle. "Seeing as we are taking a trip to Cantis, this falls under my classified assignment—top priority. But I still have to do the paperwork."

Raiden followed Caeruleus down the hall. Directly ahead stood the formidable double doors of the Council's chamber. They passed several ordinary-sized doors bearing plaques like Licensing Office, Civil Complaints, Taxes, Scribe Office. Caeruleus turned toward a door labeled Public Order Department and opened it.

Inside there were several desks. Behind each someone was sitting quietly writing on forms or pressing a seal into the bottom of a page. Caeruleus walked over to a desk where a slight young man with deep-brown skin and nearly white blond hair sat performing the same repetitive motions as everyone else but with distinct grace that did not suit the tasks.

"Leigh, could I trouble you for a temporary-departure form?"

Leigh smiled just at the sound of Caeruleus's request. "Anything for Caeruleus," he said when he looked up. He raised a hand and snapped his fingers. One of countless filing drawers behind him slid open, and a single sheet of paper slipped out and flitted across the space into his hand. "Here you are," Leigh said, handing the form over. "Is this our new guy?" Leigh asked, leaning just a little to eye Raiden with his violet gaze.

"That he is. This is Raiden," Caeruleus said, pulling him forward and patting him on the back. "He doesn't start until tomorrow. Ray, this is Leigh."

Leigh smiled. "Word of advice, we're a lot more chipper at the start of the day around here, in case you need anything." He didn't make an effort to quiet his voice.

As Raiden took a glance around, he noticed a few tiny smiles at the corners of the other workers' mouths. "I'll remember that. It's a pleasure to meet you."

"He's as polite as you," Leigh said to Caeruleus as he leaned back in his chair.

"That's not surprising," Caeruleus said as he filled out his form on the corner of the desk. "We grew up together, after all. His mother practically took me in." He signed the bottom of the page with a final flourish of his pen.

Raiden fought back the odd wave of heat conjured up by the mention of his mother.

"Thank you, Leigh," Caeruleus said, handing the form back.

Leigh tossed it over his shoulder, where it vanished with a spark. "Anytime, handsome. See you around, Raiden."

"All right, off we go then, Ray," Caeruleus said, hooking an arm around Raiden's shoulders and escorting him through the door.

Nicole and Roxanne slowed to an exhausted trot, their footsteps echoing around the cement below them and brick around them. Many of the school's classrooms were accessed from the outside courtyards and walkways.

"Here," Roxanne said, turning to a classroom. "Mrs. Lecker's room." She tried the handle, but it didn't turn. "Shit."

"Here." Nicole grabbed her friend's hand tight and shut her eyes hard as a flare of heat rushed through their clasped hands.

Nicole's head was swimming in magic, spinning her into a pit of nausea for a moment. She couldn't open her eyes. It was Roxanne's reaction that told her it had worked.

"Whoa! How'd you do that?"

"Same way I did everything else," Nicole said with a bitter chuckle, still waiting for the fluids in her skull to stop swirling. She dared to open her eyes. They were standing inside the classroom beside the door. "Would you believe me if I said it's all magic?"

Roxanne looked at Nicole with a stony expression for several seconds. "Honestly, I can't say anything else would even make sense at this point."

"That's how I felt too," Nicole said, on the verge of laughter.

"This is why you missed school, why you haven't been around for a *week*?"

"Remember last week when you called before school, when I told you I was on my way but didn't show up to class?" Nicole couldn't believe that was only last week.

"Yeah," Roxanne said with a shrug.

"I didn't make it to school because a portal opened in my backyard," Nicole said, laughing this time at how ludicrous it sounded to her even now—and *she* had been there.

"You see, somehow that makes total sense," Roxanne said. "I mean there was a *lot* of bizarre shit going on this past week. And frankly, how can I argue with mutant plants taking over outside?"

"Yeah." Nicole was caught in a strange place between chagrin and amusement.

"So is that why you left?"

"That's where this all gets unpleasantly complicated," Nicole said. "There are people from this other realm who are looking for me."

"That guy out there?"

"He's just one of them."

"Does he want to kill you?"

"I don't think so. I think he's with the people who want me alive. The reason why is still a little unclear." Nicole stopped herself when she saw the horror in Roxanne's blue eyes.

"Wait, people who want you alive? So there *are* people who want you dead?"

"That's still a little unclear too, frankly. The leaders of the other realm think I'm some kind of threat. All I know is they apparently got rid of all the others that were like me."

"People are legitimately hunting you," Roxanne said in a state of shock, her eyes frozen open wide.

"I've been trying to figure out how to tell you about this since Raiden came through that portal," Nicole confessed with a bitter smile.

Roxanne shook her head. "I was so mad at you," she muttered, and then she lurched forward and hugged Nicole. "I can't believe I was mad at you."

"To be fair," Nicole said, still trapped in the hug, "there's no way you could have guessed things were this serious."

Roxanne released her. "What the hell are we supposed to do now?" She threw her hands up in exasperation.

"You're going to stay here, and I am going to go out there." Nicole nodded toward the door.

"I don't like that plan."

"Neither do I," Nicole admitted.

Vinderek could hear the girls speaking through the door, their voices muffled. He was in no hurry. His new plan should work as well as his previous one, although he would have to rely on only one person as leverage. He strolled into the center of the smaller courtyard, midday sunlight spilling over a few raised planters that doubled as benches.

"Where's that bloody spell?" he grumbled as he searched his pockets for the piece of paper with the words he needed. Once he had a portal open, he would be ready.

Raiden bent over, propping himself up with his hands on his knees, and took a deep breath.

Caeruleus laughed. "Not used to those big jumps, are you?"

They were on the shore of Cantis, the smooth, polished stones of the beach underfoot. Unlike in Atrium, the sky was clear; the sun was just peeking over the edge of the ocean at their backs.

"I didn't think I would ever see this place again," Caeruleus said quietly, his jovial tone gone.

Raiden straightened himself up and sighed. "A week ago I didn't think I would leave this place alive."

"What *were* you doing a week ago? For these past nine years?"

"I was just trying to survive at first. I scavenged. I hid. I read spell books to learn how to protect myself and thought about revenge to pass the time. Surviving eventually turned into preparing, searching for a way to repay that woman for what she did."

Caeruleus said nothing as the sun climbed up the sky behind them.

Raiden looked up at the castle, visible from the beach. He turned his gaze toward the city. Its silent buildings stood waiting for them. Down the beach to the south and toward the city were the docks. Even at a distance it was apparent that the docks were dilapidated, the lower docks sagging into the water. The remains of one of the taller docks stood like a chain of wooden islands leading out to sea.

They walked along the water's edge toward the docks and the road merchants had once used to cart their goods into Cantis.

"I have to confess," Raiden said, beginning to craft his new reality, "I wasn't at all interested in the Council's offer. I didn't read the letters for days. I never went looking for the portal. All I cared about was going after Moira. It's all I have cared about for years."

The stones grumbled and clacked under their feet.

"I don't blame you," Caeruleus said. "When I heard about what happened, that's all I could think about too. You weren't alone."

"I *was* alone," Raiden said with a bitter sigh. He could feel his friend's guilt in his silence. Part of him wanted to tell him about meeting Nicole. Finding her had been his path out of that cold solitude. He wanted Caeruleus to know he hadn't been entirely alone, but he couldn't let on that there was anything between him and Nicole. Even if Raiden could trust Caeruleus, he couldn't trust the Council. The fact was that the only information safe from the Council was information no one remembered.

Raiden sank into the morose task of mapping out his new memory. The pieces he chose to share with Caeruleus would remain, while everything he concealed to protect Nicole would be buried so deep in his psyche he might never remember. Reuniting with her was the only sure way to exhume those memories, but the possibility of that seemed to shrivel. He tried to trust that whoever he would be tomorrow would end up helping her somehow and crossing her path. For now he tried to enjoy the memories he was preparing to give up, the ones he could not risk the Council ever getting from him.

"With the letters from the Council and someone else from the courts potentially getting involved here, I decided it was time to confront Moira. The Council didn't concern themselves with Cantis back then, and I wasn't about to risk them getting in the way." It was safest to remember as little as possible involving Nicole.

"I understand. It was your fight to finish," Caeruleus said quietly.

"A few days ago I finally had my chance to face Moira," Raiden continued, glancing up at the castle. As far as Caeruleus could know, he hadn't met Nicole before reading the Council's letter, hadn't gotten to know her or care about her, hadn't decided to help her despite the Council or attempt to infiltrate the courts to help her—that stupid plan that had landed him near death up in that damned castle.

"I should have known she would have the upper hand in that place. She could have killed me quickly, but I guess she thought it was more fun to draw things out."

From the corner of his eye he saw Caeruleus cringe.

"Then the fera showed up. I don't know how or why she was there," Raiden said, deciding to keep the moment Nicole had found him to himself. "She ran into me, quite literally." He let himself laugh, so quietly it was lost in the grumbling of the stones underfoot. He wondered if Caeruleus had heard that bittersweet, involuntary sound.

"The fera?"

"She's the only reason I'm alive." His voice was heavy with the weight of that truth. At least he would get to remember that much. He hoped he would appreciate that fact when he remembered nothing else.

"What happened, exactly?"

"I don't know. Moira left me bleeding on the floor to go after the fera— somehow Dawn knew she was there. I could barely pick myself up and walk. I'd only made it through the door when she ran into me. It all happened too fast. It didn't even occur to me who she was at first. She tried to help me. Moira caught up with her and had us cornered, the door to the chamber sealed. You should have seen her break the seal. I've never seen anything like it. She ran, and Moira followed." Raiden shrugged.

"Then what?"

"By the time I got there, Moira was dead. All I know is that woman was crazed; all that mattered was capturing the fera for her master. She said something about the fera belonging to him." Raiden would not complicate the story with Gordan. No one needed to know Nicole had an ally or about the collapsing of the bridge or Raiden's discovery of his wings. He wondered if Caeruleus had earned his yet or if the Council was still using that as incentive.

"So?"

"After all that she helped me get out of there. She didn't have to. She could have just left me there. That's how I met her. She had no idea who I was, just that I needed help. I was in no state to do anything but stumble and fall. She helped me get home. She even healed me. Her magic is … raw, instinctive, and mostly accidental."

"That's not all that reassuring, Raiden. She killed someone."

"Can you really blame her? I had every intention of killing Moira too. She was defending herself. Would you treat me like an unstable threat if I had been the one to kill Moira instead?"

Caeruleus responded with silence.

"I didn't know what to do about the Council's request at that point. I slept almost a whole day and thought about it. With Moira dead I didn't have anything else to do, so I went looking for the portal. I'm not even sure why. To thank her or just to find out more about her maybe," Raiden said, surprised the lies were so easy. "When I showed up through the portal and managed to find her, she was leaving. I don't know where she was going, but that was about the time when the Council summoned me." He finished with a sigh of relief to be done with the story.

They were at the edge of town.

"You know it's not like the Council is trying to hunt her down like prey. They just want to ensure that everybody in both realms is safe. The other fera did a lot of damage, Raiden, and rather than waiting for things to get out of hand, they are hoping to bring her in before things get out of control. If Dawn is looking for her, all the more reason to deliver her into the Council's custody. Atrium is the safest place for her."

"That's not the way the letters sounded to me," Raiden said.

"You said it yourself, Ray: she uses her magic instinctively and accidentally. With as much power as all the other fera had, can you honestly say she isn't a risk out there? That she might not hurt someone or unravel the barrier that keeps Veil safe, even if it's unintentional?"

This time Raiden had nothing to say.

"The Council just needs to evaluate her, monitor her. If she cooperates, there is no reason for her to meet the same fate as the other fera," Caeruleus said with casual ease, as though they were discussing matters of minor importance.

Raiden kept his mistrust to himself, held back his cynicism, and resisted the urge to frown.

"I don't suppose we came all this way just for you to tell me about the fera," Caeruleus said.

"No," Raiden answered. "I didn't get the chance to say goodbye." His words filled the eerie, empty stillness between the buildings of the city.

Caeruleus was silent for several steps. "Neither did I."

12. Hunted

"Just stay here. *Don't* open the door," Nicole said.

Roxanne looked at her with outrage in her wide eyes, but her fear seemed to keep her lips stitched shut.

Nicole took a deep breath and let the surge of magic roll through her. It swept her up in a hot current, scattered her into a frenzied haze of confusion, and whisked her through the door and outside into the courtyard. She lurched forward onto solid ground, staggering as she felt herself solidify.

The courtyard was still. Silent sunshine spilled around her. Then a glimmer caught her eye. The air seemed to ripple like a mirage, and the air prickled her skin for just a moment. In the center of the courtyard, a portal twisted the air, creating a porthole in the barrier through which she could see the trees of Cantis. On the cement below the portal a lopsided circle had been drawn with scattered handfuls of dirt.

"Oh no," she exhaled.

"So you can see it, fera." The voice bounced around the courtyard.

She whirled around, searching, but saw nothing, only the cement and brick of benches and planters, the slight forms of the young trees shuddering and growing in their beds.

"We're going back to Veil, you and me," he said.

"Like hell I am," she murmured, trying to pinpoint the source of his voice.

"You have a thing or two to learn about hunters," he said.

She could have sworn he was moving, circling her, but his voice slipped around the courtyard, and she couldn't be certain where it was coming from.

"We're patient. We will catch our quarry no matter how long it takes."

Nicole moved away from the portal, trying to change her vantage point and catch some movement that might give him away.

"And to be an effective hunter you've got to master camouflage."

Nicole's eyes went wide as she searched for someone she suddenly realized she wouldn't be able to see. "Do hunters have to be full of themselves, or is that unique to you?" she asked, raising her voice.

A chuckle seemed to come from the far side of the courtyard. She kept moving, kept searching, trying to think of some spell that might help her, but everything she'd read seemed to disappear under pressure.

"Search all you want," he said with a laugh.

All she could think was that he must want her to be distracted for some—

A sudden pressure cinched around her ankle. At first she thought it was a gray snake coiling around her leg, expanding, growing, but she saw no head and realized it was a plant.

"Plants seem to like you, fera. I'll leave you to get acquainted with the creeper of the Wastelands, and we can continue this conversation later," Vinderek said, appearing beside her before heading toward the classroom where she'd left Roxanne.

Her magic surged as her heart raced, and the creeper doubled in size, twisting around her thigh and encasing her foot. Panic stoked her magic into a wildfire in her chest, and the strange vine only grew faster. She pulled at it. A wriggling tendril broke away in her hand but immediately began to grow from its severed ends, wrapping around her wrist and up her arm. She screamed, yanking a handful away from her forearm with her other hand, and yet again the plant sprouted new growth.

Back in the classroom Roxanne heard Nicole's scream and looked up from the cabinet. Her hesitation vanished and she bashed the heavy base of the microscope into the windowpane. The crash of breaking glass rattled through her head. Broken glass crunched under her feet.

"Shit," she muttered as she fumbled with the contents on the shelves. She grabbed a long glove from the box on the bottom shelf and shoved her hand into it. Lastly, she snatched a bottle from the shelf.

Roxanne crossed the classroom with anxious steps, holding the bottle in her gloved hand. She placed herself beside the door, took a deep breath, and carefully opened the bottle. She struggled to hold the bottle steady with her shaking hand, taking deep breaths to keep from spilling it on herself.

The sound of the door unlocking made her heart drop like a stone. The handle turned, the door opened, and Vinderek appeared. Roxanne yelped, throwing the contents of the bottle toward his smug face, turning her head away from the splash as the acid hit both flesh and door. Some of the contents splashed back, but only a few stray droplets burned through her sleeve.

His terrible scream filled the classroom and the courtyard as he staggered away from the door and fell back, clutching his face.

Roxanne let out a frantic shriek as she pushed the door open and ran past Vinderek. "Nicole!" she yelled, her voice crashing through the courtyard. Then she heard a muffled cry.

Roxanne ran around the planters and came to a bizarre, wriggling mass of what looked like pale-gray roots, a distinctly human-sized cocoon.

"Nicole?"

"Don't touch it." Nicole's stifled voice barely made it through the vines.

Suddenly there came a hissing sound, and some of the vines burned, crumbled, and fell away, revealing hands and forearms glowing with heat. The growing tendrils recovered with new growth, grasping at Nicole, but were singed immediately.

"It's working," Roxanne cried, both horror-struck and relieved.

Nicole pulled at the vines, and they burned and shriveled in her hands. She freed her face, gasping for air, and pulled the plant away from her head and neck. It was persistent, crawling up her back while she cleared her shoulders, wrapping thicker around her waist when she pulled new growth from her neck.

Then Roxanne felt a hot growl at her ear, and a pair of massive arms clamped around her. She shrieked.

Roxanne's terrified cry wrenched Nicole's attention from the vines. Panicked, she saw Vinderek with his arms locked around Roxanne. He picked her up off her feet. His face was a vibrant red burn with a nose and a sneer.

"No! Stop!" Nicole cried, craning her neck to keep them in sight as the vines crept back around her.

"This is what I came for," he said.

Nicole pulled, tore, yanked, and ripped the creeper as fast as she could, burning terror building in her chest.

"The answer is always the right bait. Your friend and I are going on a little trip. When you finally get free from that weed, you can come find us in Veil," he said in a smug grumble as he backed toward the portal.

Roxanne kicked and squirmed against his hold. Nicole lost herself in a wave of anger and a flash of white-hot light. The ceaseless advance of the creeper withered into dust. She scrambled to her feet, unsteady, blinking the blinding light from her eyes, her movements slow from the receding heat in her limbs.

She could barely see Vinderek and Roxanne through her blurry eyes. She staggered forward, leaning on the nearby planter, the bricks cool against her skin. As her eyes focused, she saw something flash in the sunlight. Roxanne pulled something from her pocket, slim and silver, and fumbled to remove its protective cap—a scalpel from the science room.

Roxanne plunged the scalpel into Vinderek's thigh. He let out an animal roar of pain and rage, dropping Roxanne. Nicole's stride grew stronger, her equilibrium steadied. Roxanne ran toward her.

"Let's get out of here," Roxanne said.

Nicole didn't answer.

Vinderek pulled the bloodied scalpel from his leg and dropped it. Then his form seemed to flicker, and he was gone. Nicole ran, keeping her eyes on the blood dripping out of nowhere onto the cement, leaving a trail as he retreated, skirting around the dirt that marked the portal's presence.

No, she thought. *You don't get to hide.* She stooped to grab the scalpel and lunged forward, driving the little blade toward something she couldn't see. It hit flesh, and she yanked it back, surprised that she had made contact.

A terrible gurgled yell filled the air, and blood hit her in the face. Vinderek flickered before her again, his neck gushing blood through his fingers, his eyes wide with crazed anger. He swung at her with his other hand, and Nicole jammed the scalpel into his neck again, scraping against finger bones before squishing into arteries. She pushed him with every ounce of strength she had. His body fell back into the portal and vanished.

She stood there gasping for air through a chest crowded with fury, trying not to asphyxiate on rage as her hammering heart reluctantly slowed. Her anger deflated slowly into shock, and the pounding in her head finally quieted. She listened to each deep breath she took as she wiped her bloody hand on her pants.

"Nicole." Roxanne was there beside her, and the sound of her voice snapped Nicole out of her shock.

"Are you all right?" Nicole asked, searching her friend's face and eyes.

"Are *you?*"

"I'm fine," she insisted, and despite her speeding heart, she could believe that for now. "Goddamn, Roxie, you kicked his ass. You scalpeled the guy."

"Yeah, I threw acid in his face too. Motherfucker deserved it," Roxanne muttered.

Nicole let the tension in her chest break, and it came out as laughter. All she could think to do was hug her friend.

"You took care of him, though," Roxanne added. "Thanks."

"He would have come back," Nicole said with certainty. "After what he tried to do, he didn't deserve to slink away and lick his wounds." Nicole heard the darkness in her own voice. "Come on; let's get the hell out of here."

"What about that?" Roxanne asked, nodding to the portal.

"I believe I can help you there," a voice said from the roof.

The girls looked up together in time to see Gordan with his silky black hair and odd gray complexion jump down into the courtyard. He was barefoot, and his tunic was askew.

"Gordan," Nicole heaved his name from her chest and broke into a run. She threw her arms around him, and he held her up. "What happened to you?"

"You lost me during the jump. It can happen. I assume you and the truck made it in one piece, though?"

Nicole forced a laugh.

"I'm sorry—who is this? Nicole?" Roxanne kept her distance, and Nicole didn't blame her.

"Roxie, this is Gordan. He's a dragon."

"Oh, is that all?" Roxanne said with a sarcastic head roll.

"Let's worry about the portal now and introductions later," Gordan said.

Raiden and Caeruleus stood before the only house surrounded by the multistoried buildings of the city. As a child Raiden had never thought to ask his mother why their home was surrounded by three-and four-level apartment buildings. Raiden supposed he would never know.

"It looks exactly the same," Caeruleus said.

"It doesn't feel the same," Raiden warned. He opened the gate and crossed the little yard.

Caeruleus hesitated, still standing out on the street. Raiden turned to see him looking more like the Caeruleus he remembered from their childhood, perhaps because he wore an expression of fear and heartache in his eyes. This had been his home too. He was seeing the streets of Cantis empty for the first time, something Raiden had had almost a decade to grow accustomed to.

Raiden could almost see him arguing with himself. Did he want to see the house he had spent so much of his own childhood in—where he had stayed when his father had been constantly away on business, where he had preferred to be even when his father had been home—now a shell, silent and dark?

Before Raiden could speak, Caeruleus took a determined step forward and crossed the yard. "I need to see," Caeruleus declared. "I could have come, but I made every excuse I could. To think you were here the whole time." He forced a sad smile through his angry frown. "I need to say goodbye too."

Raiden tried to smile back, but Caeruleus was making him feel like a lost boy in an empty city again. He turned back to the front door and touched the knob. The protective spell unraveled easily, and he wondered if he even needed it any longer. The door creaked as it opened.

"Never fixed that, huh?" Caeruleus said with a soft chuckle.

"Mother always said she liked that sound," he said.

They stood in silence for what felt like ages.

"I'll be down the hall. Take your time," Raiden said as Caeruleus took a long, slow look around the front room.

Caeruleus didn't answer and didn't follow, a relief to Raiden as he moved toward the door at the end of the hallway, the one that would take him to the room upstairs. Only he could pass through it. If Caeruleus tried to follow, the door would open to a lonely closet.

Raiden wasn't expecting to feel so at home when he stepped into the book-filled room. Perhaps part of him thought he might open the door and find Nicole here. He could almost laugh, remembering that night she'd found the Council's letter and used the jump token to get away. But the room was dark and empty, save for the mounds and piles and stacks of tomes that had kept him company through the years. His old friends welcomed him back into their world of dust and silence.

This was the only place he could think to leave a message for Nicole. He removed a folded piece of paper from his jacket and unfolded it, reading his scrawl to take one last chance to consider his choice.

Nicole,

I hope by leaving this letter here it makes it into your hands. I cannot predict why you might be in Cantis now, but I implore you to stay with Gordan. No one else knows about him, except me. The mainland is a more dangerous place for him than it is for you. Dragons that return to the mainland are most often killed on sight. The safest place for you both would be with the other dragons in the Wastelands. I doubt the Council or even Venarius would think to look for you there. As much as I hope to meet again, I cannot deny that the safest place for you is with Gordan and far from the Council. You were right. We were stronger together.

It has only been a day since my departure. Unfortunately, time is not on my side. I have a difficult decision to make. The Council seems to trust me, to some degree, but I cannot rely on that trust, and I must ensure that I keep my secrets from them. I know things they could use against us. The day they stop trusting me is the day they might take what I know by force, so I must urge you not to come to Atrium. Someone searching for me in the city would be suspicious when I have no living family or friends from Cantis. And I don't want you anywhere near the Council.

I write this in hopes to ease any worries you might have. In fact, I have found an ally in the city willing to help me protect my secrets. Which brings me to the main reason I'm writing this letter. The only way I know to protect all of us is to forget. They can't know about Gordan or how much you mean to me. There is no way they can discover anything I know about you or Gordan if I have forgotten it all. Assuming the spell works as planned, these memories shouldn't be lost forever, just buried too deep for me to remember. It would seem the only thing working in our favor at this point is how short our time was together. A week is not so much time to lose and easy enough to alter in the mind.

It's a risk, but when have we had any options without risk? I don't know how much more time has passed as you read this letter or what will have happened to me by now. If all goes according to plan I should still be in Atrium, still untrusting of the Council, and hopefully accomplishing something that will help us.

Whatever you do, be safe.

Raiden

He sighed. This was the right choice, and at least it would only be a painful one for a few more hours. He placed the letter on the desk, removed a pocket watch from inside his coat, and set it on top. Then he proceeded to open each of the desk drawers, having forgotten where he'd last seen his stash of money.

It had taken a while for him to figure out how useless money was after the massacre. But he'd still been a kid, so of course he'd picked up the money he'd found in the empty city. He'd realized how useless it was after the first time the other survivors had stolen all his food. They'd searched his safe place and taken every bit of food and every useful tool, but they'd left that woven purse of money behind.

That had been the day he'd stopped thinking about life going back to normal. He had stopped imagining that people might return to Cantis to bring the city back to life and had stopped believing he might need the money someday. He'd never picked up a coin from the streets or the shop floors again.

In the bottom drawer of the desk he found the faded woven purse that had been his mother's. It was small, just longer than his hand and almost twice as wide as his palm, but it was heavy, laden with wealth collected by a foolish boy. Not so useless anymore.

"Raiden?" Caeruleus's voice was distant, coming from downstairs.

Raiden looked hard at the note and watch, hoping Nicole would come here and notice them. It was the best he could do. He turned toward the door, snapped his fingers once, and turned the knob. The door opened into a different part of the house. He stepped through the doorway into the upstairs hall. Across the way was his childhood room, the door closed. He passed that door and stopped at a narrow table with several dust-veiled picture frames, undisturbed for years.

He picked up the frame on the end, one he had picked up countless times in the first few years of his solitude. With his sleeve he removed the dust from the edges of the frame and then wiped half the glass clean, revealing his mother's face as she sat close beside a man, still shrouded in dust. Seeing his mother's smile after so many years of letting it lie hidden brought a sad smile to his own face. Raiden continued on his way down the hall.

When he reached the landing, he leaned over the banister. "Up here."

Caeruleus appeared from the hall downstairs looking confused. "You said you were down the hall. Why are you—?"

"I had to take precautions. There were a few other survivors—two, maybe three. Stole my food too many times," he said, nodding toward the stairs. The first four steps at the top were there, then a pile of timber, and the last three steps at Caeruleus's feet. "That was enough to deter them. I don't know who they were, but they were either incapable of interbounding or not willing to risk using magic."

"After what happened, I wouldn't blame anyone for being too terrified to risk exposing their presence. Dawn clearly wanted Cantis empty."

Raiden closed his eyes and took a steady breath, picturing himself downstairs. In a blink his feet were firmly on the wood floor beside Caeruleus. He straightened his spine and twisted his neck, which let out a pop—interbounding had the tendency of leaving travelers somewhat more compressed than they had been.

"It makes me wonder," Caeruleus said.

"Wonder what?" Raiden asked.

"If Dawn wasn't here for the fera from the very beginning," he said. "Not *all* the seers in Veil work for the Council—you know that better than anyone. Dawn could have some in their ranks."

Raiden tried not to fidget at the mention of seers. Everyone knew the Council had rounded up the seers after the Dragon Wars. Most of them had been lured to Atrium by the righteous undertaking of creating a better future for Veil. Those who had wanted no part in it had been tracked down and ... convinced. His mother had told him rumors that people were well paid for turning seers in after they stopped advertising their abilities.

"Sure, or they have someone in the courts," Raiden suggested.

Caeruleus turned a severe gaze to him. "Stars, I hope not," he said with a heavy sigh. "But either way, think about it. They were determined to be here, to make sure no one was around for the next ten years, and then the fera appears. Why else? The Council said their seers knew about her arrival for a long time. What if Dawn wanted it to be easy to find the fera? She couldn't blend into a crowd if there wasn't a soul around."

"Ruleus, come on," Raiden said.

"No, it makes sense, Ray. Whether they have a seer of their own or someone in the courts, they knew. Everyone in Cantis, your mother, they're all gone because of Dawn. And why were they here? Because of this girl, the fera."

Raiden's skin went cold. He remembered how he'd felt when he'd finally understood that Dawn had wanted a secure place to hold a dragon prisoner, how much he'd loathed Gordan for being the reason so many people had to die by Moira's hand. His mother was dead and he'd spent nine years alone because they hadn't wanted to risk anyone finding a dragon in an abandoned tower. Now Caeruleus had made that same connection to Nicole, and Raiden couldn't refute him. He had to keep Gordan a secret. Nicole needed an ally that the Council didn't know about.

"You can't blame the fera. She didn't ask to be what she is." He tried to hide his protective anger with a steady voice and a reasonable tone.

Caeruleus just gave him a look that seemed to say, *Why not?*

"After what Dawn did here, I'm not about to let them get what they're after. I don't care what it takes. I know you think she deserves to be treated like a person, and I don't disagree, Ray. But getting to her before they do is what's most important. We can explain to her later."

"That gives us the right to commandeer her life, abduct her?" Raiden wondered if he should be testing his friend's tolerance for challenge when he was the only other ally Raiden had in Atrium, even if he was on the Council's side.

Caeruleus didn't respond—whether he was refusing to answer or unsure what to say, Raiden didn't know. Then the silence was shattered by a sudden shrill ringing, a frequency so high Raiden thought the grime-choked windowpanes might break.

"What is that?" Raiden asked, raising his voice over the sound as he closed his hands over his ears.

Caeruleus fumbled in his pocket. "A portal," he shouted.

"What?" Raiden asked, shocked and hoping for a different answer than what he'd clearly heard.

Caeruleus pulled a compass from his coat. The device went quiet as soon as he held it up. "A portal opened nearby—let's go!"

He bolted for the front door, and Raiden broke into a desperate chase to catch up. He followed as Caeruleus loped down the street, checking the compass in his hand repeatedly. They were headed toward the forest.

Come on; close the portal, Nicole, Raiden pleaded as he ran.

They made their way through the city, running down the center of the empty streets, their reflections racing along with them, flashing in the fragments of windows left in storefronts. Each time Raiden caught a glimpse of himself from the corner of his eye, he couldn't help taking his eyes off Caeruleus ahead of him. They reached the neighborhood of silent houses and kept running. Caeruleus seemed to pick up the pace, and Raiden suspected they were getting closer.

The white forest of snow and bare trees lay ahead, almost too bright for his eyes.

"Up here," Caeruleus called.

Raiden had to push hard to close the distance between them. If they were about to find themselves in Nicole's backyard, he would have to make a choice—play along with Caeruleus or stand with Nicole. As he caught up with him, Caeruleus came to an abrupt halt. Raiden barely stopped himself before running into him.

There on the forest floor lay a body in a thick bed of red-stained snow. A slender silver implement protruded from the bloody flesh of the dead man's neck, and his hand hung limply over the wound. His eyes were half open, their gaze distant and unseeing.

"Stars," Caeruleus whispered.

Raiden looked down at the dead man. The sight stunned him, and he tried to reason that it shouldn't. Nicole had defended herself before—the kelpie, Moira—but not like this, not with such a gruesome result. As unbelievable as it was, though, an overwhelming wave of relief washed through him. Whoever this man was, he had failed.

"Why didn't you just interbound?" Raiden asked, more interested than ever in conversation with a portal that would lead right to Nicole was wide open over a dead man.

"I can't," Caeruleus answered with shameless annoyance in his voice. "Never have been able to get farther than across the room. You know."

Raiden did know, but that had been when they were younger. He hadn't expected that to be the same after all these years.

"Recognize this guy?" Raiden asked, anxious to know if the Council had multiple people trying to find Nicole, and to stave off the next logical step, the one that would take them through the portal.

"No, he's not one of ours. I'm the only one assigned to the fera."

"So he must have been with Dawn," Raiden said as he looked around. There was nothing but the thin white tree trunks, their black marks creating a sea of eyes that watched. Raiden and Caeruleus were the only ones in the forest.

While Caeruleus studied the body, Raiden examined their surroundings. Aside from their own footsteps, the snow surrounding the body was completely undisturbed, which had to mean the man had been in the other realm but hadn't gotten there through this portal. A hand of cold dread gripped his heart. When had this man arrived in the other realm if not now through this portal? Not knowing what had happened over there drove him mad.

Caeruleus remained silent, looking down at the dead man. His jaw clenched.

"That could have been me," he said, wrenching Raiden away from his anxious thoughts.

"Caeruleus." Raiden had no idea how to stop what his friend was thinking, and despite his need to defend Nicole, he couldn't blame Caeruleus for this sinking realization because Raiden felt it too.

"Are you not seeing this? What she did to this man?"

"Whatever he tried obviously pushed her to extremes to defend herself." Raiden's mind spun into a blur of possibilities and dread. He saw more than self-defense in this lifeless man. There was anger carved into his neck. Had he only threatened Nicole, or had someone else been hurt? He fought back the idea that the worst could have happened to her father or Mitchell.

"This isn't going to happen to you," Raiden insisted. He knew if he kept trying to justify Nicole's actions to Caeruleus he would end up destroying the fragile trust founded in childhood and strained by the years and events that had put them on different sides. The truth was Raiden didn't want this to be his friend's fate. All he could hope to do was influence Caeruleus in a way that would give Nicole the upper hand without leading Caeruleus to the same fate as this man. "I have an idea that might help you get close to the fera."

Calling her that made his skin go cold, but he had a plan that he hoped would buy her enough time, for now. Then a sudden slap of icy wind hit their faces.

"What was—"

"Bloody stars," Caeruleus said, looking at his compass once again. "It's gone." He kicked at the snow, scattering fluffy crystals of ice over the body on the ground.

Raiden's heart reeled with relief.

"What do we do now?" Caeruleus asked.

Raiden had to do whatever he could to keep Caeruleus from going after Nicole now. They could still open another portal right now so long as Nicole was near enough. He had to give her time to get away. He didn't think it would be too hard to convince Caeruleus of his plan with the evidence of how far Nicole was willing to go lying at their feet.

"Look, if you go barging into the other realm, she will know you're an enemy, and we know what kind of mood she's in at the moment," he said. They both looked down at the dead man. "If we hurry, we should be able to get back to Atrium and return while we still have the chance to open a portal." Truthfully, he hoped that would be enough time for Nicole to get the hell out of Yuma once again.

"What's in Atrium?"

"I have the clothes I got from the other realm. If you can blend in, you can get close to her," Raiden said.

Caeruleus nodded and looked down at the dead man in his heavy leather boots and common cloak laden with tools. "I see."

"Are we going to report this to the Council first?" Raiden asked, searching for yet another way to eat up time.

"Forget it; let's get what we need. Reports can wait."

"How long was the portal open?" Gordan asked as the three of them stepped through the gate into Nicole's backyard.

"I don't know—maybe five, ten minutes?" Nicole answered with a shrug.

"That shouldn't be too much of a problem. But the Council surely knows it was there, no matter how brief it was."

"What does that mean?" Roxanne asked.

"It means that they know I'm here, and they can open another portal if they want. That's why I left. If I'm not around, it's more difficult to open one."

"So you have to leave again?"

"Yeah," Nicole said.

"Our high school is a Brothers Grimm crime scene right now. Suddenly there are invisible hunters, portals, dragons … and I'm supposed to just go home and go back to my life after today? Knowing my friend is some magical oddity on the run from psychopaths from another realm? I don't know if I'll go crazy wondering if I'm crazy or worrying about you."

"Well, now you know why I haven't been answering my phone for the past week. It was easier to not answer than to lie or explain all this, but since the pink elephant just came stampeding into the room, maybe we can move on. Text me, call me, whenever you want. I promise to let you know I'm alive."

Roxanne squinted at her. "Every day?"

"Every day," Nicole said with a nod. "If I'm alive," she added.

Roxanne scowled and smacked Nicole's shoulder repeatedly, pairing a word with each strike. "That. Is. Not. Funny."

"If you don't want to be left in the dark anymore, you're gonna have to accept that what's going on is serious. No jokes. Those are the stakes. I'm not waiting around for them to find me, so hopefully you don't have to worry."

Roxanne responded with a skeptical frown.

"Keeping her alive is my job," Gordan said.

"That's true," Nicole said. "Think of him as my bodyguard. Feel better?"

"A bodyguard who was stranded in the sand dunes when you could have used his help," Roxanne muttered.

"You two handled yourselves perfectly well," he said in a disinterested tone as he turned toward the house.

Nicole forced a smile, and Roxanne sighed.

"Fine. I guess I can handle portals and dragons—as long as you answer your goddamn phone from now on."

"*Promise*, a hundred thousand times," Nicole said, grabbing her friend's shoulders and giving her an emphatic shake.

Roxanne's eyes suddenly went wide. "Mom and Dad haven't seen me since I left for school yesterday. They don't know where I am."

"Let's get you home, then," Nicole said.

13. Plan

Nicole drove Roxanne to her house two streets over.

Nicole was struck with dread, imagining what it must have been like for Roxanne to have a stranger climb into her car, threaten her, force her to drive somewhere to hide the vehicle, and then abduct her.

"I'm so sorry, Roxie," Nicole said, staring at the steering wheel in shame. "I never wanted you to get pulled into all of this."

"I'm all right," she insisted. "Just ... don't disappear from my life, okay?"

"I won't." Nicole managed to raise her head above her guilt and look at her friend.

Roxanne leaned across the cab and hugged Nicole before climbing out of the truck. Nicole watched her friend hurry into her house. Satisfied that she was safe inside, Nicole imagined she heard the door lock and left.

By the time she got back to the house, her father's work truck was parked in the driveway. She pulled in beside her dad's vehicle, the little '86 unnamed model looking like a relic next to last year's Tacoma, nearly twice as big and the paint still glossy.

Nicole jumped out and ran inside, where her dad was waiting for her to come through the door. Bandit bounded toward Nicole, oblivious to the tension in the house. They questioned each other at the same time.

"What is going on?"

"What are you doing here?"

Gordan answered, "He called the house. I told him it was safe to return."

Nicole noticed her father's gaze, not on her face but staring wide at her clothes and she looked down to see just how much blood there was on her shirt, probably her face too. *I shoved a scalpel into a man's jugular,* she reminded herself. Heartbeats and silence ticked away the seconds as her father looked at her. She guessed it was finally sinking in. After a week of golems, portals, magic, strangers who could see the future and apparently be dragons, tales of the enemies out there who were searching for his daughter, *now,* seeing her bloodstained and harrowed, now it seemed he finally felt the weight of reality pressing down on him.

"There was someone here, Dad," Nicole said, feeling like she was coming apart at the seams and she needed to be held together, but she couldn't judge the look on her father's face. Was the shock in his eyes and the fear lining his face a reaction to her or what she had just said. She didn't dare step toward him, he closed the distance instead and her relief nearly broke her.

"In the house?" Michael asked, concern thick in his voice.

"He was collecting leverage. He had Roxanne," she said into his chest. "He was taking his time, just waiting for me to come back. I think he planned on using everything and everyone he could against me, to make me follow him back to Veil."

With her face against her dad's chest, the place where bad things were supposed to go away, she found that this innocent magic from her childhood had vanished and she would have to reassure herself now. Vinderek was gone. Her dad was safe. Bandit was safe. Roxanne would be all right, she hoped. Gordan was with her. Everyone she loved was fine, for now at least—she tried to ignore the tiny voice of uncertainty uttering Raiden's name in the back of her mind—so she could take a deep breath and quell her racing heart.

Then she remembered the portal with a sudden gasp. "We've got to go!"

"What? Why?"

"He opened a portal," she said. "Gordan closed it, but there is no telling how soon the Council will be in Cantis. They can open another if I'm still here. We can't stay here. Dad, grab Bandit."

Looking confused, he took hold of the dog's collar. Nicole grabbed her father's hand and held her other hand out to Gordan. "I won't lose you this time," she insisted, but Gordan looked unconcerned as he took her hand.

"What is that supposed to mean?" her dad asked, but Nicole didn't answer. Her mind was locked on Gordan, her father, and Bandit. Then the building wave of heat and light enveloped them.

The four of them appeared in Anthony's living room in a burst of light.

Bandit erupted into a fit of barking. Michael jumped, looking around and patting himself as if checking his limbs were still attached. Gordan offered Nicole a quick smile.

"Well done," he said, releasing her hand.

Anthony stood in the doorway between the kitchen and the living room with a look on his face that indicated a very real possibility that he might drop the plate of food in his hand. In an instant he broke free from his stupor.

"Coming, going, make up your mind," he said, shaking his head while giving his father a one-armed hug. "Hey, Dad."

"Uh, hi," Michael said.

Bandit rushed around the house, sniffing cheerfully.

"Jesus Christ! What's going on?" Anthony finally took in the sight of Nicole in his living room, her clothes sprayed with blood.

"Everyone's fine, Anthony," Michael insisted in an attempt to assuage the panic in his son's face.

"Yuma isn't safe right now," Nicole said, undercutting whatever relief her dad had supplied.

"Wait, what?"

"It's a long story. Where are Frances and the girls?"

"They were bummed about you leaving, so Frances took them to a friend's house for a sleepover," Anthony said. "She'll be back soon. What do you mean Yuma isn't safe?"

"We had an intruder in the house the past couple days," Michael said.

Anthony's face went pale, and only the sound of Bandit's sniffing occupied the silence. The click of a turning knob and creak of a door alerted them to someone entering from the garage. Then came the light clunk of the door closing and footsteps crossing the kitchen before Frances appeared in the doorway. She stopped abruptly behind Anthony when she noticed her crowded living room.

"How on earth—" she started to ask but stopped herself with a hand over her mouth. The red stains of Vinderek's demise seeped through her shirt and into her, making her skin crawl with the grim awareness of her intimate relationship with death.

Michael turned to Nicole and asked, "How did you know he was in the house?" She felt certain this was an attempt to move past the bloody elephant in the room.

"You told me that picture was missing. We thought Mitch might have taken it, and I didn't think much of it. Until I remembered that Mitch has a copy of that picture in his apartment. He didn't take it, and I know I didn't.

Then this morning you said Bandit was acting weird, growling at the door to Anthony's room. Something got me thinking about it. He never does that. It all gave me a bad feeling."

Everyone listened with stony expressions.

"I didn't know for sure, so I told Dad not to go home and took a shortcut to Yuma. I ended up losing Gordan along the way—"

"You went into the house alone?" Michael demanded.

Nicole let out a little sigh of exasperation before she continued, "I didn't find anyone in the house, but when I checked the shop, I found Roxanne taped up in the bathroom."

Frances covered her mouth, but her horrified eyes peering over her hands said it all.

"She's fine," Nicole said. "A little shaken up. We ended up across the street on campus. This hunter, he opened a portal and tried to take Roxanne as bait to get me to Veil, but Roxie threw acid in his face and jabbed a scalpel in his leg."

"Where is this guy now?" Frances asked.

"Gone. He won't be coming back," Nicole said.

"But how do you know that?" Michael asked.

"Well, because I put the same scalpel in his neck when he tried to run for it," Nicole admitted, looking down at the floor for fear of seeing the horror on her loved ones' faces. "Gordan closed the portal, and we got out of there."

When she raised her gaze, Anthony stepped forward and hugged her. "Don't waste a second of guilt on him. I'm proud of you," he murmured in her ear.

"Wait, you left a dead body at your school?" Michael asked.

"No," she said. Anthony released her. "I pushed him through the portal. The body is in Veil. But since a portal was opened and we'd already had one unwanted visitor, we had to get out of town fast, and I didn't want Dad to be the welcoming committee if anyone does show up."

Everyone exchanged looks. Nicole couldn't decipher the emotions in the room. She looked to Gordan, wondering what he sensed in the air.

"Sweetie, you made the right call," Michael said with a nod, hooking his arm around her.

"Hopefully I didn't just make things worse with all the magic it took to get us here," she said.

"Would now be a bad time to announce they issued an earthquake alert on the news not long after you left?" Anthony asked through a cringe.

Nicole sighed. "There's a big surprise. That just reaffirms my decision to leave earlier. I should get to Tucson and fill Mitch in on everything that's happened."

"Not so fast," Frances said. "You have time to catch your breath, clean up and eat a little something."

"She's right," Gordan agreed gently. "What difference will another hour make?"

Nicole shrugged, her fears drastically different now than they had been an hour ago. *After an invisible hunter kidnapped my friend, what's scary about an earthquake,* she thought, almost laughing at the comically sudden change to the Richter scale of her fears.

Caeruleus lurched forward out of the ether and onto the shore of Cantis once again, alone this time. His head spun for a moment from the magic of his jump from the interbounding platform in the courts. He checked his hand for the jump token that would return him to the platform before tucking it into his pocket. He regained his balance and found himself standing before a familiar shop. He recognized the sign over the broken windows. Nearly all the letters had fallen from the brick wall, but a few remained, spelling IN ME. It used to say KEEPING TIME. The shadows inside were heavy with the unnatural silence. The simple music of ticking clocks and chimes was just a ghost in Caeruleus's memory now.

It had been a risk taking time to go back to Atrium, but now he was wearing Raiden's clothes from the other realm that should allow him to go unnoticed by the fera. He reached into the rear pocket of the durable blue pants, which were much snugger than he typically wore, and retrieved a small, palm-sized book.

He thumbed past the few pages of his identification and authorizations sealed by the Council to the various banned and heavily regulated spells. The delicate sound of paper sliding and turning was enough to fill the silence of the empty Cantis street. He found the spell to open portals through the barrier. Caeruleus spared one more sad glance at the old clock shop before turning away and marching toward the forest.

As he walked, he dragged his hand over the page of his book, stroking the magic in the silent spell-casting ink to life. The black ink glowed yellow, and the light sprang off the page to flutter through the air with light, erratic movements, like a butterfly or a leaf on the wind. The spell danced along, seeking weakness in the barrier, a tiny draft of magic through an unseen crack that could connect one realm to the other.

Caeruleus followed as it led him back to the dead man he and Raiden had found earlier. The little trembling scrap of light twitched and glided around trees until he spotted the body ahead, lying precisely as it had been only twenty minutes ago. The sight unsettled him again, and now that he was alone, standing beside the body disturbed his confidence in Raiden's plan. The spell fluttered in a sporadic circle, and Caeruleus's heart lurched up his throat in anticipation.

Then the yellow light of the spell froze in midair and burst with a pop and a hiss. Nothing. No portal. His adrenaline perished in his chest, turning into rancid frustration that he expelled with a grumbling sigh. His breath was hot and white in the cold morning air, but his heart calmed, and a shameful relief settled around him. As committed to the mission as he was, he couldn't help feeling grateful that he had more time to prepare, that he didn't have to face the fera while she was still agitated by her last enemy.

Caeruleus took a deep breath and looked down once more at the dead man. "Just you and me today," he muttered.

It was time to get back to Atrium. He now had a day of reports and paperwork ahead of him. This man was not so long dead. They might even be able to learn something valuable from his fading memories if Caeruleus could get him back to the courts quickly.

"I'm not going to make the same mistakes as you," he declared. He retrieved his handheld glass from a different pocket of his strange new trousers. He tapped the glass in a sequence: thumb, index, ring finger, index.

"This is Agent Stone. I'm coming in with a body."

There would be another opportunity. He took another calming breath and told himself to be patient. Dawn's man had failed today, and Caeruleus chose to see that as an advantage.

Now he was the only one on the fera's trail. Dawn would be a step behind him. He couldn't let them succeed after what they had done to Cantis. Moira had met her fate, but this was bigger than her, and it had to be bigger than the fera.

Raiden left his apartment, locked his door, and turned his compulsion to pace into momentum toward Tovar's shop. All he could do was hope that what he had just done would indeed help Nicole since it was the last thing he could knowingly do for her.

He couldn't deny that a part of him worried about Caeruleus and what Nicole might do to him while defending herself. By the time he reached Tovar's shop, he was relieved that he wouldn't have to suffer the distress of those thoughts for much longer. When he walked through the door, Tovar looked up from dusting a shelf of enchanted trinkets, including a solid brass owl that occasionally blinked and turned its head and a painted ceramic frog that opened its mouth and snatched a moth as it flitted past the shelf.

"Here so early?" Tovar asked without turning around. "I would have thought you would need more time to sort out the memories and enjoy the ones you're giving up."

"To be honest, any more time with them might weaken my resolve," Raiden said.

Tovar put down his rag and brushed his hands on his trousers as he turned to face Raiden. "Well then, if you're sure, we can get started. It takes some time."

"Let's get it over with," he answered, his voice darkened by the storm of regret already churning in his chest.

Tovar nodded, and the two of them made their way to the back of the shop and the hidden door.

Frances gave Nicole a clean pair of Anthony's jeans—since she was shorter and a size smaller than Nicole—which only stayed up thanks to the girth a few good years of squats added to her hips and butt. Then Frances handed Nicole a folded T shirt before disappearing with the bloodied garments. Nicole watched Frances go wearing a troubled wrinkle on her brow and unease in the corners of her mouth.

Nicole pulled the fresh Brood Nine shirt over her head, suddenly realizing how deep the pit of hunger in her stomach had become after all the magic she had used. She rolled up the extra inches of pant leg and put her shoes back on before she stalked into the kitchen searching for something to eat, suddenly feeling frantic with hunger.

She found a container of leftover white rice in the fridge and peas in the freezer. She threw the rice and peas in a bowl and started them in the microwave for a couple of minutes as she retrieved an egg carton from the fridge. She took the bowl from the microwave, rice and peas halfway reheated, and cracked a couple of eggs in before nuking it all again for a couple of minutes more. Then she gave the food another stir, breaking the yolks and mixing everything together. She added a little soy sauce and began shoveling her meal into her mouth. Some of the peas were still cold, some of the rice barely warm, but she didn't care.

Once she had hastily chewed and swallowed several mouthfuls, she let out a sigh of relief.

"I didn't realize that's what happened." Gordan's voice drew her focus away from her food briefly.

"I'm having a hard time believing it myself," she said, but her eyes shifted from the spoonful of food hovering over her bowl to her fingertips, where blood still lingered, dried in her nail beds.

She thought she heard a low growl from Gordan's throat, but it was so quiet and brief she couldn't be sure.

"Had it been me, his demise would have been far less … humane. I'm sorry you had to do such a thing today."

Nicole sighed. She didn't want to keep reliving that moment. "I'm fine," she said. "I appreciate everyone's concern, but I really am fine with what I did."

There was silence for a few bites. With her hunger dissipated, her chewing slowed. She tried to focus on the squelches and rhythm of mastication, but her thoughts were stuck in a loop of that moment on replay—shoving a bloodied scalpel back into Vinderek's neck. Then she suspected that Gordan was listening the way he did, and when he spoke, she knew she was right.

"You may never forget the lives you have taken, but don't forget the ones you have saved," Gordan said softly.

Nicole smiled and set her bowl on the counter so she could catch him in a hug. "Best decision I ever made," she said, noticing his stiff reaction to her arms around him. "Still not used to hugs yet?"

Gordan finally reciprocated her embrace. "I'm getting there," he said with a quiet chuckle.

"You realize you're a part of this family now, don't you?" she said as she backed away and picked up her bowl.

"I … No … it did not occur to me," he muttered.

"Well, you are," she mumbled through her food.

Nicole scraped every last grain of rice out of the bowl before placing it in the sink. She turned on the faucet and watched the bowl fill with water. Someone cleared their throat, and Nicole looked up from the sink. Frances stood in the kitchen with a grim expression.

"What's up?" Nicole asked, glancing at Gordan.

"I wanted to talk to you before you leave," Frances said. She looked at Gordan but didn't seem deterred by his presence.

"Yeah, sure," Nicole answered, shutting off the faucet and turning to face her sister.

Frances crossed the kitchen and took Nicole by both hands. "Now you listen to me," she said, her stern brown eyes peering into Nicole's. "I know you think the right thing to do is to run, to play it safe and avoid any more confrontations like the one you had today. There are times when running might be the right choice, but you can't run forever. You're not going to get your life back by running. If you want to *live* your life, you are going to have to fight for it. You belong with your family, Nicole. Don't let these fuckers chase you for the rest of your life, got it?"

Nicole was stunned into silence by Frances's words, and she almost couldn't find her voice to answer.

"Okay."

"All right then," Frances said, giving Nicole's hands a little shake before releasing them. "I'm going to go find the guys. I think they went outside to talk about Anthony driving Dad back to Yuma in a few days."

Gordan watched as Frances left through the door to the garage, leaving a trail of worry in her wake. He and Nicole stood in the silent kitchen. He listened to her take a deep breath, slow and careful, before letting it out. He could feel Frances's words sinking in as Nicole's nervous surprise darkened into strange mix of relief, adoration, and anger.

He wanted to express his agreement with Frances, tell Nicole she would only regret exiling herself. He wanted to ask her what she was thinking. He wanted to say something, anything, but he found his vocal cords knotted up by the same flood of emotions that stifled Nicole's voice as well.

The floor quivered beneath his feet. He looked up at the light fixture hanging from the kitchen ceiling as it shuddered. He looked to Nicole. She closed her eyes for a moment and pressed her lips together. In a matter of seconds everything was still and silent again.

Gordan cleared the lump from his throat, and Nicole seemed to break free of her thoughts.

"Right," she said. "Did you want anything to eat before we go?"

"No," he answered, still trying to chase down something to say, feeling his chance was lost.

"Guess I better say goodbye," she said through a forced smile.

All Gordan could do was huff and wonder why, when he wanted to encourage Nicole to fight for herself, his words fled from him. She didn't move from where she stood, though. Sure enough, a second later Frances, Anthony, and Michael all came into the kitchen from outside.

"Did you two feel that?" Michael asked.

"Yeah, I think that's our cue to pop on over to Tucson to see Mitch," Nicole said, swinging her arms and snapping her fingers.

"I told you she'd be quick to leave," Anthony muttered.

"Yeah, yeah," Nicole said, rolling her eyes. "Let me know when the earthquake warning is called off, and we'll stop by again. Sound good?"

"That's fair," Frances said, cutting off any argument from Anthony. "Tell Mitch we miss him."

"Promise me you'll stay there longer than you did here," Anthony grumbled.

"Okay, I promise. I'm hoping Tucson has a better tolerance for magic," she said with a chuckle. "Unless there's some secret magical community already opening portals out in Wildcat country, I think I should be good there for a while."

"Good," Michael said, stepping forward to hug Nicole.

Gordan was caught up in observing them and enjoying the moment of peace Nicole was having in her father's arms. He didn't notice Anthony had crossed the kitchen until he was standing right in front of him.

"Gordan," Anthony said.

He was taken aback for a second. Nicole was usually the only one to address him so directly. Anthony extended his hand to him. Gordan mimicked the gesture and offered his own hand, but Anthony did not shake it. Instead Anthony pulled Gordan in and put his other arm around him.

"Thanks for looking out for her when we can't be there," Anthony said as he clapped Gordan on the back and released him.

It was over so quickly Gordan wasn't sure it had even happened, but he could be sure he felt the gratitude wafting off Anthony. Worry and affection filled the kitchen when Anthony looked at his sister. Gordan understood. Anthony wasn't referring to protecting Nicole from enemies but from solitude. Everyone in that room knew full well Nicole could protect herself from harm— how many times had she proven that now? But she couldn't protect herself from the isolation that came with this new life full of enemies.

Both Anthony and Frances took their turns embracing Nicole. Michael turned to Gordan and extended his hand. Reluctantly, Gordan took it. This time it was only a handshake, but the look in Michael's eyes spoke louder than Anthony's brief embrace and hushed words. Their silent exchange was quick, and Gordan looked over at Nicole, who was still captive in Frances's arms.

"I'll be fine, really," Nicole said as she emerged from her sister's arms. She gave Gordan a sideways glance. Then she took a step closer to stand beside him.

"Be careful out there," Michael said. There was a weight in his words that hadn't been there the last time he said goodbye to his daughter.

"I will," Nicole answered, holding up her hand to Gordan. "Ready?"

Gordan took her hand in a firm grasp.

"Does Mitchell know you're on your way to his place?" Anthony asked.

"Nope," she said.

Michael raised his index finger and said, "Shouldn't we call—"

"Where's the fun in that?" Nicole insisted. "See you soon."

Gordan braced himself, gritting his teeth at the thought of his previous experience interbounding with Nicole. The heat of her magic burned in their clasped hands as though melting them together and washed through him in a flash.

He tried to keep his focus on their connected hands as they were scrambled into light, slipping through space. His thoughts were scattered into a dizzy blur for what seemed like ages.

14. Forget

Nicole blinked, but there was only darkness in her eyes. She could feel Gordan's hand in her grasp. When she put out a hand to feel through the space around them, her elbow hit something hard with a thud.

"Ow," she hissed. "Gordan? You make it in one piece?"

"Yes, well done," he answered. She thought she detected a hint of irony in his voice.

Suddenly the darkness in front of Nicole's face split open, and light crashed against her eyes.

"Nicole? Gordan?" Mitchell said, standing in the doorway. "How did— what are you doing in the closet?"

"I was aiming for the living room, actually, but not losing Gordan was more important," she said with a shrug as she stepped out into the short hall between the living room and the apartment's two bedrooms.

"I thought you said you were driving here. Wait, losing Gordan? What?"

"Still no roommate, right?" Nicole asked, nodding toward the bedrooms.

Gordan stepped out of the closet, examining his surroundings, and for a second Nicole thought he was checking that he had all his fingers.

"Not since last semester. Nate dropped out, and the complex hasn't had any new applicants for a two-bedroom," he said.

"We had a few hiccups today," Nicole began, wandering into the living room. She sat down on the arm of the couch.

"Like what?"

"Oh, you know, some earthquakes in California, a psychopath hiding out back home and kidnapping my best friend." Although her tone was nonchalant, her skin went clammy at the thought of what Vinderek had done to Roxanne and how close Nicole had come to losing her friend. She let herself fall backward onto the seat cushions, her legs still draped over the armrest.

"Whoa, whoa, whoa," Mitchell said. "Is everyone okay?"

"Yeah." Nicole's voice sank a little. "Dad and Bandit are in Ventura. Roxanne is shaken up but doing all right, and the bad guy got what was coming to him," she said, her voice dark as she returned to that place for a moment. She looked up at the ceiling.

"What about you?" Mitchell asked.

She turned her head to look at him standing sideways like a hallucination in her vision, and she saw something she rarely witnessed—her brother's serious eyes. Mitch always found a way to laugh about things, some reason to smile. Nicole could count on one hand the times she'd seen this look on Mitchell's face, his mouth compressed into a stern line and his eyes narrowed. The last time she'd seen that face was when they'd found out about their parents' divorce; he had asked her—

"Are you okay?"

"I'm good." She unintentionally answered the same as she had back then. She wondered if he was remembering that moment too. Nicole turned her eyes back to the ceiling and closed them.

"No you're not," Mitchell contested.

"But saying I am gets me there quicker," she answered, her eyes still closed.

"What happened exactly?" Mitchell pressed.

Nicole sighed, accepting that she was doomed to relive the events of that day in a loop—probably until dawn—so telling the story again wasn't going to make any difference. Forgetting wasn't an option, and Mitchell deserved to know.

Raiden huffed.

"You're certain you are ready to do this?" Tovar asked.

That answer was far from simple. He was ready to be done with the agony of this decision but not ready to lose that friendship so soon after finding it.

"Yes," he answered.

"Right then," Tovar said with a nod as he locked the door to his hidden workroom and turned toward a tall cabinet. He opened the cabinet door and pulled out a box, which he brought to the worktable.

Inside the box there were several candles of varying colors, and Tovar proceeded to remove some of those candles and set them upright on the table—a thick black candle, a short white candle, a yellow, an indigo, and finally a violet candle. Once they were set on the table, Tovar closed the box and removed it, the remaining candles inside rolling and clunking within.

"Now, you must concentrate only on those memories you wish to bury," Tovar said. He snapped his fingers, and all five candles lit simultaneously. "And we can begin."

Raiden took a deep breath and bid Nicole a silent farewell.

Nicole rolled over beneath the blanket, fighting to stay asleep, but she couldn't find the passage back into her dreams no matter how many times she rolled over. She flopped onto her back, peering through the dark room toward the ceiling. Dreams darkened by Roxanne being kidnapped and by having to plunge a scalpel into Vinderek's neck again and again as he refused to stay dead seemed to be the price she had to pay for a full night's sleep.

"Sleep well?" Gordan's voice floated in the darkness. There was a sarcastic edge to his words that suggested he knew the answer already.

Nicole rolled to the edge of the bed and searched the floor to find Gordan lying on his back, his arms folded behind his head. "You know you can sleep on a bed," she said.

"I've been sleeping on a wet stone floor for a decade," he said. "Carpeted floors are luxurious compared to that."

"Can't argue with that," Nicole said, rolling onto her back again. "But you can still sleep on a bed."

She heard a huff and then saw Gordan's shadowy form stand up. He crossed the room in a few strides and eased himself backward onto the bed beside Nicole. They both lay there looking up at the ceiling.

"Well?"

"Well what?" she asked.

"What is the plan now?"

"I don't know," she evaded. "Enjoy a few days while we can, I guess."

"I'm glad you're finally taking my advice," he said.

Nicole sat up and then groaned.

"What?"

"My bag, it's still in the back of the truck … in Yuma," she said as she fell back onto the bed. "Oh fine," she muttered and took a deep breath. Her body ignited with a flood of magic. A flash of light shattered the darkness of the room, and her large camping bag dropped out of the air directly above her. The bag fell into her arms, and she laughed as it half knocked the air out of her. She heaved the bag off her chest, and it fell to the floor with a thud—she was glad Mitch lived on the ground floor.

"You coming with me?" she asked as she got up and dug into her bag. "I want to get out there before I miss the sunrise."

"I think you know the answer to that," he said as he sat up.

She shed her brother's borrowed shirt and boxers without a care. The chilly air chased her into her fresh underwear and clean clothes. Even the garments were cold, and she let out a shudder.

After tracking down her shoes in the dark and getting them onto her feet, she yanked her red hoodie from her bag and pulled it on. She turned to Gordan. Even through the shadows she could see his plain trousers and loose tunic, like he was some colonial extra in *The Crucible*, the same clothes he had been wearing the first time she'd seen him in her backyard.

"Okay, we need to get you some clothes," she said, shaking her head.

"I'm wearing clothes."

"You don't even have shoes," she said.

"I don't need them. The cold doesn't bother me, and I have never worn shoes in my life."

"It's not for function. It's so you look a little more normal," she said, laughing as she left the room and turned to the neighboring door. She let herself into her brother's room.

Gordan lingered in the doorway, his attention on Mitchell's sleeping form on the bed.

"Don't worry about him; he sleeps like a rock," she muttered, but she still kept her voice low.

After opening various dresser drawers and snatching a few articles of clothing, she turned and tossed the wad of fabric at Gordan. He caught it.

"There. Get dressed," she whispered as she shuffled to the closet and slid open the door to find a pair of shoes. She knew Mitchell's pants would be too short and loose for Gordan's tall, slender frame. In the back of the closet was a pair of tall hiking boots that Mitch probably didn't wear all that often. She grabbed the boots and a belt hanging on a row of hooks on the door and then snuck back out of Mitchell's room to find Gordan in the hallway in a pair of jeans and a shirt, pulling on a dark-blue University of Arizona sweater. There was a good three inches of ankle showing over his bare feet.

"You'll fit right in," she said, handing him the boots. Raiden suddenly entered her thoughts. A sigh expanded in her chest, and she couldn't contain it. While the morning darkness concealed her frown, she knew her gloom wouldn't go unnoticed by Gordan. For his sake she wished she could forget about Raiden and worrying about him and—she admitted to herself—missing him, just for a day.

"Ready?"

Gordan stood, boots on his feet. "Ready."

Gordan preferred time alone with Nicole, mostly because being around so many people and all their emotions was overwhelming. Nicole was easier to read without anyone else around. After half an hour of walking along the side of long, straight Anklam Road, it was still quiet in the early morning. Few vehicles passed them at all. Nicole and Gordan came to a streetlight that changed dutifully between red and green even with no cars around. At the light Anklam turned right, and straight ahead the road had a different name. The first blush of dawn was drowning out the stars to the east. Several minutes later Gordan broke the silence for the first time since they'd left Mitchell's apartment.

"Where are we headed?"

"Here," Nicole said, gesturing to a sign in the dark. She snapped her fingers, and a tiny orb of light appeared, revealing the white letters on the blue sign: UA Science—Tumamoc.

"Oo-ah Science—Tumamoc," Gordan read.

Nicole laughed. "UA—it stands for University of Arizona. They have science buildings up on the hill. Better place to catch a sunrise than the roof," she said.

They turned off Anklam onto a paved road that led into the darkness and up the first long slope of Tumamoc. Nicole's little light followed her like a firefly. On either side of the paved road, they were surrounded by all manner of desert bush and cacti crowding the darkness. The cold, biting air carried with it the smell of rain despite the clear sky overhead, and the sound of concealed creatures scurrying through the dirt and brush filled Gordan's keen ears.

Soon he saw Nicole's little yellow light glinting in countless curious gazes, or perhaps he was projecting his own curiosity in those flashing eyes. The creatures in this realm had probably never tasted magic in the air in their lives, certainly not anything like Nicole's.

Gordan inhaled deeply. The air around Nicole had a certain charge that he could feel percolating in his lungs and invigorating every particle of his being, like that first gulp of fresh air he had taken after all those years in his dank dungeon, or the air above the clouds that tasted more of freedom than the air closer to the ground. It was a mixture of electricity and petrichor.

When she held her magic in, anxiously keeping it to herself, he would have to stand right beside her to catch that scent of energy. But in her carefree moments he could be far beyond arm's reach and still detect that brilliance in the air.

Gordan stopped, letting Nicole put distance between them. He watched her march onward up the slope, waiting for the taste of magic to slip away as his breath made little white puffs in the morning air. She stopped and turned to see him far behind her. The space between them was enough that she looked small enough to stand in his hand.

"What are you doing?" she asked, a laugh in her voice.

"Just observing," he answered as he moved his legs again. "You seem to have sparked a lot of interest this morning." He nodded toward the flora and fauna beyond the pavement. In the growing light several animals' faces could be seen—cottontails and quail, a pair of deer. Nicole looked around, and her face lit up with surprise and delight.

She mashed her lips together, containing a smile. "Oops," she said.

Gordan wished that spark of happiness wasn't doomed to be fleeting. Nicole deserved that much, to be herself without fear of how the world would react around her, without having to hide. It only now occurred to him that she provided precisely that freedom to him. A life in Veil meant only one thing for Gordan, exile with the other dragons, hiding from their violent past and the shame of their crimes. Here, in the old world with Nicole—even bound to her in debt—he had the freedom to simply *be*, a delight he hadn't known for so long.

Nicole talked beside him as they walked, but he couldn't quite focus on her words. He wanted desperately to tell her what she had done for him, explain the opportunity she had given him that he never would have found in Veil, to lift her spirits and prove to her that she was a gift to this world, not a curse, not a threat. But he couldn't bring himself to say it, to tell her how free he felt beside her while she lived in her own exile, hiding and running from her enemies. It seemed cruel to boast of his freedom to her even if it was *because* of her.

"Helloooo—Gordan, can you hear me in there?"

"Yes, of course," he answered. What he knew he should tell her was that she deserved her own freedom and that she would have to fight for it. He wanted her to have that freedom, he truly did, but his heart was equally as selfish in its desire for her safety and his own happiness here with her.

"What did I just ask you, then?" she demanded.

Gordan tried to remember some fragment of what she'd said, any word that might have made it through his thoughts. "You've got me; I haven't heard a word."

She laughed. "Well, now I'm torn between asking my question again and finding out what you've been thinking about instead."

"Apologies—they were frivolous thoughts. What was your question?"

"Why are they so interested in us? Are you sure it's not you? Can't animals sense that you're ... different?" Nicole nodded toward the gathering creatures, some even trailing after them along the paved road.

Gordan's eyes met the curious stare of a rabbit close behind them, which immediately whirled around and bounded behind a bush.

"I'm quite certain it's you," he said. "Magic is a natural force, like sunlight, the energy of life itself. Living things are drawn to it. How many times have you witnessed your effects on plants, how they grow much faster when your magic is in the air?"

"The plants I get, but why animals?"

"I can't profess to know what you are, Nicole, or to explain to you the power you harbor within you, but I can tell you what I have felt," Gordan said. "When your magic fills the air, the fog of this world clears. It chases away exhaustion. It sharpens my senses."

"Wow. I, uh, don't know what to make of that," Nicole said with a laugh.

"I think you need to understand that for you there is no place to hide in this realm. Once they get here, they will find you. That is a fact. These creatures cannot help being drawn to you because you are the only source of magic there is here. You're an oasis in a desolate place."

Nicole was silent for a long time as they trekked up the steep incline, following the road as it switched back and forth, zigzagging up the hill. As they trudged up the steep slopes, Gordan could hear Nicole's heart pound in her chest and the force of each deep breath she took. He could not fathom what her thoughts were, but her magic rolled off her in ever-increasing waves, permeating the air.

They reached the top before the sun broke the horizon.

"Are you saying I would be harder to find in Veil?" she asked at last.

"The more magic around you, the less yours would stand out," he said.

"A voice in a crowded room versus an empty hall," she said.

"Yes."

Nicole took a long, steady breath and released it. Gordan could sense no anxiety, no fear, no anger.

The first pool of golden sunlight swelled over the jagged line of the horizon as the sun emerged over the mountains in the distance, and Gordan watched the light hit Nicole's face. There was a subtle smile at the corners of her mouth.

"What?" The longer he spent with her, the weaker his tolerance for her mysteries seemed to become.

"Nothing."

"You do realize I can sense emotions, right? A state of nothing is impossible, not even in death."

She laughed. "Fine. I was just thinking it's funny—bizarre actually—that I can feel … almost free. Despite how worried I am that I'll drag my family into this, how guilty I feel about Roxie, how scared I am. Despite the fact that every decision I make now is a direct response to the threat of my enemies, I don't feel as trapped as I know I am. Not yet anyway. Maybe it's all you. You help me feel normal and sane. I guess having a dragon held captive by a debt to call a friend eases the feeling of being an alien trapped in a cage I can't see. I wish there was some way I could repay you for that—it doesn't seem as simple as lifting a latch."

She looked at him, a smile defying the sadness. Then suddenly that faint pull between Gordan and Nicole snapped like a fragile, old string. His debt was gone—inexplicably paid. He was stunned into silence. There was no way he could have repaid his debt; he had done nothing. Could Nicole forgive that debt without payment? He had never heard of such a thing.

"I mean, I know you *have* to be here, but I'm still glad you are."

His inability to understand what just happened halted his attempt to explain to Nicole before she continued.

She laughed. But then her heart sank into the depths of some cold dark thought. "I don't like dragging you into whatever's coming for me. I wish I didn't have put you at risk, but a debt is a debt, right?" She made an attempt at another laugh, and Gordan swallowed back the news in his throat. If he told her, would she try to disappear? If she knew he couldn't follow that tether to her, would she leave him to keep him safe like she planned to do with her family?

"Right," he answered.

They watched the sun climb up out of the mountains and into the sky, staining the clouds in the distance magenta and gold.

"That's the university campus over there," Nicole said, pointing. "It's kinda crazy to think if it weren't for the Council and Venarius I would be finishing high school this semester like any other girl, going to school here next semester, and you would just be following me from class to class, not from city to city running from enemies."

"Do you want that life?"

"It doesn't matter anymore, does it? I've always thought it was self-destructive to want what you can't have," she said. "I do my best to avoid pining after the impossible."

"Well then, what do you want in *this* life?"

"I want the chance to figure out who and what I am, without worrying what effect I'll have on everything around me or how everyone will see me," Nicole said with a shrug. "What about you? What do you want?"

"Believe it or not, there was a time when the only thing I wanted was to be with the person I loved. Unfortunately, I lost that chance long ago."

"What happened?"

"He chose death over me." Gordan spoke the words for the first time in his life, and his heart ached with a sharp pang.

"Oh." Nicole turned toward him, surprise in her gaze. "I can't imagine— I'm so sorry."

"It was centuries ago. After that I found other things to occupy my life."

Nicole looked at him for several moments, her lips pressed firmly together. Then he noticed the sound of at least two people coming up the paved road behind them, still hidden from view.

"I'm telling you the air feels different this morning. It *tastes* different," a woman spoke, her voice carrying up the slope.

"Well," Nicole said, taking him by the hand, "let's not waste any more time finding out what we want." She smiled, and a surge of prickling energy rushed through their joined hands, raising his scales and hair.

A trio of hikers came up the final slope as Nicole's magic swept her and Gordan up in a vivid flood of light that rivaled the rising sun.

Nicole's and Gordan's feet hit the floor of the kitchen in Mitchell's apartment.

"I like that more and more every time," Nicole said, grinning as the light around them receded. She enjoyed the buzzing rush of magic lingering in her head. "It's a lot easier when you aren't going so far."

"I have never been one for interbounding," Gordan confessed. "Always preferred flying, even if it is rather slow by comparison."

"I never could get the hang of flying," Nicole grumbled. "Not for lack of trying."

"It's easier for those of us with wings. Flying is just a matter of development, strength, and coordination, like learning to walk. But flying without wings is an entirely different matter. I wish I could help you there."

"That's all right," Nicole said with a shrug.

"What are you two doing up so early?" Mitchell mumbled from the hallway as he shuffled out of his room. His light-brown hair was disheveled, flattened against one side of his head and standing straight up on the other side. The air in the apartment was brisk, and Mitch was groggily pulling a sweater on, one arm at a time, covering his bare back. He wandered into the little living room, his eyes barely open, wearing unicorn slippers on his feet and plaid pajama pants.

"We walked over to Tumamoc and caught the sunrise at the top. Figured you would rather sleep in," Nicole said.

"You were right, and yet here I am ... awake," Mitchell said, twisting a knuckle against his eye.

"You'll live," she said.

"And what are you two going to do now that you're squatting in my apartment?" he asked, shuffling into the kitchen.

"I don't know. I could always make money doing kids' parties," Nicole said, opening the fridge to see what kind of provisions her brother had.

"Yeah, you would make a great clown," he said with a chuckle.

Nicole stood up and eyed her brother over the fridge door. "Those pants look rather loose, Mitch."

Mitchell took hold of the elastic waistband. Nicole gave him a smug grin, glancing at Gordan, who stood silently leaning against the short kitchen counter, his eyes slanted toward her brother.

"That's what I thought," she said, turning back to the virtually empty fridge. "Do you have *any* food in this apartment?"

"Unless you count protein powder and some questionable milk, no."

Nicole huffed. "You're hopeless," she muttered, closing the door.

"I haven't had the chance to get to the store yet, okay?"

"Yeah, yeah." Nicole rolled her eyes and thought of the summoning spell from Raiden's book. "*Evoco,*" she said while thinking of all the things she wanted. The refrigerator shuddered for a moment. When she opened the door again, the fridge was full.

Mitchell crossed the kitchen to peer into the fridge. "Whoa," he cried. "Wait, there's an awful lot of green stuff in there."

Nicole leaned in to grab the carton of eggs. "Do you want breakfast burritos or not?"

Mitchell put his hands up in surrender.

"That's what I thought." Nicole's mind ticked through the preparation of everything they needed—eggs and hash browns cooked, ham diced, tortillas warmed. It was so easy to let her magic out, let it spread through the kitchen like extra arms and eager fingers.

Mitchell backed up to the counter and stood beside Gordan, watching the kitchen become a flurry of ingredients, cookware, utensils, and spices.

"For someone who's trying not to open portals, you're awfully comfortable getting your Merlin on over breakfast," Mitch said.

"Should I spend all my time worrying about it?" she said, grating a couple of potatoes over a bowl with her own hands while a frying pan floated over to the stove and the burner clicked on. "It's here whether I hold it in or use it. It's a matter of how long I'm here, not how many times I tap into what's always here. Making myself uncomfortable isn't going to make a difference. Being miserable isn't going to keep a portal from opening."

"Oh," he said. "I guess that makes sense."

She dumped the potato into the pan.

"For a second there it seemed like you didn't care about opening one anymore," Mitchell said.

"And what if I don't?" she asked, realizing for herself that it no longer induced the cold, creeping panic in her veins like it did before.

"It's just a complete one-eighty, that's all. You were adamant about keeping portals closed just the other day. You didn't want them to get to this realm yesterday; now all of a sudden you don't mind?"

"Maybe a part of me doesn't," Nicole mused. The kitchen went silent for a moment save for the sizzling of hash browns. "It's going to happen sooner or later—why not get it over with, don't you think? I don't want to see anyone else I love get dragged into it, but I don't want to be running and hiding and looking over my shoulder for who knows how long until that day comes." She sighed while the procession of breakfast carried on around her.

Mitchell was silent for a minute or two. "I knew this was going to happen," he said, shaking his head.

"Sure you did," she scoffed.

"Nikki, you can't back down from a fight to save your life."

"You're exaggerating."

"Remember the kid you hit on the playground when he told you girls couldn't play with them? And the girl you cussed out in front of the teachers after she called Roxie a name? You've never let anyone else deal with your problems, not a teacher, not Tony or me or Dad."

Nicole scowled at him.

"Hey, I get it," Mitch said. "I know you're angry about what happened to Roxie and worried the same or worse could happen to the rest of us. But as your brother I'm allowed to worry too. These guys aren't some pisshead kids on the playground. Don't think for a second I don't want them to end up like that prick from yesterday. I just don't think you should do something stupid like go up against people who have a whole army at their disposal by yourself."

So basically, run for the rest of my life, she translated in her head. Nicole tried to smile at him. "Aren't you sweet." He was her brother. He worried. He loved her. She reminded herself that it was his own selfish desire to keep her alive even if it meant asking her to run away, to be afraid. He didn't know how slowly it would suffocate her.

"I'm a brother; it's what I do," Mitchell said.

Nicole shook her head, turning back to the stove. "Were you lucky enough to grow up without siblings, Gordan?" she asked, ready to change the subject.

"I had eighty-two, actually," Gordan said.

Nicole turned to look at him with an open mouth and saw Mitchell doing the same.

"Dragons brood their young collectively. The eggs are nested together, hatched together, and raised together," he said as matter-of-factly as someone announcing the time. "Dragons rarely single out their own offspring. The young are raised by everyone."

"Wow," Nicole said.

"Yeah," Mitchell agreed. "Eighty-two brothers and sisters."

"My relationship with my siblings was nothing like yours," he said with the slightest smile.

"Not the kind to make you breakfast burritos in the morning?" Mitchell asked as he hitched his thumb toward Nicole.

"No, not at all," Gordan said.

"Well, you've got us now," Nicole declared as three tortillas folded and rolled up around hash browns, scrambled eggs, and ham. "*And* burritos." The burritos plopped down onto their plates.

Mitchell crossed the kitchen and bear-hugged Nicole, lifting her off the ground. "You're the best insufferable little sister a guy could ask for," he roared, giving her a little shake in the air.

"He's happiest when he has food," Nicole explained with a strained voice.

"I can tell," Gordan said with a chuckle.

Mitchell set her back down. "What about salsa?"

"Oh." Nicole looked around the kitchen, but she'd forgotten about salsa. "Why don't you get us some?"

"Come on; after all that you want me to drive to—"

"No, numbnuts," she interrupted. "I mean why don't you try the conjuring spell. Don't you remember what Raiden said? Most people can do magic; they just never get the chance here."

"You just want me to make a fool of myself, right?"

"Maybe a little," she said. "Just try, Mitch."

Mitch gave her a nervous glare. "Fine," he said. He thought for a moment and then said, *"Evoco."*

A jar of salsa appeared out of thin air right in front of Mitchell's nose.

"Shit!" Mitch cursed as the jar fell. He caught it, fumbling. "Holy shit," he said, turning the jar over in his hands in disbelief. "I just did that. I really fucking did that."

"Congratulations," Nicole said with a laugh. "Now can we eat?"

15. Peace

*N*icole enjoyed the silence as they ate, chewing her way through her thoughts.

"So, Gordan," Mitchell said as Gordan took another bite of his breakfast burrito, "I didn't expect you to eat human food."

Gordan looked up at him.

"I mean, you're a dragon," Mitchell added.

"I am," Gordan answered with a slight curl on his lips. "But in human form I can subsist on the same things you eat. I can even enjoy it," he said.

"So when you *aren't* in human form," Mitchell pressed, "your diet is a little more … raw?"

"Yes," he said.

"Ever eat a human?"

Nicole choked a little on her mouthful of food, coughing the half-chewed wad back up.

Gordan raised his eyebrows but offered neither denial nor confirmation and took another bite of his burrito.

"Damn," Mitchell said, taking a devastating bite of his own breakfast. "That's kind of badass," he mumbled through his food.

Gordan turned a look of mild surprise at Mitchell, then at Nicole. *Maybe he expected disgust*, she thought.

She shrugged. "Whoever it was probably deserved it," she said before returning her focus to her plate. Who was she to judge after what she had done only yesterday?

After they finished eating, Mitchell disappeared to get dressed. Nicole waved her hand at the three empty plates and shooed them off to the kitchen. Dismissed, the plates zipped through the air and settled into the sink with a few clanks.

"So what's this dream team gonna do today?" Mitchell asked, emerging from his room dressed in jeans and a teal flannel shirt.

"We could always show Gordan around downtown," Nicole suggested, "and see what kind of trouble we can get into." She decided not to acknowledge the look of scrutiny that Gordan gave her.

"Great," Mitchell said with a clap. "Ready to go?"

Nicole smiled and hooked one arm around Mitchell's and one around Gordan's. She felt like she was being pulled in every direction as they made the jump. Clinging desperately to Gordan and Mitchell and concentrating on them was the challenge while the surge of magic scattered them through space and tried to scramble the very thoughts in her head. But it only ever lasted a fleeting moment or two, the time spanned by a few beats of a racing heart.

By the time their feet returned to solid ground and their bodies lurched into solid form once again, Nicole's heart had reached top speed. She felt a broad grin on her face and realized that the more she used her magic freely, the more natural it felt. What had been a fiery panic burning her from the inside seemed more like an exhilarating rush that she wanted to taste again and again. The residual burn was still there, though, faint and fading away like a ghost—she was starting to like that burn.

"Sonovabitch," Mitchell hissed as he swayed and sandwiched his head in his hands to steady himself.

"I take it that was your first time interbounding," Gordan said.

"Inter—what now?" Mitchell said with his eyes closed. Finally he straightened up and pried open his eyes to look around.

They were standing in a tiny corner parking lot beside a store called Antigone Books.

"Christ, Nikki, Fourth Avenue in broad daylight?" Mitchell's voice cracked.

"Calm down. It's Sunday morning. Look around," Nicole said, rolling her eyes. It was still quiet on Fourth Avenue. Almost every storefront—the little boutiques, the tattoo shops, the bookstore—was still dark and closed up tight with its metal gates, except the co-op across the street in the red brick building and the café on the other side of Antigone Books. Down the street the bars, smoke shops, and hookah lounge were all dark. Fourth Avenue was a vivid place, with the buildings painted in bright yellows and blues and, farther down the street, the Goodwill with its pillars and arches painted lime green and desert orange. There was no sign of the trolley either.

"What if someone had seen us just …" Mitchell whipped his arms up, apparently as a gesture of sudden appearance.

"You're right." Nicole feigned sudden concern. "They would probably tell the first person they saw."

A couple walking down the sidewalk with paper coffee cups in their hands passed the parking lot.

"Oh, hey," Nicole called to them with wave. She trotted over to them. "I just saw those two guys appear out of nowhere—no joke. It was actual magic," she said with a straight face.

The couple made a valiant effort to contain their laughter for a moment as they looked at each other, but their chuckles slipped out, and they kept on walking.

Nicole turned back to her brother with as much smug on her face as she could muster. Mitchell closed his dumbfounded mouth and scowled at her.

"Who the hell is going to run around telling people something like that, and who would believe them? Even if someone caught it on camera, would anyone take it seriously in a world where the exact same 'magic' has been created in six-second videos?"

Mitchell was silent for a moment, and his expression softened into something like intrigue.

"Okay, that's a valid point," he admitted, nodding. Slowly the devilish Mitchell she knew returned.

"Finally sunk in, did it?" she teased with a laugh.

"Yeah," he answered shamelessly.

"Good. Let's go then—I need coffee," she said, turning left toward Antigone Books and making her way down the sidewalk.

Gordan and Mitchell caught up in a few seconds.

"Have you thought about what you're going to do when you don't have to deal with those pricks in the other realm anymore?" Mitchell asked.

"Haven't thought that far ahead, actually, but I get the feeling you have," she said, both amused and grateful for her brother's optimism, no matter what idea he had in his head.

"You could go into the hero business, for real," he said with severe sincerity. "I mean, come on! How badly does this world need a legit comic book hero? You know I'm right."

Nicole laughed.

"What is a 'comic book hero'?" Gordan asked.

Mitchell and Nicole looked at him and gasped in unison before breaking into a deluge of laughter.

"We'll educate you," Mitchell promised, giving Gordan a pat on the back.

"After caffeine," Nicole added.

"I don't know how you drink that," Mitchell said.

"After four years of college, I don't know how you *don't*," Nicole retorted with a laugh. "You have the best cafés here," she accused, raising her hand up to the oval Café Passé sign hanging over the sidewalk as they arrived. The warm, welcoming scent of brewing coffee greeted them as a woman opened the door and stepped out onto the sidewalk. Her eyes lingered on Gordan as she passed.

"I'm starting to wonder if I'm at all convincing as a human," Gordan said, lowering his voice as they all stepped inside.

"If Trump can pass as human, you're fine, man," Mitchell said, laughing at Gordan's confused expression.

"It's the eyes," Nicole said as they stepped up to the counter. "Good morning," she said to the barista with straight bangs and a straight black ponytail swinging behind her head. Her name tag read Ash. "Can I have a double cappuccino please?"

Ash smiled, raising the tiny silver ring in the corner of her lower lip. "Sure thing. Anything else?"

"That's all, thanks."

Ash answered with a nod, rang up Nicole's fix, and got started.

Nicole turned back to her brother and Gordan. "Violet eyes are kind of unusual," she said with a shrug as they moved to a table and took their seats. "People can't help but stare."

"And, you know, you're a little … gray," Mitchell pointed out, slapping his hand onto the table beside Gordan's to compare their complexions.

Nicole couldn't help smiling as Gordan studied his hand and forearm beside Mitchell's.

"I am a bit gray," he agreed.

The barista arrived with Nicole's cappuccino. She placed the oversized mug on the table and tucked the serving tray under her vibrantly tattooed arm. Nicole caught a glimpse of neon kittens and skulls.

"Thank you," Nicole said, placing her hands around the mug.

"Sure thing," Ash answered, turning away slow enough to give Gordan a quick once-over.

Nicole chuckled into her cappuccino. "Could be the fabulous hair too," she said. "It's inhuman, really."

Gordan turned his head to look at her, and true to her observation, Gordan's long sheets of black hair swung like heavy strands of silk.

"People are more likely to think you're a cosplay enthusiast than a dragon," Mitchell said, nudging Gordan's arm with his elbow.

Nicole took a look around. A copper-haired man with thick-rimmed glasses sat across the room holding a mug in one hand and a book in the other, and the barista was busy tidying up behind the counter. Nicole turned her focus to the little bar with sweeteners, milks, creams, and toppings. She held out her hand, and with a little squint a couple of yellow packets appeared on her palm.

"Nikki," Mitchell scolded as she poured the sweetener into her drink.

"What?" she replied, turning her hands toward the ceiling with an innocent smile. Then the cinnamon shaker blinked onto the table beside her mug. "No one is watching." She stirred her cappuccino and shook a little dusting of cinnamon over the top before taking a sip.

The hot drink slid down her throat, almost too hot, reminding her of a surge of magic spreading through her. She wondered how long it would take for a portal to open. The waiting was terrible. If she kept up this life on the move, never staying anywhere long enough to let a portal open, she would go mad. Just three days of it already made her want to scream.

That question—*how long do I have?*—was always in the back of her head, chasing her where the Council could not, running her out of every place she wanted to stay. Strangely enough, deciding that she no longer cared about a portal opening was a relief in a lot of ways. She was still anxious about *when* the portal would open, but only because the more she thought about it, the more she wanted to get it over with. She wanted to show whoever came that she was done running and it was their turn to be afraid.

Heat spread through her, and she knew it had little to do with the hot cappuccino sliding into her stomach. As she fed her brain's need for caffeine, Mitchell explained the world of comic book heroes and cosplay to Gordan, who listened with rapt attention and a look of fascination in his eyes.

This is my *goddamn life*, Nicole thought with another surge of fire through her veins. Gordan and her brother made her laugh, and in a strange way that joy stoked her anger even further. *They aren't going to take this from me.*

Nicole's cell phone jingled. It was a text from Roxanne. "You alive?"

She smiled at her phone. She texted back, "Still alive."

The vision of the woman with silver hair shattered Raiden's sleep. He lurched upright in a moment of confusion. He had forgotten where he was. The last thing he remembered was his trip to Cantis with Caeruleus and coming back to his apartment to get the clothes to help Caeruleus blend in. After that, he must have been more exhausted by recent events than he'd thought, because the day was gone. It was dark outside.

He pinched the bridge of his nose, rubbed his eyes, and raked his hand through his hair, fighting back the grog of sleep. As his eyes cleared, he was able to read the clock hanging on the wall. He was astonished to see it was after four in the morning. He hadn't just slept through the day; he'd slept a whole day and night away. He supposed the years of sleeplessness and the last week of chaos had finally caught up with him.

His two days for acclimating were over. His half scowl was an involuntary reaction. He lived in Atrium now. He worked for the Council, and in an hour his duties would begin. A little bile crept up the back of his throat as he tried to get used to the idea.

I work for the Council, he repeated like a mantra to desensitize himself. *Like my father*. The notion made his jaw clench, and he had to start a new mantra to ease the tension. *I am not my father*. He sighed.

No, his father had worked for the Council, and Raiden vowed to work against them. They'd failed the thousands of people in Cantis when they'd turned a blind eye to Dawn's activities. All those lives lost, and the Council hadn't done a thing. They'd never even come looking for survivors, and yet they cared about tracking down the fera. Raiden seethed. The Council had known he was alive in Cantis. Now they had the nerve to care about Dawn's movements.

He wanted to know why the Council was so adamant about finding the fera. He couldn't help thinking the righteous claim to protect the people of both realms from a being with volatile powers and to safeguard the integrity of the barrier that sheltered Veil was a convenient justification to disguise a different motive. Anyone else might have believed that stack of lies, but Raiden had seen firsthand that the Council didn't care about innocent lives.

He would learn what he could about the Council. Caeruleus might be willing to help him gain access to more information. Caeruleus cared about the fate of Cantis as much as Raiden did. Raiden couldn't help but wonder how difficult it was for Caeruleus to reconcile his loyalty to the Council with the fate of Cantis now that he had seen what remained firsthand.

Remembering the look on his friend's face as they'd stood in the empty streets of their childhood, he wondered what the chances were of that pain changing Caeruleus's feelings toward the Council. At this point Raiden didn't foresee Caeruleus shifting the blame away from Dawn. The Council remained blameless to Caeruleus.

Raiden stood and crossed the room to the small dining table in the kitchen where the court records on Atrium's rebel movement were spread out. As ready as he was to play the game, there was an anxious pang in his chest. *Why would they take me off the fera mission only to put me on assignment with the rebels?*

If they didn't trust him with the delicate matter of the fera, a problem that could have devastating repercussions to their reputation throughout the realm, it made little sense to trust him with a problem of virtually equal significance challenging their reputation in their own city.

He shook his head, examining the pages of information scattered across the table. If the Council was at all suspicious of him, giving him a task with so much freedom could very well be some kind of bait. After all, if they wanted to keep a close eye on him, they could have assigned him to some job in the courts where he would always be under someone's watchful eye. He would just have to accept that the Council's reasons would have to remain a mystery for now.

Sitting among the Council's various reports on the rebels was the purse and the picture frame he had retrieved from Cantis. This picture was all he had left of his life before coming to Atrium. In an hour he would report to training for his first day as one of the Council's agents. He hoped it wouldn't take another nine years to find justice for his mother and all the other lives lying framed and shrouded in the dusty homes of Cantis.

Raiden stepped out his door and took a deep breath of the misty morning air. He took the long way to the courts, avoiding the crowded thoroughfares that led more directly to the court building at the center of the city. He was in no hurry, enjoying a leisurely pace along the quiet, lamplit streets.

By the time he ascended the steps to the court building, the streetlamps were dimming. Caeruleus was outside waiting.

"Ready for your first day?" he asked.

"I suppose."

"Good. I'm assigned to training today too. We'll meet Loak in the training hall—come on." Caeruleus nodded toward the open doors.

"Who is Loak?"

"Loak Clyson, the training sergeant," Caeruleus said as they walked the corridors. "He's just about the most experienced agent in the courts. Been here longer than anyone else."

They reached a pair of tall doors, propped open and leading into a high-vaulted hall. There were large mats on the floor and several training dummies in one corner, and overhead a ceiling of glass panes let in the gray light from outside. Having just been outside in the dim morning, Raiden suspected that the windows above were enchanted to amplify the cloud-diffused light from outside.

A voice boomed across the hall from where a man stood tall and large even in the vast training hall. As Raiden and Caeruleus got closer, Raiden realized just how large the man was. His bald scalp was a head and broad shoulders above Raiden. He had a complexion like coal and eyes the striking orange gold of a harvest moon.

"Stone," the massive man greeted Caeruleus and then turned his eyes to Raiden. He straightened up with a look of interest on his face and asked, "Cael, is that right?"

"Yes," Raiden answered, fighting back a sneer.

"Everybody in! Come on, then!" His command nearly shook the hall.

Raiden glanced over his shoulder to see about ten other agents filing into the chamber. All the men and women reporting for training appeared to be human—no mixed-bloods or fey, which Loak clearly was, in the lot. There had been so many mixed-bloods in Cantis that Raiden was a little surprised there were virtually none in this lineup of the Council's agents.

"Singleir, Baran, Loudain, the last one to get their sorry spines in line will be sparring Tolmack today," Loak boomed.

The three men lagging at the back of the approaching pack all picked up their pace as the first agent of the group arrived, a grin on her face. Raiden assumed this was Tolmack. She had a sleek rope of copper hair plaited down her back and a fading purple shadow under her eye that stood out in stark contrast against her alabaster complexion. Tolmack was clearly unafraid of confrontation. Raiden suspected she wasn't the sort to pull her punches in the training hall, judging by the way the other guys reacted to the prospect of training with her.

Loak scanned the faces of the eleven men and women who had lined up beside Raiden and Caeruleus.

"Where's Lander?" Loak demanded.

On cue a man came trotting into the training hall, not taking his time but not exactly trying to make up for being the last one in line. He had a slender build and angular face that suggested there were elves in his lineage, but by wearing his fair hair short and exposing his round ears, Lander was more convincing as a human.

"Let's get to it, then," Loak said. "Pair up; we're sparring. Objective: seize your opponent *without* the use of spells."

Raiden tried not to let his disappointment show. Spells he knew. He was even decent with a sword against golems, but hand-to-hand combat was a skill he'd never acquired as a boy, let alone in the nine years he'd spent alone.

Caeruleus and Raiden moved off to claim a space.

"Why no spells?" Raiden asked.

"Our uniforms are enhanced with standard-issue protection spells, and our gear equips us to deal with assailant magic," Caeruleus explained. "We work on our magical strategy sometimes, but Clyson prefers to train nonmagical tactics."

"Great." Raiden tried to muster enthusiasm.

"You'll pick it up in time," Caeruleus said. "Ready?"

Raiden raised his hands, but before he could answer, he felt the Sight crawl into his mind through the doorway of dread and anticipation of what was to come. He saw Caeruleus make the first move, striking with an open hand. Then Raiden's eyes refocused, and Caeruleus was standing there still waiting for his answer.

"Ready," he said with uncertainty.

But Caeruleus moved precisely as he had in the vision, and Raiden slipped to the side with ease.

"I can't go easy on you," Caeruleus warned.

"By all means," Raiden said, a smile creeping into his mouth. "Don't."

It didn't take Caeruleus more than a few minutes to realize what was happening as Raiden effortlessly evaded him. A grin spread across his face. "You're supposed to be attacking. Aren't you going to try?"

"No," Raiden said, ducking below a hook.

Caeruleus laughed as he advanced, and Raiden evaded. Caeruleus's grin began to fade, and Raiden could see him focus harder through his fatigue, trying to be spontaneous, but by then Raiden had encountered all his preferred moves.

"Not bad," Loak said as he observed Raiden and Caeruleus. "But you won't apprehend a suspect if all you do is avoid, Cael."

Raiden's jaw clenched hard at his father's name, and he took his eyes off Caeruleus. As he glared at Loak, a jolt of the Sight hit him, and in the blink of an eye he saw Caeruleus catch him off guard. But Raiden stepped to the side as his friend came at him, seized Caeruleus by the arm, and locked it behind his back.

Loak raised his eyebrows.

"Ah," Caeruleus let out with a laugh. "Fine, you got me."

Raiden released him. Caeruleus turned to him with an amused scowl on his face and held out his hand. They clasped each other's wrist for a moment.

"I will get you for that," Caeruleus grumbled through a grin.

"You know I'll see it coming, right?" Raiden murmured, and Caeruleus let out a laugh.

Around the hall the pairs shook hands and slapped backs as they finished the first round of sparring.

Loak raised his voice to the whole hall. "Spells are not the only threat out there. We must never discount the chance that nonmagical tactics will be used against us or be the deciding factor in gaining the upper hand when dealing with an assailant. Most of us have relied on magic our whole lives."

Caeruleus elbowed Raiden in the ribs.

Loak continued, "The Council thinks that the court-mandated procedures and complex spell technologies are all you need to do your job out on the streets of Atrium. All I can say to that is there's a reason we all still carry the standard-issue short swords. I cannot guarantee that you won't be disarmed. Your protective antispell masks can be removed. Our weekly sessions are about keeping you from getting comfortable, complacent.

"We will finish today with the usual equipment drills with your guns and latest spell cartridges, but the majority of this session will focus on restricted hand-to-hand sparring as well as some unrestricted sparring to challenge your creativity when you have neither your masks nor your guns. Now everyone switch partners, and let's go again."

Loak turned back to Raiden. "Cael, you'll be with me this round. Stone, see to it Lander's ego doesn't get the better of him. Go three with him and Tolmack."

Raiden answered with a stiff nod.

Caeruleus laughed and said, "Yes, sir."

Loak craned his head toward the far end of the hall. He took long, slow steps that Raiden had to match with almost twice as many strides to keep pace. Once they were far from the others, Loak said in a low voice, "Right, since the Council wants to throw you right out onto the streets to track down the rebellion, what you need is the intensive course. Agents don't need much training to wear a mask and point a gun, but you're not going on patrols. You're going to be out there without a uniform, without our equipment. I don't know what the reports said, but you need to know that several agents have died trying to infiltrate the rebels."

Raiden's jaw clenched. That fact had not been in the reports. A vision flashed before his eyes like a hallucination, and he saw Loak's arm turn into a blur before seizing his shirt and hurling him down onto the floor. Raiden blinked the vision away, startled. Loak was still standing there, his arms folded across his chest.

"First thing you've got to learn," Loak said.

Raiden sidestepped and caught Loak's arm. Using Loak's momentum against him, Raiden pulled Loak forward off his feet, and the giant man hit the floor with a great thud. Everyone across the hall stopped and looked over in stunned silence. Loak picked himself up, chuckling quietly, which sounded more ominous than jovial to Raiden.

"I thought as much," he muttered to himself. "Back to it, you lot!" His voice startled the others out of their frozen stupors.

Raiden's chest swelled with pride as he watched Loak straighten up. As Loak turned back to face Raiden, he took a large step forward, mashed his massive foot onto Raiden's, and hit him square in the chest with a flat hand. Raiden toppled back and hit the padded floor with a loud smack.

Loak knelt down beside him as Raiden looked up at the ceiling with stunned wide eyes and empty lungs. "Now you listen to me," Loak said. "The Sight can be beat by spontaneity. You may not be able to avoid visions, but you better learn when to act and when *not* to act on what you've seen."

Raiden swallowed a sudden lump in his throat and convinced his lungs to expand.

"Keep using the Sight like that, and eventually someone you can't trust will figure it out. Don't be stupid, Raiden," Loak said, offering his hand.

Raiden hesitated, confused by Loak's use of his first name, but accepted the gesture. Loak stood and pulled him off the floor, practically yanking him off his feet entirely. Raiden took a deep breath, his chest sore, and he imagined a hand-shaped bruise forming there later.

"Back to business, shall we?" Loak asked.

"Yes, sir," Raiden said, uncertain about Loak and unnerved by the exposure of his secret but unable to deny that he needed to learn anything and everything he could even if Loak was not trustworthy.

16. Quiet

ordan looked up from the vividly colored illustrations of Superman catching a falling bus. Nicole was lying supine on the floor. For a few seconds she defied gravity enough to put an inch or two of air between her spine and the floor.

"What are we doing for dinner?" Mitchell asked.

Nicole plopped back onto the floor with a huff of exasperation. "I've been domestic enough for one day," she muttered. "Dinner's on you tonight."

"The only thing I'm making is a call for takeout," he said. Then he snapped upright, jerking away from the couch cushions beside Gordan. "I have a brilliant idea."

"What?" Nicole asked.

"Spencer Makenzie's."

"No."

"Can't you just pop over for a minute? Real quick?"

"Mitch, I left California trembling yesterday—literally. If I go back, I could send the San Andreas into an all-out fit. I'm not going back to Ventura. Not even the world's best fish tacos and ahi pockets are worth the risk."

"Fine," Mitchell said, deflating in defeat.

"Pick anything that isn't located in an earthquake hotbed," she suggested, folding her arms across her chest.

Nicole returned to levitating her body, managing an inch for a few moments longer than the last attempt. Gordan thumbed a few pages ahead in Mitchell's issue of *Superman*. Several other comics lay scattered on the cushion beside him.

"How about ..." Mitchell said, trailing off for some moments of thought, "something raw tonight, for Gordan?"

Nicole sat up. "Sushi sounds good to me," she said, seeming to have read her brother's mind. "I'll call it in," she said, grabbing her cell phone from the coffee table.

"What is sushi?" Gordan asked, looking up from the comic.

"Raw fish and rice. You'll eat fish, right?"

"Certainly," he answered simply as he closed the comic and chose another from the pile beside him. He glanced at Nicole pacing in the kitchen as she spoke to someone about caterpillars, rainbows, and seaweed salad. Then he reached for a different comic, one titled *The Flash*.

"Thank you," Nicole finished on the phone and returned to the living room. "Good choice—the Flash is my favorite." She lowered her voice to say, "He's the best," but Mitchell heard her.

"No he's not," Mitchell sang back. "No offense to the Scarlet Speedster, but Superman will always be the best. It's just a fact. His only weakness is a rare alien mineral."

Nicole rolled her eyes but smiled.

"Why is he your favorite?" Gordan asked.

"He's funny. He makes me laugh. Even in the worst situations he still has his humor. Plus, well, he's a runner," she said with an even broader smile. She turned and headed down the hallway.

"Where you going?" Mitchell asked.

"To get my shoes," she called.

Mitchell and Gordan exchanged glances.

"These tales," Gordan said, nodding down at the comics, "it's strange how much of her I can see in them."

Mitchell smiled. "That's not surprising. She grew up on them. Anthony and I read them to her since we didn't like reading her little-kid books," he said with a fond smirk. "Mom hated that, said they were too mature and violent, but Nikki loved them."

Gordan looked up, wondering why Nicole was still gone. Mitchell seemed to have the same thought and got up to wander down the hall, but before he could make it out of the room, a pulse of magic rolled through the apartment, a passing wave of warm air charged with static. It crackled over Gordan's skin and raised his hair.

"I can't imagine what a nightmare babysitting her would have been if she'd had her magic from day one," Mitchell said.

"I'm sure she did," Gordan replied.

"What?"

"Have her magic from day one. It might have been nothing compared to what it is today, but she would have had it. It would have only taken time to virtually disappear, though. Odd or unsatisfactory behavior in children can usually be deterred easily enough, and the most powerful force in either realm is belief—the will of the mind is the driving force of magic and lack thereof in this realm. Most of us accept the rules of the world we live in—be they the rules of your family, your culture, your society—and by doing so we submit ourselves to limitations. The people here in this realm have buried themselves in their limited beliefs, rejecting many things, not just magic and the beings that aren't like them. My guess is Nicole must have accepted what everyone else in this realm accepts, that magic isn't real, isn't possible. I dare say the suppression of her magic was just as much her own doing as it was this whole realm and its absence of magic."

"So you think Nicole could have had magic all her life." Mitchell crossed his arms. "But just buying into everyone else's idea of what the world is, or isn't, stopped her?"

"We all limit ourselves," Gordan said as he looked down at the vibrant illustrated pages of the comic. "People are only ever capable of doing what they believe they can. Throughout the centuries magic fled to Veil, and that exodus left behind a sort of vacuum in which minuscule amounts of magic became even more difficult to find. But it is the overwhelming belief that magic doesn't fit into the world that defines this realm. Most people deny their own potential to some extent or another. It's just that people in this realm suffer from that pitfall to the greatest extent, and they are suffering dearly for it. A world without magic is a dying world."

"So you're telling me there is no magic in this realm because people don't believe in it?" Mitchell asked with a laugh. "That sounds like some Peter Pan logic. If you say you don't believe in fairies, does a fairy drop dead somewhere?"

Gordan tried not to laugh at the notion. "No, not quite. But rejecting a whole group of people is enough to chase them away, make them seek safety and refuge from hate. Fear and hate inevitably become violent. Those feelings shaped the fate of this world. People and creatures of magic chose retreat and self-preservation."

"Do you think they should have fought? They had every right to stay here."

"I do, and perhaps many of us thought so, but we were afraid, and with fear often comes silence." Gordan read a few panels. "You know, I once thought the ability to sense the emotions of others meant I could understand them better than anyone. But looking at these"—he nodded down at the comic—"I feel like I understand her better now knowing that these were her bedtime stories."

Mitchell laughed. "Yeah, I'll give you that one."

"You know Nicole far better than I, growing up with her, reading her these stories … I wonder, then, why you would encourage her to run away from the coming fight."

"Of course I'm encouraging her to avoid danger, to keep herself safe," Mitchell scoffed.

"Running doesn't make her safe. She's not safe here in this realm, even with the barrier between her and her enemies. You said this morning that she never backed down from a fight—that's who she is. Why ask her to deny who she is? Sooner or later they *will* find her."

A look of discomfort and annoyance pinched Mitchell's face. "So wanting her to stay alive is a bad thing?" His words were hard and defensive, but Gordan could feel his anxiety, his fear for his sister sheltered in his shell of anger.

"No," Gordan said. "I can relate. But can you ask her to spend her life running knowing it will smother her? It won't prevent the fight from coming. But running, cultivating that fear, could very well defeat her before they even find her. If she has any chance of beating this, it will be as the Nicole you know, the one who stands up for herself—and for those she has no obligation to defend. Her enemies have already taken her life hostage by looming over her, by taking Raiden, threatening her family and friends."

"I know her, Gordan," Mitchell said, shaking his head. "She will try to go it alone."

A wave of energy erupted in the middle of the living room, Nicole appearing at its center, a full plastic bag dangling from each hand.

Mitchell jerked away in surprise. "Sonova—jeez, Nikki!"

"Sushi time," she announced.

"Scare the living shit out of me," Mitchell muttered under his breath.

Nicole gave Gordan a devious smile, her eyes bright with satisfaction. She set the bags down on the low table between the couch and the television. "Okay, ready?"

"For what?" Mitchell asked, annoyance lingering in his voice.

Nicole straightened up, took a deep breath, and, with both hands moving downward in unison, snapped her fingers in command like a music conductor. On cue a blue light flashed bright enough to swallow the whole of the table, and when it dissipated, their food was carefully laid out for them on dishes, ready to be eaten.

"Yes," Nicole hissed, shaking a fist in triumph.

"Wow," Mitchell said, nodding in approval.

Gordan took in the spread of food before them. Pieces of bright raw meat lay over little knobs of rice, and there were some long, segmented rolls, one topped with something green, another with several different colored slices of flesh. There was a plate of little dumplings beside an empty saucer, a small bowl of what looked purely like seaweed, and a bowl of some pungent yellow root, thinly shaven. Finally, there was a roll containing a rainbow of fish but wrapped in something crisp and green rather than rice.

"Wow," he agreed with Mitchell.

"Let's eat," Nicole said. "I don't know about you, but I'm ravenous. Something about using magic makes me so hungry." She chose a side of the low table and knelt down beside it, picking up the bowl of seaweed.

"You're using energy; it drains you like any other activity. Breathing fire is the same for me. It's more taxing than you might think—conjures up quite the appetite." Gordan lowered himself to the floor on the long side of the table with the couch behind him.

"No kidding?" Mitchell sat down on the floor across the table from Nicole.

"I didn't know you could breathe fire," Nicole said with awe in her voice.

Gordan picked up a pair of chopsticks for himself. "Much harder to master than flying was," he said, trying to decide what morsel to take first.

"You two sure know how to make a guy feel utterly ordinary," Mitchell said, grabbing a dumpling with his fingers and popping it in his mouth.

"Well, you could always move to Veil and see what sort of talent you have for magic," Nicole suggested.

"Yeah, you know, they might have some great graduate programs over there," Mitchell said, laughing. "I'm sure I could put my ecology and evolutionary biology degree to good use."

"I might live there someday," Nicole said, then delivered a wormy green mass into her mouth.

Everyone was silent, and Gordan wondered what thoughts were hidden within the pang of anxiety he felt ring in Mitchell's chest. For a moment Gordan thought Mitchell was seriously considering what Nicole had said.

"What, and deny this realm its first real superhero? How could you?" Mitchell's mocking tone turned into laughter.

Nicole didn't seem to mind her brother's lack of seriousness. She laughed as well, seemingly happy to be distracted by food and jokes.

Gordan trapped a piece of dark-pink meat atop an oblong ball of rice between the ends of his chopsticks and stuffed the whole thing in his mouth. Both of the siblings watched him with interest as he chewed.

"Well?" Nicole asked.

"Much nicer without all the scales and bones."

They laughed.

Raiden lay on the mat looking up at the shimmering skylight above, wondering if it was the magic enhancing the gray daylight or head trauma sparkling in his eyes. The white brightness flooded his pupils and filled his brain while his body ached in more places than he could count.

"Same time next week, everyone," Loak announced in his thunderous shout. "Now get out of here."

Raiden sat up, scowling at the twinge in his side where one of many bruises was forming. As the others congregated and made their way to the tall double doors, Raiden picked himself up and spotted Caeruleus crossing the hall.

Loak quieted his voice but could not diminish his deep baritone. "Learn when to display your strengths and when to keep them a secret, Raiden. The Council doesn't know about you having the Sight, but trust me—if they find out, you will know it. They'll have you downstairs before the Sight can warn you."

Caeruleus strolled into earshot, and so Raiden said nothing, unsure whether or not Loak's words were a threat or advice. The Council didn't know about his gift, but Loak did, and he could tell them anytime it suited him.

"Next week, you two," Loak said, giving them a nod.

"Enjoy your first day?" Caeruleus asked.

"Immensely," Raiden answered with a sarcastic grimace, eyeing Loak's broad back as he walked away.

"Never seen him train someone personally for an entire session before," Caeruleus said. "What was that all about?"

"He said he wanted to make up for my lack of training before I'm out on the streets," Raiden said.

"Well, he knows what he is talking about. The rebels are more organized than they first seemed. They managed to cause a lot of problems and commotion when they started. Now it seems like they've up and quit, but we're pretty sure they're just being careful these days."

"I gathered as much from the information the Council provided, which wasn't all that much," Raiden said, tempted to make a snide remark about the volume of paperwork on incidents but very little real information on the rebellion.

"Which is why they need you out there, someone who doesn't think like every other agent here. I imagine that's why they chose to put you on this assignment," Caeruleus said.

"Yeah, that must be it," Raiden agreed, swallowing the sour disdain in his throat.

"I've got to report to the Council for a briefing," Caeruleus said as they walked out the doors of the training hall and into the corridor. "I'll see you around, though."

"I guess that means my work starts now." Raiden tried to sound enthusiastic. "Although, I can't see much good in having someone who's trying to locate and infiltrate the rebels openly coming and going from the courts every week."

"You can get authorization to interbound in and out," Caeruleus said as he stopped Raiden and steered him down a corridor to their left. "You just have to apply for access to the interbounding chamber—prevents anyone from popping into the courts wherever and whenever they want."

Raiden bobbed his head in understanding as they made their way down the narrow corridor.

"Aside from the risk, you've probably got the best assignment here," Caeruleus said. "I mean, you can virtually come and go as you please. Not having to serve patrol or do the regular check-ins throughout the day, you probably have the most freedom of all of us in the courts, aside from the fleet."

"The fleet?"

"The agents with their wings. The Council only trusts the best with the skies," he said with a laugh, and Raiden got the feeling this was some kind of joke among the agents that he was missing.

Raiden was suddenly confused. Why had no one mentioned the fleet to him upon his arrival? Hadn't the Council granted him wings that night he'd encountered the fera? The memory seemed foggy now, but he had been under a lot of stress in the last few days.

He had been in the tower of the castle, as good as dead. The fera had interrupted Moira's torture, sparing him the conclusion of a painfully slow death. Moira had pursued the fera, leaving Raiden alone. As he'd made his escape, he'd witnessed what the fera was capable of and had seen Moira finally receive the fate she'd so deserved. When the bridge had begun to crumble and the fera had needed help, he hadn't even hesitated. He hadn't been thinking about what she was or the Council's letters. She had just saved his sorry life, and she'd needed his help in return. The fact that they'd survived the fall thanks to the Council's wings left a bitter taste in Raiden's mouth.

Caeruleus was still prattling on about wings. "I'm hoping after this whole fera business is settled I'll finally get mine," he said.

"What's it like? How does the Council do it?" Raiden asked. Truth be told, he had no idea. He just assumed that if they could grant agents wings, certainly distance wasn't a complication. They had his father's blood, after all; they had summoned him with it. Surely that vital key to a person's body allowed them access for other spells—otherwise how else had Raiden ended up with his?

"Landor is the only agent to earn his wings since I've been in Atrium. They hold a big ceremony here in the courts where the recipient accepts the responsibility and makes a pledge before the permanent transfiguration is performed," Caeruleus explained.

"I see," Raiden said, choosing not to mention his experience back in Cantis. It seemed unlikely that the Council had given him his wings after all.

"Here we are," Caeruleus said, stopping at a door with a plaque that read Authorized Interbounding Commute Office. "You just need to let them know who you are and fill out some paperwork, and they will have you on your way in no time. I've got to get to my briefing."

"Yeah, thanks," Raiden muttered as Caeruleus trotted off down the corridor, leaving Raiden looking up at the plaque, still thinking about wings.

For a fleeting moment the only things on Nicole's mind were Mitchell and Gordan and their laughter filling the apartment.

Mitchell let out a groan of annoyance. "I guess I better get to bed. I've got class tomorrow—can't stay up all night."

He stood up from his place at the coffee table. The plates had been cleared of every last morsel of sushi. Only stray grains of sticky rice, knobs of wasabi, and smears of sauce remained of their dinner.

"I'll clean up," Nicole volunteered with a raised hand and a grin. Her arm tingled with magic, and she brought her hand down flat, striking the table with a loud smack. The energy in her hand transferred into the wood with a pulse like the release of static, and everything on the table disappeared.

"All right, show-off, I'm going to bed," Mitchell said, turning away and disappearing into the hall while shaking his head.

"Don't be jealous, Mitch," Nicole called. "Drop out and become a wizard instead. It's never too late."

"Wake me up when my Hogwarts letter gets here," Mitchell called back, his voice muffled, and Nicole grinned.

"I suppose we should get some sleep too. Unless dragons don't really need sleep." She turned a curious gaze toward Gordan.

"I need sleep," he confirmed.

"Okay," she said with a skeptical nod, unfolding her legs and standing up. She turned off the lights in the living room and kitchen, where the time jumped out at her in sudden darkness: 11:37. The numbers glowed green and seemed to make her recognize how tired she really was.

After waking up so early and using magic all day, her body felt utterly drained, which was strange since she could still feel that ever-pulsing source like gentle electricity deep in her core. How she could possess a constant source of energy and simultaneously be so worn out was baffling to her, like having energy but a sore body. They passed Mitchell's door. The room was already dark.

The second room, still unassigned by the student apartment complex after Mitchell's roommate had graduated a semester early, was bare and empty save for the bed and desk.

Nicole kicked off her shoes, and Gordan removed his awkwardly. It was clearly not a task he was accustomed to. He took his side of the bed, still fully clothed, and lay looking up at the ceiling while she changed into her boxers and sleep shirt. Then she climbed into the bed and burrowed under the blanket before pointing at the light switch and flicking her finger as she would to flip the switch down. The light blinked off.

"Is your brother right? Are you hoping a portal will open here?" Gordan asked, his question quiet in the darkness.

"I ..." she tried to respond before she even knew the answer. "I guess I just don't want a repeat of last time, where I leave thinking I've kept a portal from opening and it turns out one did anyway. It seems like the best way to avoid that is to stick around to be the welcoming committee, show them that I will stand my ground. It's not like I plan on running right to the Council or Venarius; I just don't want them to see me running *from* them anymore."

"I understand," he said. He let the silence remain undisturbed after that.

Nicole wasn't sure whether or not he was sleeping. She thought about the people in Veil waiting with rapt attention for the next portal to point them in her direction. Days ago it had seemed so simple—stay on the move, don't open any portals, and ... what? Life would have been a grand adventure?

She almost laughed into the night. Only three days into her farewell-to-my-family tour she had set off a chain of earthquakes in California, unknowingly left a hunter at home with her dad, and nearly gotten her best friend abducted. At least it hadn't taken any longer to figure out how nonsensical the plan had been. Better to realize that sooner rather than much later, before she ended up surrounded by the enemy while thinking she was out of their reach.

No, she would much rather stand her ground. Maybe she would only end up provoking even greater forces to come after her. But she'd rather go down facing this fight than running from it.

Part of her knew that this change of heart wasn't really about her family or her friends' safety. She had killed a man, and not just out of self-defense, not like Moira. Maybe she hadn't been trying to kill him, but she had. She'd gone after him with that scalpel, full of hate and violence. The memory still made her pulse quicken. Her body went hot, and her stomach went queasy. That was what had changed her. Although she feared what kind of change it was, she could accept that the line had been crossed. There was no going back. She certainly didn't want to do it again, but at least now she didn't have to fear stepping over that line if she had to.

Go ahead—try me, she thought, half angry and half amused, as she drifted off to sleep and dreamed of portals.

Raiden's feet hit the floor just inside the door of his apartment. He froze for a moment while his head recovered from the rush of interbounding. He had to gather his thoughts. The jump from the courts to his living room had scattered them.

So the Council was far more selective when bestowing wings than he had thought, and from the sound of things they certainly never would have doled out such an honor so carelessly even if they could do such magic across the distance between Atrium and Cantis. Now that he thought about it, he wasn't sure the magic to transfigure someone's body could be performed across such a distance. He had been so surprised by the appearance of his wings that night that it had been easy to believe the Council had been responsible. Still, he was baffled that they could have been his all along and he'd simply never known about them, never discovered them.

He crossed the apartment to the table in the kitchen where he had left the photograph of his mother, the thick layer of dust still concealing his father. She had been a seer who had renounced the Sight, and his father had been one of the Council's agents. That was all he really knew about them. Unless his father had been away on missions, the Council didn't exist to them, and his mother had never spoken of her childhood with the Sight.

Raiden picked up the frame and studied his mother's face, the soft smile she had always worn when she hadn't been laughing or beaming at him. He could hardly remember a time when she'd been solemn, except the day she'd learned her husband would never return and the few grief-shrouded months that had followed.

The picture was all shades of gray. The dark gray of his mother's skin and the light gray of her eyes would have been a mystery to anyone else, but Raiden saw the cinnamon hue of her skin and the pale blue-green irises of his mother every day in his own reflection. He pushed his hand through his deep-auburn hair, the same thick tresses as hers.

His hair was stiff with dried sweat and the powder from the mats back in the training hall. His body ached. He felt grimy. His rumpled clothes reeked of physical exertion. Then his stomach chimed in with a furious grumble adamant about food. Raiden opted to get into the shower and wash away the stink of his humiliation in the training hall.

Inside the little bathroom just past the small kitchen, he flicked on the light and looked around. Before now he hadn't paid much attention to the basic commodities besides the sink and toilet. Soap, shaving ointments and razor, and even a comb were all present. They had to have been there before he'd arrived, but he hadn't even stopped to think about them. He could understand why the Council would want someone assigned to infiltrate the rebels to be housed away from the court barracks, but he felt baffled that they would have gone so far as to equip his lodgings with every little essential.

Raiden picked up the shaving ointment, opened the cap, and smelled it. His heart pounded as he recognized the warm, spicy scent. A memory hit him, of his father picking him up as a small boy and holding him high overhead. He closed the bottle and set it down before looking up at his reflection in the mirror. The realization came hard and left him feeling foolish for not understanding sooner. This had been his father's apartment when he'd been away from Cantis, when he'd been gone for days and sometimes a week or more at a time.

His father had looked into this mirror every day. Raiden looked around again, seeing every wall and door differently. This was where he had paced when he hadn't been at home in Cantis, pacing the kitchen over some trouble he'd kept to himself. It surprised Raiden how much he suddenly remembered about his father.

Strange, how one small whiff of that shaving balm could summon those faded and buried memories from the darkest reaches of his mind. Raiden took a breath and went about his business, trying not to let that man back into his thoughts.

He showered, resisting the surreal feeling that he was suddenly living his father's life, becoming him through the sheer act of performing the same rituals in the precise place he once had. Raiden pulled clean clothes out of the drawer and put them on, trying not to imagine himself looking in the mirror and suddenly discovering that he now had his father's golden hair, brown eyes, and fair complexion.

For a moment he thought he shouldn't look in the mirror at all. As he rustled his hair, shaking out some excess water, he returned to the bathroom, keeping his eyes down and pretending it was natural to do so. *I'm not him*, he intoned like a spell in his head as he looked up. He sighed. His hair was still a deep, dark auburn, his mother's clear teal eyes looked back, and the same brown skin remained, assuaging his childish fears.

Raiden was not that man. His father had belonged to the Council, and Raiden would do anything he could to defy them. Raiden dropped his head back in exasperation. He'd drive himself crazy with his own psychological obstacle course while his stomach proceeded to devour itself. So he shrugged on his coat and headed for the door, resolved to track down something to eat.

Before he could grasp the knob, he halted with an idea. Turning on his heel, he strode through his apartment and into the bedroom, where he found his uniform and mask lying in the drawer. He took the mask and slipped it back into a deep inner pocket of his coat. With that he hurried out the door, following the demands of his gut toward food.

Not too far from his apartment the hot scent of breads fresh out of the oven nearly dragged him in off the street. The inside of the bakery was the antithesis of the dreary, chilly gray day outside. The ovens in the back glowed orange and red. The air was warm and welcoming, the sweet smells enticing his stomach to growl and softening his hungry irritation.

"What can I get for you, love?" a woman with a friendly round face said from behind the counter. The baker wore a smile and a simple cotton bonnet to contain her hair while she worked. Her cheeks were rosy from the oven heat, and there was a delicate veil of flour on her person.

"I honestly don't know," he said. "I could eat anything at this point."

"Lucky yer nose led you here," she said with a wink. "I've got just the thing to sort you out."

She straightened up, and Raiden noticed that she was standing on a platform several steps high. As she descended the steps, her stature became apparent; she was no taller than the counter. Behind the counter she went to one of the many trays of cooling baked delights stacked atop each other. There she pointed at what looked like a large, round loaf of bread, its crust shining in the warm light of the bakery. The steaming loaf lifted itself off the tray as she opened a paper bag, where it deposited itself.

The baker walked back up her platform and returned to face Raiden with the same smile as before. "Belly bun," she said, handing it to him. "It'll fill you right up."

"How much?" Raiden reached into his pocket. Handling money was strange after nine years without needing it.

"Three and a half coppers," she answered.

The coppers were small, square coins, about the size of this thumbnail, and the half coppers had holes in the center. He fished out a handful of coins, mostly square coppers, but there were a couple of silvers there too—slender, rectangular coins twice as long as the coppers. Searching his palm for the coppers he needed, he plucked up the three and one half before dropping the remaining coins in his pocket. The baker handed him the paper bag as he placed the coppers in her hand.

"Thank you," he said.

"Come back again," she sang.

He waved on his way out the door. When he opened the bag, enticing tendrils of steam unfurled into the cold air. The belly bun was as big as both his hands cupped together. He pulled it out of the bag and took as large a bite as he could. His teeth sank into mostly bread, but it was soft, hot, and heavenly.

By the weight of the bun, he knew it was filled with something. His second bite managed to reach the savory contents—salty, gooey cheese and some kind of meat so thoroughly spiced he couldn't identify whether it was lamb or beef. The spices captivated his taste buds, and his stomach's rampage was silenced. But as he ate and walked, he couldn't help feeling as if he had forgotten something. The nagging suspicion that something was missing seemed to persist with every bite. He just couldn't figure out what it was.

With his appetite placated, he could turn his attention to a more productive endeavor.

17. Friend

The grand double doors opened for Caeruleus, and he hurried across the vast expanse of the Council's great chamber, his reflection hanging upside down in the polished deep-green floor beneath his feet.

"Caeruleus, come in, come in," one of the councilmen said with a distracted air. "We have much to discuss regarding the events of your most recent report."

"Yes, sir," he answered.

"We are aware Raiden was there with you when you encountered the portal and found the body of an unidentified man," a councilwoman on the far left said.

There was a rustle of paper as the councilman on the outermost left seat raised Caeruleus's report. "And it says here that you two went to investigate the scene of Raiden's encounter with the fera. Was that all you did while there?"

"No, that wasn't the only reason. Cantis was my home. I left before the massacre, and I needed to see it for myself—what Dawn had done. I believe it might be connected with the fera. We didn't actually make it to the castle before the portal appeared," Caeruleus explained.

"We respect your need to mourn," the councilwoman replied. "We value your dedication to this mission, Caeruleus, but we must insist that you refrain from including Raiden in any further work regarding the fera."

"I don't understand," he said.

Another councilman three seats away said, "We are unsure how trustworthy

Raiden is at this time. You may have known him when you were a boy, but we cannot overlook the fact that he was the only survivor of that terrible massacre almost ten years ago. That is either extremely lucky or highly suspicious. Cantis became a hub for Dawn's activities, and there is a strong likelihood that he could have connections with Dawn one way or another. We took a great risk reaching out to him when our seers saw the fera's arrival in Cantis. Sending someone risked alerting Dawn's own person already occupying the island. Only after receiving no response from Raiden and fearing we would lose our opportunity did we send Sinnrick."

"Furthermore," another councilman continued, "the deceased man managed to get into the other realm so swiftly. We must consider the possibility that Raiden could have been helping Dawn's efforts rather than our own. In your report you said that the portal closed soon after it opened, but you returned to Atrium before attempting to open it again. You stated your reason as simply 'retrieving supplies.'"

"I did not think it was wise to confront the fera in an agitated state without being prepared. I returned to Atrium to change my clothes for garments that Raiden secured from the other realm before his arrival in Atrium. After seeing what she had just done to her previous visitor from Veil, I felt success would hinge on my ability to blend in and get close to the fera. Unfortunately, by the time I got back to Cantis, I could not open a portal."

"And this plan was yours?" a councilwoman sitting toward the center asked.

"No, ma'am," he said, hesitating to reveal the truth now that they suspected his friend of traitorous action. "It was Raiden's idea. He offered the clothes to me. Although we don't know what happened between the fera and the dead man, he believes that the danger lies in threatening her. I am certain he was only interested in my success and well-being. Yesterday was the second time he witnessed a life taken by the fera. The man we found can only be one of Dawn's men."

"We are investigating the identity of the man in hopes of determining Dawn's current location and perhaps gaining some insight into the failed tactics he may have used in pursuit of the fera."

The councilman in the center of the crescent said, "It is true that the safest approach when dealing with the fera may be to get close and gain her trust, but we do not have the luxury of time in this matter when the most prominent faction of dark magic in this realm seeks the fera for their own purposes. We don't know the true extent of their following or their resources.

We cannot afford to take our time in securing the fera and keeping her from Dawn's influence."

The Council stood.

"Do not forget, Caeruleus, that the last time Dawn managed to intercept a fera before we could was disastrous. The entire Candhrid peninsula was swallowed by the fera's destructive rampage. We may not know what Dawn intends to do with the fera, but we have seen the power her kind possesses. In Dawn's hands there is no telling what the fera will bring upon this realm."

A different Council member continued, "Getting the fera to Atrium and protecting both realms from her means preventing Dawn from finding her, even if that means bringing her here by force. Do not risk this mission by taking Raiden's advice. As far as we can see, all he did yesterday was buy Dawn more time."

"We have the seers watching tirelessly for any glimpse of another portal," another Council member said. "We have agents upon the alatus ships throughout the realm in hopes of tapping into any trace of magic in the other realm strong enough to open a portal, but even with all our ships in the skies out searching we have had no luck. With so little magic left in the old world today, all we can do is wait for the fera to weaken the barrier again. When one *does* open, you must be prepared to bring the fera back by whatever means necessary. Try to convince her to come willingly if you like, but you are expected to return with the fera."

Caeruleus swallowed the lump of anxiety in his throat. "And if she puts up a fight, how am I supposed to apprehend her? So far two of Dawn's people have tried and died in their attempts."

"We advise that she not be given the chance to resist. Incapacitate her before she knows you are there. You have the full disposal of the court armory; they'll be expecting you there. If Raiden has led you to believe that the fera can be approached, reasoned with, or even befriended, then he is sabotaging us all. Great though her powers may be, she is still new to her magic. Use that to your advantage."

"Yes, sir," Caeruleus said, straightening his spine as much as he possibly could.

"Good. You will remain here in the courts and continue preparing for this endeavor while we await sign of another portal. Be ready to leave and prepared for the worst."

"Understood," he said.

"You are dismissed," they said in unison.

His heels squeaked on the floor as he made an about-face and headed for the massive doors with the Council's words spinning in his head.

Raiden glanced up at the cottony grayness hanging over the city of Atrium. He walked the narrower streets, away from the late-afternoon crowds, as he pondered how he would switch his mask with the mask of another agent. No one had come to training in uniform, and those on patrol were supposed to wear their masks at all times according to protocol. He decided he would worry about that challenge after he'd rigged his mask with some spells of his own.

With the slew of wards, charms, and spells already woven together into the mask, tampering with it to add his own magic could prove to be troublesome, but if done right, he could have ears in the courts. The only problem with this idea was the challenge of meddling with intricate magic without undoing or distorting what was already there. He knew he had nowhere near the skill required for such an endeavor. He was well studied, yes, and proficient with active spell casting, but the intricate combination of so many spells together was beyond him. He could try but very well might end up ruining all the magic work or even the mask itself, and then he would have nothing to plant in the courts.

The chime of a door opening rang in his head and made him look up from his feet. His eyes fell on the hanging wood sign ahead of him: TOVAR'S CHARMS AND TRINKETS.

The sign swung a little in the air. When he reached the shop, he saw the same words upon the window and dozens of different enchanted objects on display behind the glass. For a moment he was mesmerized, watching an enchanted quill-and-ink set as it carefully wrote a paragraph upon crisp parchment. "... Better than your own personal scribe, this quill will pen your dictations with care and flourish without any unsightly inkblots or smears. Not for the writer in a hurry, but for those who seek to make an impression upon the page ..."

Charms were usually written off as simple magic, but while their functions often seemed simple, the magic required could be remarkably intricate.

"Maybe," Raiden murmured with a shrug. If this shop owner did his own charm work, he could very well be capable of accomplishing Raiden's troublesome task.

Raiden stepped inside, and the door chimed above him again. The shop was filled with freestanding shelves, no taller than his shoulder, lined up parallel to one another in two columns on either side of the shop. More shelves filled every wall from floor to ceiling. He looked around, expecting to spot the customer who had set off the doorbell moments before him, but saw no one other than the shop owner perched atop a ladder organizing various bobbles on a high shelf. Had he imagined that first chime, or had it come from another shop? No, he was sure of it. His thoughts seized in the sticky sensation of déjà vu. He felt as though he'd been here before.

"Looking for anything in particular?" the shop owner asked without turning away from his task on the high shelf.

"You're Tovar, I presume?"

"Indeed I am."

"How do you organize your merchandise here?"

Tovar set down a ceramic lion, which began to prowl the shelf back and forth. Then, taking care to hold on to the ladder, he turned to look down at Raiden. His eyebrows crept up his forehead.

"You'll find those shelves there are mostly of whim and fancy," he said, pointing to the shelves near the window. "Nothing all that useful. These shelves here will have more-practical items," he said, pointing to the shelves below him and opposite the center aisle toward the center of the shop. "And as you move farther back, you will find items with more-complex functions."

Raiden gave a grateful nod and turned to examine the man's portfolio of work. He tried not to hurry to the shelves in the back too eagerly, but he wanted to know what Tovar was capable of, whether he could possibly help him.

"You do all your own spell work? Repairs too, in case anything needs it?" Raiden asked casually.

Tovar paused with a peculiar look on his face. Raiden couldn't decide whether he seemed amused by the question or uncertain of his answer.

"All mine," he confirmed, "and yes, I provide maintenance on my own work, no charge." Tovar climbed down the ladder as he answered.

"I see," Raiden murmured, examining a shelf of kitchenware, kettles, mugs, dishes, and utensils. Little plaques on the edges of the shelves told what each item did.

Polite Kettle—no unpleasant shrieking. That kettle had to require a noise-canceling charm to stop the obnoxious whistle and also some kind of alert charm triggered by the activation of the other.

Everwarm Mug—keeps hot drinks hot but doesn't burn you. Raiden supposed that was a heat charm and a containing spell.

Drop-Resistant Dishes. This one had no further description, so Raiden picked up a plate and let it fall from his hands. The plate dropped but stopped itself halfway to the floor and reversed, flying back into his hands. He couldn't begin to count how many different charms this plate used. Surely it had, at the very least, a reversal charm and an antigravity charm, but it also would require some other magic that activated the others based on the speed at which the plate was moving. Just trying to work it out required searching the repertoire of spells in his head, and still he couldn't be sure he knew which ones this object used.

"Find anything you like?" Tovar asked in passing as he returned to the long, narrow counter at the back of the shop. He sat down on his stool behind the counter.

As Raiden considered his answer, he noticed a barely audible hum that seemed to come from the walls, but it lasted only a moment. In fact, it was so brief his thoughts were easily possessed once again by the sense of familiarity in this shop.

"I wonder if you might work on something that isn't yours? For compensation of course," Raiden said.

This man could very well do what Raiden needed, but could Raiden trust him? Tovar would recognize the mask, and the moment Raiden explained what he wanted, Tovar would understand that Raiden was committing treason—not to mention that Tovar would be guilty as well. For some reason Raiden had the sense that he *should* trust this man, although he could not fathom why a complete stranger should instill such confidence.

The moment Raiden convinced himself not to take the risk, he noticed something odd again, this time the slightest pulse in his head, as though a ripple of atmospheric pressure had rolled through the shop. He'd definitely felt that and had heard the hum without a doubt. There was something hidden here beneath a cloaking spell. Raiden was particularly good at sensing them, but it was not something he had learned from his books. He'd learned this exceptional skill by accident nine years ago, the day his world had been torn apart.

Memories of that day seemed to be lashing out from his subconscious with a vengeance the last few days, hitting him as hard as visions did. He remembered his mother apologizing before pushing him into the tiny closet and locking him in. Then the terror of Cantis had begun. While he'd been trapped inside, all he'd had to do was listen for those countless hours. The reason he'd never been found, why the blood in his veins hadn't been sniffed out by the golems: a cloaking spell. After all those hours, he'd eventually grown numb to the sounds of screams, the cacophony of chaos as people tried to fight back but drowned beneath the tide of monsters and blood. His senses had found solace in something else, that infinitesimal pulse and hum of the cloak his mother had placed on the door.

His heart gave a sharp knock against his chest, rapping against the closet door of his memory and recalling him to reality. Tovar had a secret—there was a cloaking spell at work here.

"Perhaps," Tovar answered. "What sort of thing needs work?"

"Something the Council can't know about." Raiden risked it and waited for Tovar's response, hoping he wouldn't have to hold the illegal cloaking spell as leverage.

"Meddling with the Council's affairs—that is a dangerous game you are asking me to play." Tovar's voice was far more lighthearted than one's should be when discussing treason, and he looked almost on the verge of smiling at some joke Raiden wasn't privy to.

"I get the feeling you know the game well enough," Raiden answered, somewhat perplexed by Tovar.

"Indeed I do," he said with a chuckle as he moved out from behind his counter and crossed the shop to lock the door.

"So you're willing to commit treason for a stranger ... just like that?" Raiden grew wary, wondering if Tovar was being a little too trustworthy.

"Oh, I think you'll find there are more than a few people in Atrium who are willing to defy the Council," Tovar said, turning back to face Raiden.

"You have ties to the rebellion, then?"

"Most people in this city are rebels; they're just too afraid to admit it. Treason laws, you know. Me, I like a good challenge. What have you got for me?" he asked, rubbing his hands together.

Raiden reached behind his back and pulled the mask from the inner pocket of his coat. He thought briefly about how he could possibly spin this to the Council if Tovar were to turn him in, but he insisted to himself once more that the man had a cloaking spell in his shop. Tovar was hiding something too. Raiden was resolved to take the risk.

"I want to hide a listening spell in this," he said, giving the mask a little shake as Tovar closed the distance between them, his eyes alight with fascination. "Without compromising any of the magic already there, and it has to be completely undetectable," he added.

"Naturally," Tovar agreed. "May I?" He extended his hand in request to take the mask.

Raiden held it out for him to take.

Tovar turned the mask over in his hands. "That's a lot of magic to sort through," he murmured, nodding.

"Of course, I understand if it's too much to ask," Raiden said.

Tovar raised his eyes to meet Raiden's. "Nonsense. I'll need assistance since many of these spells will only be active when the mask is being worn. Shall we start?"

"Now?"

"I was about to close up anyway."

"You don't want to know why or discuss payment?" Raiden could almost laugh at how ridiculous this seemed. "You don't even know my name."

Tovar smiled. "Well, you haven't told me your name."

"It's Raiden."

"All right, Raiden, I might hazard a guess that if you're willing to commit treason, then whatever your motivations are, they must be rather personal. Seeing as we're going to be spending quite some time together, I presume you will tell me eventually. And as for payment, I can't determine the cost of this job until after I know how much work it will require. This is a tricky one," he said, holding up the mask.

"Right," Raiden said with a slow nod.

"Come on." Tovar waved at him to follow as he moved back behind the counter once more.

Caeruleus's footsteps echoed around the great hall as he returned, surprised to be called back so soon. The door closed automatically behind him. He carried a bag over one shoulder, with the clothes Raiden had given him and a few other items crucial for his carefully crafted plan to apprehend the fera. After receiving the message to report directly to the Council, he was anxious to hear that a portal had finally opened. The anticipation was worse than the risk.

"Has a portal opened?" he asked from a greater distance than he should have.

"Our seers have glimpsed a portal at sea in the near future."

Caeruleus sank with disappointment. He knew this was no guarantee that a portal would open. What the seers had seen ten minutes ago could change in an hour if the fera were to change her mind and do something differently, like leave wherever she was and thus avoid opening a portal. He had hoped they were sending him to an already open portal. But the potential for *something* was better than nothing and another night in the courts on a cot instead of his own bed.

"Where?"

"Somewhere between Cantis and the mainland. We have a ship heading that way, and they are expecting your arrival," one of the councilwomen explained. "The ship is equipped to determine the precise location. Once you're in the other realm, the fera should be easy to trace—she cannot hide her magic there."

"We don't care how you do it, so long as you bring the fera back to Atrium," the councilman at the center of the crescent said in a severe voice.

"Understood," Caeruleus answered.

"In that case we will send you on your way."

The room spun before he had the chance to brace himself, but he regained his balance before his vision even cleared. The walls around him were curved, as if he were standing in the long belly of a beast.

"Good. You made it," a woman's voice said.

He turned around to find who had spoken. A woman sat reclined on a pile of cargo, tapping the toes of her boots together. She had only an inch or so of straight black hair and wore a pale teal jumpsuit paired with a large slate-gray jacket.

"I hate to think anyone hasn't," he said, looking around. He was standing on a circular platform.

"Well, not since they started using the beacon platform," she explained as she stood up. "Made of crystal—acts as a sort of magnet for anyone interbounding in so they don't miss. Moving target, after all. Captain Rhee." She held out her hand.

"Caeruleus." He shook her hand.

"Aren't you the pretty one?" she added, looking him up and down once. "The Council likes the pretty ones. I suppose the people respond better to attractive law keepers." She chuckled.

"You're the captain—shouldn't you be on the deck?"

"I don't fly this thing all by my lonesome. Besides, I wanted to welcome you to the *Tempest* myself. Not to mention when the Council demands you drop your cargo orders to fly halfway to the middle of nowhere late at night, you can't help being a little curious."

"I can't exactly tell you what my mission is."

"What can you vaguely tell me, then?"

"What did the Council tell you?"

"Gave us a location in the middle of the ocean and an order to get there fast. Said to expect one of their men and that we're out here looking for a portal. That's it. All this trouble to close a portal? Didn't think those things were a problem anymore."

"I'm not assigned to close it. I have business in the other realm. That's all I can say."

"In that case it might get pretty boring in here while we wait," she said, returning to the pile of cargo to sit back down.

"I can't help what's classified," Caeruleus said with a shrug.

She nodded and rubbed her bristly head. "True. But when it comes to the Council, 'classified' usually means something borderline or outright illegal. Of course, when you make the laws, you can bend them."

"What do you mean? Has the Council given you assignments that are illegal?"

"That information is classified," she said, folding her arms behind her head. "I'm just here to bring you to a portal."

Caeruleus sighed, lowered his bag to the floor, and pulled off his coat and tunic.

"I'm not *that* bored," Captain Rhee chuckled.

"I'm just changing my clothes," he clarified as he pulled on the long-sleeve shirt from the bag.

"No sense of humor," she said. "Stakes must be high, then."

"You've got that right," he muttered.

"What are the chances you get yourself killed?"

"Well, if I prepared for this right, I'm hoping it's unlikely, but realistically … fifty-fifty," he said.

"In that case, do you need to say any last words?"

"Yeah, I probably should have said goodbye to my friend," he said with a dry laugh.

18. Foe

The blaring of a foghorn jerked Nicole out of her slumber. When she realized it was Mitchell's alarm, she shoved her face back into the pillow, waiting for the alarm to turn off. An obnoxious minute of monotonous foghorn blasts passed, and then another. She let out a groan muffled by memory foam. At last there was silence. Her body relaxed into the bed once more, and her mind sank easily back into bizarre dream soup.

It felt like only a few seconds later that Mitchell shouted, "Oh, shit! How did I not hear my alarm?"

Nicole opened her eyes wide with a sudden guilty realization. "Uh-oh," she moaned, realizing she had unknowingly silenced the alarm earlier.

She could hear Mitchell cussing and hissing in his room, closing drawers with careless bangs, so she jumped out of bed and dug through her bag for some clothes. Once she had her hands on a pair of athletic leggings, a thong, a bra, and a loose gray shirt, she set them in a wad on the bed. With one look down at her pajamas and a mental tally of her garments, she nodded, let her magic race through her and into her hands, and snapped her fingers. The air around her flared with heat and a spark-like static. The clean clothes on the bed were suddenly on her body, and the sleep clothes were in a heap on the bed instead.

She looked down at her bare feet and groaned, "Ugh, socks." Her bag wiggled, and two socks ejected themselves from among the other contents and flew into her hand. With a victorious smile she yanked the socks on and shoved her feet into the nearest pair of shoes, her running shoes as usual.

In less than a minute she was in the hallway outside Mitchell's room.

"What's up, Mitch?" she asked, cringing because she already knew he was late. That was obvious, and it was her fault. Nicole suddenly realized she hadn't seen Gordan. She looked around, leaned back to peer into their room, and saw the bed was empty.

"It's eight fifty, and my class starts at nine," he said as he pulled on his chucks.

Nicole wandered down the hall and found Gordan sitting on the couch studying the comic books again.

Mitchell appeared behind her. "If I hurry, I'll only be ten minutes late." His attempt at optimism sounded more like dread as he hunted down a textbook and shoved it in a mostly limp backpack with mermaids riding T-rexes all over it. "Keys, keys, keys."

"Oh, come on," Nicole said. "Gordan, let's go with Mitch."

Gordan set the comic book down. "Where are we going?"

"I don't think that's a good—"

"Just think of the bathroom closest to your class that will hopefully have an empty stall. Otherwise things will get really weird."

"What? You mean I'm steering?" he said with a nervous laugh.

"Yep," she said, grabbing his hand and Gordan's. "One."

"Nikki, I don't know—"

"Two. If you don't pick a destination, I have no idea what will happen," she said.

"Okay," he caved.

"Three."

A clanging, deafening alarm sounded, reverberating in the mostly empty cargo hold.

"Sounds like your portal finally opened," Rhee said, wiggling a finger in her ear after the alarm went silent. She didn't seem as startled or disturbed by the sound as Caeruleus.

"Have you always had portal locators on this ship?" Caeruleus asked as he consulted his own compass.

"Naturally. All ships have 'em. Wouldn't want to run into one by accident when you're cloud sailing. Not that it's really a problem these days since the

Council's relocation efforts. I've only had about, what, three portals across Veil in the last ten years? That's including this one. Wouldn't know about the Wastelands, though. None of us fly out there."

"There have been as many in Cantis in the last week," Caeruleus said.

"Has there now?" Rhee sat up with interest. "I suppose you know why."

"I do," he said. "But that's—"

"Classified, yeah, I've heard," she said with a chuckle.

"Captain," a mechanized voice said overhead, "we've got the portal in sight. Where do you want us?"

Captain Rhee went over to a box on the wall—Caeruleus suspected a vox system like the ones used in the courts to connect the agents' masks. She flipped on a switch beside the box. "Back us up to it and open the cargo door. Get us as close as you can, Pep."

"You got it," Pep answered, and the ship gave a little lurch and a dip.

"Pep can fly this thing better than I can," Rhee said. "Should be able to get us right up to it so you can stroll on through."

"Great," Caeruleus said, wobbling a little with the ship's movements and trying to hide the grimace of nausea on his face.

"This is your first time on an alatus ship," she observed. "Takes a while to get used to, but everyone does eventually. I've spent so much time on the outside of the ship that I couldn't stand my hair anymore." She rubbed her hand over her head. "Had to shave it. Just drove me nuts out there."

Before Caeruleus could remark, the massive door at the end of the cargo hold opened with a clang and great metal moans. Outside was a dark landscape, the star-smattered blue sky over a vast black ocean reflecting the moonlight. As soon as the door was open, the cargo hold became a whirlwind. His own black hair, although not overly long, broke into a chaotic dance, slapping against his ears and whipping at his eyes. He could understand Rhee's choice now.

They walked to the opening, having to lean against a gust of wind as they got close.

"They aren't easy to see," she said. "Hence the alarm system and the sensors."

"That's why I have this." Caeruleus held up his compass. With a flick of his fingers, the middle of the compass turned out on a hidden hinge. It was a round glass like a large monocle—a druid's glass, made from stones with naturally occurring holes. Looking through the hole allowed one to see things otherwise unseen, like portals. Alchemists could transmute the stones into glass while leaving the magical properties unaltered.

He held up the glass, and Captain Rhee leaned in, bumping her cheek against his to look through it as well.

The seascape was muted and colorless in the druid's glass. The naked eye could see only a moonlit sea and stars drifting endlessly toward the watery line of the horizon. The glass revealed a bright, swirling pool of light.

"Well, there you go." Rhee sounded impressed. "Portal straight ahead," she said, pointing out the open cargo door. She chuckled. "You might want a running start, though."

Caeruleus said nothing, trying not to choke on his apprehension or think about his distinct inability to interbound or about how the Council hadn't given him wings yet and they would be pretty useful right about now. He took a few steps back and looked at the three body lengths of running surface he had.

Before he could muster up the courage to run, he thought of something. "The ship is going to stay here, right?"

"Call her by her name, please." Rhee folded her arms.

Caeruleus sighed. "The *Tempest* will be here waiting for me to return?"

"The Council didn't mention it," she said. Then she laughed at his horrified expression. "Relax. Of course we'll wait. But you did say your chances were fifty-fifty. I've got no way of knowing what's going on over there. We can't wait forever, you know."

"Of course not," he agreed and thought a moment. "Give me three hours?"

"I'll give you until sunrise; that's about six," she said, extending her hand once more to him.

He gripped her hand with the force of his gratitude. "Thank you."

"Good luck over there, whatever you're up to."

He nodded and took a deep breath and one last glance through the druid's glass to verify the portal was dead ahead before closing up the compass and putting it back in his pocket. Then he ran as hard as he could, keeping his eyes trained on the stars straight in front of him. He reached the end of the cargo door and jumped.

Gordan, Mitchell, and Nicole emerged from the air abruptly to find themselves wedged into a bathroom stall.

Nicole laughed when she heard Gordan let out a sigh of relief.

Mitchell let out a groan of nausea.

"Aim for the toilet, Mitch," Nicole said, trying not to laugh as she pushed her way past the stall door, Gordan close behind her.

A guy standing at the sinks, leaning close to his reflection to examine his face, looked at Nicole in the mirror.

"Hey," she said with a nonchalant wave.

The guy raised his eyebrows, turned, and left.

Gordan gave her a questioning look.

"It's the men's room," she explained.

"Oh," he said but still looked confused.

Mitchell finally staggered out of the stall. "That was worse than yesterday."

"Don't look at me," she said, putting her hands up. "You were driving this time."

He answered with a grunt.

"Well, you better get to class. We're going to wander around campus," she said as she strolled out of the men's bathroom. Gordan and Mitchell followed.

"Yeah, see you later." His voice still sounded a little sickened.

Nicole and Gordan made their way out of the science building to find the sky crisp and blue overhead. Although the air was chilly and the breeze biting, the sunshine was warm during brief still moments.

"I love this campus," Nicole said.

There were students everywhere, making their way to classes in the surrounding buildings. She felt a pang of sadness as she looked around at the red brick buildings and the streams of students flowing around them. As grateful as she had been to escape her mundane, cookie-cutter high school life, she had been looking forward to this, choosing her own path, courses, and future.

"This is where you want to be," Gordan said, looking around at the campus scene.

"Yeah." Her answer was wistful. "It's not so much about the place as finally getting to direct my life, figure out which direction I want to go and who I want to be. How do you move forward when you're constantly running from your problems?" she muttered.

They crossed the long, open mall, its grass yellow. As her magic slowly seeped out of her and sank into the ground, the grass turned green, but with so many people walking across the mall, it wasn't obvious that Nicole was the cause. Students stopped where they were, marveling. Several bicyclists and skateboarders on the paths on either side of the rectangular space stopped in awe when they noticed the transformation.

Nicole kept walking as if she didn't notice. To their left, at the end of the mall, was the Old Main building, standing like a monument to the old west with white wooden stairs leading up to its wraparound porch. Across the mall was the massive modern structure that housed the bookstore, student union, food court, and Canyon Café.

Before they stepped inside the café, the door opened, and the thick, warm scent of coffee and sticky, sweet pastries hit their faces.

"Would I be right to guess we are here for a … cappuccino?"

Nicole laughed, putting an arm around Gordan as she did to her brothers and her dad. "You catch on quick," she said.

His heart lurched into a frenzy. He sailed briefly through the cold, salty air, certain he would simply fall down into the black ocean. But as quick as the thought crossed his mind, the night around him disintegrated into blinding white sunshine, and he fell just a few feet to land on solid ground.

Caeruleus was frozen in shock and relief for a moment, his hands and knees partly buried in loose dirt. He picked himself up, suspecting that he had fallen no more than his own height. Brushing his hands clean and then swatting the damp sand from his legs, he looked around and realized he was in a mostly dry riverbed of some kind, although the dirt banks on either side were unnaturally steep.

He picked up his bag and dug through it to find his anchor, an old, dingy potion bottle, and jammed it down into the moist sand so that it stood upright, partially buried. Quickly, he checked his pocket for the bottle stopper, a little brass rose atop a piece of cork—the jump token that would return him to the anchor. Getting the fera back to the portal and into Veil as swiftly as possible was key. He tucked the stopper back into his pocket.

Not far from him, the dirt banks became less steep and shrank down to almost nothing, and there was a bridge that spanned the wash. When he reached the shade of the bridge, he noticed a low, rumbling whoosh that sounded overhead at varying intervals. A stone staircase led up to the bridge. As he ascended the steps, he pulled out his compass.

There were three separate arrows on the compass, each pointing toward the nearest sources of magic in the area. The gold arrow indicated the direction of the magic closest to him, the silver arrow pointed toward the second-nearest source of magic, and the black arrow pointed to the next-closest source.

Once on top of the bridge, Caeruleus studied the face of the compass. The silver and black arrows both pointed steadily to the northeast from where he stood. The gold arrow was pointing to his left, north, toward the portal down in the wash, but the gold arrow was not still like the other two. Every second or so the gold arrow twitched toward the northeast, in the direction of the other two arrows.

"Easy to find," he muttered and made his way across the bridge heading east, holding the compass before him.

Nicole and Gordan were seated at a table outside, her with a steaming paper cup in her hands, carefully balancing her worries and hopes—with the help of cinnamon-dusted cappuccino foam—into a moment of contentment.

"Here, try it," she insisted.

Gordan took the cup with a skeptical look.

She laughed. "Just try it."

He took a sip and handed the cup back. "That's rather ..."

"Delicious?"

"Interesting," he finished.

"I'll accept that answer," she said, taking a drink.

Nicole's gaze drifted around the campus. The expressions and gaits of the various students told her whether they were late for class or had nowhere to be, or just didn't care that they were late. Friends walked in pairs and trios, and people hurried along while looking down at their cell phones. There was a steady stream of students heading for a morning coffee or a quick breakfast from the student union.

Her mind wandered, and she hardly seemed to see the people passing through her gaze. What was Raiden doing in Veil right now? Assimilating to his new life? Maybe the Council trusted him and he could actually live something like a real life there. She smiled at the idea of him being so lucky.

Then she realized her eyes had locked on a young man with jet-black hair. There was something familiar about him that had forced its way through her thoughts. The bottom half of his long-sleeve shirt was dark gray with horizontal white pinstripes, and from the collar to the elbows the shirt was turquoise.

Her heart hammered against her chest before she even understood why. This man was wearing Raiden's clothes—she couldn't possibly be imagining it—and he was walking right at her, his eyes fixed on her.

"Nicole?"

She could hear the confusion and concern in Gordan's voice, but it was nearly drowned out by the thunder in her chest. Her mind raced. *Get away.*

Don't let that primal instinct take over. Don't fight with all these people around.
She jumped up, pushing away from the table and knocking her chair down
with a clang, and ran.

Gordan involuntarily tensed as the air around Nicole turned into a cloud of
dread. She jumped up and practically turned the table over as she whirled
around and broke into a run. A man bolted after her, and finally Gordan
understood. He lurched to his feet and bounded after them, his eyes locked
on the man in pursuit of Nicole.

Gritting his teeth, Gordan struggled to catch up, not for lack of speed but
from avoiding the people in his path. A pack of pedestrians crossed in front
of him, and he gave up his human pretenses, leaping clear over the crowd of a
dozen or more students.

A chorus of "Whoa!" and "Did you see that?" met his ears as his feet hit
the ground, and he bounded ahead. Nicole and the man in pursuit ran down
the campus mall. Gordan glared angrily at the man's back, recognizing his shirt
as the one Raiden had been wearing the day he'd been taken from them. The
adrenaline flooding his mind kept him from understanding what that meant.
All he could do was close the distance the pair had put between them and him.

For a split second he considered now might be the time to shed his human
form altogether and get Nicole out of here.

Ahead of Nicole a statue of a large wildcat shook with life and leaped
down from its pedestal. Nearby students screamed at the incredible sight as
the statue came bounding to Nicole's aid, pouncing over her and pinning the
man in Raiden's clothes to the pavement. Gordan sailed over the statue and its
catch, landing on the other side with Nicole.

Gordan halted beside Nicole, both of them facing her adversary, who was
stuck beneath a stone paw. Students all around the mall stood frozen, watching
the unbelievable happen before their eyes. Gordan kept his eye on Nicole. Her
hands were balled into white-knuckled fists, and her whole body was shaking.
Waves of anger rolled off of her. The sheer force of that rage stunned him.

"No," she murmured to herself, barely audible. Then she raised her voice
and it trembled with hate. "I am *done* running from you." The pavement
under her feet cracked, and fractures slithered through the cement as her anger
radiated off of her.

"Nicole." Gordan spoke her name in hopes of breaking the strange trance
she was in. She appeared to be enchanted, enthralled by her blinding fury that
only seemed to be growing.

"What gives you the right?" she demanded, approaching the man under the statue as he struggled to squeeze out from under the massive paw on his chest.

"You're"—he struggled to answer, but answer he did—"a threat. To both realms."

"No, just to you," she said with venom.

Gordan glared at the man squirming and realized he was trying to reach the bag he'd been carrying, just out of reach beneath the statue's belly. Before Gordan could act, the man managed to retrieve something from it. Gordan didn't recognize the object, but the man pointed it at Nicole, and it fired at her like a strange, explosive wand.

Gordan grabbed Nicole by the shirt, yanking her aside without a second thought, pulling her off her feet as the humming violet spell slipped by her. Nicole hit the ground, untouched by the spell. People around them screamed. In that moment the statue shuddered, seized by a spell that sucked it into a small metal box in their visitor's hands. Gordan lunged for the man as he scrambled to his feet, scooped up the box, and opened it. The statue was expelled from the box the moment the lid opened, catching Gordan and knocking him to the ground under its incredible weight. He was barely able to shift it off of him.

Nicole picked herself up with fire in her eyes. In fact, Gordan thought he saw a glint of green, a spark of the power inside her.

The man held his weapon at arm's length and fired again, three successive blasts of the same buzzing purple spell. All three slowed to a halt before they could get to her, and suddenly they reversed, shooting back at him with double the force. He dived out of the way as he took another shot. This one flew toward Gordan instead of Nicole.

The spell only grazed his leg, but the effects took hold. Gordan's leg went numb, useless. It buckled under him, and he fell to his knee, his leg paralyzed.

Seeing Gordan fall, Nicole froze in a moment of terror. A fresh wave of outrage crashed over her.

"It's only a paralysis spell," Gordan said, as though that made it okay.

But Nicole was seething, seeing red. There was nothing but fire in her veins. She held out her hand, and a flood of magic shot through her arm, extending her reach across the space between her and her enemy. When she closed her hand, her magic took hold of the man's gun. She could feel the pressure of her magic's grip around the gun as though her actual hand had a hold of it. She pulled as hard as she could. The gun didn't break from the man's grip, but he was pulled toward her, his feet slipping against the ground. His blue eyes went wide with panic, and he fired again.

Instinctively, she opened her hand and held it up as a shield against the spell. The purple bolt nearly hit her palm, but a pulse of energy erupted from her hand. As the two opposing forces met, she was pushed back, her own feet sliding against the pavement. Then the gun's spell reversed course, turning black and tearing through the air erratically before it struck the man in the face.

He fell backward and hit the ground, a terrible cry of agony escaping his chest as he writhed, one hand clutching his face. Nicole cringed. His other trembling hand disappeared into his pocket, and in a blink he was gone.

Nicole pushed her fingers up into her hair and took a firm grip against her scalp. She couldn't hear anything but her pulse pounding in her head, her body humming and surging with adrenaline, her heart crashing savagely against her rib cage as she tried to slow her breaths.

"Gordan." Her mind lurched back to him, and she removed her hands from her hair, turning to him. She ran to his side and sank to the ground. She took his arm and wrapped it around her neck to help him stand.

"It's not serious," he insisted.

The sound of his voice stood out in stark contrast to the remarkable silence surrounding them, inhabited only by the whisper of the morning breeze and the birds singing their usual songs. Students all around the mall stood dumbfounded. Some were holding up their cell phones; others merely stared openmouthed. Anyone arriving to the scene halted as though there were something contagious in the air.

"I think it's time to go," she muttered, holding on to Gordan more tightly before letting a burst of magic out of her core. It swept them up, and they escaped, slipping into the silence.

Caeruleus landed in the dirt beneath the portal, hardly able to perceive anything but the blinding pain in his head, his eye a red-hot coal inside his skull. Fighting against the waves of agony that seized his body, he felt around him with his free hand, searching the sand for the bottle.

At last his hand knocked against the glass, and he grasped the neck of the bottle. He managed to sit up, still clutching his face. With a shaking breath, he hurled the bottle into the air overhead. He let out a great sigh of relief as the anchor disappeared into the portal.

Then he reached into his pocket with the desperate hope that the jump token would still work if the anchor was broken.

Captain Rhee returned to the cargo hold with a steaming tea spiked with a vigil's brew to stave off sleep. She took a sip of the warm drink, studying the view out the open cargo door, closing one eye and then the other in an attempt to see the portal. Suddenly a glinting object flew right at her face. Her hand moved reflexively, snatching it from the air before it could hit her.

"A bottle?"

Then almost immediately Caeruleus appeared at her feet, slumped over on his hands and knees, hissing in pain.

She dropped the bottle and her cup, spilling her tea across the floor as she crouched beside him.

"What happened?" she asked as she took his shoulders and sat him upright. His head lolled back, turning his face up at her, and she saw. The left side was swollen, his eye a bulging, bleeding mass.

"Oh ..." She had to swallow back the disgusted shock that rolled up her esophagus. The sight made her stomach churn. "Come on," she said, choking back her nausea and helping him to his feet. "We have a healer on board."

She placed herself under his arm like a crutch and managed to get him to the doorway out of the cargo hold. Beside the door was a speaker and a switch. She flicked the switch up and barked into the little box, "Pep! Wake up Alek. Get us back to Atrium, and close the damn cargo door."

19. Return

Nicole held Gordan's arm and wouldn't let go as he sank down onto the couch.

"Really, I'm fine."

She let go. Then the pacing began. He watched her cross the living room over and over.

"He was wearing Raiden's clothes," she said.

"I noticed." It still troubled his thoughts as well.

"What does that mean?"

Gordan considered his answer for a moment. "I think it means he was trying to send you a message, to warn you ... and it worked. You realized who that man was before he could even get close." He refused to entertain any other possibility.

Gordan turned his thoughts to the man's plan. The man had come prepared with a spell to paralyze her and an enchanted box to contain her. That strategy could have been quite effective if Nicole hadn't spotted him and run. Of course, the spell would only have lasted so long. There was no telling how long it would have affected her, and not being able to move would not have prevented her from using her powers against him. Even if the magic of the box could have contained her powers, it too would not have been able to hold up indefinitely.

But if the man had not been wearing Raiden's clothes, if Nicole had not recognized him when she had, Gordan imagined the man would have walked right up to them and maybe even succeeded at paralyzing them both before they'd realized what was happening. The thought was chilling.

Nicole let out a frustrated sound between a sigh and a groan. "I'm done with this," she said.

"Pardon?"

"I'm not playing this psychotic whack-a-mole game, waiting for them to come through portals so I can hit back." She shook her head. "They use *guns* that shoot magic. I'm not inviting that bullshit into this realm again. And they say I'm the threat to both realms," she growled through her teeth.

Gordan studied her expression, a shadow of that same look from only minutes ago. He could detect no more fear there, as if it had been burned out of her. Just that morning he had wished she could be free of that fear, but he worried about the anger that had replaced it. He knew she was still reeling from the encounter. Even he was still attempting to process what he had seen, how she had changed before his eyes.

"What's our plan, then?" he asked.

She looked at him with fury still burning in her eyes, and he knew she couldn't even find the words for what she wanted to do. Maybe she didn't really know, or maybe it was too terrible to say.

"We're going to Veil," she finally answered.

Caeruleus could hardly focus on what the people around him were saying. His eye was ablaze inside his head, and he was sure it would burn everything inside until it was black and empty.

He could feel hands holding his arms and pushing him back onto a hard surface.

"Can you do something for him?" Captain Rhee snapped at someone.

"I need to know what spell hit him."

"It was," he stammered through his urge to shout, "my own spell—paralysis …"

Caeruleus could see nothing but light and blurs when he opened his good eye.

"What? What's wrong? You said you needed to know the spell; he told you."

"There's still magic in this wound, and it's not a paralysis spell at all. Either he's mistaken, or the spell was changed somehow. This is behaving like an acid hex—"

"Well, do *something*, Alek," Rhee yelled.

"I can numb the pain, but we should get him to the court healers."

"Pep said we'll be there in less than an hour."

There was a moment of silence. Caeruleus tensed with another wave of pain and for a blurry second he saw Alek give Captain Rhee an uncomfortable look.

"What?" Captain Rhee snapped.

"If it takes that long, he'll lose the eye."

"Pep!"

"Yes, Captain?" Pep's voice came as a thin, wobbly answer through the ship's vox system.

"Do we have any translumination cells left?"

"One, Captain."

"Use it."

The raging agony in Caeruleus's head suddenly dissipated, making room for another fire to burn deeper into his thoughts, a berserk hatred for the fera.

Nicole grew more resolute with every passing heartbeat, still heavy with adrenaline and outrage. She turned on her heel and stalked down the hall. Her hands moved without thought as she plucked a hair tie off her wrist, gathered up her curls in both hands, and then pulled the elastic band around her ponytail—it was a ritual to her now whenever she prepared for something serious or strenuous. Until now it had been the start of her challenging herself, setting out for a run or preparing for a heavy lift. Now her hands seemed to know this new challenge called for the ritual. She stepped into the bedroom and grabbed her bag. The books at the top tumbled out along with underwear and a hiking boot.

For a moment she looked at the boot and thought about where she was going. Then she hunched over to pull off her running shoes. She dug out a pair of long, thick socks and shoved her feet into them. Mechanically, she pulled on the boots and laced them up, wrapping the extra-long laces once around her ankles before knotting them. She left her running shoes on the floor beside the bed.

When she picked up the books and stuffed them back into the bag, she noticed her phone on the bed, a notification on the screen. It was a text message from Roxanne: "Marco."

"Polo," she texted back before dropping the phone into her bag and closing it up.

In the silence of the apartment she realized her heart was racing again—or still—but now for a whole new reason. She threw her bag over her shoulder and returned to the living room.

"We're leaving now," she said. She didn't want to wait. She didn't want to lose her nerve. It was time to bring the damn fight to them. She wanted those bastards to know what it was like to be afraid.

Gordan nodded in agreement and stood up, gingerly putting weight on his paralyzed leg. The leg buckled. He cringed but didn't topple over.

"Some feeling is coming back," he said. "But I'll still need assistance." He raised his arm, inviting her back as his crutch.

She suspected this was more for her than him, but she smiled nonetheless and obliged. With the tiny shift in her expression, there came a strange relief. The heat in her body cooled; her heart rate slowed. Her anger receded, but her resolve to go did not.

With Gordan's arm around her neck, she felt a little calmer. She made a silent apology to Mitchell for disappearing as she took one last look around the living room. A surge of hot energy passed over them. In a flash they were standing in the living room of her home back in Yuma. They both shuddered a little at the chill that hit them immediately after the heat of her magic departed.

Everything looked precisely as it had only yesterday, the empty couch watching the silent black television.

"Hello?" Nicole called into the house. There was no answer, no distant sound of Bandit scrambling to get up and greet her.

Her heart sank a little, but she was glad no one was here. She didn't want to tell anyone what she was doing, that she was leaving for Veil to turn the tides on the Council, make *them* the target for once. A fresh tide of anger in her chest lifted her low spirits back up.

Gordan hobbled toward the back door.

"Hold on," she said, holding up a finger. "There's one thing I need to get."

She set her bag down and trotted up the stairs. The silent house felt so wrong to her. It was dark too. Every light was off, and only diffused gray light from the cloudy day outside seeped in through the windows. Up on the landing the hallway was even dimmer, and she felt strange walking down the hall to Raiden's room.

Just inside the door his packed bag still sat against the wall. She crossed the room and dropped to the floor to peer under the bed, where Raiden's sword lay in the shadows, gleaming even in the absence of light. She closed her hand around the metal scabbard, and she was greeted by the same mysterious comfort as when she'd held the sword before. She dragged it out from under the bed and straightened up. She had forgotten how bizarrely light the weapon was. As she swung the sword onto her back, her stomach dropped with anticipation.

She took one last look around the room, glanced down at the bag, and left, crossing the hall with purpose and descending the stairs.

Gordan stood waiting by the back door. "Wise choice," he said as she bent down to pick up her bag and swing it back onto her shoulder.

The yard was still yellow and dry, save for the green path across the yard to the shop. It was a foreign place to her after seeing it so green the past few months. The smooth blanket of clouds overhead felt like a death shroud waiting to drop on her. This was her life now, destruction looming over her instead of tests and assignments, a sword on her back instead of a backpack full of homework. An ironic laugh stirred in her chest but couldn't quite escape the weight of her psyche. For as drastically different as her life now was, it was somehow also the same, still full of people who wanted to tell her who she was, lay down a path for her, and force her into their equation to achieve their goals, whatever they may be.

A deep toll of sadness struck her heart like a bell, and she let it roll off of her freely, releasing the magic always waiting below the surface. It washed over the yard, and in a remarkable instant the scene transformed into the emerald haven it had been before. A thick carpet of clovers sprang up from the ground, and the stiff, scraggly remains of the rosebushes erupted in green leaves and brilliant blossoms. The yard around her was bursting with life again. She could feel it humming against her skin like an echo of the force inside her.

For a peaceful moment she took in the sight, feeling at home again. It gave her the surreal sensation of being back in time, standing in the world as she'd known it a week ago. She half expected to see herself and Raiden walk out the back door of the house or to look up and see Gordan at his post on the roof. But he was beside her, his arm draped over her shoulders. She gave him a grateful squeeze.

"Ready?" she asked.

"As ever," he said.

The place where the first portal had opened seemed as good a place as any to open one last one to leave her life behind. She let her magic expand and form a sort of bubble of charged warmth around her and Gordan. Her view of the yard—thick rosebushes, the still blue pool, the red brick walls—gradually became transparent as she allowed her magic to pour out of her. It was a relief, like exhaling painfully stale air after holding it in for too long. Letting that energy out, although it burned, was as welcome as stepping into the scalding heat of a summer day after being cold soaked.

Then suddenly there came a current of icy air through the warmth, crisp and alive. She knew the taste of this air, filled with magic that raised the hair on her arms. It was Veil.

"Shall we?" Gordan raised his hand toward the portal in invitation.

To Nicole's eyes, the portal was a slightly hazy window through which she could see the forest of Cantis. Raiden hadn't been able to see portals like she did. He claimed most people didn't.

"Can you see the portal?"

"I can see the shimmer around the edges," he said, tracing the oblong shape of the portal in the air with his index finger. "And it looks like a mirage from the corner of my eye," he explained.

They stepped through and emerged on the other side to find it was the middle of the night. The moon overhead was full, and the snow on the ground glowed in the moonlight. Nicole turned back to the portal. The breeze twirled and twisted in little eddies where it met the edges of the portal, and tiny flurries of powdery snow danced, almost glittering, on the ground around her feet. She closed her eyes and felt the Veil air moving around her.

The air tickled her face like the faintest touch of an ostrich feather. Something told her this sensation was the frayed edges of the barrier fluttering and tingling. It was time to stitch those edges back together. Extending her magic out like extra arms, she felt the crackling edges of the portal and pulled them together.

"And you didn't even need the book," Gordan said.

Nicole opened her eyes and reached out in front of her, searching the icy air for the portal. There was nothing but swirls in the snow where the portal had been.

"I don't think I have a mind for spells," she confessed. "I can rarely remember them when I need them. So I have to wing it."

"Well, they're just commands. Spells are merely a manifestation of your will. Your thoughts can be expressed with more than words. Incantations are just one way of teaching magic with uniformity, to bring a little order to the chaos."

"So could I use music to cast spells if I wanted?"

"Certainly. Words are just one of many ways to express our desires and intentions."

Nicole looked around, expecting to see the cliff and the dirt road from when the very first portal had opened into her backyard, and realized they were out in the middle of the forest.

"The portal didn't open in the same place as before," she said.

"As I understand it, Veil isn't fixed to the other realm. It floats in a way, in a separate plane of existence," Gordan explained as he pointed past the trees to the black shape of the tower in the distance. If the tower was there, then the city of Cantis lay in the opposite direction.

Nicole steered them toward the city, their feet crunching in the snow. "So it kind of moves around?"

"Yes, somewhat like death. Death is separate from this realm, and it's strange and fluid. Time does not flow steadily, nor does it always flow in the same direction. It—" Gordan stopped when he glanced down at Nicole.

She was looking at him with both confusion and awe. "You mean death is another realm, like this one?"

"You could say that."

"How do you even know that sort of stuff about death?"

"I met a necromancer in my youth," he said.

Nicole laughed. "You barely look past puberty."

"When I was younger, then," he amended.

Nicole shook her head. "I'll be dust before you even look a year older," she said, stumbling as the terrain became rockier.

"Indeed," he answered with a chuckle. "Now watch where you're going. If you fall, you're taking me with you."

"Yes, Gramps."

Gordan's heart drummed an ominous rhythm whenever he glanced up at the tower in the distance, a bleak reminder of his and Nicole's shared enemy. They still had no idea how they were tied together, but Dawn had plans that somehow involved both him and Nicole.

As time and distance passed beneath them, Gordan gradually put more weight on his leg until he finally managed to walk almost normally. He kept a hand on Nicole's shoulder as they went, his gait uneven with a slight limp caused by a lingering sensation of needles. By the time they wandered past the first silent house and onto a stone-paved road, his strides were even and steady again.

The silence in the presence of the empty streets and buildings was somehow entirely different from the silence of the snowy forest. Their hike through the forest had cooled Nicole's anger into anxiety and almost even something bordering on calm. But now, as they reached the stone-paved streets and empty buildings of the city, Gordan felt her grow uneasy. He understood her need to break the silence.

"I can't believe Raiden spent ten years here when he could have left," she said.

"Revenge is a persistent hunger." Gordan knew this all too well, and he had the feeling Nicole might be feeling those pangs in her own heart.

Gordan took in their surroundings with a solemn gaze. Once or twice his mind tricked him into thinking he saw a pale figure standing in the darkness of a building looking out onto the street and watching them pass. But then he would catch Nicole's or his reflection in the remnants of glass clinging to the window frames.

Nicole broke the silence again. "I think it's this way."

"What?"

"Raiden's house."

Gordan walked beside her as she took slow, uncertain steps and paused to look around and decide between directions. At a T-shaped intersection, she walked out into the middle of the road and checked both left and right.

She pointed left. "It's down there. You can see it, the house between the apartment buildings."

Gordan didn't see it until they were standing in front of it and suspected some kind of spell at work. Perhaps Nicole could see it because she had been here before. He glanced back down the road at their two trails of footprints in the thin layer of snow on the stones. This time he thought he saw a white human shape disappear around a corner, but everything around them was dusted in snow—of course he saw something white. His mind was creating ghosts, probably an unconscious attempt to fill the emptiness where there should have been life.

"You coming?"

Nicole's voice drew his attention back to the house before him. She was already at the front door. He hurried along to follow her inside.

Nicole stepped into the darkness inside the house, only moonlight slipping in through the front windows. She was glad Gordan was right behind her. Despite the real horrors in her life now, darkness still made her uneasy. It felt like a portal through which nightmares could creep out of her mind and into reality. They surveyed the front room—all shades of gray in the limited silver light, furniture coated in veils of dust, the staircase mostly destroyed.

Taking it all in, she walked across the room carefully, as though a careless step might shatter the remains of Raiden's life. She moved into the kitchen. It was dark. A soft white glow from the window revealed only the sink below the window and the once-polished wood counter. Crossing her arms in front of her to block out the cold isolation in the air, she turned to look around.

Gordan was still standing in the living room, taking in all Raiden had lost with an unreadable expression. She didn't have his empathetic gift or even the ability to read his thoughts, but somehow she knew Gordan had never had a home to lose.

She sighed, stepping out of the kitchen and turning left down the short hall, where the light from the front room did not reach. She moved toward the narrow closet door she could barely make out in the shadows. The door creaked as she opened it, revealing only the narrow, rectangular black hole of the closet behind it.

She let out a perplexed "Huh." The magic that had been here was gone. Her heart gave a curious thud. *Has someone been here?* The rhythm of her pulse suggested it had been Raiden.

"What?"

"This door used to … Never mind. Guess we take the stairs."

"What stairs?" Gordan asked with a quiet laugh.

She returned to the front room and looked at what was left of the staircase in the dim shadows of the house.

"Right," she said and took his hand.

They popped from the front room to the landing. The second floor was even dimmer than downstairs, so Nicole summoned a little light that swelled into existence in front of her heart.

She drifted over to the door on the right, her light hovering ahead of her and bouncing off the door. She turned the knob, but the door didn't open at her initial push, so she shoved her shoulder against the wood. The hinges let out a short groan as the door swung open, and she stumbled forward into the room. She stood there a moment, looking around as her light swooped in after her.

The floorboards creaked underneath her as she stood there shifting her weight from one leg to the other. There was a bed for one in the middle of the room. The ceiling above was painted into a dark ocean of stars, and every wall was a window to some distant sky. The wall straight ahead, across the room, was a vibrant sunset terrain of mountainous clouds that spilled onto the neighboring wall, where the sky turned blue and birds soared among the cumulous mounds. She turned to face the wall behind her, where Gordan stood waiting outside the door in the hall. The continuous sky turned into a sunrise on this wall, with the great glowing disk sliced in half by the horizon of the floor. On the fourth wall, behind the bed where Raiden had slept as a boy, the sky became dusk, a faint gradient of the sun's pink and orange light fading into the starry ceiling.

Nicole was almost dizzy from turning around to take in the mural. She wondered whether Raiden's mother had painted it, what it had been like growing up in a room that made you feel like you were flying, what it had been like to have that life crumble around you. Her head spun with sadness and awe, eyes stinging and throat clenching.

She left the room abruptly, closing the door again behind her.

"Wrong room," she said, crossing the hall to the other door, which opened more easily.

This time Gordan followed as she entered. The room came alive as Nicole's light chased after her, turning the large black mounds around the shadowy room into Raiden's great nest of books. It looked exactly as it had the last time she had been here, so much so that she felt she had stepped back in time again by walking through that doorway.

Nicole heaved her bag onto the bed but left the sword hanging between her shoulder blades. She liked the feel of it there, its soft weight unbefitting its size and the strange calm it seemed to imbue through contact. She turned back to Gordan.

"Here it is." She smiled. "Last time I was in this room, I found my way to you."

Gordan looked around. "It's remarkable, isn't it? To look back and see the clear path formed by chance," he said in a distant tone.

"Yeah," she agreed, looking around for herself. Her eyes fell onto the desk, where a pocket watch sat atop a piece of paper folded in half.

"And what about the path ahead?" he asked. "Where do we go from here?"

Nicole picked up the pocket watch and turned it over in her hands. It was brass, smooth, ordinary, and yet its weight in her hand felt tremendous. Her heart fluttered with some knowledge her brain was slow to accept.

"We head for the mainland, I guess," she said as she passed the watch to her left hand and picked up the folded paper with her right. Her heart pounded harder. These things had not been here the last time she had been in this room. The pocket watch and the folded paper—a note—had been left here sometime after that night.

Her heart skipped. The note was from Raiden. She was suddenly nervous, uncertain whether she wanted to read it or not. Not now at least. She didn't want to read it in front of Gordan and subject him to whatever emotional roller coaster might be waiting for her inside. Mostly she was afraid of what she would feel when she read it. So she slipped the paper into her pocket and turned back to Gordan.

"It *would* be best to fly to the mainland under the cover of night," Gordan said. "Not a bad night for flying either," he added. "It's clear, and the moon is full."

"Someone once told me people out in the middle of the night are probably up to disreputable things," she said, trying to hold back her grin.

"Well, he would be right—a fera and a dragon sneaking across the sea to the mainland where neither is welcome?" he said with a subtle curl to his mouth. "What's that?"

"Just a pocket watch," she said, opening it to check the time. The numbers on the watch face went up to thirteen, and she couldn't help smiling at the simultaneous strangeness and similarity of Veil to the world she knew, both foreign and familiar to her. Being here was enchanting and frightening all at the same time. The hands on the watch face indicated that it was 12:17. *Less than an hour until midnight.*

"I suppose we should get going. I just felt like I should come back. It's the only place I know here."

"I understand," he said.

She stepped over to the bed and tucked the pocket watch into one of the small outer pockets of her pack before she picked it up and swung it onto her shoulder. "Okay, let's go."

They left the room of books behind, and on the landing Nicole took Gordan's hand to interbound them from the second floor down to the front door. Although she knew that she might never come back and that Raiden might never come back either, she felt the need to close the door and lock it behind her, to protect the memories inside perhaps. With her hand on the knob, she let her magic rush down her arm and into the door, filling it with her intent to keep intruders out.

"And no one ever opened it again," Gordan said as though narrating.

Nicole let herself laugh, feeling indecent making such a carefree sound in such a sorrowful silence.

"A *day* with Mitchell, and he rubs off on you," she said, shaking her head. "One day." Her tone sank as she heard herself—perhaps their last day with him ... *No.* She wrenched her thoughts in the other direction. *I won't accept defeat before the fight.*

"Are you quite finished with that little internal struggle of yours?"

"Oh, shut up and mind your own emotions," she warned, trying not to let him see the smile attempting to seize her lips or hear the laughter behind her words.

He chuckled. "We should head to the beach."

"Why?"

"Vertical takeoffs are not my forte," he confessed.

Nicole looked around. The streets were narrow and crowded by buildings three, four, and five stories high, and whoever had planned Cantis had had something against a grid system. She had no idea which direction they were even facing after their hunt for Raiden's house.

"All right, which way?"

"That way," he answered with utter confidence, pointing down the street.

"How do you even know?" she demanded.

He tapped his nose twice and smiled.

"Of course," she chuckled. "Lead the way."

20. Beach

Gordan led them through the maze of city streets and buildings by following the salty scent of the ocean in the air and listening to the call of the winds singing over the sea. At last they were upon the main road leaving the city proper and heading to the piers where Cantis most certainly had had an industrious relationship with the sea and her fruits.

They were headed toward the southern end of the crescent-shaped beach where the short Cantis peninsula curled southeastward out to sea. The city's streets and structures were clustered directly west of the beach but did not extend onto the peninsula, which was inhabited entirely by trees and rocks.

The beach was in sight ahead of them, the tiny patch of forest on the peninsula off to their right. He caught sight of a pale figure among the trees, and this time he knew it was no trick of snowy reflections in old windows. There was someone else here on this island, someone who was following them.

He didn't want to alarm Nicole or their unknown voyeur. Unsure whether this person was with the Council or Venarius, Gordan decided to be discreet.

"Go on down to the beach. I will follow soon," he said, stopping on the road.

"Why?" she asked, looking around, her light still floating over her shoulder.

"I've got to"—he searched for a lie—"relieve myself," he finished with a shrug.

"Oh," she laughed. "Take your time, then." With that she proceeded toward the beach.

Gordan turned and marched into the trees where he'd last glimpsed the stranger. As he wandered out to the end of the peninsula, the terrain grew ever more rocky. Great, jagged boulders protruded from the earth around the slender, bare trees.

He continued until he could see the sea and several little rocky islands off the end of the peninsula through the last of the trees. Here, the mysterious figure appeared again. He stepped out from behind a tree, turning to Gordan with a politely neutral expression on his face. He was young, not young enough to be considered a boy but not quite a man. He was entirely pale—not just pale but faint and insubstantial, even slightly translucent.

"You're a keeper of death," Gordan said, understanding at once.

"I am," he answered.

"I don't need to ask you why you are here, then." Gordan knew the keepers often lingered in places like this, once full of life, turned silent by a sudden wave of death. "Still, I wonder ..." he continued. This death keeper felt familiar, but his features were so pale that they were almost undistinguishable, lost in the whiteness of his form. "Why have you been following us?"

"To observe," he answered.

Those words struck Gordan with an eerie familiarity. The keeper wasn't a threat. He wasn't truly here but in death. Strange as this being was, like all keepers were—old souls, too tired to live another life, too worn and scarred to take any more pain or pleasure, mere reflections of people, no longer capable of either compassion or malice—perhaps he might be helpful.

"Can you tell me if anyone has been here recently, since the day nearly everyone joined you?" Gordan ventured.

"I can."

Gordan took a careful breath, feeling irritation creep across his face. "Will you tell me about them?"

"Only if you tell me about her," the death keeper answered, and his eyes shifted toward the beach.

Gordan's spine went rigid.

"That one is intriguing, not like the others, not like any of the others," the keeper said.

Reluctantly, Gordan agreed, "No, she's not."

"Even I cannot help being drawn to such a ... tremendous presence," the keeper mused. "Is that, I wonder, why *you* keep her company? You do not bear the weight of a debt upon your soul, dragon," he accused.

"No, I don't, and that is not my reason for being with her." Gordan shifted defiantly at the keeper's questions.

"I tried to warn Raiden." The keeper paused, the corners of his mouth pulled back in what might have been an attempt to smile. "*That one* will lead him to death. She will lead many here. Are you willing to follow her still, with such a path before her?"

"Yes," Gordan answered easily. "Yes I am."

The keeper merely stared at Gordan, tilting his head ever so slightly to the side with a tiny, uncanny jerk. He rolled his head around once as though taking in sights and sounds beyond Gordan's senses and then looked at Gordan once more.

"Of course, I can only see her potential. There are many possible fates for one like her," the keeper said. "Perhaps Raiden would know."

Gordan huffed impatiently, not at all surprised at the mention of Raiden. If the keeper had been here all these years, there would have been few other souls left for him to observe in all that time.

"Are you satisfied?" Gordan asked as he glanced through the trees to the north at the bay below. He could see the speck of Nicole's light through the darkness.

"Indeed."

Nicole wobbled now and then while the smooth stones shifted under her feet, clacking and grumbling as she crossed the beach. The shoreline was long and curved inward, cradling the little bay that was bookended by outcroppings of land, their silhouettes harsh and rocky in the moonlight.

She stood near the water's edge at one end of the beach. To her right a rocky peninsula shielded the bay from harsh waters. Waves rushed and roared in the night, crashing around the several little rocky islands extending off the peninsula. To her left the beach extended in its long curve to the other outcropping of high cliffs leaning over the churning waters below. In the shelter of the bay there were several piers reaching out toward the horizon. Most of them were sagging into the water, some broken into fragments, little man-made islands on stilts.

Nicole set her bag down, followed by the sword. She inhaled the salt of the ocean air and tried to absorb the soothing sound of water rushing up against the beach and then hissing in retreat.

While she waited for Gordan, she bent down to pick up a stone and hurled it out at the ocean. It hit one of the dilapidated piers slanting into the water with a thump against the sodden wood and then plunked into the sea.

There was a single pier that remained intact. She wandered closer, her curiosity winning out. Her hovering light revealed the pier clearly in its yellow glow. With careful steps she tested the first several planks, which proved to be sturdy under her boots. Killing time, she gave every plank a good tap with her foot before stepping wholly onto it, and in that manner she made it all the way to the pier's end. Her heart swelled with her tiny triumph.

The thought of Raiden's letter waiting in her pocket was an itch demanding to be scratched. Since she had a private moment now with Gordan in the trees taking care of business, she could read the letter without him scrutinizing every flutter and fall of her heart.

The light still floated over her shoulder as she dug the paper out of her pocket. She unfolded it and with her finger directed the little orb to hang just over the page.

Illumination washed over the paper, and the black ink of Raiden's writing mesmerized her for a moment. This was the first time she had seen his handwriting. His letters were crowded together, the strokes of the pen sloppy with urgency.

Nicole,

I hope by leaving this letter here it makes it into your hands. I cannot predict why you might be in Cantis now, but I implore you to stay with Gordan. No one else knows about him, except me.

Nicole relaxed a little, knowing Gordan was a secret.

The mainland is a more dangerous place for him than it is for you. Dragons that return to the mainland are most often killed on sight. The safest place for you both would be with the other dragons in the Wastelands. I doubt the Council or even Venarius would think to look for you there. As much as I hope to meet again, I cannot deny that the safest place for you is with Gordan and far from the Council. You were right. We were stronger together.

Nicole clutched the paper with anger shaking in her hands. She could punch that idiot. Of course they were stronger together. She had tried to tell him that the day he'd decided to go off and solve her problems all on his own. And now that he was stuck in Atrium trying to do just that, he finally understood. With a deep breath she managed to return to the letter.

It has only been a day since my departure. Unfortunately, time is not on my side. I have a difficult decision to make. The Council seems to trust me, to some degree, but I cannot rely on that trust, and I must ensure that I keep my secrets from them. I know things they could use against us. The day they stop trusting me is the day they might take what I know by force, so I must urge you not to come to Atrium. Someone searching for me in the city would be suspicious when I have no living family or friends from Cantis. And I don't want you anywhere near the Council.

I write this in hopes to ease any worries you might have. In fact, I have found an ally in the city willing to help me—

A sickening crack wrenched her attention away from the letter, and suddenly she was falling. The plank beneath her feet gave way, and she slipped, tumbling, grasping for a hold on anything as she and the broken wood crashed into the black water below. Her light went out. The salt stung her eyes, and she surfaced frantically, trying to search the water around her through blurred vision for the letter.

The water was deep, icy, and dark. The letter was gone. Her heart sank. She tried summoning the paper to her hand, but her thoughts were seized with the trembling cold that gripped her body, the struggle to tread water while heavy with clothing, and the panic crawling out of the darkness around her and into her mind. Then something clamped around her ankle and yanked her down below the surface before she could even utter a sound. It felt as if she'd left her heart above her as she descended to the sandy ocean floor below in a rush.

In the shadow of the pier and through the stinging salty water in her eyes, she could hardly make out what was happening around her. There seemed to be at least three strange moving shapes, one still clutching her leg with almost-human hands.

Her lungs ached, pulling desperately against her shut mouth for air. A spark of magic expanded around her, and a bubble of air bloomed around her head and shoulders. She gasped for one glorious moment, and then one of the dark shapes lunged at her with a horrible screech, breaking through the bubble and swiping at her. Nicole jerked away from the webbed hand and the grim, pale, mostly human face. The creature's eyes were larger than normal, cloudy and white, and its face looked stretched tight, its mouth a gaping maw of needlelike teeth. With her bubble of air broken, the water slammed shut against her face.

As the water hit her eyes again, she shut them hard. Then several more hands took hold of her, at her other ankle, her hair, her arm, her wrist. Her panic swelled in an instant. She dared to open her eyes as her magic burst forth in a vivid yellow burst that spread through the water like fire. Shrieks warbled through the instantly hot water. Every hand that had a grasp on her pulled away, tearing at her clothes and yanking the elastic band from her hair. The blurred shapes fled, and she thought she caught a fuzzy glimpse of a massive fishtail as they disappeared into the shadowy waters.

Free at last, she swam furiously toward the surface, fighting against the weight and restriction of her clothes. To her horror, when she broke the surface of the water, she saw that she was at least twenty feet away from the end of the pier. They had taken her farther from the shore. She moved her arms and legs as fast as her frantic heartbeat against her ribs.

All she could hear was the water splashing and churning around her. Then, at last, she was at the pier. In her mind the creatures of the water were at her heels. Stretching her arm as long as it would go and with as hard a kick as she could muster, she reached for the wood overhead, but her fingers just grazed the edge of the plank. A fresh surge of panic seized her heart as she sank back into the water, knowing the hands would surely come out of the darkness to drag her back down.

Gordan just wanted to be done with this death keeper. He did not like the sense he kept getting that the keeper knew him.

"Has anyone else been here?"

"One man arrived and disappeared through a portal, but he returned to die. And dear Raiden brought another man who saw his future in the dead man's eyes. All those who set foot upon this unlucky island are drawn into the same fate." The keeper's voice was just audible over the roar of the crashing waves behind him.

Gordan thought he heard a challenge in those words. He stole another swift glance at the beach and saw the distant speck of light, reassuring him that Nicole was there.

"Perhaps the curse of this place is strong enough to follow Raiden to the mainland."

"Death does not follow anyone," Gordan said defiantly. He heard a splash—another crash of water that almost swallowed his words.

"We shall see," the keeper replied, and this time his mouth did curl in an unmistakable smile, an unsettling sight.

Gordan jerked his head to check for Nicole. Her light was gone. There was nothing but a dark beach and the moonlight upon the water.

Nicole fought to tread the frigid water. Her boots felt like two anchors on her feet. She heard a splash behind her, and her heart reeled again. As something grasped her shoe, she kicked her legs twice as hard and fast in another attempt to reach the pier. She nearly missed a second time, but a welcome hand appeared and caught her forearm. Gordan pulled her out of the water with ease and set her on her feet on the shore side of the gap in the pier.

There came a spitting hiss from the water below, and Gordan answered with a deep, guttural snarl. Nicole peered around him and saw the creatures from before sink down until only the top half of their heads remained on the surface. They glared at him a moment with their large, milky eyes and then sank into the black waters.

Gordan spun around and stepped over the gap in the pier. "You're all right?"

Nicole nodded, the movement barely distinguishable from the severe shuddering of her body.

He gave a sigh that sounded like a quiet growl, and then he hugged her. For a moment her mind couldn't form a coherent thought. She couldn't believe he had just done that even while his arms were still clutching her.

"I can't recall the last time I was that scared," he muttered. "I thought I warned you about attracting mermaids."

"I—guess—I—forgot," she stammered with a laugh. Her shivering seemed to fight against Gordan's secure embrace. He released her.

"And now you're freezing."

"Just—give me—a second." She had to sort through her surprise, the numbness, and the shaking of her body to find her magic. As soon as she had been plucked out of danger, her magic had recoiled inside her, her surge of energy now a snapped rubber band. It could be so alive, more aware of the world than she was. Sometimes it seemed like a cohabitant in her body with its own consciousness.

When she found that smoldering concentration of energy, she dragged it back out, summoning heat to flood her veins until it seeped out of her very pores and into the air around them. The warmth in the air tingled against her skin as it dried her faster than Yuma's summer sun.

"What happened?" Gordan asked as they walked back toward the beach.

Nicole looked down at the planks with every suspicious step, but Gordan's question rekindled her memory of the moments before the pier had betrayed her. She looked up at him. "Just curiosity," she confessed, feeling a little childish for letting a curious whim get the better of her. "It seemed fine the whole way out there, and I got distracted by a letter from Raiden."

"A letter?"

"I found it back at his house. It was sitting on the desk with the pocket watch."

"Ah," he said with a nod. "That's what you put in your pocket that made you so flustered."

She felt her face grow hot at Gordan's perception of her conflict upon finding the folded note. "I was reading it, and the plank broke right out from under me. I didn't get through it all, and it's gone now."

"I see," he said. They reached the beach. "What did the letter say?"

Raiden's letter came rushing back into her mind. "He said I should hide with you in the Wastelands and that he'd found an ally, but I didn't get to read the rest." Raiden's words about the treatment of dragons on the mainland made her stomach twist. Dragons would be killed on sight. Knowing that, she didn't want Gordan traveling with her, but she didn't want to say goodbye to anyone else.

Then a tidal wave of realization hit her. Gordan had just paid his debt—hadn't he? Or had he done so back in Tucson when he'd pulled her out of that gunshot's path? She supposed it didn't matter; he had certainly repaid her twice in the span of a few hours.

"I think we can safely say our Raiden is actively opposing the Council. I choose to believe the Council's agent wearing Raiden's clothing is proof of that. But I wonder how long he can keep his treason a secret," Gordan said, pulling off his sweater.

Nicole fell into a sinkhole of thoughts. Raiden was a veritable prisoner in Atrium, trying to do anything he could to deter the Council. At the very least he had someone there on his side. Now here she was in Cantis. How long before the Council knew she was in Veil?

Since deciding to leave her realm behind, she hadn't actually thought about what she was going to do. She had already decided she wasn't going to run anymore, and she wasn't going to hide in the Wastelands either. That only left one path. If the Council wanted the fera so badly, that was what they were going to get, but on *her* terms.

Then she realized there were no shoes on Gordan's feet. Mitchell's sweater was a shadowy heap at his feet. He peeled off his shirt and began unfastening his jeans with clumsy fingers unfamiliar with the denim and button.

"What are you doing?" she asked through her disbelief and laughter.

"I can't fly you to the mainland like this," he said, raising his arms to emphasize his half-clothed human form. "The transformation is uncomfortable enough without being constrained by clothing during the process. And they would be ruined."

"Of course," she said, raising her gaze to the stars as his pants dropped to the ground. She held her laughter back. This was her life, chatting with a dragon while he undressed on a beach.

"You might want to take a step back," he warned.

21. Farewell

ordan closed his eyes and released the tension in his body. Transforming back from his unnatural human form was like the moment Nicole had released him from his chains. His wings tore free with painful relief. His skull elongated into a wide snout, ridges carving themselves along his scalp as straight, slender horns sprouted from the crown of his head just above his ears, now large and horselike. His bones expanded inside him, joints cracking, sending violent shudders through his changing body. His skin erupted with scales.

When he opened his eyes, he saw Nicole trip and fall back. The vertebrae in his neck grew in bursts of agony, and as the ground got farther away, Nicole seemed to shrink. His tail extended out behind him as his spine was forcibly stretched. It was both torture and splendid relief.

He snaked his neck through the air, adjusting and popping everything into place. He stretched out his dark, leathery wings, still stiff and achy from confinement. He filled his lungs with as much air as he could, and his great rib cage expanded blissfully to its limit. He shook, from his head to his hind legs, and his sleek mane rustled around his horns, his ears, and down his lengthy spine. The stones of the beach grumbled and shifted under his weight.

Gordan dropped his gaze to see Nicole on her butt, leaning so far back she was almost lying in the stones as she looked up at his transformation in awe. He gave his tail a swing, and one last tuft of hair sprouted with a swish. She climbed to her feet, still looking at him with the same incredible wonder in her eyes as he had seen the night they'd met in that dank tower.

"I'd almost convinced myself this version of you had been a dream," she said, shaking her head and reaching out.

He dropped his head against her open hand and could feel her heart rate pick up its pace through her palm. She slid her hand up his muzzle and forehead, stroking the fine scales there. Then she let out a timid laugh. Her hand drifted to his neck and traveled down to his shoulder.

It was such a relief to have his body back, to be seen and accepted as himself. Nicole walked around him, and he twisted his long neck around to look over his shoulder at her. She stood about as tall as his back while he was standing. He lowered his belly to the ground.

"We better be going," he said, inviting her to climb onto his back with a nod of his head.

She jerked her gaze back to his face, and the shock in her eyes made his chest rumble with a gravelly chuckle.

"What? You didn't think I could speak in this form?"

Her look of surprise broke into chagrin. "How stupid of me," she said through a laugh.

"You might want to put on an extra coat," he suggested.

She nodded. "Good point," she said, digging into her bag. In a few minutes she had pulled on a pair of gloves, a second sweater, and a large brown leather jacket that looked too big for her. She zipped the jacket up, closed her bag, positioned Raiden's sword across her back, and then put her bag over the top of the sword.

"Get on, then, human," he grumbled with a grin at the corner of his mouth.

"Who knew dragons were so impatient," she chuckled as she placed her hands on his back.

With him lying down, his back was only as high as her hips, and she climbed on easily. She settled herself on his shoulders, her legs straddling the base of his neck. As he stood up, he felt her lurch forward and secure herself to his neck. He turned and bounded northward up the beach, spreading his eager wings wide. He had been dreaming of this moment for ten years, escaping Cantis and returning to the skies. As lift finally caught him up, Nicole's grip tightened, and he realized this was far better than he had imagined. He beat his wings, leaving the ground behind him.

The rush of wind around him made his heart thunder, and he turned, dipping his right side down to avoid the rocky outcropping at the other end of the beach. Nicole gave a little yelp, clinging to his neck as his course curved eastward and out over the ocean.

Laughter expanded in his chest and escaped his throat in low, halting grumbles. But as he cast his gaze at the dark horizon where the starry sky hit the black line of the sea, he thought of their destination, and his moment of joy turned to stone in his stomach.

They were both fugitives in their own way, but Nicole at least was blessed with anonymity that might very well get her all the way to Atrium. But even in his human form, he would be recognized as a dragon in Veil. His willingness to take the risk aside, marking Nicole as a dragon sympathizer—even if the Council weren't hunting her—would earn her equal hatred and perhaps even the same sentence that awaited him for setting foot on the mainland.

He wanted to stay by her side, but he wanted her to succeed above all. It didn't seem likely that they could get to Atrium without meeting a single person, and even if they could, there would be no hiding his identity or his presence in the city.

Gordan could not bring himself to condemn her like that. This entire realm would be her greatest camouflage, people who didn't know her face, her name, or her abilities, such an abundance of magic to surround her, conceal her. How could he compromise that?

The wind buffeted and roared in his ears. He felt Nicole push her feet against his shoulders and slide herself up his neck, which was almost as long as she was tall it seemed, until her chin rested atop his head.

"Hey," she said into his ear. "How's it feel to be flying again?"

"Magnificent," he answered, and it was true, even as he made his heart-wrenching decision. "Perfect opportunity for flying lessons," he teased, and he wasn't surprised to feel her grab hold of his horns and tighten her hold on him.

"I think I'll pass and just enjoy the ride," she said through a nervous laugh.

"Very well." That was perfectly fine to him, as he enjoyed having her warm voice in his ear—it was a welcome change to have a different voice in his head.

"How long does it take to get to the mainland?"

"We should be there before dawn," he answered.

Cold as it was atop a dragon flying over the ocean on a winter night, Nicole couldn't think of anything more incredible than this, the opportunity for the two of them to just be themselves, undisturbed, soaring between a sea of stars and an ocean of darkness.

The wind howled in her ears, but Gordan's voice was so deep that she could hear him easily over the noise. Since she could speak right into his ear, they conversed easily and happily as they went. To Nicole it still felt like the beginning of the day, it being morning back home in her realm. This must have been how Raiden had felt his first few days in the other realm, his internal clock completely screwed up.

She thought about Raiden. As angry as she was that the Council wanted to hijack her life, she felt twice as angry over them seizing Raiden's too. Who the hell did these people think they were? In an attempt to quell her fury, she tried to recall the letter—the part she had managed to read—and commit the words to memory, but she found she already couldn't remember most of it and cursed the ocean below—and the mermaids too.

"What has got you so worked up now?" Gordan asked.

"Mermaids," she grumbled, happy to channel all her frustration over losing Raiden's letter to them.

"They cannot help it," he said. "It's their nature, deeper than mere instinct—they aren't like other creatures."

"I don't understand."

"Mermaids are not born; they do not breed. The story goes that the first mermaid came to be when a woman grieving the betrayal of her lover and a broken heart threw herself off a cliff in her sorrow. As I told you before, magic does not require incantations. The heart can cast some of the strongest spells with an all-consuming desire. She cast away her life, sacrificed her own body, to escape her pain. But in her last violent moments among the rocks and waves, she must have desired one thing above all else—to hurt him as she had been hurt."

"Jeez," Nicole muttered.

"Some magical theorists suggest that such a transformation would require the darkest of magic and that the woman might have sacrificed more than just her own life."

"You mean she might have been pregnant too, sacrificing two lives?"

"It would support her desire to hurt the man who broke her heart. Of course, magical scholars will never know. Mermaids are not ones to have informative conversations, nor are they capable of introspection anymore. They seek only a few things: to kill any men they can get their hands on; to kill those who dare to love, even women; and to convert those who have had their hearts broken. That is how mermaids come into existence. If a woman with a broken heart is unlucky enough to meet a mermaid, she has the choice to become one of them or let them put her out of her misery."

"And to think we have stories about them saving sailors and falling in love," Nicole said with a humorless chuckle.

"Oh, you're talking about merrows. They are commonly mistaken for mermaids. Unlike your friends with the murderous personalities, merrows are natural immortal children of the sea. They're known to warn ships and towns of coming storms. I've met one myself, actually."

"Well, lucky you," she said through a twinge of jealousy.

"Should I ever meet her again, I shall introduce you. But I wouldn't get your hopes up. There is a lot of ocean out there."

The hours passed like this, just talking. Nicole felt painfully aware of the time slipping by. As they drew ever closer to the mainland, her time with Gordan dwindled, and her position as a rider felt more and more like the desperate embrace of a child who didn't want to let go of the one who kept the monsters away. When the dark sliver of land could be seen out ahead of them, her heart sank. The black waters of the ocean reflected the moonlight, but the land on the horizon was a dark mass that did not shine in the night.

The harder she willed time to slow, the faster it went by, until the first blush of dawn lightened the sky and the mainland became clearer. The shore was sandy, and not far from the water's edge a hill ended in an abrupt ledge, as if some force had taken a cleaver to the land.

"It didn't used to take so long to reach the mainland," Gordan said.

Nicole was immediately confused. Had the ocean expanded? Was Cantis drifting around the seas of Veil?

"The Candhrid peninsula and islands used to reach across the sea. Cantis was the capital of Candhrid, the kingdom's gem perched upon the farthest island in the chain, safest from its enemies—well, its enemies on the mainland."

"Cantis was the first to fall in the Dragon Wars," Nicole recalled.

"Yes, and after the capital fell, the rest of Candhrid went right along with it, and the Candhrid royal family was killed."

"But what happened to the peninsula?"

"I don't know. It wasn't lost during the wars; I can tell you that much. Sometime in the last fifteen or twenty years some catastrophe befell it. The whole peninsula and its islands disappeared into the waves. All I know is it was there and then it wasn't."

"So you have been flying close to the mainland since the wars ended," she accused. No wonder he'd gotten himself captured. He hadn't been staying where the rest of the realm felt he belonged, in exile with his own kind. *But why keep him?* she still wondered. What had Dawn wanted with a dragon? To cause some stir on the mainland maybe, manufacture panic for some reason that would expedite their political ends?

"Guilty," he admitted.

When she felt Gordan begin his descent, her stomach lurched. *No, not yet,* she wanted to cry. Instead she just held on tight to him, relishing the last few moments she had. When they touched the sand, she would have to ask him to return to exile. Just thinking about saying those words made her feel sick. After all he had told her about life in the Wastelands, about how exile had been no better than a decade in chains, how could she ask that of him? She didn't want to send him back to that life, but she didn't want to risk losing him on the mainland either.

He glided over the waves rolling onto the beach, close enough for her to hear the low rushing of the water gliding up the sand, the hissing as it receded, and the roar as it churned in the surf. When their combined weight hit the sand, she thought she might actually throw up. *How am I supposed to do this?*

"Nicole?" His voice rumbled in his neck beneath her. "Are you going to come down?" He lowered his head closer to the ground so that she could climb off.

"No," she answered in a pathetic whimper.

He laughed, and she committed the sound and the vibrations of it against her body to her memory. She clutched him tighter as her eyes and nose started to burn.

"I cannot come with you, Nicole," he said, and she lost her grip, stunned. She slipped off his neck and fell into the sand with a thud.

"What?" She scrambled to pick herself up, not bothering to brush the sand off her clothes.

"My company would only put you at risk here on the mainland. I cannot accompany you any further and profess to care about your safety at the same time. Your success here depends on being able to blend in. I'll be recognized, and the only thing worse than a dragon to the people of Veil is a dragon sympathizer. I cannot do that to you."

His deep, heavy words sank into her mind and her heart. Her nose was on fire, and her eyes burned, but somehow laughter slipped past her lips, mixed with sobs. For the past several hours, while she had been agonizing over keeping him safe, he had been doing the same. Words failed her, so she nodded, supporting his decision.

For completely different reasons they were in agreement that this was goodbye. Her face twisted with sadness, and she took it upon herself to wrap her arms around him. With her cheek pressed against his forehead, she managed to encircle his head and clasp her forearms in her hands.

After several moments she managed to convince herself it was time to let go, and she released him from her arms.

"I need you to know something," he said. His low voice was so soft it was almost lost in the sound of the waves.

"What's that?" she asked, wiping tears and snot from her face.

"The circumstances of my debt," he began.

"Oh. I already know you've paid it. Was it the mermaids or earlier—"

The shake of his head was so subtle she barely saw it. "It wasn't when the Council's man attacked, and it wasn't even when I pulled you out of the water tonight."

Confusion pinched her face.

"You released me from my debt when you thanked me for being there with you. I didn't fully understand it myself, but I felt the weight of it disappear. The debt was gone."

"I guess I don't understand either," she said apologetically.

"You didn't save me from a death in chains, Nicole. You saved me from solitude, from misery ... from a fate far worse than death that I had been lost to long before I was forced into chains. I thought you should know that."

She took a shuddering breath, her eyes stinging once more. "Thank you," she managed to utter before the tears came. "For getting me this far."

"You'll go a lot further without me," he said, something like a smile curling his scaly mouth. "But before I leave you, I can give you something that might be helpful along the way."

"What's that?" she asked, looking around for a silly moment. What could he possibly give her?

"Put out your hands," he instructed.

She held her hands out, palms up.

"Together," he added.

She obeyed, cupping them together.

He hung his head over her hands. He inhaled and let out a hot breath, then again, a deeper inhalation and an even hotter exhalation into her hands. The third time he inhaled she heard a sort of crackling deep in his throat, like a roaring fire in the distance.

She didn't even stop to think, or worry, as he exhaled into her hands again, flames spilling from his mouth this time. The fire filled her hands, curling and lapping at her skin without burning. The heat was gentle and tingled with that telltale sensation of magic. This was more than just fire.

The pool of flames in her hands formed a little ball. Then the dancing, feathery substance went still and became a solid mass of what she could only describe as a wad of gold the size of a baseball. She was already dazed with astonishment, but then the golden object moved.

As it uncurled itself, she realized that it was a slender, serpent-like creature the length of her forearm, with half its length belonging to its tail. It crawled around her hands on little swift legs, circling her palms, scrambling around the back of her fingers, and making figure eights around her wrists. Rather than having the weight of a solid-gold baseball, it was light, although its body was indeed firm and metallic.

"Dragon's breath is eternal," Gordan explained. "Let it light your fires, keep you warm, and be a reminder from me to stay safe."

Nicole almost couldn't take her eyes off it. While it traversed the surface of her hand, she raised it to her shoulder, where it continued its curious trek, over her shoulders and the nape of her neck, through her tangle of long, windblown curls, over her bag and Raiden's sword.

"Thank you is starting to sound meaningless," she said with a laugh.

"Avoid roads as much as you can. Keep your encounters to a minimum. The fewer people who know your face, the better. We don't know if the Council knows what you look like."

"Right."

"And keep to the forests. If they're out searching for strong sources of magic, you will be harder to detect among the trees, but still keep your spells small and to a minimum."

"Okay," she said, nodding. "I'll find a way to contact you," she promised.

His great mouth curled again. "They don't deliver post to the Wastelands, remember?" he said with a sad chuckle.

"Then Raiden and I will meet you in the Wastelands once I've ... settled things with the Council," she said, trying to keep her voice confident as she remembered that the Council had effectively exterminated the rest of the fera before now.

"I'll be waiting."

The sky grew lighter, and Nicole had a better look at Gordan than ever. His scales were a dark brownish green like oil and were iridescent like oil as well, wispy rainbows slipping across each scale. His back stood as tall as her truck. She could just peer over him when standing beside him. The scales of his body were small and tightly packed together, except for those under his jaw, down his throat, and down his chest—those were larger, like protective plates of armor shielding his jugular, heart, and underbelly.

"I guess this is the part where we go our separate ways." She nearly choked on the words.

"I suppose it is."

He lowered his head again and pressed his forehead against hers. Nicole thought her heart might shatter, and her goodbye got stuck in her throat. All she could do was watch as he turned away and broke into his long, galloping strides down the beach.

From a distance Gordan struck her as a giant pangolin, except he had a much-longer, slender neck and a head like a horse. As he beat his wings and climbed into the air, her heart ached. She stood there for what felt like ages, watching him shrink into the distance.

Then a great lamenting roar, nearly lost in the sky, rang out across the water. Nicole didn't want to turn away until the blue mouth of the sky swallowed him up out of sight, but while he was still a winged shape on the winds, she wrenched herself away and started up the beach.

22. Search

Raiden's mind was starting to feel numb. He'd lost track of the time, his eyes too tired to focus on the hands and numbers on the clock for the last few hours. His body grew steadily heavier with exhaustion, his bones and muscles telling him it was probably sometime near dawn.

Tovar rubbed his hands together as he straightened up from his worktable. "All right then. I'm just about finished. Then we can test it out."

Raiden felt drawn to the bookcases around the room while Tovar fiddled with spell work that didn't require Raiden's assistance.

"They don't get much company anymore," Tovar said.

"Are they all … valuable?"

"Oh, that depends on the kind of value," he chuckled. "They are worth a fortune in knowledge. Some of them are worth a lot of time in prison."

Raiden searched the spines as though the criminals would jump out for him. A crimson-red spine of a familiar title caught his eye, *Blood Magic* by R. Blackheart—he'd read this book.

"I have been rather detached from Veil for a long time," he said, spotting a book bound in pale leather, its title seared into the spine. He pulled the book out and saw the title was similarly burned into the cover—*Traversing Death*. It had no author. "Is necromancy still illegal?"

"It is," he said. "I don't suppose that will change anytime soon."

Raiden nodded, still holding the book.

"How long?" Tovar asked.

"I'm sorry?"

"How long were you 'detached' from the rest of Veil?"

"Nine years," Raiden answered, "but I can't really say how connected the people of Cantis were with the mainland even before—"

"Bleeding skies!" Tovar looked up at him. "You never told me you were from—" He stopped himself and started again. "Were you in Cantis *during* the massacre? They were so certain there weren't any survivors."

"Yes, I was."

"Forgive me; it's just … you're a piece of living history, Raiden. There are no accounts about what happened in Cantis. The Council … well, they laid blame where they always do: postwar instability and Dawn's resurgence. They have been pointing at Cantis for years to frighten people into buying their unity."

"I can't offer much of an account beyond the darkness of my hiding place," Raiden admitted, feeling a new weight of shame as he realized how important it was for the story of Cantis and its people—the story of his mother—to be heard. If he got himself killed, would anyone ever know what had really happened there? Or would Cantis be written off as a protracted casualty of the Dragon Wars and forgotten, lost through the cracks of written history?

"I hope to hear that story sometime, but I will have to wait, I suppose," Tovar said. "Right now we've got this to worry about."

Raiden looked up from the book cover, suspicious that he had lost several minutes of time although it had seemed like mere seconds glancing at the book. Tovar was finished, so he returned the book to its spot on the shelf and walked back to the worktable.

"Best be careful with that one," Tovar said, nodding to the bookcase. "You can lose days in the pages of that book. Anyway, the mask." He clapped. "Now, this beauty should be able to provide you with three very important things: its location, no matter where it is; the ability to listen whenever you want, regardless of it being worn; and the ability to even see what the mask sees, but only when it's being worn. That spell had to be anchored to the other vision charms in the mask, and the whole network is only active when the mask is on. But all together these spells should get you some worthwhile information."

Raiden was at a loss for words. "I—wow—that's more than I expected. How do I monitor all this?"

"Ah, yes," Tovar said, pointing to the ceiling. "This here"—he picked up a palm-sized mirror—"is yours. It's a portable looking glass. They've been around for decades, but they have especially caught on in recent years. This will allow you to find where the mask is, see what the user is seeing, and listen in when you want."

Tovar placed the glass in Raiden's hand. It was rectangular, about the size of his hand, its corners cut instead of sharp.

"The commands are pretty simple. Touch the glass with one finger for three heartbeats to get the mask's location. Touch the glass with two fingers for three heartbeats to have access to what the mask is seeing—if the mask is being worn, of course. Touch the glass with three fingers for three heartbeats to listen. Pass your palm over the glass when you wish to deactivate its functions."

"I can remember that," Raiden said.

"Good. Now let's have a go, shall we?" Tovar said, putting the mask on.

The mask had an entirely different effect when it was being worn than it did lying on a table. Attached to a body, it looked more alive and bug-like with the large amber glass lenses set in the segmented silver faceplate. The segments allowed flex both for fit and jaw movement. The moment Tovar pressed the mask against his face, the segments spread, and the mask became almost a helmet. The segments extended back over the crown of his head, covered his ears, and fit under his jaw.

"Rather stuffy in here," Tovar said, the lower segments of the mask elongating and contracting as he spoke.

"I'm glad I don't have to wear the uniform," Raiden said as he placed two fingers on the glass and counted three pulses in his fingertips. The glass went cloudy, and then suddenly he was looking at himself.

"There I am," Raiden said, almost laughing as he looked down at the glass to see himself looking down at his hand. He waved at Tovar while watching himself wave in the glass. "Well done, Tovar."

Tovar removed the mask and took a gulp of air. "I enjoyed the challenge," he said, holding the mask out to Raiden. "I already checked that the location and ears work. Just had to get those eyes right—needed help to test them."

"It's perfect." Raiden slipped the handheld looking glass into his pocket.

"Who are you going to plant that on?"

"I honestly don't know yet. I have to keep my eyes open for an opportunity to switch mine with someone else's."

"I see. Be careful with that, Raiden. The closer you get to someone's secrets, the more viciously they will protect them," he said with a nod at the mask.

"I'll bear that in mind," Raiden assured Tovar as he tucked the mask into his belt. "What about payment?"

Tovar thought a moment. "I haven't decided yet. Not all payments must be made with money. I might prefer some help here at the shop or some favor of equal worth. Let me think on it. I've got to open up shop."

"Sure," Raiden said, fairly certain he didn't have nearly enough money for what Tovar's services were worth.

As they left the back room, Raiden took one last glance toward the bookcase before stepping out into the shop.

Raiden closed the door behind him and took in the sight of his apartment with a gratitude he hadn't yet experienced. After spending the entire night in Tovar's workshop altering the mask, he just wanted to drag himself to his bed and throw himself down. He'd just set the mask down on the table when a knock at the door made him groan with dread.

He returned to the door and opened it to see a messenger with an envelope marked urgent.

"What is it?" Raiden asked as he took the envelope, but the messenger just shrugged and departed.

Raiden let out a huff of annoyance as he shut the door and fumbled to tear through the paper. Was *everything* a matter to be concealed in letters? Didn't anyone in the courts *speak* to one another? At last he yanked the note free from the envelope and gave it a hard shake to unfold it. It was from Caeruleus. "Come to medical ward."

The exhaustion pulling on his limbs and eyelids vanished. He stuffed the message into his pocket and turned abruptly on his heel without hesitation. His form dispersed into the air where he stood, and he went zinging through the space between his front door and the designated interbounding arrival platform within the courts.

His abrupt arrival at the platform jarred his legs, and his head was spinning as he reemerged into a solid being. He had the sneaking suspicion he and someone else had crossed paths midbound, as he stood there with a piece of toast missing a bite in his hand. His stomach gave an interested gurgle.

"Happens all the time," the attendant said from his desk, apparently having noticed the utter confusion on Raiden's face over the toast.

Raiden jumped down from the low platform, putting the piece of toast into his mouth to free his hand so he could adjust his clothes, which had twisted and bunched during the interbound. The woman on precautionary guard at the door didn't seem to be paying any mind to anyone coming or going, but when Raiden turned to her and asked, "Medical ward?" she seemed to awaken and pointed him down the hall with a vaguely amiable expression.

By the time Raiden reached the medical ward, he had both finished the piece of toast and decided the interior of the courts was far more expansive and complicated than it appeared from the outside. The great square, domed, column-lined building was like a sprawling maze on the inside. There had to be magical expansions at play.

He walked through the door and down the long, rectangular room that was the medical ward. There were partitions up between all the beds, the mattresses clean and wrapped tight in crisp white linen. A pair of people stepped away from one of the beds toward the end of the room. One of them carried a piece of paper in her hands with a smudge upon it that looked like nothing. The two marched toward the door, passing Raiden without a glance.

There was a set of legs in view upon the bed where the two people had been. Raiden recognized the shoes, the blue jeans—articles of clothing he had given Caeruleus. His heart gave a swift thud against his chest as he realized Caeruleus must have encountered the fera. It surely hadn't ended well if he was in the medical ward.

Sure enough, when Raiden came around the partition, there Caeruleus was, sitting upright against several pillows piled up behind him. He had bandages around his head concealing his right eye.

"Raiden." There was a note of mirth in his voice.

"Stars! What happened?"

"Got hit with my own paralytic spell, but it was distorted somehow. The healers have no idea how her magic changed it, and without knowing precisely what she did, they can't undo it." He sounded like he was reciting his healer's words, mocking jovially when he should surely be upset, angry, disappointed, something.

"You mean they can't heal you?"

"They have healed the damage, but they couldn't reverse the fera's magic," he explained, lifting his bandages enough to reveal his eye.

Raiden's shock seized his face. Caeruleus's eye was no longer an eye but a mostly healed, still red and angry depression of scarred flesh in his eye socket.

"Looks worse than it feels at the moment," Caeruleus said with a chuckle as he lowered the bandage. "Numbing spells are a wonder."

"But how? What happened? *When* did this happen?"

"Last night. The seers found a portal. Went out to wait for it, and when it opened, away I went. Wore this like you suggested," Caeruleus said, giving his shirt a little tug over his chest. "No one looked at me twice the whole time I was tracking the fera down, but she knew. I don't know how, but she spotted me immediately and *knew*. I think she might read minds, Ray. That thing—whatever she is—is dangerous."

Raiden felt angry for what his friend had lost but not at the fera. This was the Council's fault for sending one man up against a fera. He felt guilty for the sympathy he had for the girl, especially after what she'd done to Caeruleus. Raiden's heart seemed unable to reconcile the fera that had tried to kill Caeruleus with the one who had saved his life only days ago—one he could hate, and the other he could not. He fought the urge to let out a groan of self-loathing.

"Oh, and you won't believe it," Caeruleus said, lurching forward and throwing his legs off the bed in his excitement. He paused a moment, his one eye wide and brilliant blue as he waited for Raiden to lean in with anticipation. "She had a dragon with her."

Raiden's initial reaction was one of aversion. If it was bad for Dawn to get their hands on the fera, how bad would it be if the fera aligned herself with the dragons? Being from the other realm, she of course couldn't know about the Dragon Wars, but that didn't mean her befriending the dragons was any less dangerous for Veil. The gratitude he felt toward the fera was being buried under all this new knowledge of her.

"You know," Raiden said, pushing his friend's legs back onto the bed, "you seem to be far too happy about this whole situation."

"I had to give him a little elation tonic," someone said before appearing around the partition. "He was in an absolute rage when he arrived. The crew that brought him in had already numbed his eye. Their healer may have botched the spell—numbed the physical pain but increased his psychological duress. I've seen it happen before, but I don't know what he's usually like."

The healer was a slender young man, so delicate of frame Raiden couldn't even picture him taking on a violently upset patient. His skin was a faint shade of plum, and his pale-blonde hair was plaited into a long, straight rope.

"Oh, I will be paying her back for this," Caeruleus declared cheerfully as he pointed to his eye. "Believe me," he chuckled.

Raiden and the medic exchanged an uncomfortable look. The potion-induced elation made Caeruleus's promise far more unsettling.

"His emotions should return to normal in a day," the healer said quietly to Raiden through an uneasy smile.

Not far from the beach, Nicole found herself among a forest very different from the one in Cantis. The trees were great gnarled things, with twisted trunks and tangled, bare canopies reaching up toward the encroaching clouds that crawled across the sky out of the east.

The dragon's breath got caught in her hair, reminding her it was there. Wincing and cursing, she removed the little golden dragon from her tangle of salty, windblown curls. Once she had it free of her hair, it proceeded to scurry back up her arm. She plucked it off her shoulder. As it scrambled around her fingers, she turned her hand over and placed her other hand in its path. She continued in that vein for a couple of minutes. Watching the little creature crawl endlessly around her moving hands summoned up a smile through her gloom.

"I guess I need something to call you," she said.

As it darted over her knuckles and then across her palm, she noticed the ridge of tiny spikes along its little spine. It paused occasionally to look up at her, blinking its golden lids over its wet golden eyes, which seemed to shine even more with fire than the rest of its body.

"I'm sorry," she muttered. "I'm not feeling very creative at the moment." So she returned the dragon's breath to her shoulder, where it ran a few circles around her arm, back, and chest before sneaking into her jacket and settling around her neck beneath the collar.

In fact, she was feeling a little tired but mostly hungry, having had nothing but a measly little cappuccino since she'd woken up in Tucson. Her stomach reminded her with a scolding grumble that she hadn't thought to pack any food for this trip. So she held out her hand and conjured an apple out of the air. The fruit popped into existence and plopped down onto her palm.

She ate as she walked, taking in everything around her. This forest was filled with sound. The chirping of winter birds was almost strange to her ears, as she had gotten so used to the eerie silence of the Cantis forest. Sometimes she even thought she heard the occasional trill of a flute in the distance, and she wondered what all lived here.

After a couple of hours of trekking through the trees, she came upon a dirt road that seemed to head back toward the coast. Taking Gordan's advice, she put several paces between her and the road before continuing on, following it from a distance.

When her head began to ache and she felt a little dizzy, she convinced herself it was still a symptom of too little food. She sat down against a large boulder entangled in the roots of a tree and shrugged her bag off her shoulder. The bag toppled over, and something tumbled out. It was the little leather-bound book she had found in Raiden's home in Cantis, hiding deep under his bed, which she realized now had actually been his parents' bed.

The thought of a young Raiden, alone, curled up where his mother had slept, hit Nicole so hard she was glad she was sitting down. She shook her head to shoo away the thought. What she needed was something to eat and some time to regain her balance and clarity.

When she summoned up her magic from the well inside her, her head spun faster with the rush of it. She closed her eyes, feeling like a child after spinning in circles until falling down. She could hardly think straight. Realizing that she hadn't had anything to drink for the last several hours, she first focused on a water bottle, which popped into her hands. The weight of it, at least a liter, pulled her arms down, and she opened her eyes to see the plastic bottle was slightly misshapen. *I guess I'm not thinking clearly,* she thought as she twisted the top off and took several large gulps. After downing a quarter of the water, she dreamed up a nut-butter sandwich with slices of banana inside.

When she opened her eyes, the sandwich in her hands was half again as large as she remembered store-bought bread to be, and she chuckled, recognizing the danger of conjuring food on an empty stomach.

So she sat on the cold earth, eating slowly, listening to the birds and the breeze in the branches overhead. The dragon's breath poked its head out from the collar of her jacket and slithered out, running a spiral path down her arm.

"Bored?" she asked.

It spit a little burst of fire at her sandwich, toasting the corner crust into a crisp golden brown.

"Hey!" she said, more startled than anything. Then she had an idea. "Come on, then; finish the rest."

She held the remaining three quarters of her sandwich carefully so that her fingers weren't in the line of fire, and the miniature golden dragon puffed out little mouthfuls of flame, toasting the bread in small sections. After a minute Nicole had turned her sandwich every which way, and now it was crispy on the outside, warm and oozy on the inside.

"Thanks," she said, running her index finger down the dragon's back. It seemed to shudder with contentment under her touch, and then it scurried back up her sleeve and burrowed between the collar of her jacket and her neck.

The rest of her sandwich was far more pleasant being warm, and as she chewed, she pondered the simplicity of just thinking of Raiden and interbounding to him. That could work. She didn't need to know precisely where she was going in Veil, in Atrium; she could just focus on him as her destination. Of course, it was a terrible idea. There was no telling where he might be or whether it would be safe to just appear out of thin air. She was sure it wouldn't be that easy even if she dared to try. Could anyone just interbound into Atrium without the Council knowing? Maybe they were watching Raiden. Even when he was alone and asleep at night, it might not be safe.

She sighed. The smartest way to get to Raiden was to walk into Atrium the old-fashioned way, so that the Council would have no idea where she was. She supposed they would know she was coming. The Council had their seers of course, but could they see where she was if she didn't even know herself? *Guess we'll find out.* She shrugged and picked up the leather book in an attempt to drag her mind away from senseless worrying.

The pages were like a puzzle, with writing filling every bit of each page. Opening to a page in the middle of the journal, she ignored the upside-down words filling the space between the original writing and read, "I saw this very house, old and dim, silent and abandoned. My mother would say it is a useless vision, but I'll still write it down. I will write them all down. I think there is importance in each and every glimpse through time. It may mean nothing to me now, but it will mean something, someday ..."

The passage, or perhaps the chill in the air, made her shudder. If this was Raiden's mother's journal of her visions, why were there *so* many if she'd renounced the Sight when she'd been young? Would she have kept writing them down? Nicole turned to the very first page of the journal, hoping there would be a date or something. She didn't even know his mother's name, but that soon changed, as she saw "Althea Gweldith Divale" was written across the first page.

Nicole opened to another page in the book, combing through the tangle of writing for a decipherable string of words. "I sometimes wonder if I am really there in those moments. The visions are so real. Am I standing in those moments, in the future? I have yet to meet another seer whose visions are as tangible as my own ..."

Nicole stopped. Althea's visions were intensely vivid like Raiden's but apparently not normal as far as the Sight went. She let out a dry chuckle at the thought of normal *anything* in this realm. After closing the journal, she held it in her hands a moment. Had Raiden given up on reading this for some reason, or had he not even known it had been under the bed?

Instead of wasting time on questions no one could answer, she returned the journal to her bag, pulled the cord tight, and gathered her energy to stand, letting out a little groan of self-pity as she got up. Her body was tired, her head still somewhat achy. Her toe struck something with an odd sound, and she looked down to see a toadstool with its red cap knocked over.

"Oops," she muttered with a guilty cringe as if she had bulldozed an innocent creature. She couldn't help wondering if things were more alive here, if the trees were wide awake and listening, unlike the trees back home trapped in some endless cursed slumber. Thankfully, the mushroom didn't cry out, and no tiny fairy leaped out to accuse her of vandalism.

After bending down to grab her bag and standing up to swing it onto her back, her brain did a little spin inside her skull, and she closed her eyes for a steadying moment. The warmth of the little dragon's breath pulsed like a heartbeat around her neck. She took a deep breath to stoke her motivation and set off again.

With as drained as she felt, she found herself wishing she had that same fire in her as she'd had when she and Gordan had left Tucson. She watched the ground as she walked. She watched the trees slip by her, the tangle of branches overhead. There didn't seem to be any encouragement to find anywhere. The trees went on, her footsteps kept going, and there was no destination to achieve but onward for who knew how many days. Her march warmed her up at least, so the fact that this forest seemed to exist inside an infinite refrigerator didn't matter much to her.

It wasn't long before she found herself recounting the morning's events in Tucson. Just the memory of that man's face, him walking toward her casually in Raiden's clothes, sent a pulse of anger through her. When he'd taken aim at her, when he'd hit Gordan instead ... every flash of that encounter made her even more furious. After a moment she realized the heat of her fury had nearly doubled her pace.

Suddenly she understood how Raiden had been able to live all those years in a silent, empty city, keeping to the same room, walking the same streets alone. He'd had his books to break the monotony and his pain to fuel each day.

Well, if running on anger was what it would take to get her to Atrium, so be it. She needed it now. She needed that part of herself that scared her. There was no one she loved around that she could hurt. Why not let herself be dangerous, terrifying, everything the Council accused her of being? To them that was what she was, and she could happily deliver. Her strides felt easier. Her anger was a strong wind at her back supplementing her momentum.

As Raiden paced away from Caeruleus's bed, the healer was preparing for another treatment spell that might reverse some of the damage to Caeruleus's eye, but he didn't sound like there was much hope that a salvaged eye would be worth much.

As Raiden walked out of the medical ward, he couldn't help wondering whether someone like Tovar might be able to help. The trouble with magical wounds was residual magic lingering in the body, and so part of treatment often required someone capable of dispelling remnants of the magic that had done the damage.

Raiden walked down the long corridor, its passage narrow but its ceiling high overhead, passing people who looked only ahead to where they were going, their minds focused on whatever tasks the Council had assigned them. Would Caeruleus's encounter with the fera shake his confidence in the Council? Part of Raiden hoped his friend would see how little the Council valued their agents, but the other part of him knew how dangerous that realization was. The Council's side was the safer side. So long as they didn't send Caeruleus up against the fera again, he would be better off loyal to them than not.

Just as Raiden turned a corner, his face nearly ran into the chest of Loak Clyson.

"Cael," Loak said.

Raiden glanced around at all the passersby. Loak had used Raiden's first name yesterday when no one else had been able to hear. As oblivious as these people around them seemed, Raiden couldn't help wondering whether everyone in the courts was always listening for the Council. Whatever the reason, Loak apparently didn't want anyone to hear him speaking to Raiden on such familiar terms.

"Sir," Raiden answered, fighting back the disdain in his voice. Loak knew more about him than the Council did. So far he was keeping Raiden's clairvoyant secret, but for what price? Raiden couldn't help feeling that he should trust Loak even less than the Council.

Loak looked over Raiden's head and down the hall toward the medical ward. "Just been to see Stone, have you?"

"I have."

"I didn't realize Caeruleus had been assigned to the retrieval of the fera until today. If I'd known, I might have been able to prepare him better," Loak said.

Raiden got the distinct feeling that Loak was fishing for some kind of information from him, anything about Caeruleus's encounter perhaps. It didn't surprise Raiden that the Council would keep special assignments classified. If Dawn had someone in the courts, he or she would want to know who was going after the fera. Come to think of it, Dawn would need someone with authority in the courts to get any noteworthy information, someone like Loak Clyson.

Raiden did his best not to sneer as he looked Loak in the eye. "Is there something you wanted to speak to me about? Sir." He wasn't about to play games with this man, but he was smart enough not to anger him when he knew the one secret Raiden desperately needed to keep from the Council.

Loak scrutinized Raiden for a moment with his fierce golden gaze, looking like he was considering something. Then he shook his head. "Not at all. I'm sure you're busy with your assignment. Those rebels can be trickier than a fera, but I dare say having a new mind—that doesn't think like the rest of us—on the task might finally yield some progress."

With that Loak gave him a departing nod and carried on down the hall, past the medical ward, and around a distant corner.

Raiden was slow to regain his pace as he pondered Loak's words. He grew increasingly annoyed by Loak's hints that he *knew* Raiden. *A mind that doesn't think like the rest of us.* Raiden couldn't be sure if Loak was referring to the Sight or to the fact that Raiden wasn't loyal like the other agents serving the Council.

He made his way back to the interbounding chamber, energized purely by his desire to be out of the court building and its dizzying maze of halls and offices with gold plaques above every door.

28. Clues

aiden had no intention of going back to his apartment to sleep. He stopped at a potions shop and walked straight back to the owner behind the counter to ask for a couple of bottles of wakefulness. The woman unlocked a cabinet of brewed potions and removed two small, clear bottles filled with sky-blue liquid.

She placed them on the counter, and he placed his payment down beside the bottles. They each took what was theirs, and Raiden left, downing one of the potions before he was out the door. The potion hit his stomach and spread through him, flooding his mind with a buzz that turned the fog to clarity and dissolved the weight in his limbs. His heartbeat picked up, and he felt as if he'd just woken up from a full night of sleep, his body energized, his senses alert.

Another dreary gray day over Atrium did not dim the rush of potion-induced energy as he made his way through the streets to Tovar's shop. He even took the busier streets, unfazed by the crowds, his mind so focused on his destination and gaining momentum.

When he strode through the door of the shop, Tovar looked up from his counter at the back, where he was tinkering with a tea set. The cups kept hopping off their saucers, the sugar bowl lid had trapped the spoon inside the bowl and refused to let it out, and the teapot kept turning its handle away from Tovar's hand as he reached for it.

Raiden's vigorous pace didn't slow as he crossed the shop and stopped at

Tovar's counter. Tovar seemed to notice and looked up at Raiden with a curious gaze. "You look like a man with purpose," he remarked. "I thought I wouldn't see you until tomorrow."

"No," Raiden replied. "I bought myself some sleep so I can get to work."

"Ah, wakefulness. That potion has gotten me through a number of troublesome projects."

"It's a long shot, but the Council wants me to find the rebels. Well, I plan on doing just that and helping them bring the Council to an end." Raiden could feel the wakefulness stirring his thoughts into a frenzy as the potion still churned in his stomach, which let out an incredible grumble. "And finding something to eat, apparently."

"Besides the wakefulness, what's brought about this sudden vigor?" Tovar asked.

"A friend lost his eye for the Council. I'm not going to watch him lose anything more."

"In that case, I suppose—" Tovar was interrupted by the chime of the door. His eyes shifted past Raiden to the customer walking in, and Raiden looked over his shoulder to see a woman stroll into the shop and over to the shelves with various lamps.

"I'd recommend Mat Street," Tovar said simply. "I'm a little preoccupied at the moment. This tea set's charms have been reversed somehow, and the owner will be back for it this afternoon."

Raiden nodded, turning toward the door with a small wave.

He knew the way to Mat Street since he had wandered around so much of the neighborhood the night before. With the warm buzz of the potion still humming in his body, he felt consumed by the need to accomplish something today. He needed it as desperately as his gut needed food. Caeruleus had lost an eye because of the Council, and they were sure to keep sending him after the fera until he succeeded or didn't come back at all.

If Raiden could find the rebels, maybe the Council's downfall would come before they could send Caeruleus into another death trap. Raiden got the sense that their desire for discretion in matters of the fera was their weakness. They kept trying to handle this quietly, and he didn't need to understand why to use that against them.

He made it to Mat Street and stepped into a gentle current of delicious scents. His stomach growling, he let his nose lead the way to food. He studied the street as he navigated the maze of smells, wondering where the rebels were gathering to spread their message. Where were they recruiting if their presence had left the streets? He supposed they had found some private place to house their movement—a business perhaps, where rebels could stroll in under the ruse of patronage and safely discuss the controversial and incriminating ideas that they had once shouted from the corners.

A place called Oracle Leaves appeared to be both a tea shop and a fortune-telling destination. Raiden let out a sardonic laugh and kept walking. All the lampposts on Mat Street were coated with various posters and flyers for the surrounding businesses.

As he passed one post, he noticed some of the posters appeared to be Council propaganda. The word *unity* filled the top quarter of each of these posters in all caps. Some then had a paragraph of inspiring text beneath the word, and others contained different images—like a row of the Council's winged agents backed by rays of light with "Freedom for All, Protection for Veil" on a banner under the illustration.

Raiden let out a snort.

"Back again. Are you going to try one of the pies this time?" a gentle voice asked.

Raiden turned to see the Meat Pies & Sweet Pies shop behind the young woman who had spoken to him. She stood there smiling, with the palest-blue cascade of hair spilling around her shoulders. A broom swung back and forth, sweeping on its own beside her.

"A fresh batch just came out of the oven," she added.

Raiden was lost in his thoughts, recalling his recurring vision of the woman with silver hair. He hadn't thought about that vision in weeks it seemed, and now he felt as if he were practically having it again seeing her standing before him.

"Uh, sorry," he said, managing to find words. "My thoughts were … elsewhere."

"Sounds like you must have skipped breakfast," she said, laughing. Her eyes were the same icy blue as her hair.

"Dinner and breakfast, actually," he said with a mournful laugh, pushing his hand through his hair as though doing so might manage to sort out his thoughts.

"Gwyn," she introduced herself, extending her hand.

"Raiden," he replied, taking her hand. He shook it, relieved that visions didn't rush in. He supposed the Sight no longer needed to point him in her direction.

"Better get over there," she said, nodding toward where several people were already in line at the pie shop. One person walked away with a half-moon-shaped pie in her hand, wrapped in paper and steaming in the cold morning air. "The fresh ones sell out fast."

Raiden obeyed with a grateful smile, dazed by the strangeness of someone who felt so familiar upon first meeting. As he wandered over to the pie shop's window, his mind was swimming in a daze of hunger, drifting along in the idea of her. He wanted to know how far away that future was, the one he had seen so many times with her in his arms. Then he realized that she had commandeered his thoughts. He needed to focus on finding the rebels and freeing himself and Caeruleus from the Council.

It occurred to him that he was standing at the window, lost in his thoughts. A young man wearing an apron stood on the other side of the window.

"What can I get you?" he asked, greeting Raiden with a warm smile. He looked so much like Gwyn that they had to be siblings, only his eyes and hair were the palest green.

"Anything warm," Raiden said with a shrug. He just needed his stomach to shut the hell up so he could think.

"Certainly," the young man answered, producing a paper-wrapped pie. Steam curled into the air as he handed it to Raiden. "That'll be four coppers."

Raiden dug a handful of coppers out of his pocket to pay for the half-moon pie. "Thank you," he said as he handed over the money.

"Enjoy."

As he turned away from the window, his gaze met Gwyn's as she passed on her way back inside the shop. She smiled, but he already had the pie in his mouth, so he waved and kept walking. The crust was crispy and flaky, crackling loudly. The filling was some kind of root, potato, or parsnip, sweet and seasoned with cinnamon and cardamom.

Weaving through patrons back to the street, he looked around, considering everyone he saw, but everyone was either seated at outdoor tables eating or bustling along the street on their way somewhere else. He stopped, finding himself beside the streetlamp again, and rolled his eyes at the Council's unity posters. He wondered how many people believed this. After all, Tovar had said most people were rebels even if they didn't identify as such. Was the Council aware of the changing sentiments of their people? He peered at the posters, no longer tasting the pie as he chewed mechanically and studied the propaganda. Was this the Council's fear or confidence plastered all around the city?

Then he spotted a poster that didn't seem quite right. Like the others, the word *unity* dominated the top quarter of the poster, but below was a map of Veil, each state separate from the others like islands with walls illustrated around them all. A banner that read Protection through Division occupied the space beneath the image. He studied the image and slogan, and a smile crept across his face.

The rebels were still on the streets after all, mocking the Council and spreading opposition right under their noses, disguised as their own propaganda. He nearly choked on his mouthful of food when a laugh slipped up his throat. Leaving the rebel poster behind, he hurried the rest of the pie into his mouth and set out, stopping to examine the abundant posters plastered on lampposts and walls throughout the city.

Among the posters glorifying the Council was the occasional disguised message from the rebels. Each one Raiden found brought a spiteful grin to his face. He grew more confident with every one he found, knowing that somewhere in these dissenting posters was the key to finding the rebels.

He found another mock unity poster in a long line of posters spaced precisely along a building's wall. Every single poster bore the same image—a posterior view of a winged man aloft over the city. The banner below the image on all the Council's posters read "Freedom for All, Unity for All," but on the rebel poster the banner read "Freedom for Some, Unity for None."

He studied the rebel counterpart, searching for some tiny message that might be hiding in the illustration. His scrutinizing gaze found nothing. Then as he straightened up, he saw a pair of eyes, one on each side of the *i* in *unity*. The eyes blinked at him, and all he could do was blink back.

A mouth appeared below the eyes. "Moonstone." Then both the mouth and the set of eyes were gone.

Raiden stared at the poster for a moment, and his face froze in a dumbfounded expression between confusion and triumph. He didn't have a clue what "moonstone" was supposed to mean, but he knew it was an invitation.

Nicole thought she felt a tiny pinprick of icy cold hit her cheek. Then she felt just a drop of moisture sink through the roots of her hair. She searched her scalp with her fingertips, felt the water, and looked up. The sky had been gray most of the day, but now the first drops of precipitation began to pitter-patter through the branches above her and against the earth.

Before she knew it, an assault of rain came down over the forest, and the leafless canopies offered no protection.

"Shit."

She looked around as if there might be some shelter that hadn't been there before, but there was nothing to offer her sanctuary from the frigid raindrops.

Holding her arm up, she let her magic flow through her hand. Creating an unseen shield overhead required no effort at all. As the rain rolled down the invisible dome over her, she continued walking. To pass the wet, gray minutes, she weighed what she knew about the Council against her plan.

To be safe, she had to assume the Council already knew she was in Veil, that their seers had glimpsed her intent to make it to Atrium. She absolutely had to assume that the Council already had people out searching for her. She had no way of knowing how well concealed she was among the trees and rain, but she trusted Gordan, and he said the trees' magic would cloak her if she kept her own use of spells to a minimum.

The hiss of the rain was her company as she walked, navigating the forest to stay on higher ground. Tree roots were exposed like crisscrossing bridges over puddles, and she ran her hand along the trunk of each tree that helped her keep her boots dry. Eventually the rain eased up into a drizzle, and the rivers streaming off her invisible umbrella were reduced to droplets and trails wriggling down around her.

The light rain continued for the next few hours, and her body grew clumsy with exhaustion. She wondered what she was going to do about sleeping in a wet forest. Even if she came to a town or just a lone house, she thought she should avoid everyone, even if they seemed friendly—friendly didn't mean trustworthy.

She would heed Gordan's advice. The less people who saw her face, the better, so she would have to figure out how she was going to keep dry and get some sleep. The hope that the drizzle would eventually stop if she just held out long enough kept her going. The forest grew more troublesome to navigate as an abundance of great stones littered the ground, some of them enveloped in roots and others carpeted in moss.

Then Nicole came upon a tree that appeared to be the solution to her dilemma. In fact, it appeared to be two trees that made up one massive, twisted entity. The twisted trees stood in an uneven bed of mossy stones, and each tree looked to be almost twice as big as the neighboring trees of the forest. Where the two trees met there were large nooks sheltered by the trees' huge, gnarled branches.

Each of the Siamese twin trees seemed to be a great, sprawling canopy of knotted branches atop a mass of tentacle roots without much of a trunk to distinguish between top and bottom. Nicole scrambled over green stones and roots, making her way to a nook formed by a gap between the two trees where one leaned drastically toward the ground and the other twisted underneath it.

She let her dome of magic dissolve into the air as she crawled into her cold but dry shelter. There was just enough room for her to shrug off her bag and prop it up behind her. She slipped the sword off her back so that she could lean against her bag like a cushion. Scooting her heels up to her butt and her knees toward her chest, she settled in, crossing her arms around the sword and pinning it to her torso, a teddy bear and a weapon tonight.

The cool metal against her body, although it didn't help to warm her, seemed to soothe her anxiety as she let her heavy eyelids close. The dragon's breath crawled out from under her jacket collar; its tiny, clawed feet prickled against her neck as it went. She opened her eyes to see it curl around the top of the sword's sheath, just below the hilt. She closed her eyes, mildly perplexed by the dragon's breath behavior but too tired to dwell on it. Then in a minute she felt the sword grow warm, and she wondered whether the dragon's breath knew the sword could conduct its heat.

A sleepy smile pulled at her lips, but her eyelids were too heavy to open again. Fleetingly she wondered what time it was, but she was drifting off to sleep before she could even consider pulling the pocket watch out of her bag.

When she opened her eyes what seemed like just moments later, all she could see was darkness and the orange-red glow of the dragon's breath, which was scurrying around her in circles. In the darkness, she assumed it was the middle of the night or just before dawn. But a strange sound registered in her mind, a low creaking, and she realized that the tree seemed to be shifting beneath her.

A sliver of light appeared, and she could see that the darkness was a mass of branches all around her. The hairline gap closed, and she was in the dark again. Her brain finally caught up. The tree was closing up around her.

Nicole let out a distressed shout as she lurched forward, hitting her head against bark as she searched blindly for a gap that wasn't there. Her thoughts were a string of profanities she couldn't even articulate. The sudden panic had her heart racing and her blood burning with magic. The cramped space writhed around her—shrinking.

"Hell no," she growled through clenched teeth, and she let her fire out. The tree burst open, a fist unfurling its many twisted fingers to release a hot coal.

Nicole jumped down from between the singed, knotted branches, stumbling as she ran away from the tree. The sword was in one hand; in the other hand was her bag, hitting her leg with every stride. Not until she felt like she was out of the tree's reach, beyond its roots, did she turn around.

The two twisted trees now leaned away from each other after being blasted apart, and not a single twig was moving. She sighed, suddenly remembering how plants had always reached for her, grasped at her, as though they craved the magic inside her more than sunlight. It had never occurred to her that a tree might try to devour her whole.

She stood there while she caught her breath. The sky over the forest was clear, a couple of stars still hanging on as dawn stretched from the east to the west. As the sun rose, its light swept through the trees, shining like a beacon. The sun was rising to her right, and she realized how turned around she had become.

She shook off her disbelief, took one last suspicious look at the twisted tree, and gladly left it behind her as she marched once again toward the east.

"That tree actually tried to eat me," she muttered to herself as she walked.

The rapid rhythm of the dragon's breath's scurrying steps across her chest, around her shoulder, down the back of her jacket, around her waist, and then back up the front of her jacket coaxed a weak smile past her lips.

"You woke me up," she said, realizing that maybe it had done so on purpose. It crawled over the collar of her jacket and wriggled its way into its favored spot around her neck. She chuckled. "My hero."

She spent her morning hike deciding how best to scold Raiden about not warning her that trees would try to eat her. A dull headache competed for her attention, but she decided it was just a lack of caffeine. She ignored the foggy pain in her head as she trudged along, hoping for a quiet, boring day ahead of her.

Raiden rolled over and sat up, his head still reeling from the vision of embracing the woman with silver hair. His mind was a confusing combination of the lingering elation from the future and groggy exhaustion of the present. After the wakefulness potion had worn off last night, he'd felt like a dead man walking. Even after a full night of sleep he could still feel the effects of that crash after the high of magic-induced energy. He coaxed his eyes open by rubbing the sleep from them.

The room wasn't dark, but it wasn't exactly light either with only the dull glow of a dreary day coming through the window. As much as he relied on that vision as a tiny beacon of hope, he would like to enjoy uninterrupted sleep for once. *I understand that future now,* he thought at the Sight as if it were a living entity squatting in his head. *You can give that vision a rest.* If he had to suffer the Sight while he slept, he would like to get something more useful to him now, like a warning that the Council was onto his treasonous motives or something that might help Caeruleus.

A knock on his door pulled him from his thoughts. He was slow to drag himself out of his bed. By the time he crossed his apartment and opened the door, there was no one standing there, but there was an envelope on the mat. He swiped it up and closed the door.

There was nothing written on the envelope, but the Council's insignia—two crossed keys within a laurel wreath—was pressed into the wax seal. He hesitated for a moment before opening it and then scanned the page swiftly. Caeruleus was earning his wings, and Raiden was being summoned to appear for the ceremony.

"Today," he read, annoyed.

The ceremony was in just a couple of hours. He was instructed to come in uniform, including sword and mask. This might be his only chance to switch his mask with someone else's. He sighed and hoped a shower would wake him up and miraculously grant him the mental fortitude to walk through the courts in the uniform he had hoped he would never have to wear.

His mind returned to the rebel clue. Moonstone. He had visited every last stone-and-crystal shop he could find in the city and asked the owners about moonstones, but not a single one had seemed to glean a hidden meaning from the inquiry, and so Raiden would have to make sense of the clue some other way.

He shuffled his feet across the hardwood floor of the apartment, heading for the shower. As he crossed the kitchen, he dropped the ceremony announcement on the table, atop the pile of information the Council had provided about the rebels. Nowhere in any of that information was there mention of the rebels' subversive posters. None of the Council's agents had noticed.

Before disappearing, the rebels' activity had started as boisterous disruptions throughout the city. They'd attempted to hold spontaneous rallies to gain traction and recruit others, but their tactics had mostly led to public confrontations with the Council's agents. The Council's information indicated that the rebel movement—being senseless rioting—had largely been fought back and that all that remained was to locate the leaders and weed out their efforts to rebuild the movement.

What Raiden saw among all this information was the Council's attempt to downplay and delegitimize the political faction. As far as Raiden could tell, the rebels had gotten smart. By adopting tactics that kept them concealed while spreading their messages of dissent throughout the city, they could safely, albeit slowly, reach out to like-minded citizens. Either the Council wanted to make it seem that they had effectively squashed an aimless rebellion, or they believed they had.

Raiden found himself admiring the rebels. Patience was more valuable to their movement than anything, and it meant they could survive to make a difference. He just hoped he could find them and help expedite their efforts.

Taking a shower, getting dressed, and going down the street for another potion took twice as long as it should have. But he couldn't be sure whether it was lingering effects of the potion from yesterday or just the dread of the ceremony in the courts.

At least today he would have the opportunity to trade his mask with someone who could carry his eyes and ears closer to the Council's secrets. He would even get to see how the Council granted wings to their most trusted servants. He frowned. His friend was one of them, but he still had hope for Caeruleus. *He's not mindless*, he thought, *just completely deceived.*

He stood in front of the dresser, putting off the moment he had been dreading quietly in the back of his mind: putting on the uniform. He huffed and opened the drawer. The sight of the folded uniform made him scowl.

It was slate gray with silver buttons and embellishments. After lifting it from the drawer, he begrudgingly changed out of his casual clothes and into the uniform. The Council's emblem was pinned to the breast of the coat, and the silver pin of the twin keys forming an X and the surrounding laurel wreath stood out against the dark bluish-gray fabric.

Also in the drawer was his standard-issue short sword, tall black boots, and a black belt. He put on the polished boots, looped the belt around his waist, fastened the sword to the belt, and straightened his spine to stand tall as he clasped the stiff collar of his jacket closed around his neck.

Reluctantly, he stepped into the bathroom to take a look at his reflection. He could barely see his mother in himself now. Wearing the Council's uniform, he could only see his father looking back at him. His lips tightened in distaste, and he turned away from the mirror.

All he had to do was show up for the ceremony. His boots clunked across the hardwood floor as he crossed his apartment. The mask was sitting on the table with all his rebel information and the Council's announcement. He picked it up, hoping he wouldn't have to wear it. It seemed as good a time as any to interbound into the courts. With a firm grip on the mask, he departed in a whirl.

Nicole couldn't shake the dull headache, not by distracting herself, not by sheer willpower. Not even her magic could soothe it. When she stopped midmorning for a short rest and a breakfast of a conjured banana and two hardboiled eggs, she noticed a small slash in her pants just above the ankle of her hiking boot.

Examining the tear, she found a dark scar there that she didn't recognize. It looked to be healed, but it was grayish instead of the usual pink that it should be. It had to have been from the mermaids' claws—the hole most certainly had not been there when she'd put the pants on. She didn't think much more about it once she stitched up the tear in the fabric with a little surge of magic.

Nicole sat for a while, picking the shells off her eggs and listening to the quiet music of the forest, hearing a faint melody in the distance again. She was sure this time: there was someone playing music, an airy and delicate sound from some kind of flute. For a brief moment an ache in her chest distracted her from the one in her head. She didn't want to be alone anymore, even if just for a moment, but the prospect of seeking company was a dangerous one for her. She had to accept the silent company of the trees like Raiden had. *I have his mother's journal,* she reminded herself. Even if it was only from the pages of a diary, she had someone to keep her company.

Patting her bag where the journal waited patiently for her return, she felt encouraged to get up and continue on her way. She could spend some more time with Althea at the end of the day and get to know her some more.

"All right," she muttered, standing up and heaving the bag onto her back. The dragon's breath stirred at the vibrating sound of her voice in her neck, and it emerged from beneath her jacket collar to make several laps around her torso.

"I'm still thinking of a name, buddy," she said, grateful to have something to talk to. It seemed to run even faster in response. So she shifted the ache in her head aside and made room for the task of finding a name for her little companion. She had nothing but time after all.

24. Wings

Raiden straightened his uniform as he stepped off the interbounding platform in the courts. He wasn't surprised to see two more people appear beside him, two women in the same uniform as his, one with her blonde hair only a few inches long and the other with her jet-black hair twisted back into a tight, sleek bun.

As the two women passed him, he noticed their masks were attached to the right shoulder of their jackets. He turned his face to his shoulder, and sure enough, there was a small strip of fabric and a button there for securing the mask in place. But he hesitated, concerned about how he would switch his mask with anyone else's once his was attached to his uniform.

He bumped into someone with a patch on his face and a bright-blue eye.

"Caeruleus," he said, surprised at his delay in recognizing his friend.

"There you are," Caeruleus said, distracted by trying to attach his mask to his shoulder. Since the mask went on the right shoulder and his right eye was covered, he couldn't see what he was doing.

"Let me," Raiden said, taking the mask before Caeruleus could protest. It couldn't have been easier. He attached his own mask to Caeruleus's shoulder and kept Caeruleus's mask for himself.

Caeruleus let out a frustrated grumble. "Thank you."

"Of course," Raiden answered, fastening his new mask to his own shoulder.

"Come on," Caeruleus said, nodding in the direction they ought to be heading. There were several other uniformed agents walking ahead of them.

"There better not be any elaborate formations for this ceremony. I haven't got the slightest idea what I'm supposed to be doing here," Raiden said, trying for lighthearted conversation. He felt like his insincerity was glaring, but Caeruleus didn't seem to notice.

"You'll be fine. You just have to line up with the rest of us and stand there for the ceremony," Caeruleus said, a hint of amusement in his voice. "Lucky me—I get my wings today, *and* my best friend will be there. If someone had told me as much when I joined the courts' ranks, I would have laughed in their face."

"I would have too," Raiden said wistfully. He certainly hadn't seen this coming. He almost laughed, but the attempt got caught in his throat by his disgust.

"I'll admit," Caeruleus said, lowering his voice so that it almost disappeared between them, "if anyone had told me I would have to lose an eye to earn these damn wings … I don't know."

They walked in silence, listening to the many rhythms of footsteps clashing and clattering around the hall with theirs. Raiden's heart strained with reluctant hope that Caeruleus was starting to doubt whether the Council and their agendas were worth his sacrifices. The thought brought a trace of relief to Raiden's many worries. A current of uniformed men and women migrated toward the great hall where the Council received their audiences.

As they strode through the massive double doors, Raiden saw the hall fully lit for the first time. Its true size was dizzying—almost to the point of seeming like an illusion from some enchantment. It seemed more vast inside than the whole of the courts even appeared from outside.

Everything was marble—the floor, the pillars, the walls. The green marble floor was so highly polished that the massive white pillars were reflected in the floor, creating the illusion that they were taller than they were. The white marble bore a faint green tint and green veins, giving the impression that the floor was a dark-green pool of water that had come trickling down the walls and pillars.

High above their heads the ceiling was made up entirely of intricate gold-leaf molding with swirls and flourishes radiating out from a crystal dome that protruded from the ceiling like the bottom half of the sun itself. The Council's representation of the sun was so true to its nature that the ceiling was almost too intensely bright to look at.

"Now you know why they keep the lights off," Caeruleus said with a dry chuckle. "They would never have anyone's attention if they didn't."

Raiden almost laughed—no, the Council preferred to address people in a void of darkness inhabited only by their presence at their sprawling crescent-shaped pulpit.

A collective murmur filled the space as the Council's agents streamed in and lined up on either side of the hall, the gargantuan pillars looming behind their backs. Just inside the open doors of the hall, everyone else who worked in the courts gathered to watch. Raiden spotted the slender form of the healer who had tried his best to help Caeruleus. Since Caeruleus now wore a patch over his eye, Raiden didn't have to guess whether or not the healer had managed to make any improvement.

The lighthearted murmuring in the hall slowly faded into an immense silence that somehow made the space feel larger still. At the other end of the hall the crescent bench at which the Council usually sat was empty. However, once total silence settled in the hall, a tall narrow door opened behind the bench, and a single-file line of people wearing billowing silver robes paced into the hall, walked around the crescent pulpit, and stood before it.

The Council's ceremonial robes moved and rippled like sheets of silver liquid, ethereal garments quite unlike the somber black robes they had been wearing when Raiden had first laid eyes on them. They moved in sync, their footsteps echoing through the hall in perfect unison so that there seemed to be one large set of feet crossing the emerald floor. All thirteen of the Council members were bald, so from afar they all looked alike, differing only slightly in stature and some variation of skin tone.

The man standing in the center of their semicircle said, "Let Caeruleus Stone step forward." His voice rang out, magnified and slightly distorted by the magic that helped his voice fill the hall.

Caeruleus glanced at Raiden and stepped out of line, his footsteps echoing in the hall like a timid solo performance. Raiden's heart sped up, but he couldn't quite pinpoint the source of his anxiety at watching his friend approach the Council. Maybe it was his distrust of them or his concern that Caeruleus had both proven his loyalty and now doubted it, which was a dangerous place to be for any of the men and women standing in this room.

The councilman at the far left stepped out of the semicircle and approached Caeruleus with a scroll in hand. Simultaneously, the councilwoman at the far right stepped out of the formation with a ceremonial dagger glinting in her grip.

Again the councilman at the center spoke. "Please recite the pledge."

The councilman unrolled the scroll and held it before Caeruleus for him to read from while the councilwoman stood waiting.

"I, Caeruleus Stone, do pledge my loyalty to the Council and their work for the people of Veil. I solemnly vow to devote my mind and my body to the preservation of the courts and the people that they stand to protect. I will defend this institution of unity against any who threaten it." Caeruleus paused for a breath. "Upon the honor and the wings you have granted me, I swear to protect this city, this realm, and all who call it home. Let blood bind my words in truth."

The councilwoman took his hand and raised the dagger in her other hand. She drew the blade across his palm in one swift motion. Caeruleus didn't even wince. He placed his bleeding hand against the scroll, beneath the words he had just finished reading aloud, smearing a vivid red band at the bottom of the contract instead of a signature.

With a grave nod the councilman retracted the scroll and stepped back into his place while the councilwoman handed Caeruleus a long bandage that was silver and fluid like her robes. Then she too inclined her head and stepped back into her place with the rest of the Council.

Caeruleus quickly wrapped the silver fabric around his hand.

"Now, if you would please remove your coat and shirt."

Caeruleus did as he was told. A young man seemed to materialize from behind the crescent bench, carrying with him a delicate pedestal and a bowl. He set the pedestal beside Caeruleus and placed the bowl on top of it. Then he stepped forward to take Caeruleus's coat and shirt and moved off to the side of the hall, his light, scurrying footsteps barely audible.

Bare from the waist up, Caeruleus turned around, presenting his back to the Council. He stood tall, facing the witnesses in the hall. One by one each member of the Council stepped forward, took a brush from the bowl on the pedestal, and painted on his back. After the first six Council members had made their marks and walked away, Raiden realized that they must be painting alchemic symbols on Caeruleus's skin.

So they used alchemy to transfigure their agents. It was the most complex form of magic there was, the only kind that could achieve permanent physical transformations. A successful transmutation required impeccably drawn symbols, and the more complex the transformation, well, the easier it was to mess up.

Raiden shifted with anxiety. He wondered whether there had ever been a mishap during one of these wing ceremonies. All he could do was take solace in the calm silence surrounding him as he watched the Council paint on

Caeruleus's back. The last member of the Council stepped up to their human canvas, but instead of picking up the brush, she laced all her fingers except her index fingers together, forming a triangle.

In the overwhelming silence Raiden could hear the councilwoman's soft murmur before the hissing of burning skin slipped through the hall. Caeruleus arched his back, and his face twisted in a teeth-bared cringe against the pain.

The sickening sound of bones popping and flesh twisting crept through the hall as two growths protruded from Caeruleus's back between his shoulder blades. The force of the Council's magic rolled through Caeruleus, and he curled forward. Raiden cringed and resisted the urge to look away from the forming wings, bizarre, deformed arms reaching out from his friend's back.

At last the growths took on the telltale shape of wings as they lengthened and bloomed with a sleek black plumage. The fully formed wings stretched wide, and Caeruleus straightened up, dropping his head back in relief. His chest expanded with a deep breath, and Caeruleus sighed, folding his new wings behind him as the hall erupted with jubilant noise.

Every agent and court employee burst into applause and cheers, but Raiden was still processing. His eyes fell on Loak Clyson across the room. Loak clapped, lending his hands to the cacophony, but the stoic look on his face seemed to indicate that his participation was unfelt and obligatory. Raiden followed suit and clapped, still unsure about Loak.

Did the man really have everyone here buying his loyalty to the Council? Raiden looked around. Surely someone else noticed Loak's lack of enthusiasm. Then again, Raiden supposed it was his own lackluster participation that allowed him to recognize it in Loak. He was almost certain the man wasn't loyal to the Council. Raiden considered for a moment. Loak could be with the rebels, but there was also a chance he could be with Dawn, and so Raiden still couldn't trust him.

Raiden forced his attention back to Caeruleus. One of the councilmen placed a pendant hanging from a long cord around Caeruleus's neck and said something to him. Caeruleus nodded, and his wings shuddered, melting into yellow light before shrinking into his back. The young man from before returned his clothes, and Caeruleus pulled his shirt on with careful movements.

The entire ceremony lasted no more than twenty minutes. Once Caeruleus was dressed again, the Council presented him as their most dedicated agent and commended his sacrifice, although Raiden noticed they chose not to mention the fera. He couldn't help smiling to himself, amused by their secretive praise.

He busied himself during their closing words by scanning the hall and wondering how many people could possibly be eyes and ears for Dawn. Loak was a likely traitor, maybe even the healer—yes, a healer would be a good source of information with access to the Council's agents and their secrets while in the medical ward.

Suddenly the lines of agents broke, and everyone dispersed. Many of them seemed eager to shake Caeruleus's hand as he crossed the hall. It occurred to Raiden that these might all be agents that were in the Council's fleet. Raiden recognized one of the men who shook Caeruleus's hand as Landor from their training session. Raiden was close enough to hear their voices through the low roar of conversation throughout the hall.

"I look forward to flying with you, Stone," Landor said.

"Likewise," Caeruleus answered, his smile looking more like a grimace as Landor turned away.

He nodded at Raiden as he passed, and Raiden reciprocated.

"How do you feel?" Raiden asked.

"A little light-headed," Caeruleus confessed with a laugh. "I've got a lesson in morphing later, so I won't need this to put my wings away." He lifted the cord around his neck, and the pendant swung like a pendulum. It was a simple piece of white quartz.

Everyone migrated toward the double doors, and Raiden couldn't help eyeing the mask on Caeruleus's shoulder, trying not to feel guilty about the trick. He would have preferred to tell Caeruleus, work with him to learn the Council's secrets. After all, Caeruleus wanted justice for Cantis as much as Raiden did. But Raiden didn't want to incriminate his friend. If the Council ever interrogated Caeruleus over leaked information, he could truthfully deny knowing about it or having any part in it, even if the Council searched his memories. Raiden was sure it would be best if Caeruleus didn't know.

The two of them were the last to wander from the hall. Before they could step out the doors, the light that filled every corner of the room went out, and a heavy curtain of shadows shut on them.

"How are things going on the rebel front?" Caeruleus asked.

"Nowhere at the moment," Raiden admitted. "Can I ask ... how's your eye?"

"Oh, it's still gone," he said. "People stare less at the patch."

They weren't more than three steps outside the hall before the doors closed behind them.

"I'm sorry about that, Ruleus," Raiden said with a sigh.

"Why? It wasn't your fault," he replied in a light, dismissive tone, but Raiden suspected that his anger was still alive and well.

"You shouldn't be going up against the fera alone," he said, his anger toward the Council coloring his voice.

Then one of the massive doors opened, and the young man who had held Caeruleus's uniform during the ceremony poked his head out to look down the corridor. His face lit up with relief when he saw them.

"Oh, there you are," he said. "The Council needs to see you—urgently."

"He must mean you," Raiden said.

Caeruleus nodded and slipped through the opening to return to the now-dark hall. A realization struck Raiden so suddenly that he almost gasped aloud. With the altered mask on Caeruleus's shoulder, he could listen in, but he couldn't listen in the corridors of the courts. He ran for the interbounding chamber without a care for the looks he was given as he went.

To his surprise, Loak Clyson was loitering in the corridor outside the interbounding chamber. He looked ready to address Raiden as he approached, still running.

"No time—got a lead," he said as he blew past Loak and turned into the Authorized Interbounding Commute Office. He didn't slow down. He didn't even come to a stop on the platform before he was gone.

Raiden lurched out of thin air at a run, skidding to a wobbly halt in his apartment. He pulled his small looking glass from his pocket, fumbling with it as his head spun from the jump. He pressed three fingers against the glass. Three heartbeats sped by, and as the reflection went dark, voices came from the void.

He almost couldn't hear anything over the pounding of his heart in his ears and his heavy breathing.

"She is making her way toward Atrium," a councilman said.

Raiden supposed "she" had to be the fera.

"The seers do not have a clear image of where she is now, but they have seen her on the western coast and walking the streets of Atrium." There was a pause. "They have also seen hazy glimpses of destruction in the courts."

Another councilman spoke up. "We need to intercept her before she reaches Atrium."

Raiden was stunned for just a moment, seized by a mix of thoughts and emotions. He knew the Sight; seeing a moment in the future did not reveal the path to that moment. If the seers saw her in Atrium, it was because she'd put herself on the path to Atrium, but how could they know what might lead her to bring destruction to the courts?

He worried about Caeruleus. The fera seemed to grow more dangerous with every encounter. Regardless of where her violence came from, the

Council's repeated threats to her freedom and life would only guarantee her lashing out at Caeruleus again and might even inspire her to teach them a lesson in meddling with someone's liberty. If they wanted the fera so badly, let *them* risk their lives. They were powerful, weren't they, with their combined lifetimes of experience and skills?

The silence seemed to go on far too long. What was Caeruleus thinking? Raiden wished the mask could hear those thoughts.

At last Caeruleus answered. "How do you propose we intercept her?" There was skepticism in his voice. Raiden could hear it, but could the Council?

"As you know, someone came to the medical ward to retrieve her image from your memory yesterday. We are preparing to send out a force of agents to alert the townships between Atrium and the coast, to make sure everyone knows her face so we can find her."

"Do you plan on telling people what she is?"

"We do not want to spark panic. All the people need to know is that we are searching for the young woman in the picture."

"What if someone tries to apprehend her themselves and the worst should happen? If people are not warned, any injury or death is on us," Caeruleus said.

Raiden cringed.

There was a pause.

"We agree. We will warn people not to intervene and to instead notify our agents. All agents involved in the search will work in pairs."

"Will the other agents know we are searching for the fera?"

"We want to keep the fera's identity confined to a select few for the time being. Rest assured every agent will be adequately prepared. She can and will be apprehended, just like all the others."

"With all due respect, I don't think anyone can be prepared to face the fera if they do not know what they are up against."

Raiden's eyes went wide. "Caeruleus, what are you doing?" he murmured to himself. The Council's silence worried him.

"I've seen what she can do," Caeruleus said, "and how unassuming she appears. If you still want to keep this matter secret, then I request that I retain sole responsibility for bringing her in. I have firsthand experience with the fera's abilities. Send out the ships to scan for her, but let me front the search. Please do not send in agents who don't know what they are facing."

There was another pause from the Council, and Raiden paced his apartment. He suspected Caeruleus was more concerned with getting to pay the fera back for his eye than he was with the safety of his fellow agents.

"We will grant your request. The flyers will be distributed, and we will send out the airships to search for unusual spikes in magical energy. Any word of sightings or abnormal readings will be reported directly to you."

"Thank you."

Raiden brushed his palm across the glass. The dark void faded like clearing smoke, and the reflection of the room and his face returned. He wanted to scold Caeruleus for criticizing the Council to their faces right after receiving their highest honor. Then again, part of him was a little proud. Caeruleus had gotten away with it, after all. The Council probably thought Caeruleus's scrutiny was all about his devotion to his mission. Using his personal vendetta to exude loyalty was brilliant in some ways, and absolutely mad in others.

The repeated clunk of Raiden's boots against the wood floor while he paced reminded him that he was still in his uniform. He removed his coat as he made his way back to his bedroom, where he tossed the stiff garment into the corner. As he removed each piece of the uniform—one boot, then the other—he tossed it all into the corner with no intention of folding the clothing with care or wearing any of it ever again.

He put on a pair of brown pants and a cream shirt before he sank onto the bed in thought. The mattress rustled, and the wire net beneath it creaked under his weight. He had to figure out how to contact the rebels. "Moonstone" was still a mystery to him, and then there was the knowledge that the fera was on her way to Atrium, whether she arrived on her own or in custody. There had to be some way this could all work together to bring down the Council, and hopefully without Caeruleus going down with them.

Nicole listened to her footsteps crunch over forest debris and thud softly against moist earth. She listened to the sound of fabric sliding against fabric as her thighs rubbed together with each stride. The rustle of her bag as it bounced and shifted with her movement, the whisper of the chilly breeze, the happy chirping of winter birds high in the trees around her—it all became a sort of symphony while she hiked.

She couldn't hear the mysterious flute in the distance anymore, and she supposed with disappointment that she had been moving away from it and not toward it all along. But still she listened for it, missing the idea that there was someone who might be a friend to her out there.

I have a friend, she thought, reminding herself of the little warm dragon curled around her neck, a piece of living jewelry. *And he needs a name*, she insisted to her undisciplined mind that kept wandering away from its task.

She fished the pocket watch out of one of the outer pockets of her bag on her back and flicked it open. Almost noon. She felt more tired than she should for only noon, but then, spending the night huddled up in a tree probably didn't result in quality sleep. As she walked, she saw a road ahead, crossing her path almost perfectly perpendicular. She wondered whether it was a different road or the same one she'd been vaguely paralleling the day before.

Then she heard the distant thudding rhythm of horses' hooves. Down the road, just coming into sight around the bend, were three horses and their riders. Her heart jumped up her throat. She ran for the nearest tree and pressed herself against it. As the sound of hooves drew closer, she sidled around the tree to keep herself from view. When they were close enough that she could hear the horses' snorts, her heart accelerated.

At that moment she heard the flute that she had heard earlier, playing the same melancholy melody in deep, soothing tones.

"Would you shut that thing up?"

"It's a bloody fairy flute, idiot. They play on their own."

"Why did you take it, then?"

Nicole didn't dare peek around the tree to see which voice was whose.

"Feeling a bit sentimental for Meridian, are ya?"

"Hey—"

There came a whistle like a musical cry. Then the flute landed just two feet to Nicole's left. Her heart stopped, and her body went rigid.

"Leave it. I'm not listening to it anymore. The damn thing will only warn people we're comin'. It's why we found the last guy in the first place."

Nicole convinced her lungs to breathe again, and she scooted along around the tree, away from the flute, as the men on horseback passed and continued on out of sight. She sank down to the roots of the tree and sat there, waiting until she could no longer hear hooves against the earth. The flute was still playing, its song faint and partly muffled in the dirt.

Once she was sure they were gone, she got up and circled the tree to pick up the flute. It was a simple four-pipe flute. She brushed the dirt off and listened to the music for a minute before she decided to nestle it in the crook of a tree's low branch and leave it. She would have loved to keep it, but as the flute had apparently given away the presence of some other traveler, she knew she shouldn't.

She crossed the road and kept going. Her ears were trained on the music until she could hear it no more. The rhythm of her footsteps and the accompaniment of her bag's rustling was hardly a replacement for the airy voice of the flute. With her hearing now tuned for horses' hooves, she convinced herself that she was better off with silence.

The dull ache in her head seemed to spread to her neck and shoulders. She tried to convince herself it was just the weight of her bag hanging off her body. But as the afternoon wore on toward sunset, she started to think she might be sick.

The sun had started to dip toward the horizon behind her, throwing a long-limbed, alien shadow out in front of her. She began picking up stray sticks and twigs as she went, deciding she would have a warmer, more restful night if she could. By the time she had collected a large bundle of wood and kindling under her arm, she was happy to call it a day, even if there were still a good couple of hours of daylight left.

"What good is 'tremendous power' if you still get sick?" she grumbled to herself. The rational part of her brain supposed that if being sick could make a strong body weak and achy, drain its energy, and meddle with its senses, then her magic was no more exempt from being affected than any other part of her. The logical explanation did not help in the least, and she sighed.

She didn't particularly like the idea of sleeping up against another tree, so she kept her eye out for a better option, an open-enough space between trees perhaps. She tried not to imagine trees lifting their roots and crawling toward her like spiders while she slept. There were several odd rock formations around, and the forest floor grew more uneven. Her body was so drained that she decided on a large rock formation at the top of a nearby slope.

After setting her pile of wood down where she could mostly conceal a fire among the large rocks, she shrugged her bag off her shoulders. The rocks were mostly bigger than her, and the largest looked as though more than half of it was buried.

As she appraised her firewood, she realized what she had probably wouldn't last long, so—after a cursory look around the forest and up at the sky—she summoned up a little magic from her core.

It was slow to respond, and the small surge burned as it had in the first few days of using her magic. In almost two weeks, she realized, her tolerance had in fact grown. Only now her sick body seemed sensitive, delicate. She managed to duplicate her stack of firewood a few times before she couldn't take the searing pain that kept building. For such a miniscule feat of magic, the effort left her feeling as drained and fragile as she had that night on the bridge when she'd lost all control of her powers.

Feeling defeated, she sank down to her butt. "Okay, I'm definitely sick," she grumbled. She felt utterly useless as she constructed some of the firewood into a suitable structure.

"Hey," she said, lifting a shoulder to disturb the dragon's breath around her neck. "Wake up. This is your area of expertise."

The little golden dragon emerged and scurried down her arm as she held her hand out toward the firewood. He hopped off her fingertips and onto the old, broken branches. He dived into the pile and disappeared. Just when Nicole was tempted to lift a branch and look for him, there came a pop, and the kindling ignited, sending the first tiny wave of warmth her way.

Her achy body sagged with relief to feel the air grow warmer. After lifting the strap of the sword over her head and setting the weapon down beside her, she propped her bag up against the rock and sank down against it, fidgeting and shimmying until she felt almost comfortable. This resting place was no softer than on her first night, but with the fire it was far warmer.

She looked around the forest with an anxious gaze before grabbing the sword and positioning it between her chest and folded legs. The flames whispered their secrets, cracking and spitting occasionally. The warmth lulled her closer to unconsciousness with every passing moment, and she watched the little dragon slither and scurry around in the fire, frolicking among the burning branches.

She closed her eyes, and when she opened them again what seemed like a moment later, the forest around her was dark, the last vestiges of the sunset lingering in the sky above. The fire had died down to smoldering embers. The dragon's breath was curled up in the glowing remains of the fire like it was a nest. When she put a new branch down beside the dragon, he sprang into his same excited routine as before, so she piled on a lot more of the firewood. As soon as the waves of heat rolled over her again, sleep dragged her back down.

25. Elude

*R*aiden returned to Tovar's shop seeking answers from the books hiding in the back workroom. He spent the day poring over some of Tovar's books. Books always had answers when he didn't know what to do. They'd had the answers he'd needed to survive in Cantis by himself; surely they could help him decipher the meaning of "moonstone" and lead him to the rebels, especially since several of Tovar's books seemed to be historical texts that contained less-than-complimentary accounts of the Council's actions since their establishment after the Dragon Wars.

But by the end of the day, Raiden could hardly apply anything he had read to meaningful ideas. His head was full of thought soup, and it was pointless to try to organize what was all just sloshing around in a matrix of exhaustion after a long day. He needed sleep to solidify everything in his head and create some order from it.

Even after spending the whole day in a diligent search to get closer to the rebels, he stood up feeling utterly dissatisfied with himself. He sighed. Did he dare to try interbounding home, or would he end up in someone else's bedroom on the next street? It was probably best if he walked, as slow and unbearable as that relatively short distance would be.

The trip across the room took longer than usual. He placed the doorknob in the door and knocked.

Tovar knocked once in response—*wait*. Raiden dropped his forehead against the door, hoping the customer was on his or her way out.

When two knocks came from Tovar's side of the door, Raiden was startled awake, shocked that he'd dozed off on his feet. He stepped back and opened the door to see Tovar waiting for him.

"Any luck?" he asked.

"Not today," Raiden answered. "I'm going home."

"Good idea," Tovar agreed.

"See you tomorrow."

Raiden left the shop and turned down the street, trying not to think of the distance between him and his apartment. Instead, he just focused on the distance between each streetlamp as he went.

When Nicole woke up, she thought she heard a quiet voice, murmuring indistinctly. She opened her eyes to a sleep-blurred view of a dimly lit forest, and she blinked to clear her eyes, realizing it must be cloudy or foggy. The forest wasn't dark, but it was hazy.

An extremely short figure stood hunched over the embers of her fire, snatching repeatedly at something and occasionally striking the still-hot embers instead. He spit in pain and grumbled, trying to catch the dragon's breath.

"Tricky gim," he muttered. "Shiny gim, all mine."

"Hey!" Nicole lurched upright, her hand flashing out to grab the manlike creature by the back of the neck before he could make another snatch at the dragon's breath.

The shrunken man creature shrieked and wriggled furiously, pulling at her hand, trying to escape her grip, but he was small and she was big. In a blur the dragon's breath ran up the goblin's leg and body to her hand and across her arm to his safe place around her neck.

"Mercy, mercy," the goblin squealed, managing to wrench himself free, but he tripped and nearly fell on the embers.

She muttered through gritted teeth, scrambling after him. "Oh, you thieving little—" The sword fell onto the rocks with a metallic clatter, ringing into the forest.

On all fours the goblin crawled out of her reach and jumped up to face her, raising his tiny, bony hands. His skin was an odd orange hue and wrinkled like an old man's. He wore a little, tattered kilt that looked to be made out of scraps of once-luxurious garments, and a sash that was something like a vest, covered in shining bits of jewelry and bobbles.

"Just admiring the pretty gim." His eyes flashed to the dragon's breath. "I didn't take. No harm done." The words tumbled from his mouth as he picked himself up.

"I caught you first," she countered.

"Yes, yes," he said. "You caught me. You win. You are master, master of shiny fire gim. Whatever you want, you can have." He presented his collection of glittering objects, all manner of things: rings, broken jewelry chains, an ornate doorknob, a tarnished silver spoon with an intricately designed handle of flowers and vines.

"Oh, no," she laughed, shaking her head. "No thanks. I'll pass. Just go away."

"You want nothing?"

"I want you to leave me and my 'gim' alone."

By the ugly look he gave her, he had no choice but to obey. "You look human," he said, squinting at her. "But the trees say strange things."

She screwed up her face back at him, and to her surprise, he made his scowl even nastier still. Then he wheeled around and darted away so fast she couldn't have caught him again if she'd tried. Absently, she reached for her neck, and the golden dragon crawled onto her hand.

"That ugly hobgoblin tried to steal you," she grumbled. The dragon's breath spit a tiny bit of fire no bigger than a candle flame that disappeared into the air. "Come on, you tricky little gim," she said. She stopped and tilted her head. "Gim," she uttered and thought that had a nice ring to it. "How about Gim?" she asked and he proceeded to sprint up her arm, across her shoulders, and down her other arm.

When she stood up, her head spun a little. She tried to ignore it, but her balance swayed. She stooped to grab the sword by the strap and swung it onto her back. It was funny, how natural wearing a sword felt when just two weeks ago she'd been wearing a backpack full of schoolwork instead.

As she reached for her bag, she heard a snap and froze to listen. There was only silence first and then a voice.

"I'm telling you I heard something that way," someone said, keeping his words low.

Nicole took a frantic look around, crouching lower into the shelter of the rocks. Perhaps the dragon's breath had Gordan's ability to sense her emotions, because her sudden alarm had turned his playful mood into somber caution. She returned Gim to her neck and carefully maneuvered her bag onto her back.

"Half the time you're hearing some goblin or gnome," another man accused, less cautious with his volume.

"No, I heard a human voice out here. You know travelers who stay off the roads have better stuff."

"I think you're right—you smell that?"

"Woodsmoke."

"Sure is."

Nicole's heart hammered against her chest. *Shit, shit, shit*, she thought as she looked down at the remains of her fire. She cringed at every tiny, gritty sound of her shoes against the stones, each shuffle of fabric against fabric that seemed to shatter the silence. She could not see the bandits anywhere within sight down the slope, so they had to be somewhere behind the cluster of rocks.

Taking a deep breath as slowly and quietly as she could, Nicole racked her brain for what to do. Hide or run, magic or no magic, avoid or confront? She could take the risk on using her magic, but her body was still achy.

Running might be more doable than magic right now, especially knowing how using her magic affected her while she was sick. With the way she'd felt after her little trick with the firewood last night, she didn't think she would be able to run after taxing her body with any spells.

There were no sounds of horses' hooves or footsteps. Wherever the bandits were, they were still and waiting, surveying the area.

"That way," one of the voices whispered, close enough for her to hear.

Her body shuddered with adrenaline. She had to fight the urge to bolt, waiting, straining to hear their approach over the pounding of her heart in her ears. If she was going to run, she needed to wait until she knew which direction they were coming from. She didn't hear any sound that indicated they were on horseback, not the creak of leather stirrups or the heavy breaths of horses.

To her relief, she finally heard the sounds of their footsteps moving through the forest. She listened hard, hoping to determine which side of the rocks they might come around. If they were smart, they would approach from both sides. She would have to hedge her bets and hope she could climb over the rocks quietly.

The crunching of their footsteps over the earth drew closer. At her feet there were some shards of rock. She took a palm-sized piece of stone in each hand. Her heart thundered as she hoped to time her plan right. The sounds of their footsteps diverged and moved to either side of her. *Now*, she thought in a panic.

As quickly as she could, she lobbed each stone high into the air, over the heads and line of sight of those approaching, each stone in the opposite direction. The stones arched high through the air. She didn't need to fool the bandits, just to turn their attention for a few seconds. The stones fell, one with a thud against a far tree, the other with a clack against a large forest rock.

She turned toward the massive stones at her back, and as soon as she heard her rock shards strike, she scrambled over the top, using the space between boulders as her path. She could hear the sound of the bandits' footsteps behind her. The tread of her boots gripped the sandpapery surface, and the grit scraped against the flesh of her palms. She reached the top of the rocks and kept herself low as she distanced herself, trying to take long and quiet strides.

"Told ya someone was here," one of the voices said from behind the cluster of rocks.

"Throwing stones—they're still here somewhere," the other said.

"Oy, look!"

Nicole straightened up and shifted into her highest gear.

"Move it—come on!" one of the men yelled.

She ran, her head spinning with adrenaline, trying to convince herself the forest wasn't tilting back and forth beneath her feet. Trees whooshed by her as she resisted the urge to look back.

"No, no—the horses!" one of them shouted in the distance behind her. Try as she might to push herself harder, she knew no amount of distance she put between them would matter when they reached their horses.

"There, that way!"

With sudden dread she knew she couldn't get out of this one without magic, without setting the fire loose through her ill body. She ducked behind a large, twisted oak and pushed a burst of magic out, denying herself any moment for a second thought.

Like hot cement under bare feet, her whole being burned, but gravity retreated and allowed her to float just enough that she could pull herself up into the canopy with swift ease. All she could feel was the fire beneath her skin as she half flew, half climbed. She couldn't feel the bark under her hands or even the twigs that she knew were scraping against her face, her neck, her arms—she could only feel the fire.

The sword and her backpack got caught on branches as she went, until she couldn't go any farther. At a high, thick branch she stopped, closing her magic back into her core. Wincing, she embraced the massive branch as if it were Gordan's neck and waited in agony for the residual burn to dissipate.

She tried desperately to slow her breathing, to calm her heart rate, to disappear into the silence of the forest. As the low rumble of horses' hooves against the soft earth approached the tree, she dared to sit up. The movement sent pangs of pain through her like bell tolls.

"No—this way," a voice said below.

Every muscle in her body, large and small, protested as she repositioned herself in the tentacle tangle of bare branches, trying to keep herself out of sight while determining where the bandits were. She managed to place her feet under her butt and straighten up to stand against the tree's great trunk. Taking a peek around the tree, she spotted them.

There were three horses and three riders. One of the riders had almost porcelain-pale skin but with a distinctly green tinge and sleek golden hair hanging just to his shoulders around long, slender ears. Where there probably should have been pointed tips at the end of his ears, there was a harsh, flat edge, as though they had been cut. The rider beside him appeared human, with thick, dark hair, a thick neck, and tanned skin. These two accounted for the male voices she had heard.

Lastly, the third rider and horse trailed just behind them, a woman. She had dark-blonde hair braided intricately from her widow's peak down the middle of her head to the nape of her neck. The sides of her head were shaven. She leaned forward on her horse, looking around with seemingly little interest.

Nicole didn't want to resort to magic again, not while her body was still stinging from her ascent into the tree. As the bandits passed right below the tree, Nicole kept close to the trunk, skirting around it with careful steps from one branch to the next to stay out of sight.

"Come on; we'll check the road," the woman said in a disinterested voice that was completely unlike the other two voices Nicole had been listening to. It was soft, low, and commanding.

Both men let out grunts of annoyance.

"I *was* right," one said.

"They're round here somewhere still. Can't get far on foot."

"If you idiots don't shut your mouths, they'll stay well out of sight, and we won't find them," the woman said. The softness of her warning was threatening.

Nicole remained pressed against the bark as she listened to the horses moving away from the tree, three sets of four-beat rhythms fading into the forest. She did not dare take any more looks around the tree to watch them go in case they had gotten suspicious and taken to searching the branches overhead.

It wasn't until she couldn't hear a single hoof against the ground that she dared to glance around her hiding place. They were so far in the distance she could only see them now and then through the trees. Slowly, she made her way down through the old, gnarled branches until she dropped from the lowest bough to the ground.

She couldn't be sure where the sun was in the hazy gray sky. She didn't know which way was east anymore, but she knew she wanted a different direction from the three thieves. Not two strides from the tree, a sudden weight hit her shoulders, and she was yanked backward.

"Knew you were up there," a voice grumbled behind her—the female bandit. The woman was trying to wrestle Nicole's bag off.

Nicole grabbed her bag's straps, one in each hand, to secure it to her and turned hard, throwing her assailant against the tree, but the woman's grip held. *Fine*, Nicole thought angrily, slipping out from the strap and whirling around with a ready fist. The woman tried to lean away, but Nicole's knuckles struck her hard in the face. The woman's grip faltered. Nicole yanked her bag free and ran.

The woman wasn't thrown off for more than a second, and Nicole could hear her cursing close behind, keeping pace. The trees whipped by as Nicole ran. Then suddenly a high-frequency buzz and a pulse of heat flew past her and struck the trunk of a tree.

She didn't have to look over her shoulder to know the woman had a gun, like the one the Council's man had been armed with in Tucson. But Nicole had no way of knowing what kind of spell this woman was shooting at her, and she sure didn't want to find out. The woman fired again, two shots.

The pounding of Nicole's feet against the earth echoed in her head, which felt light and empty. Only instinct moved her, her ache-ridden muscles still capable of speed even if it was less than her best. Adrenaline had provided an override—the illness in her body did not matter now—but it did not steady her head or clear her vision. She didn't know how long she could keep pushing. Then the forest went strange all around her. The varying trees suddenly seemed to be an army of straight and slender duplicates lined up in unnaturally perfect rows.

At first she thought she must be out cold on the ground, just imagining she was still running, her head spinning, confused. But then the word *orchard* came to her mind, and she spotted a house and a barn ahead. She choked on a cry of relief as she gasped for air. She tried to push her legs just a little faster, but she knew that she was slowing and her pursuer was not. As Nicole's body failed her, her vision blurring around the edges, a firm grasp seized her bag.

The woman threw on the brakes, and Nicole lurched forward against the sudden stop before falling backward. The woman wrestled Nicole's bag to the side and latched a firm grip on the sword. Nicole realized then that the woman wanted the sword, not the bag. The bag slipped off Nicole's back and hit the ground with a thud. Nicole threw elbows back blindly but couldn't turn around to face her opponent *and* keep her hands locked on the strap that kept the sword attached to her torso.

"Hey," a voice shouted, and Nicole looked up to search for its source.

There was a figure approaching. Nicole tried to blink through the distortion of her pounding head. The person carried a long object, a bat maybe—no, a long gun. The figure raised the gun at them.

"Get out of my orchard," the person commanded with such severity that Nicole wanted to get the hell out of there.

The woman gave the sword another yank. Nicole was pulled to the ground, but the sword did not come off its sturdy leather strap. The woman gave up, releasing the sword. Nicole tried to get up, but she couldn't even determine which way was up and which was down in her spinning head. She sank to the ground as darkness closed in around her vision.

Raiden opened his eyes to the sound of banging from the opposite side of his apartment. His head was still heavy with sleep and confused by dreams. Was he reliving yesterday? No, of course not. This banging refused to stop. He stumbled out of bed. As his rested body gained momentum and his mind cleared, he grew more annoyed at the sound. He yanked the door open, already prepared to snap at the person on the other side.

It was Caeruleus. Raiden's annoyance recoiled. It was morning, after all, and he had gotten a full night's sleep.

"About time," Caeruleus said, stepping inside before Raiden could utter a word.

"Come in," Raiden answered, closing the door.

"The fera is in Veil."

Raiden raised his eyebrows, trying to mimic surprise.

"I spent all day yesterday in one of the ships out scanning for her. Wanted posters are being distributed to the surrounding towns too. Someone will spot her eventually and we'll find her, but I need your help. I get one more shot at her, and *I'm* going to win this one."

"Whatever you need," Raiden said. Of course he would help. Sure, it would be grand to see the Council crumble tonight and Caeruleus walk free from his duty to their backward justice and secretive assignments, but Raiden wasn't any closer to finding the rebels today than he had been yesterday, so he figured he might as well ensure Caeruleus was prepared to survive his next encounter with the fera.

"Great," Caeruleus said with an exuberant nod.

A warm, gentle voice crept into Nicole's head. "Miss?"

A woman's voice.

"Honey, can you hear me? Can you tell me your name?"

Nicole had every intention to answer. Her name was right there in her head, but she couldn't make her mouth form it, couldn't find up or down or anything solid around her. Her head was in a dizzy sea of darkness.

"Do you know what's wrong with her, Keren?"

"Her eyes are clouded black—looks like odum fever. Asi, please get her bag. Fen, let's get her inside."

Nicole drifted away, wondering what the woman meant about black eyes and odum fever.

Caeruleus shook his head, pacing the living room while Raiden sat reclined on the couch.

"Don't you think I should have—"

"No," Raiden said, dropping his head back. Then he sat up, leaning forward away from the back of the couch. "I'm telling you, this is all you need. Up against someone like the fera, this kind of protection is *also* your ammunition."

Caeruleus stopped to give him a skeptical squint with his one blue eye. "Fine," he said. "But if I lose my other eye ..."

"You'll come find me, will you?" Raiden said, attempting to contain his laughter and failing. He leaned back against the cushions. "Trust me—I have read more books than a damned master of sorcery in the last nine years."

Caeruleus rolled his eye. "So where am I supposed to get a nettle ward?"

Raiden heaved his weight off the low couch. "I know a man who might be able to point us in the right direction."

"Lead the way," Caeruleus said, reaching for the door and opening it for Raiden.

Raiden and Caeruleus walked into Tovar's shop. Raiden had a belly bun in his hand, and Caeruleus moved with a stiff anxiety in his stride.

"Hello, Raiden," Tovar greeted. "Who might this be?"

"My friend Caeruleus. He left Cantis when we were young."

"And here you are reunited in Atrium. It's nice to meet you. I'm Tovar," he said, offering his hand.

"Likewise." Caeruleus took his hand and gave it one swift shake. "Raiden said you might be able to point us in the direction of a nettle ward."

"I see." Tovar pressed his mouth against his fist and then raised the same hand, pointing casually toward the ceiling. "You know, I think you'll find one on Moon Street at Silent Sorcery. Tell Madam Yama I sent you."

"Great," Caeruleus said, making a triumphant fist. "Thank you. I've got to run. Catch up with you later, Raiden." He was out the door before Raiden could swallow his mouthful of food and answer.

"In quite the hurry," Tovar remarked with the slightest hint of amusement at the corner of his mouth.

Raiden sighed. "The Council is tracking down a fera, and Caeruleus is assigned to the task. He lost his eye the first time he tried to bring her to Atrium. I don't want to see him get hurt again."

"A fera?" Tovar repeated. "They're supposed to be gone."

"Well, one escaped to the other realm, I guess, and then she showed up in Cantis."

"You never said—" He stopped himself. "You didn't mention the Council had found a fera."

"It's not my mission, not my concern. I do like to think she'll teach the Council a lesson. The court seers have apparently seen her in Veil and on her way to Atrium. I thought the rebels were the key to bringing down the Council, but the Council might have sealed their own fate with the fera." Raiden shrugged. "I just don't want Ruleus to lose any more than he has."

"Does this mean you're done tracking down the rebels? Going to leave it to the fera?"

"No, no. I've got to keep looking. I can't count on the fera—certainly not if Caeruleus succeeds the next time he meets her. The Council got rid of the others, after all. As much as I would like to see them fail, they have a successful record behind them."

"The books are right where you left them," Tovar said, raising his hand toward the back of the shop.

"Thank you," he said, heading for the back, but he stopped and turned to Tovar. "You don't seem concerned about the prospect of the Council falling.

Your business, your life here in this city might fall apart with them. Why are you okay with that?"

Tovar smiled. "There are more important things."

Raiden's face pinched in a brief frown as he wondered what made a man like Tovar want to defy the Council, and then he turned back toward the rear of the shop.

When Caeruleus stepped into Silent Sorcery, two people were bickering at the counter, their language unknown to him. They both spouted simultaneous streams of syllables at each other, and it seemed to Caeruleus that neither of them could possibly hear what the other was saying.

It appeared they were arguing over the box of various stones sitting on the counter between them. The woman behind the counter, with white hair and age-spotted face, shook her head at the man across from her. The man had a handful of rectangular silver pieces—payment for the supply of stones, Caeruleus supposed—but obviously wasn't pleased with the amount. He kept repeatedly jabbing the counter with his finger to emphasize his point. The woman's expression was so sour that her entire face puckered, her eyes getting lost in her wrinkled frown.

"Ah!" She threw her arms up, took the box in one arm, and shooed the man away with a wave of the other arm.

The man let out a huff of exasperation, closed his hand around his payment, and turned to leave. Caeruleus thought for a second that the man might walk right into him in his flustered exit; he seemed utterly oblivious to Caeruleus standing there just inside the door.

The woman turned to place the box on a shelf behind her. She didn't seem to realize Caeruleus had walked into the shop either. He looked around. The shop was filled with all kinds of relics, amulets, idols, totems, scepters, staffs—he almost went dizzy taking it all in. This sort of magic was usually expensive, but if the nettle ward could do what Raiden said it would, then it was surely worth whatever the cost might be.

Caeruleus cleared his throat and stepped up to the counter. "Pardon me, are you Madam Yama?"

The woman looked up at him, her expression blank beneath her hooded eyes.

He continued, "I'm looking for a nettle ward. Tovar said you might have what I need."

At the sound of Tovar's name, Madam Yama's face shifted into a crinkled smile. "Yes, yes. I can help you."

She came around from behind the counter and shuffled across the shop to a display of countless pendants and amulets. For a moment she stood there searching the selection, making clicking sounds with her mouth. Then she raised her shaky hand to pluck one of the pendants off the velvet board. The round pendant was the size of a large coin, a disk as thick as his little finger comprised of two half-moon pieces, one red and one blue.

"We call this the stinging nettle," she said with a breathy chuckle. "Red jasper and sapphire sealed together with nettle sap. All have potent protective properties, but *together* ..." She finished with a grave nod.

"So this can repel anything?"

"No, not *anything*," she said, and his heart sank. "It won't stop a fist or protect you from a poison if you're stupid enough to drink it. But spells, curses, magical attacks of any kind, yes."

His heart pounded hopefully.

"It will repel and rebound any harmful magic directed at you," she confirmed.

"Perfect. I'll take it," he said, reaching for the small leather purse tucked into the inner pocket of his jacket. "How much?"

When he pulled out his purse, the coins clinking within, she forced a short burst of air through her lips in a disparaging sound. At first, he thought she could tell he didn't have enough. He did have a few gold pieces among his silver, though. Just how expensive could this amulet be?

"You are a man of the courts, yes?" she asked, eyeing his uniform.

"Yes," he said, even though his uniform clearly answered for him.

"Payment for the stinging nettle is a favor," she said with a nod.

"What kind of favor?"

"I want a permit to import from every state. You bring me that permit, and the stinging nettle is yours."

"Done," Caeruleus said, turning on his heel and marching to the door. It wouldn't take him more than a few hours to get her that permit, and then he would have the stinging nettle.

26. Safe

"That's the second time a ship has flown over us. Twice in a day—we don't usually see them twice a month," a girl said.

The voice reached Nicole's consciousness as her mind emerged from the darkness again. She was glad to feel firm cushions under her, to know she wasn't lost in that consuming nothingness anymore.

"Do you think it might have something to do with her?" a different young girl asked.

"There's no way to know," a woman said. "She needed help; that's what matters."

Nicole opened her eyes to see a wood ceiling above her.

"You're back so soon," the woman said with pleasant surprise in her voice.

"Back?" She blinked and turned her head to see the woman sitting beside her. "What do you mean?"

"It usually takes a little longer for people to recover from odum fever, even with the aid of an eyebright potion. We only gave it to you a few hours ago."

"Odum fever," Nicole repeated as she tried to sit up, but she only managed to get about halfway.

"It's a minor infection you can get if you've been scratched by certain creatures. The fever makes you weak, achy, but its trademark symptom is the total darkness that clouds the mind and the eyes."

"Oh." Nicole realized slowly how obvious it must be that she wasn't from

Veil if she had no idea what a common ailment was. "Right." She hoped she sounded delirious instead of clueless.

Then she noticed there was something soft and warm curled up on her thighs. The fluffy disk of red fur didn't seem to have a head, but its bushy tail gave a little flick.

"Hope you don't mind," the girl said.

Nicole turned her head to look over her shoulder. A pale young girl with straight black hair, maybe twelve or thirteen years old, came around the couch Nicole was lying on.

"Shio doesn't usually take to strangers, but he seems to like you," she explained, nodding toward what Nicole was certain was a fox.

Her brain fumbled for words. "Oh, that's fine." She thought of the animals on Tumamoc Hill drawn to her magic, and she almost explained that it wasn't her that Shio liked but the warm furnace of magic inside her.

"What's your name, dear?" the woman asked.

"Nicole."

"Where are you from?"

"Cantis," she answered easily, deciding she would borrow Raiden's life but forgetting for a moment what that would mean to people on the mainland.

The woman's eyes went wide with surprise. "Goodness, they said there weren't any survivors in Cantis. What on earth brings you to the mainland after all these years?"

"There wasn't any reason to stay."

"Are there any other survivors?" an older girl standing beside the woman asked, looking at Nicole with hopeful curiosity. The older girl looked to be sixteen maybe and had rich brown skin and a halo of black curls around her head.

"No." Nicole's voice was somber.

"Forgive us for insisting on such a painful topic without introducing ourselves," the woman said, nudging the girl.

"I'm Fen," the girl said.

"I'm Asi," the younger girl, who was now sitting at the end of the couch, said with a smile.

Asi's black hair, cut short in line with her jaw, was so sleek and straight it almost looked wet hanging around her face. The freckles on her pale cheeks around her almond-shaped eyes made Nicole think of her sister-in-law, Frances. Asi and Fen looked nothing alike and were clearly not biologically related, but Nicole knew siblings when she saw them.

"I'm Keren," the woman said.

Nicole's eyes drifted around the room, searching before she even remembered what she was looking for—her bag and Raiden's sword. All around the cozy living room there were plants in pots and vases, many hanging from the beams of the ceiling. There was a veritable garden inside this house.

"Your things are right here," Keren said, gesturing to Nicole's bag and Raiden's sword on the floor beside the couch.

Nicole sank back into the pillows, relieved to see the sword. She sighed. "Thank you."

"Thieves don't usually bother us. We don't have the kind of valuables they want, and they would have to steal a *lot* of fruit to get the kind of money they're after," Keren said with a chuckle.

"Fruit?"

"From the orchard. Of course, they could fetch a lovely sum for certain herbs in our garden, but they would have to be smart enough to know what's what." She and the girls laughed together.

Nicole studied Keren. She was sitting on a stool, but the drastic bend of her legs and the height of her knees suggested she was tall. Her clothes were large and loose—a boxy white tunic and a long yellow vest that hung unfastened around her. She had long brown hair and eyes dark like rich soil. Her hands, which were lying in her lap, drew Nicole's eye. The tips of her thumbs and fingers were a deep green, as though stained by emerald ink. The color grew gradually fainter the closer it got to her palms, which were a suntanned beige.

"You've never met a floramor," Keren said, opening her hands in display, palms up.

Met one? Nicole had never even heard of a floramor, but she couldn't say so. She couldn't just tell them she was a rogue fera from the old world on her way to Atrium who still knew so little about a realm she sort of belonged to.

"I haven't. Meeting anyone is still"—she searched for the right word—"surreal, I guess." She remembered how Raiden had reacted to meeting her, not just someone from the other realm but a living, breathing person. Her heart ached a little, partly for thinking of Raiden and partly due to her own relief to be in someone's company.

Nicole became uncomfortably aware that all three of them were looking at her—with interest, expectation, or perhaps uncertainty.

"I should get going. Is there any way I can thank you for—"

"Nonsense," Keren said, leaning over to place a hand on Nicole's forehead.

"Your eyes and head may have cleared, but you still have a fever. Besides, as bad as that woman wanted to get this sword off your back, they will be hanging around beyond the orchard waiting for you to leave. Take a few days to recover, and let them give up."

"You'll just let a stranger stay with you?"

"Is there any reason I shouldn't?"

Nicole's immediate thought was *Yes*. The Council was looking for her. One of their agents or even a whole army might show up at the door any day.

"I'll take that as a no, then," Keren said. "I won't turn a sick girl out onto the road for the thieves. You're practically traveling with bait wearing that thing on your back and that on your neck."

Nicole was surprised that she had forgotten about Gim. She lifted her hand to her neck and indeed found the little gold dragon circled there, resting over her clavicles. Keren only seemed to think Nicole was stupid enough to be wearing a gaudy golden necklace while traveling. Needless to say, dragon's breath was probably even more valuable than a solid-gold dragon necklace.

Gim moved at Nicole's touch, and Keren and the girls all jumped. The fox on Nicole's legs bolted awake, and immediately his eyes locked onto the glinting golden creature crawling around on her chest. She knew that look and what would follow. Nicole trapped Gim under her hands before Shio pounced. All he could do was sniff and paw at her hands.

"Was that …? Is that a …?" Keren couldn't find her words.

"Dragon's breath," Nicole affirmed with an apprehensive voice.

"I've only ever heard of it," Fen said.

"How did you get it?" Asi asked.

"It was a gift," Nicole explained, "from family."

"Well, they aren't called immortal flames for nothing, are they?" Keren said. "Must've been in your family for generations."

Nicole almost laughed. *Sure, he's been in Gordan for centuries.* "I suppose."

"Well, when you do leave, best to keep that hidden. I can't think of anything more troublesome than an artifact like that on the mainland. I'm not sure what it would inspire more, greed or disdain." There was sadness in Keren's voice.

"I'll remember that," Nicole said.

"Come on, Shio," Asi said, picking up the fox and pulling him away from his concealed quarry.

Keren eyed Nicole's hands with a nervous rigor in her posture. "I'm sure you have noticed we keep company with a lot of plants," she said.

Nicole understood; Gim, the immortal flame, made Keren uncomfortable. "Do you have a fireplace?"

"Yes." Keren stood up, revealing the fireplace that she'd been blocking from Nicole's view. There were glowing embers in the blackened red-brick mouth.

"If it would make you feel any better, Gim can stay in the fireplace. He'll be happy as long as he's got some wood."

Keren relaxed a little. "I can agree to that."

Nicole sat up and swung her legs off the couch, dropping her feet to the floor, and immediately realized how out of sorts she still was. That short distance from semireclined to sitting upright had turned her brain into a spinning top again.

"Oh, you shouldn't get up," Keren insisted.

Nicole sighed. "Here." She plucked Gim off her shirt and held him out.

Keren held her hands against her chest—she clearly wasn't about to touch living fire.

"He doesn't burn," Nicole promised.

Fen stepped forward. "I'll do it."

"Thank you," Nicole said, placing Gim in Fen's cupped hands.

The fox squirmed in Asi's arms as Fen carried Gim to the fireplace and placed him at the edge of the burning embers. He crawled excitedly into the coals and nestled himself in like a bird into its nest. Fen giggled, and Keren let out a tense sigh, clearly much more comfortable with the immortal flame in the fireplace.

Asi let the fox leap from her arms. He ran across the room to sit and stare into the fireplace.

"That should keep the peace," Asi said.

"Yes," Keren agreed. "Now you lie back down," she said to Nicole.

Nicole obeyed in part and reclined halfway against the small pile of pillows, but she was afraid of resting, afraid to close her eyes and fall asleep. If the Council's men came, she might wake up in Atrium. True, that was where she wanted to be, but the Council had already succeeded in wiping out all the other fera in the realm. Though the fera had all had tremendous power, their magic hadn't been enough to survive against the Council's aims.

"I'm going to take a cursory walk around the orchard," Keren said, moving over to an arched door that was wide but almost a head too short for her to walk through fully upright. She grabbed the long-barreled gun that leaned against the doorframe, opened the door, and ducked outside.

"The house was built by a dwarf family. You should have seen us trying to live in it the week before we had a spell worker come and enlarge things," Asi said.

"Keren could barely afford that kind of magic. Her talents lie with plants, of course," Fen said. "I'm only good with potions."

Asi looked at her. "That's not true. You cast butterfly charms better than anyone." There was a hint of jealousy in her voice.

"Oh, and summoning butterflies in the spring is such a talent," Fen scoffed.

"Talent doesn't have to be practical to be appreciated," Nicole said, and Fen smiled. "So the guy who grew your house didn't make it quite big enough?"

"This was the best he could do, and he was the best we could afford," Asi said with a cheerful shrug. "I don't have to duck through the doors yet. And he was able to make the beds the proper size."

"How did you three end up moving into a dwarf house?"

"Keren wanted to settle down, and the land was cheap here since Candhrid was affected so bad by the wars and part of it literally sank into the ocean. People just don't want to live here. There aren't any big cities, just villages and lots of land," Fen explained.

"The closest village is a two-hour walk away," Asi added.

"How far are we from Atrium?" Nicole asked.

"Uhh ..." Asi answered with a blank face.

"We've never been. But some of the people from the village go to do business there. Keren's friend Eli goes in the summer, and she sends fruit with him," Fen said.

Asi wandered over to the fireplace, where the fox was still watching Gim. She picked up a short wedge of wood and placed it in the fireplace.

Movement in Nicole's peripheral vision turned her attention to the window behind the couch. Keren passed by, and Nicole couldn't help looking out at the orchard. She remembered feeling disoriented by the sudden order of the trees when she'd accidently run into the orchard.

"How long was I out?" Nicole asked.

"All day. We got you inside, and then it took Fen a few hours to brew the eyebright potion," Asi said.

"So what scratched you?" Fen asked.

"What?"

"What kind of creature scratched you in the last few days?"

"Oh." Nicole thought a moment, remembering the tear in her pants and the healed cut. "I guess it was one of the mermaids."

Both girls' eyes went wide, and they looked at each other.

The door opened, and Keren ducked through, stepping into the living room.

"Are you two letting her rest or interrogating her?"

"I was just going to brew something for her," Fen insisted, hurrying off through a door at the other side of the room.

Keren turned her questioning gaze to Asi.

"I'll go help," Asi said, whirling around to follow Fen.

Nicole laughed. "They weren't bothering me at all."

"You had siblings I take it," Keren said, leaning her gun against the doorframe.

"Brothers."

"Me too," Keren said with a sad smile, and Nicole suddenly felt the significance of "had" and the affection in her observation. "How old are you, Nicole?"

"Eighteen."

Keren nodded.

"Your girls?"

Keren smiled. "Fen is seventeen; Asi turned fourteen recently. I'm sure you can tell we aren't related, the three of us."

Nicole shrugged one shoulder in a sort of *Naturally* and *What does it matter?* sentiment.

"We sort of ... adopted each other," she said with a nostalgic laugh.

A surge of guilt suddenly rolled through Nicole's gut. Her anxiety over whether or not she could trust strangers was drowned out by the dread that her presence here might destroy this odd, happy family. She couldn't stay, but she could at least wait to leave until night, when they were asleep, to avoid their protests. Besides, she was on the mend. She had spent a whole two days hiking through the dizziness. She knew she could use a few more hours of rest and some food. She made her decision silently behind her smile.

"I really should leave you alone to rest," Keren said.

"Actually, I'm tired of being alone," Nicole confessed. But she couldn't explain to Keren how alone she was. No family to embrace her, no Gordan to accept her, no Raiden to assure her. There were no others like her to help, and their absence foretold her fate. *I am a fera*—if she said that aloud, would the name strike Keren with fear?

"All right then." Keren lowered herself into a chair opposite the couch in the small room.

Five minutes later the door across the room opened, and Fen appeared, holding the door open for Asi, who was carrying a tray in her hands. Fen looked excited as Asi set the tray down on the stool beside the couch. On the tray there was a plate with a few thick slices of bread, a steaming teacup, and a short-stemmed glass with a mysterious, cloudy white liquid, like water with a few drops of milk added to it.

"Oh," Nicole said when she saw the tray.

"Drink this first," Fen said, pointing to the milky liquid.

Nicole sat up again, slowly this time, and her head hardly spun at all. She picked up the glass, raised it to her nose, and sniffed. There was a floral scent to it.

"Is this going to make me spill all my secrets?" Nicole teased.

"No," Fen said, laughing. "It's a healing potion."

"It's really complicated to brew," Asi said, bouncing once where she stood. "She had to start it when she started the eyebright potion."

Nicole did the rough math—a potion that took at least six hours? She looked into the glass with disbelief.

Fen shushed Asi, but Keren perked up behind them. "Oh? The challenging ones always use the special herbs," she said.

"I only needed a tiny bit of everlasting," Fen said with a cringe.

"Fen, the everlasting is almost gone," Keren chided.

"The eyebright potion only clears the darkness from the head. This will cure the odum fever, guaranteed. She'll be better before nightfall."

Keren gave her a stern look.

Nicole, still holding the potion, felt bad. "Do you not grow everlasting yourself, like all this?" She looked around the room.

Keren sighed. "I would if I could get my hands on a living plant. As far as I know, it only grows on the shores of the Wastelands."

Nicole didn't need to be told it was an expensive herb for someone to have in their cabinet. She couldn't refuse the potion if it was worth that much. "Cheers, then," she said, raising the glass before bringing it to her lips and tilting it back. It went down in one gulp, and she involuntarily cringed at the taste of sour milk and bitter greens.

"Sorry. Knowing it will taste bad makes it harder to drink," Fen said. "That's what the bread and tea is for. The potion moves slow, but it kicks in after a couple hours, and just like that, you wouldn't even know you were sick."

"She is a regular wizard laureate with potions." Keren's voice softened with adoration.

Nicole reached for a piece of bread and took a bite to chase away the foul taste lingering on her tongue. She took the teacup in the other hand and could smell it was simple hot water with lemon and honey. Her appetite was nowhere to be found, but still she chewed the bread gratefully, dreading having to swallow it, as her stomach didn't feel all that welcoming.

"She's been dying to try that potion for years, but none of us have been sick with more than a cold," Asi chimed in.

"Well, I'm glad I could be of service," Nicole said, thinking hard about what she could do to repay them for their help and especially the costly herb.

27. Aid

*N*icole kept taking tiny, dutiful bites of the bread and chasing it down with sips of the slightly sweet lemon water. She knew her body needed the sustenance, even if her stomach was uninterested.

While she waited for Fen's healing potion to kick in, she wondered how Keren and the girls felt about the Council.

"I don't exactly know much about what's been happening on the mainland," she began. "Fen said you recently moved into this house. Did you not always live in Candhrid?"

"No. I used to travel around, tending to gardens and crops as I went to make money. But it became more and more difficult to get around."

"Why is that?"

"Well, the royal states haven't made it easy to come and go."

"Royal states?"

"The kingdoms with surviving royal families after the Dragon Wars. Candhrid is a free state; as you know, Candhrid's royal family did not survive the war. Neither did the royal family from—oh, I forget, Orodon maybe. The Council promised to lead the realm without borders, yet somehow all the old borders remain," she said with a dry laugh. "Some of the royal states are especially strict about travelers these days. Travel into the open states is, well, open, but people would rather be in the royal states, where they have done a much-better job recovering from the war and prospering under the Council."

"Oh," Nicole said, noticing Asi's and Fen's faces as Keren spoke of royal states and prosperity. They looked as though they smelled something disgusting. She took another bite of bread and reverted her eyes back to Keren.

"I suppose it is because they had their royal families to rally their spirits and reinstate order. Everyone was so broken after the Dragon Wars. I don't know the politics of it all, but I can tell you that the Council has never really had a strong presence in the open states. Maybe because they don't have the populations that demand attention. Take Candhrid. Here there are just scattered homes, small townships, and the occasional village with little more to offer. I've heard people call it the 'dead state' because so many people fled to the safety of the Council's new city and its walls after the Great Union."

"That's why the land was so cheap," Nicole said, understanding.

"Precisely. We're close to Witch Haven; it's a village with a decent market. We can make a good living when the trees are bearing their fruit. In the off-season we sell herbs to the apothecaries and potions supply shop. Luckily, I have a way with the trees." She raised a hand, showing off her green-stained fingers, and smiled. "I can get the trees to bloom early and again late in the season. The orchard is still new; the trees are young, and so is our relationship. Even I can't get fruit out of them this early, but I can usually get them to bear fruit in early spring, which means we have a good few months with no competition at the market."

Nicole had an idea about how she could repay them for all their help. She listened and sipped a little more of her hot lemon water, which was still remarkably hot even after sitting there as long as it had.

"So where is it you're going, Nicole? Did you have somewhere in mind?"

She nodded. "I'm headed for Atrium to find someone I used to know."

"Oh, well, you're in luck. The city isn't far from Witch Haven—a three-day journey I believe. I'd like to send some fruit to market there this year, but that can be tricky. Atrium is like its own royal state; you've got to have a permit for everything you bring through the wall."

"Is it hard for people to get in?"

"That I don't know," Keren confessed. "I can ask Eli. He sells goods in the city."

Even though she'd swallowed the potion over an hour ago, Nicole's stomach suddenly grew warm, as though she had just swallowed a large gulp of hot tea. It occurred to her that the sensation had to be the potion taking effect.

Almost as suddenly as her stomach went warm, it seized with a pang of hunger. Her aches shrank away, and her head was clear and steady again.

"Oh, wow," Nicole said, looking up at Fen, who perked up where she sat in the armchair, her legs crossed in front of her.

"How do you feel?" she asked, leaning toward her in suspense.

"*Hungry*," Nicole laughed, taking a substantial bite of her barely nibbled bread.

"Yes," Fen cheered under her breath.

"What did it feel like?" Asi asked.

"Like the time my brother gave me whiskey," she said, covering her mouth as she mumbled through her bread. She forced the mouthful down. "My stomach got really warm all of a sudden and then ... all better."

"Our Fen can brew anything," Keren said with a sweet smile.

Nicole finished the piece of bread and sighed, reaching for a second one.

"I don't know much about potions myself, but I'm impressed. How did you learn so much? Just by teaching yourself?" Nicole asked, still stunned by how hungry she was.

Fen shifted an anxious look at Keren, and Asi fidgeted on the stool, her eyes on the floor.

"I just remembered," Keren said. "We haven't started dinner. Girls, what should we have tonight?"

They looked relieved at the change of subject, and Nicole couldn't shake her confusion. Still, she managed to chime in, "Would you mind if I make you dinner tonight, or help at least, as a thank-you?"

"I don't mind. Girls?"

They nodded in approval.

"Wonderful," Nicole mumbled through another mouthful of bread.

They giggled, but Nicole couldn't forget their discomfort just moments ago. She wondered whether Fen had lost someone. Obviously they all had. Why else would these three have made their own family together? Theirs was a story Nicole was not welcome to know; that much she could understand. All she could do was be grateful for this perfectly unusual family, even if they could not trust her with their secrets and she could not trust them with hers. She finished her second slice of bread, put the third piece in her mouth, picked up the tray, and stood up.

"Lead the way to the kitchen, girls," Nicole said around the bread between her teeth.

Asi jumped up from the stool and whisked across the room to the door she and Fen had disappeared through earlier. Fen popped up from her chair and followed Nicole. On her feet for the first time, Nicole could finally tell how low the ceiling was. It was high enough for her to walk around, and Keren could stand in the room without stooping. But the doorways were certainly too short. Nicole would have hit her forehead square on the doorframe if she hadn't ducked. Just as Asi had said, she could still walk through the door without ducking, but she had only an inch or two left to grow before she too would be bending to pass from room to room.

Nicole made her mental list of chores to do before she left. As soon as they were sleeping, she could get to work. She placed the tray down on the great slab of wood that was the countertop of the island. She grabbed the bread sticking out of her mouth, taking a bite as she did so, and surveyed the kitchen.

There was a large basin sink with copper pipes and ceramic knobs. On either side of the sink the counter was covered in a mosaic of mismatching tiles of different sizes, shapes, and patterns, including some broken pieces too—the affordable leftovers of a hundred different homes. The counters were slightly lower than they should be, only as high as her hips instead of her waist. Opposite the sink was a wood-burning oven, like an overgrown fireplace and swollen chimney with an iron door. Countless hanging pots of herbs dangled from the ceiling at face height, creating a kitchen obstacle course, and there were eggs in a basket beside the sink.

There was a small, bulbous cauldron soaking in the sink and some ingredients strewn about—potion making Nicole supposed. She even caught a whiff of the floral scent of the healing potion hanging in the air.

"All right, what do we have to work with for dinner?" she asked the girls.

They rattled off what they had on hand.

"Beans, flour, oats, rice, tons of pickled vegetables," Asi said.

"We have butter, a few cheeses, and fresh milk in the cabinet," Fen added.

"In the cabinet?"

"Right here," she said, turning to a shoulder-high, freestanding cabinet with a single door. She opened the door. It was like any other cabinet, but a draft of cold air slithered into the room.

"Oh, a cold cabinet," she chuckled to herself. It was a refrigerator. *And why not?* she thought. Just because they didn't rely on electricity in this realm didn't mean they wouldn't have figured out the same basic conveniences. They'd probably had cold cabinets for food centuries before the other realm had started using iceboxes. She shook her head at herself for expecting so little of a realm full of magic.

"We have some vegetables in the garden too," Asi said.

"I can work with that," Nicole said, nodding. "Is there anything you prefer to make?"

"No," Asi chirped.

"Not at all; make what you want," Fen insisted.

"All right then. I just need your help since I don't know where anything is in this kitchen," Nicole said, looking around at the countless cupboard doors.

Raiden searched the shelves of Tovar's workroom, trying to decide which books might be most helpful from their titles alone. He thought his best bet for making sense of the rebels and their moonstone clue might lie somewhere simple that he wasn't seeing. How could the rebels recruit people if the clue was too hard to decipher? He sighed, lifting one of the glass doors closing in a lower shelf.

There weren't any books on this shelf, just jars, bottles, and vials of various ingredients and potions. To one side there was a little army of identical bottles, small and containing the same sky-blue liquid. Raiden plucked one of these bottles off the shelf and pulled it out for a closer look in the light. *Wakefulness potion,* he thought with a chuckle. So that was how Tovar managed to work on spells all night and still run his shop the next day.

He placed the bottle back on the shelf and closed the glass door. With a sigh he straightened up and crossed the room to another bookshelf. Even though he had already looked at these book spines several times, he looked again, and his eyes kept returning to *Traversing Death.* He knew he wouldn't find any answers in this book, perhaps in any book. He should be searching for answers in the city instead of books, but he felt compelled to pull *Traversing Death* from its place on the shelf.

Perhaps it was something in him, the fact that almost all the people he had ever known in his life were dead, that compelled him to know more about this book. Or maybe it was the book itself, more alive than all of Cantis, enticing him to read its pages. He pulled the book from the shelf and turned it over in his hands curiously as he crossed the room back to the worktable.

With a wave of his hand, all the open books on the table clapped shut with soft thuds and jumped into a neat pile—it was a spell he had mastered years ago. Then he sat on the table, plopped his feet onto the chair, and opened the book, holding it under his nose with one hand.

Nicole brought dinner to Keren, Fen, and Asi, all seated at the round table. She felt strangely happy as she directed four floating bowls of food to their places on the table, because Keren, Fen, and Asi didn't blink twice at her use of magic. It was as common as anything here, and so Nicole stirred cooking rice, broke eggs, and opened jars of pickled vegetables mostly without using her hands. She wasn't watched like a circus performer. She was just Nicole.

"If I had the money to hire a cook, you would have the job," Keren chuckled, looking down at her bowl of rice with green onion omelet, thinly sliced pickled carrot and radish, and roasted mushrooms all arranged neatly on top.

Nicole smiled.

"Well, if she's staying for a few days to wait out those forest thieves, she can always cook for room and board," Fen suggested to Keren while nodding eagerly at Nicole.

I can't stay, she wanted to tell Fen, *not even for a few days.* But she managed to maintain her smile as she sat down in the fourth chair.

"Well, I hope it's as good as you think it looks," Nicole laughed.

Asi plunged her fork into the bowl of food, stuffing her mouth with the first bite before anyone else could disturb their bowls. She nodded vigorously as she chewed and forced it down thirty seconds later.

"It is," she declared.

They ate their dinner with light conversation. Nicole asked Keren if they pickled their own vegetables, which they did, and the girls happily described the great to-do it was in the house when it came time to pickle. Then pickling led the conversation to jam making in the summer when the fruit harvest was at its peak. The jam was kept in the cellar and reserved for sale in the winter when there was no fresh fruit to sell.

When they were finished, the girls stood up with their bowls.

"Hold it," Nicole said. "Cleanup is my job." If she was being honest, Nicole was reveling in the fact that she could use her magic again and it was just a pleasant warm sensation coursing through her instead of that agonizing fire when she had been sick. She never wanted to be sick again. So she gathered up the bowls and washed dishes more cheerfully than she'd ever had in her life. She almost laughed to herself.

Night fell, and the house was a completely different place than it had been in the day because glowing plants now lit the rooms. Nicole tried not to make it obvious how enchanted she was by them. She had to marvel at them discreetly. In the kitchen alone there were three of these leafy green plants spilling over their hanging pots, every stem and leaf glowing with a yellow light like a living chandelier.

The rest of the night, Nicole reveled in the warmth and magic of the house and its family. Her plans to leave that night loomed in her mind, pressuring her to enjoy and memorize it all, a dream that might slip out of her memory when she walked out the door. Once everyone was asleep, she would go, but not before leaving a couple of gifts in gratitude. How easy her departure would be became apparent when the night wore on and everyone began fighting back yawns.

The small house had only two bedrooms. Fen and Asi shared the larger room, as it was the only room that could fit two proper-sized beds, and Keren had the smaller room.

"The couch is the best we have," Keren said.

"I appreciate anything softer than the rocks I slept on last night," Nicole said with a chuckle. "I assure you I will sleep just fine."

Her attempt to assuage Keren's regret seemed to work. Keren smiled. "We can at least offer you the washroom for as long as you like. I imagine if you have been sleeping on rocks in the forest, you haven't had a proper bath in a while."

"I don't even want to count the days," Nicole laughed.

In less than fifteen minutes she was locked in the bathroom with a deep bathtub full of hot water. The tub nearly filled half the bathroom. Keren and the girls might have been happy to live with short doorways and low ceilings, but a properly sized tub was as important as full-sized beds. This one even seemed as if they'd had it increased to be bigger than normal.

Once Nicole was submerged in the tub, she didn't think she would ever convince herself to get out. It seemed like more than an hour passed, but the water didn't go tepid. Then she finally realized she was buzzing happily, magic trickling out of her pores and keeping the water warm. When she was clean and prune-like, she decided she might as well get out, get dry, and get dressed to leave.

She spent a few minutes agonizing over whether or not she should dress for travel when she was supposed to be dressing for sleep. But when she peeked out the door, the hallway was dark, and the house was quiet. Keren and the girls were in their rooms. So carrying her bag in one hand and her boots in the other, Nicole went downstairs, guided by the faint, sleepy glow of a hanging light plant just over the landing.

Downstairs the red light of the fire embers lit the living room. Shio wasn't watching the fireplace, so she figured the fox was upstairs with Asi and Fen. Nicole sat on the couch to put on her shoes, tying the laces up swiftly. As much as she wanted to get her work done and go, she knew she ought to wait a bit in case her movements had disturbed anyone's sleep. To give them time to sink into their dreams once more, she pulled Althea's journal out of her bag and took it to the chair beside the fireplace. She opened the journal and let the pages flutter through her fingers before stopping at a random page somewhere in the middle and searching for discernible words.

A short section of words jumped out at her on the page due to a sudden change in the usual curly jungle of writing. As though Althea had been writing a new entry only to be seized by a sudden change in mood and topic, the swift, light scrawl suddenly turned into thick and halting scratches that stood out among the tangle of writing on the reused page. "The pillars upon the hill will fall before dawn."

Nicole frowned. These roughly written words gave her a chill. Then she flipped through the journal more carefully, searching the crowded pages of Althea's writing for more of those dark, sloppy letters. She found them on another page: "Those who seek to save us will set loose children of discord and destruction. Among them they have but one fate and will break down the walls that seclude us."

Nicole turned page after page, her eyes searching. She found another. "When chaos finds peace and peace embraces chaos, two opposed in harmony will forge the key and unlock our chains."

The more of these strange messages she read, the less she understood. She imagined these moments had been a result of the Sight seizing Althea while she wrote in her journal. A soft snoring from upstairs caught Nicole's attention, reminding her where she was and what she was supposed to be doing. Althea's visions would have to wait.

Nicole closed the journal and tucked it back into her bag, wedging it securely between her clothes and the side of the bag. Then she pulled the drawstring tight and buckled the flap down carefully so that it didn't make a loud click in the silence. She picked her leather jacket up from beside her bag and shrugged it on over her sweater. Raiden's sword went on her back first, and then she swung her bag over the top of it. With everything situated, she crept back across the room to the fireplace.

"Psst, Gim," she whispered, holding out her hand and wiggling her fingers in encouragement. Gim popped out of the embers and scrambled to the edge of the fireplace mouth, onto her hand, and up her arm.

She moved to the front door carefully, as her load seemed inclined to make every noise it could. She managed to open the door silently and slip outside. Then she relaxed a little. After closing the door as softly as possible, she looked up at the house and placed her hands against the wall on either side of the door. *Please let there be no ships out searching in the middle of the night,* she thought, stealing an anxious look around the sky overhead for any movement.

With a deep breath she braced herself for the heat and let her magic swell inside her, filling her to the brim, rushing down her arms, spilling through her hands into the walls of the house. Her magic seeped into every brick, floorboard, doorframe, and door, into every stone of the cellar beneath the house and every truss and beam of the roof, until in her mind she had a picture of everything her magic connected her to.

By the time she could feel her reach through the whole house, she could have sworn if she opened her eyes she would find herself under the sweltering Yuma summer sun. *Now grow*, she demanded, making the house in her mind expand like a bubble. Under her hands the house rumbled as bricks and stones grew. It creaked as the wood floorboards, stairs, and doorways spread. The whole house moaned in the night, and every fiber of her being grew hotter. She feared for a split second that everyone might wake up. But in a mere thirty seconds the front door, just inches from her nose, was at least seven feet tall.

She released the house, stopping the spell. The house was still and quiet. Hardly daring to breathe, she listened, waiting for sounds of anyone waking up to break the silence. But none came. Despite the low moan of the house and the shuddering of its walls, no lights turned on; no voices spoke in the night. Nicole let out a sigh of relief.

The moon overhead provided ample light despite not being full, and when she looked up, Nicole realized the moon seemed much larger in Veil than it did back home. A breeze whistled faintly across the bare forest, carrying a chill through her and making her long for the warmth of the house. In the light of the moon she could make out a dirt track leading away from the house that she was fairly sure would take her to the village of Witch Haven.

But before she could go, she had one last thing to do. No sooner had her body cooled to its usual temperature than she stoked the fires in her core once again. This time she let her magic sink through her legs and pour into the earth. The orchard partially surrounded the house, and those trees closest to her slurped up the magic from the soil as quickly as she released it into the ground. The spiky silhouettes of the trees transformed into soft, leafy shadows swaying in the night. Nicole smiled, hoping those trees would bear fruit in the coming week or two for Keren to sell.

There was nothing left to do, so she directed her feet onto the dirt track and set out, turning her thoughts to the thieves lurking nearby. Although her aim was to avoid them, she prepared to face them. She knew they were out there, and part of her wanted to teach them a lesson. This time she wouldn't run. In fact, she thought a horse would be rather helpful.

She let her bag bounce and her footsteps fall noisily, not bothering to walk carefully like she had through the house. Not long after the house was far behind her and out of sight, she felt a pang of regret. To stifle the tiny ache of sadness in her heart, she imagined Keren, Fen, and Asi waking up the next morning to find that the house had grown and that part of the orchard had mysteriously awoken from its winter slumber. She imagined the trees laden with fruit in a week or two and hoped they would make more than enough money to replace the costly everlasting herb Fen had used for her sake.

The sound of her footsteps, the soft swishing of her bag shifting against her back, and the occasional whisper of the midnight breeze all occupied her ears as she enjoyed her reverie. When she recognized the sound of several more feet approaching behind her, her heart started in terror. She grabbed the handle of the sword and pulled it free from its sheath as she whirled around.

The sudden flash of white light from the blade illuminated two faces, and the pair jumped back with a synchronized yelp. It was Fen and Asi.

Nicole let out her fear with an angry huff. "What are you two doing out here?" she demanded as she returned the sword to its place on her back. The shocked expressions on the girls' faces melted into the shadows as the sword's light disappeared.

"Looking for you," Fen said.

"Why are you leaving?" Asi asked.

"I can't stay anywhere. That's just the way it is. Now you two need to go back home."

"But the bandits," Asi whispered.

"Look," Nicole said, stepping closer. "I was sick yesterday, and I needed help. But trust me, on a regular day I am more than capable of taking care of a few—"

"That so?" A familiar voice joined the conversation.

Nicole turned around to glare as the woman from yesterday stepped out from behind a tree and onto the dirt road.

"I'm inclined to agree," the woman said.

The girls let out a gasp and tiny cry behind Nicole, and she whipped around to see the two men now accompanying Asi and Fen with hard hands gripping the girls slender arms.

"All you got to do is hand over that pretty sword of yours, and we'll be on our way," the woman said as she took long, confident strides to close the distance between her and Nicole.

Nicole sighed, looking around. "No horses, I see," she muttered. She felt Gim's presence on her right forearm as her tendons stiffened and her hands balled into fists. "Gim," she said before throwing a jab at the woman's jaw.

The woman bobbed aside, and Nicole missed, but Gim's belch of fire did not. Flames swirled into the woman's face. Nicole threw a left cross without hesitation as the woman cried out in pain. Nicole felt the heat radiating from the fresh burn as her fist hit, dropping the woman to the ground.

Then Nicole wheeled around and let out a wave of magic that blew past the girls but caught the two men and carried them up into the tree branches, two human-shaped kites flailing on a rogue gust of wind. As an extra measure she let her magic seep into the roots around her feet and then raised her hands and closed her fingers into fists with purpose. The branches overhead trapped the men in a secure grasp while they let out shouts of protest.

Nicole broke into an angry stride toward the girls, catching them by the arms and whirling them around to steer them back to the house.

"That was fantastic!" Asi exclaimed.

"Thank you," Nicole said, more flustered than flattered. "Now I am taking you two home, and you are going to stay put."

"What about you?" Fen asked.

"What *about* me?"

"Are you going to stay put?"

"I told you, I can't stay anywhere. Once I get you home, I'm going to Witch Haven and on to Atrium."

Nearly ten minutes passed in silence disturbed only by their footsteps and the wind in the trees. She marched them along until the house came into view. As they drew closer, it became clear there was someone else standing outside in the night—Keren.

Nicole sighed as they reached the front door, where Keren was waiting, her arms folded in front of her.

"What's going on here?"

"*They* were just going back to bed," Nicole grumbled to them.

The girls hurried through the front door to escape Keren's disapproving glare. The door shut behind them.

"They followed me after I left for Witch Haven," Nicole explained.

"What's this about a fire thrower and men in the branches?"

"How on earth do you—"

"Trees spread gossip like you wouldn't believe," she said flatly. "I thought you were going to wait out the thieves."

"People worse than those thieves are looking for me. I can't stay here, or anywhere," Nicole said, hoping that enough of a confession would convince Keren to let her go and not get involved. "The Council is looking for me. If they find me here, you would be guilty of defying them."

Keren took a deep breath and sighed. Nicole thought it was a sigh of acceptance.

"Then I am already guilty. Come inside for a cup of tea, and if you still want to leave afterward, we can at least send you on your way with some food."

As Keren reached for the knob, the sound of feet thumping up the stairs in a rush came from inside. "Girls," Keren called up the stairs as she stepped through the doorway, "are you going to pretend to be asleep or join us for some tea?"

Nicole hesitated a moment, knowing she was about to be lured into staying, because she wanted to, no matter how much she didn't think she should. She followed Keren through the door and shut it behind her.

28. Stuck

As Nicole and Keren walked through the living room, Keren reached up to touch the leaves of one of the hanging plants, but they were above her instinctual reach. She looked up at the plant, which was higher than it had been before she'd gone up to bed.

"Huh," she uttered as she eyed the now much-higher ceiling. She could still reach the leaves with her long arms, and at her touch, the plant's yellow glow spread through the room. Keren slowly turned her head about to inspect the room. There was suspicion in her slow movement, and then, when she stepped up to the door leading to the kitchen, taller than her by a few inches now, she finally seemed to understand.

Keren turned to Nicole, but before she could say anything, the girls thumped back down the stairs. Fen was sporting a broad smile that looked rather triumphant to Nicole, and Asi appeared to be containing a grin behind tightly pressed lips. Both stopped to give Nicole a hug, catching her off guard as they trapped her for a brief moment in their arms—a thank-you for everything from taller doorways to their safety out on the road so close to home.

When the girls released her, Nicole looked up at Keren's questioning gaze and shrugged. "I wanted to thank you," she said.

Keren shook her head slowly and closed her eyes for a moment. "Come on, then," she said, opening the door into the kitchen and letting them file in before her.

Everyone was silent while Keren went about making four cups of tea, occasionally pausing and adjusting to the new size of her kitchen, the higher ceiling and taller counters. She set the steeping teacups out around the kitchen island.

"I won't pry further into your private matters without first sharing some of our own," Keren began.

Fen and Asi looked at each other.

Nicole waited, picking up her cup. The golden-pink tea smelled of hibiscus and rose hips, lemon and chamomile.

"I used to travel Veil, from one state to the next. That was my life. I called no place home. The royal state of Taroth to the north of Candhrid was a difficult place for me to do business sometimes, but when people need a floramor's services, most don't mind that I am a woman."

Nicole frowned.

"They are … particular about the roles women play in society there. Girls cannot apprentice for practices like potion brewing for instance." Everyone's gaze flicked to Fen.

"Theirs are not my stories to tell. But I can tell you I found them hiding in my caravan long before we left Taroth and I chose not to turn around and bring them back. They made the choice to leave, and it was not my right to take that from them, so I let them come with me. In the eyes of the law, I kidnapped them. In my eyes, they would have kept running either way, and at least I could give them safety." Keren took a sip of her tea.

Nicole could only hold her cup in her hands while Keren's story sank in.

"Like I mentioned before, they adopted me. And, well, that meant the end of traveling the royal states at least. They ask too many questions at the borders, and all travelers require passports. So we settled down here in Candhrid because it's peaceful, and I thought they deserved a real life in a real home, not hiding in a caravan on the road."

"I'm sorry," Nicole said, placing her cup down.

"For what?"

"For running into your orchard and your lives. You mentioned seeing an airship twice yesterday; that's because they're looking for me."

Keren must have heard the guilt in her voice. "You couldn't have known we had anything to hide before you arrived."

"I just don't want to cause you any more trouble than I already have. Good people have already gotten dragged into my life and my problems. I can't risk breaking up your family," Nicole said, thinking about her own family and how broken it would be if she never came back.

"We live with that risk every day, Nicole, even before you arrived. That did not stop us from helping you today, nor will it prevent us from helping you tomorrow if you will let us," Keren said.

"I don't know how to say this without sounding insulting, but how can you help me? What will you do when the Council's men come knocking on your door?"

Keren smiled, looking at Fen and Asi, then Nicole. "We have our talents. Trust me when I say we can hide you."

"You aren't going to ask me *why* they're looking for me?"

"Not tonight."

Nicole didn't know what to say.

"So?" Asi prodded.

"Will you stay?" Fen asked.

Nicole sighed. She didn't know whether it was the warmth of the house or the tea, but all she wanted to do was sleep somewhere warm and soft, just for tonight.

"Sure, I'll stay."

With the matter settled, at least for the night, there wasn't much to do but finish their tea and say goodnight until tomorrow. Nicole returned Gim to the fireplace, removed her jacket and shoes, and was asleep almost as soon as she settled into the cushions on the couch.

A pounding in Raiden's head jarred him out of the words on the page, and he sat up, reluctantly moving his gaze away from the book. The banging came again, and this time he realized it was coming from the door. He hopped off the table and laid the book down, open on the page he was reading. When he placed the knob in the door and opened it, Tovar was standing there with a bewildered look on his face.

"Oh good," he said, his body relaxing. "I thought something happened to you in there. I forgot you were even here last night when I locked up. Do you even realize how long it's been?"

Raiden was temporarily hung up on Tovar's fear that something had happened in the safety of the concealed room. It made him wonder what else Tovar had in his cabinets and shelves besides books that Raiden hadn't discovered yet. Then his gaze drifted away from Tovar's face and over his shoulder, where he could see it was light outside the front door and window, or as light as Atrium ever seemed to be.

"It's morning," Tovar said as though Raiden might be slow to understand. "What have you been doing in here?"

Raiden lowered his ear to his shoulder, noticing a kink in his neck. "Just reading," he answered and removed the knob from the door.

"For twenty hours straight?"

"I suppose so," he said with a shrug.

"All right then, come on," Tovar said, placing a hand on Raiden's shoulder and guiding him out of the doorway. "I'm barring you from this room until you at least go stretch your legs and get something to eat."

Somehow during his time lost in the words of *Traversing Death*, Raiden had never had a single pang of hunger, but now that he was away from its pages, hearing Tovar mention food seemed to wake his appetite.

"Fine," he agreed, tossing the knob to Tovar on his way toward the front door. As he stepped out of the shop, the door chiming behind him, he debated whether to go right to get a belly bun down the street or to go left and head over to Mat Street for something different.

Mat Street won out when he remembered Gwyn was there, and so were a lot of propaganda posters. He could see her warm smile and maybe find another clue in the rebel posters he was missing.

Nicole couldn't ignore the red light forcing its way through her eyelids any longer. She opened her eyes for a blinding moment, morning light flooding through the window and into her retinas. Instinctively she turned away from the light, rolling over and right off the couch.

"Oh shit," she grumbled, confused for a moment. Then she realized where she was—besides facedown on the floor. As she picked herself up, she rubbed her neck and noticed that Gim was curled around it, covering her collarbones.

"Hey, Gim," she cooed, looking over at the fireplace, where there was nothing but cold ash. She could only suppose he had wanted somewhere warm to spend the rest of the night after he'd run out of fuel and the fire had died.

That got her thinking. Did Gim think and *want*, or was his personality a product of her imagination and the principle that magic was drawn to magic, as Raiden had once explained to her? Maybe it was just an imperative for a magical immortal flame to seek the warmest places, and perhaps he fed off her own energy and emotions, like Gordan in a way.

Gim stirred, scurried beneath her shirt collar, crawled across her shoulder, and came out through the sleeve of her shirt. She raised her forearm as though Gim were a parrot perched on her elbow.

"Come on," she said, escorting him to the fireplace. She tossed a couple of small logs into the wide brick mouth and held out her hand. Gim raced down her arm to the firewood. He wriggled in between the two logs, and a minute later a flame flourished around the wood.

Only now did she notice the slight chill in the room nipping at her arms, raising goose bumps. She stood close to Gim's fire for several minutes, waiting for the warmth to creep through the room and into her bones. Out of habit she returned to the couch and found her shoes. Her socks were loose and twisted from sleeping in them, so she straightened them out before pulling on her boots.

"Not trying to sneak out on us again, I hope," Keren said from the stairs as she descended into the living room.

Nicole smiled. "Not this time."

"Good. I hope—" Keren stopped and turned her head like she was listening to something.

"What?" Nicole asked.

Keren leaned to look out the window and then went for the door. She quickly unlocked it, swung it open, and stepped outside, her feet still bare. Concerned, Nicole crossed the living room and followed her outside into the cold morning air. Keren stood there looking around with awe on her face, and Nicole realized why. The trees surrounding the house were not just leafy and green; the branches were laden with fruit.

Keren obviously hadn't noticed this difference in the trees last night. She turned to look at Nicole with utter disbelief. "Did you do this?"

Nicole half grimaced, half smiled, not entirely sure whether she had done something right or wrong. "I just thought you could use—"

Keren lurched forward, caught Nicole's face in her hands, and planted a swift kiss on each cheek. Then she immediately withdrew, looking embarrassed by her sudden outburst. "How did you …?" She apparently couldn't find the words to even finish her question.

"Have you ever heard of the fera?" Nicole asked, throwing secrets to the morning breeze and partly hoping the truth might scare Keren enough to rescind her persistent offer to help.

"Well, yes, most people have, but—" She looked Nicole in the eye. "You?" Her eyes went wide. "When you said the Council was looking for you, I figured you might have done something wrong, but …"

Nicole shrugged. "All I did was exist," she said, trying to smile but only managing a sneer this time.

"But you're just a girl. You're not anything like those stories."

"So I've been told. But that doesn't really matter to them. What matters is what they believe, and they believe I'm dangerous." Nicole had accepted that, and that there would never be any convincing them otherwise.

"Then why on earth would you be *going* to Atrium?" Keren demanded. "I don't understand."

"I told you, I'm looking for someone I know. The Council 'recruited' him, thanks, in large part, to me. If I hadn't shown up in Cantis, they might have just left him alone."

"So you think you're going to march into the Council's city and leave with one of their conscripted agents without getting caught?"

"No. I plan on sneaking into their city and giving them what they want—me. They think they have the right to take me away from my life, from my family. They treat their own agents like they are as disposable as golems, and my friend is stuck there trying to help me. They've tried to get me to Atrium by force and put another friend in danger in the process. My ending up in Atrium has always been a matter of time. I've decided it's going to be on my terms."

"I see."

Nicole feared for a moment she might have proven to Keren that she *was* like the fera in the stories.

Keren sighed, looking around at the trees with a critical eye. "Well, it's a good thing you're still here. You've gone and given us a lot of work to do."

A mixture of disbelief, confusion, and gratitude resulted in a laugh breaking through Nicole's anxious silence.

"How about breakfast, huh?" Keren asked with an easy smile as she turned back toward the door, stepping past Nicole and into the house.

Nicole followed once again. "So that's it?"

"That's it."

"You're ready to get involved in something that could dismantle your family?" she challenged.

"This family believes in doing what's right."

"You barely know me."

Keren turned, halting in the middle of the living room. "I have heard the stories, and I have met you. I have seen this all before, lies that turn people into devils for others to despise, sowing fear and hate to justify treating someone like less than human. It's toted as one of the Council's greatest victories, saving the people of Veil from the fera, tracking them down and stopping their destruction. After the Dragon Wars, people were scared. They wanted unity, but it was difficult to shake the mistrust cultivated by so many generations of fighting. The Council did not unite this realm; they patched it together with fear of a new enemy. I see a young woman bearing a monstrous legacy, one the Council crafted for you. My dear, I know you better than you think."

Nicole stood there feeling like she'd been stripped down to her emotions.

"I have seen the worst atrocities, and they happen when people let their differences divide them. The Council wants you to be alone, to feel alone. Asi and Fen proved to me that people are always stronger together," Keren declared with a dangerous glare.

All Nicole could do was wonder what Keren had seen, remembering that she had mentioned she'd *had* brothers.

The fierce Keren retreated and disappeared behind a sweet smile. "The girls will probably sleep a bit longer. Shall we get that breakfast started?"

Nicole nodded.

Raiden walked the length of Mat Street, halfway through his breakfast—a pita stuffed with heavily spiced lamb, cucumber, apple, and some kind of yogurt. It was one of the few options available this early that wasn't a sweet pastry. He strolled more slowly than most, inspecting any propaganda poster he could find, making his way down one side of the street and back on the other side.

There was fierce competition for marketing space on Mat Street. The propaganda posters that he had seen the other day were already plastered over with ads for treats and deals from the surrounding eateries and then covered once again with new propaganda posters, which made him wonder who was putting up the Council's propaganda and when. Who put up the rebel propaganda for that matter?

As he finished his pita, he decided he should find out, and Mat Street might be the best place to monitor. Why languish over a clue when he could find the rebel putting up the posters and follow him or her back to the rebels' base of operations? Then his mind returned to the book waiting for him in Tovar's workroom. Returning to the pages of *Traversing Death*, just for the day, wouldn't hurt. He could always ask Tovar to remind him of the time. He wiped his hands on the paper that had been wrapped around the pita before tossing it in one of the trash bins in passing.

"You've got some on your face still," a friendly voice said.

He turned curiously toward the woman who had spoken. It was Gwyn.

She had flyers for the pie shop cradled in one arm, and with her other hand she pulled a paper napkin from her apron.

"Here," she offered through a laugh.

He took the napkin and wiped his face.

"Thank you." A momentary flash of that unchanging vision disturbed his thoughts of death like a prod from the future to leave the past alone. *Death is everyone's future*, he thought, suddenly arguing with himself with calm finality.

Every time he ran into Gwyn and each time the vision returned, he felt torn between the future and the past. Those visions had been a beacon of light in his solitude, but he couldn't just turn his back on all those lost lives, not like the Council had. It was their responsibility to protect the people of this realm, and they had failed. They would answer for that treason. He supposed he wasn't the only person who felt this way. Why else was there a rebel movement in their precious city of peace and unity? The Council had turned their backs on their promises long ago.

"Are you all right?" Gwyn asked.

"Oh—yes, sorry," he said, shaking his head. "Lost in my thoughts again."

"Are you due to be anywhere?"

"Not urgently."

"Would you like to help me put these up?"

He pondered for a moment. The book could wait. The rebels weren't going anywhere, and neither was the Council. His past would stay the same, but there was no guarantee the future he had glimpsed would always be there if he kept living in the past.

"Certainly," he said. "Where do we start?"

"Firstly, we've got to be ready for someone to show up looking for you," Keren said as they all sat around the table eating porridge with fried egg on top.

"We should probably assume that they will want to search the whole property if they think she's here," Fen said.

"That's true. We can't count on a hiding place, and we'll need a way to conceal her no matter where she may be. We've got work to do around here after all." Keren was grinning now, like the answer was obvious, and Nicole got the feeling she was the only one who didn't understand.

"Black hellebore," Fen and Asi said in unison.

"What's that?"

"A flower. When dried and ground into powder, it renders anything utterly invisible," Fen recited proudly.

"Mothers like to use it to hide things from their children, like cookie jars," Keren said.

"But it can make a person invisible?" Nicole asked.

"Yes," Asi said with a giggle. "I found Keren's stash of it once."

Fen giggled too, and Keren smiled, shaking her head.

"But if they are able to detect sources of magic, won't the hellebore powder alert them?" Nicole asked.

"All forms and sources of magic are slightly different. The magic in hellebore powder and other plants is not the same as spells and potions, which are more … potent, you could say. The hellebore's magic would be lost here with all the other plants in the house and the orchard and forest around us."

Nicole took a deep breath. "That's good enough for me. I can't argue with someone who knows more about plant magic than I do."

"Smart girl," Keren chuckled and took a bite of food.

"And Keren usually hears the trees talking about people traveling through the forest, so we have fair warning whenever someone approaches the house," Fen added.

"That's good to know," Nicole said, shoveling a spoonful of the oatmeal in her mouth.

They ate in silence for a while, and then Nicole had another thought. "What if someone comes, and they do figure out that I'm here?"

They all looked around at each other.

"If it comes to that, we have Asi," Keren said simply and resumed eating.

Nicole was immediately confused. What in the world was Asi capable of? She turned her eyes to Asi, who smiled.

"I can erase memories," she explained.

"Oh," Nicole said, nodding in an attempt to convince herself that this wasn't at all a surprising revelation being in Veil. She wasn't in Yuma anymore. No wonder they weren't afraid to take in a stranger and even share their secrets. If Nicole had proven untrustworthy at any point, Asi could have taken care of it. They didn't have to worry when they could send someone on his or her way without the memory of having met them at all. She pondered this while she finished her breakfast, always on the verge of laughing to herself. Keren, Fen, and Asi were an unassuming force to be reckoned with.

29. Found

*C*aeruleus glided along on the ocean winds high above the coast, dipping closer to the ground to look more closely. A hostile gust in the air signaled an impending storm. Out over the ocean a terrible churning formation of dark clouds rolled toward the mainland. Caeruleus watched it for a moment, the distance between the beach and the storm serving as relief for his concern. He still had plenty of time to search.

There had been no reports from the ships out searching about abnormal spikes in magical activity, but that didn't mean the fera wasn't here; it only meant she was being cautious. He wished she had stayed in the other realm.

With all the other fera the Council had relied on following their paths of destruction and chaos. From what the Council told him, the fera were virtually incapable of hiding. This one, however, did not seem to fit that mold. She seemed capable of keeping her magic under control at least, but that didn't mean she was any less dangerous or that they didn't have to keep her out of Dawn's hands. The ships were still in the skies searching, but Caeruleus didn't have much hope that this fera would turn up on the scanners.

Instead, he decided he would search for more reliable clues. He knew she kept company with a dragon. Assuming she'd opened a portal in Cantis, she would have to get to the mainland somehow. The salty air whipped against his face and stung his eye as he studied the beach. The dark sand at the water's edge was smooth from the waves, and the dry, windswept sands stretched on undisturbed, for the most part. One segment of the beach appeared disturbed by some commotion. There was a massive crater in the sand and a trail of divots that looked quite a lot like tracks, though they had been softened by the winds. As he drew nearer, his heart leaped with excitement. Those were definitely tracks left by something huge. Gliding down close to the sands gave him a rush of adrenaline. He was still learning the rhythm and balance of flying—and landing.

As soon as he was on the ground, he took a deep breath and called his wings back into the skin between his shoulder blades. The wings were a part of him, bone and sinew and feather, not an illusion of magic, all him. Magically concealing them was slightly uncomfortable. But it was nothing close to the pain of growing them, the blood magic forcing his bones to sprout and twist. He would get used to the strangeness of his new extremities and the stiffness of his wings coiled up inside him. He reached into his pocket and pulled out his small book of identification, permits, and spells, flipping through the pages until he found the spell he needed.

"*Me amosar fortiden,*" Caeruleus read aloud.

A gust of ocean wind barreled over the beach, and two faded phantasms appeared before him: a massive figure standing in the large depression where it had landed in the sand—a dragon in its natural shape—and a young woman with her back to him. Though he could not see her face, her wild curls were familiar to him. The ghostly images flickered in the breeze, moving, having an unheard conversation. With as faint as their likenesses were, it had to have been some time since this moment had occurred, maybe a couple of days. When the fera looked down at something in her hands, Caeruleus couldn't make it out. Then she wrapped her arms around the dragon's muzzle, Caeruleus scowled at her affection. He moved around them, sneering at the intimate exchange. How had she come to be so familiar with a dragon? He watched them part. She nodded and said something, and the dragon bowed its head, turned, and started down the beach.

"What?" Caeruleus wasn't surprised to see the fera and her dragon ally together, but he couldn't understand their going separate ways. The dragon galloped along the water and stretched its wings into the air. Caeruleus looked back at the fera, who watched the dragon go for a few moments, then turned away from the ocean to make her way across the beach toward the forest.

"Why did they split up?" he muttered to himself.

He turned back to the dragon only to find the strange ethereal image was no longer there. The spell extended no farther than the beach where it had been cast. Caeruleus clenched his jaw, troubled by the dragon and by not knowing where it had gone or what it might mean that an entity like the fera was closely associated with the exiled enemies of all of Veil.

The ocean wind pushed at him, a nudge back on track. He shook those unsettling thoughts from his mind. If Dawn were to find the fera, this girl could be the link between the realms two greatest threats. He didn't want to imagine what could come of an alliance between Dawn and the dragons. He directed his attention back to the fera, following the path she had taken toward the forest.

In the kitchen there was a red cabinet with the sole purpose of harboring all of Keren's herbs. Everything was dried. Some jars held full stalks of a plant, others just leaves, dried flowers, roots, or seeds, and several jars were filled with plants milled into fine powders.

Fen held a small cloth drawstring bag while Keren searched the shelves, moving jars back and forth to look at the ones in the back.

"Here it is," she said, pulling out a short, fat jar almost full of a black powder.

Fen held the mouth of the bag open. Keren shoveled out several large spoonfuls of the powder into the bag until there was a good half cup or more in there. The end of the spoon appeared to be gone after being coated in the powder, but once Keren tapped it several times against the jar, knocking the remaining hellebore off, it gradually reappeared.

"That ought to be plenty," Keren said, and Fen pulled the extra-long strings, cinching the bag closed.

"Here you go," she said, handing the pouch to Nicole, who put the strings around her neck and let the pouch hang against her belly button.

"If you need to use it—" Keren started.

"*When* I need to use it," Nicole corrected.

"Just take a handful and sprinkle it over yourself," Keren instructed.

"Got it," Nicole said.

"Okay then," Keren said as she shut the cabinet. "Let's get some work done."

Raiden headed back to Tovar's shop an hour later after helping Gwyn put up her flyers. She'd shown him popular posting places he hadn't come across himself, and he had been intent on checking for rebel propaganda posters lurking among the rest.

He couldn't recall much of his conversation with Gwyn. His attention had been torn between her, the vision, and the strange expectation for their quiet, awkward exchanges to become something so overwhelmingly vital to his soul. In addition, nagging thoughts about *Traversing Death* kept promising him some connection with his mother if he only returned to Tovar's shop to continue reading, and the idea that there might be another clue to finding the rebels somewhere in the posters he was covering up with Gwyn's flyers kept him from enjoying her company.

Gwyn had insisted on giving him a free hand pie for his assistance. He finished the warm, flaky envelope of pastry filled with stewed pork and apricot before he got to Tovar's, wary that he might lose himself in *Traversing Death* and miss at least one meal.

Raiden walked into the shop to see Tovar sitting behind the counter working on repairing a charm. This most recent project was a jewelry box that kept trying to snap shut on Tovar's fingers whenever he reached in to take out a ring.

"I never knew they could be so vicious," Raiden said.

"Ah yes, they can be when you have too many pieces of magical jewelry inside together. All their enchantments get crossed and tangled, and what do you get? A self-opening jewelry box becomes a *biting* jewelry box," he grumbled and sighed. He had obviously been bitten too many times for his liking.

"Maybe *you* could use a break for a walk and a bite to eat," Raiden suggested.

"You might be right," Tovar said in a threatening tone as he glared down at the box, which looked deceivingly benign at the moment.

"There is a deal on hand pies today over at Meat Pies and Sweet Pies," Raiden offered, placing one of Gwyn's flyers on the counter as he came around the back of it to retrieve the knob key that would unlock and open the concealed door to the workroom.

"Hmm," Tovar murmured, picking up the flyer. "They look good, but I am rather partial to belly buns."

Raiden let himself into the workroom and left Tovar to his mealtime mutterings. The book was right where he'd left it.

Caeruleus was torn between covering the distance quickly to catch up with the fera and covering it more thoroughly and actually finding some trace of her presence. He knew which direction she was headed. Her destination was Atrium. Following the phantom of her steps would be slow and keep him a day or two behind her, so he opted to fly.

He flew as low over the trees as he could so that he might see through their bare branches, but there was nothing but forest floor to see. Flying a little higher allowed him to see more, although it was a sea of prickly brown treetops no matter where he looked. Occasionally he caught a glimpse of the road through the forest. He supposed it was the one leading to Witch Haven.

The brisk wind in his face and under his wings invigorated him. When he was in the sky, he could almost admit losing an eye was worth it. Then, in the corner of his narrow vision, a flash of green caught his attention. To the northeast there was a circle of green in the sea of naked branches. If not for the vibrant leaves catching his eye, he wouldn't have noticed the house among the trees.

The Council had sent out posters of the fera to the surrounding villages and towns, but people living far outside those villages might not have gotten the word. He could spare a few minutes to pay this house a visit and ask the residents whether they had seen any lone travelers, particularly one that looked like the fera.

Keren walked across the living room, headed for the front door. Nicole and the girls followed.

"Girls, if you will go get a couple of our baskets from the barn, I'm going to take Nicole to check the water in the house tank before we get started with the fruit," Keren said as she opened the door.

Her eyes went wide, and she shut the door abruptly. Nicole and the girls stopped in alarm. "We have a visitor," she said in a severe voice that made Nicole stiffen in fear.

"Nicole, the hellebore. Girls, kitchen. He'll be at the door any—"

There came a knock. The girls jumped and ran for the kitchen, disappearing through the door in a flash. Nicole fumbled the pouch around her neck open, shoved her hand in, and pulled out as big a handful of the fine powder as she could while Keren gave her a panicked look and urgent nods.

The black hellebore powder was so fine it seemed to float rather than fall as Nicole raised her hand over her head and sprinkled it all over her. It shimmered slightly as it fell, and the inky powder seemed to melt into the air before her eyes. There were no piles of the sooty substance at her feet. There came a second set of knocks. She looked up at Keren, who relaxed a little and opened the door immediately.

Nicole's heart pounded against her ribs as she stood there frozen, watching Keren greet a man with black hair and an eye patch.

"Hello," she said, sounding perfectly curious and oblivious to who he was.

"Hello, ma'am," he answered. His voice was friendly, and his smile was charming. "Please forgive my arrival so early this morning. I am here on the Council's business."

"I see," Keren said, nodding.

He was wearing a uniform, a slate-gray jacket with what looked like a mask attached to his shoulder like a stray piece of armor. Then Nicole realized that she recognized him. With the patch and without Raiden's clothes she hadn't seen it at first, but it was the same man who had shown up in Tucson. It was all she could do to quiet her epiphany to a sudden inhalation that she hoped he wouldn't hear.

He produced a folded piece of paper from inside his jacket, unfolded it, and handed it to Keren. "You might not have gotten word, living outside of Witch Haven. We are looking for this young woman, and I have reason to believe she might have been in the area recently."

"Oh," Keren said, taking a moment to study the page with Nicole's ink image. The ink was cloudy and blurred, as though someone had dripped water in places, compromising the clarity of Nicole's features. It was by no means a photograph. It looked more like an impression from a poor memory or a hazy dream. Nicole's face was clearest around the eyes, and the most striking part of the image was the anger in those two-dimensional eyes. Keren tried to hand the paper back.

"As busy as I've been with getting the trees ready for an early harvest, I haven't seen any travelers. It's not easy waking up those trees in the winter, even for me," she said with a friendly wave of her hand to take credit for Nicole's magical deed before the man could even think to get suspicious.

"Of course," he said, placated by her explanation. "Please, keep it. We want everyone to know her face."

"And if she were to show up?" Keren asked, feigning the perfect amount of concern. "I have two girls," she added, nodding her head toward the kitchen door, through which came the muffled sounds of running water and dishes clanking.

The man looked directly at Nicole, and she went rigid, holding her breath as his gaze slipped right through her to the kitchen door behind her.

"I understand," he said with a smile. "I would encourage you to turn her away and send word to Witch Haven if you can."

"Certainly," Keren said. "Thank you."

"Keep a look out, ma'am, and be safe." He gave her a respectful nod and turned away from the door.

Nicole relaxed and let the stale air whoosh out of her lungs. She could just make out the man's shape through the thin curtain covering the window. A pair of black wings extended from his back, and he leaped into the sky.

Keren shut the door and sighed.

The door to the kitchen opened, and the girls crept out.

"Is he gone?" Asi asked.

"That was easier than I thought," Fen said, taking a few steps into the living room and bumping into Nicole. "Oops, sorry, Nicole."

"That's okay. How do I ditch invisibility mode?" she asked.

"The effects diminish as the powder comes off," Keren said. "The breeze outside should help." She held out her hand, not seeing Nicole. When Nicole reached for Keren's hand, she realized she too couldn't see her own arm. Nicole's body was just a vague distortion in her vision and Keren's hand seemed to close around a mirage.

Keren opened the front door just enough to check the sky for the Council's agent, then led Nicole outside. Fen and Asi followed. Outside the breeze washed over them, and Nicole got to work shaking out her hair and patting and brushing her clothes.

"There you are," Asi giggled.

Nicole looked down and saw that she was somewhere in between solid and invisible, with some patches of clothes and parts of her body looking less substantial than the rest of her.

"Almost," Fen corrected with a chuckle.

Caeruleus glided over the bristly treetops northeast toward Witch Haven. His eye followed the road between the floramor's house and the village, where the trees parted and the road widened. Not far from the house he spotted something strange in the trees, what appeared to be two bodies caught high in the branches.

"What is …?" he muttered to himself. A little farther down the road there was a gap in the branches where he could get through and land. He hit the ground at a run, hurrying back along the road until he was beneath the two figures stuck in the trees. They appeared to be two men, a human and a nymph of some kind.

"Hello?" he called up to them. They were so still that he feared this was that day in the Cantis forest all over again, only this time there were two dead bodies high in the trees. But both men gave a jerk at the sound of his voice.

"Oy!" the dark-haired man shouted. "Thank the bloody stars! It's about time someone came along."

"How did you get up there?" Caeruleus asked, hoping to hear his hunch confirmed.

"What does it matter? Get us down," the nymph called. "Been up here all night."

"You'll stay up there until you tell me what happened," Caeruleus said. "Did a young woman do this?"

The two men glanced at each other before the one with dark hair decided to speak. "Yeah, she didn't look like much, but the wench spit fire, and before we knew what was happening, here we were."

"She spit fire?"

"That's what I said."

"Where'd she go after that?" Caeruleus demanded.

"Back that way," the nymph replied tersely, waving his hand at the road in the direction Caeruleus had come.

"Yeah, with a couple younger girls. Really chummy they were—went back to that house she was holed up in all day yesterday."

"Shut it, toad," the nymph hissed at the other. "He's one of the Council's angels."

Caeruleus rolled his eye at the derogatory remark. *Angel* was the bastardized word for a celengel used by the people who had changed the old world and split it in two. Other fey like this nymph used the word with disdain. It was people's way of saying the Council was the same, creating rifts in the world, creating rifts in the world and debasing the image of noble fey, who stood for freedom above all else, by portraying them as servants of a divisive leadership.

"Oh, think he couldn't figure out why someone would do this to us, did you?"

"Only a toad would tell a bloody angel outright we followed someone after staking out where they were hiding."

Caeruleus tuned out their bickering to process what the man had said. She had gone back to that house with two girls. He broke into a run, not even thinking about his wings. The fera was at that house, and that woman had to know.

With the help of six other hands, Nicole had finally brushed and patted herself back into a corporeal entity.

"Did we get it all?" she asked, checking every inch she could see and turning toward the girls to check her back.

"You look completely solid," Fen assured her.

"Good."

"Oh no," Keren said, looking off toward the road.

Nicole and the girls all followed her gaze in time to see what the trees must have been talking about. The Council's man was back, heading headlong for them. He knew, and he'd spotted her.

"Oh no," Nicole repeated, accepting the coming confrontation.

Keren stepped in front of her, and so did Fen and Asi. None of them flinched as he closed the distance between them, close enough that Nicole could see the look of angry fervor on his face.

Before Nicole could object, or even think, Keren knelt down and placed her hand against the ground. The grassy earth erupted with growth between the four of them and the approaching man. The green blades grew tall and thick, impeding his advance, wrapping around his feet, his ankles, and his legs as the grass continued to grow. He let out a grumble and a shout of frustration as he struggled against the many thousands of green tethers securing him in place no more than two feet from them.

Then he twisted, reaching for the gun on his hip. To Nicole's shock, Fen rushed forward, pulling her hand out of her pocket and blowing against her open palm. A handful of white powder suddenly scattered into the air, directly into the man's face. His sneer melted away as his face relaxed and his whole body sank into unconsciousness. He slumped to the ground, a heap of dead weight.

Nicole's mouth dropped open, and she pushed her hands into the roots of her hair, baffled and in awe of what she'd just witnessed. "That was …" She couldn't even think of words to describe it. "What did you use on him, Fen?"

"Morpheus dust. Potions, poisons, and powders, a true master knows them all," she said as though she was reciting an old teacher's motto.

Since the man was limp on the ground, Keren waved away the grass, which released him and returned to fluttering in the breeze as though nothing had disturbed it.

"Now what do we do?" Nicole asked, looking down at him.

"That's where I come in," Asi said, hopping forward and bending down to touch her index finger to his forehead. She held that contact for about twenty seconds and then pulled her hand away. "Done," she said as she stood up.

"How long will he be asleep?" Keren asked.

"I used a lot," Fen said with a halfhearted cringe. "He could be out for at least three hours."

"I suppose we should get him onto the cart and take him to Witch Haven, let him wake up there," Keren said.

"I can get him there," Nicole said. "It won't even take a minute."

"Fine, but you don't want to be seen. It will be busy this time of the morning, but most people will be at the market. Take him to the old manor on the far end of Witch Haven. No one is ever there."

"One problem—I've never been there. I have no idea where I'm going," Nicole said.

"I can fix that," Asi said, reaching up to touch Nicole's forehead.

Nicole didn't even have the chance to wonder what Asi meant before her head was suddenly filled with memories of Witch Haven—Asi's shared recollections of countless visits to the village. It was the strangest sensation, to know she had never been to this village and yet find her head flooded with memories of it—the wooden sign that greeted travelers from the road when they first got to town, the main road paved with cobblestones, and the crowded market where people gathered around carts and tents to investigate the wares. Asi provided every moment of walking through Witch Haven, past the shops and houses, to the edge of town, where an old manor stood silent and empty.

Several memories of this manor played through Nicole's mind, each one shifting slightly in perspective and light. Nicole could make out three stories, but there were too many slender windows to count before Asi removed her finger and the influx of images stopped.

"Whoa," Nicole said. "That is the single strangest feeling I have ever experienced," she confessed with a laugh.

"Does that help?" Asi asked.

"Immensely," Nicole said, placing her hands on Asi's shoulders. "Thank you."

She stepped closer to the man unconscious on the ground. He looked like some drunken fool passed out in a stranger's front yard.

"I'll be right back," she promised, taking hold of his arm and focusing on the memories of the manor Asi had shown her. Her magic engulfed them both in a flash.

The jump with dead weight was different from any other. He seemed harder to pull through space, and it took several seconds for them to materialize at their destination. The momentum of their arrival sent him rolling, pulling his arm from her hand. He came to a stop facedown. With a sigh, she bent down to pull him over onto his back. After all this she felt like she ought to know the guy's name.

She straightened up and looked down at him lying on the ground, looking a little less awkward now that he was perfectly supine. His eye patch was slightly askew, though, and she knelt back down to straighten it. In that moment her brain seemed to process the eye patch and their last encounter.

"I did that to you," she murmured to herself. Somehow she couldn't rekindle her burning hatred from that day. When he wasn't trying to track her down and bring her back to the Council, this guy couldn't be all that bad. He had seemed so genuine and kind talking to Keren. Though the man truly believed Nicole was dangerous and did whatever the Council told him, no doubt he thought he was doing the right thing to protect people like Keren and the girls.

She stood up, angry at herself for not being able to hate this unnamed man as she had the day he'd attacked her in Tucson. The guy was brainwashed and unconscious; he'd gotten what he deserved today, just as he had the first time they'd met. She didn't regret fighting back.

"This is where I leave you, asshole," she muttered, on the verge of summoning another surge of magic, but she looked up and halted at the sight of the manor.

Standing in front of this place and knowing she was seeing it for the first time was at odds with her transplanted memories of the structure. There was a fence around the manor, tangles of curled iron segmented by pillars of brick as tall as her shoulders. On the pillar beside the gate there was a brass plaque that read Divale Manor. She stared at the plaque far longer than she should have to recognize that name. *Divale*, she thought, *Althea Gweldith Divale!*

"Holy shit," she whispered, putting her hand into her hair and turning this way and that, unsure where to face or what to do about this revelation other than stare in awe at the house as a flood of questions filled her mind.

Then the man on the ground stirred, and she jumped. He was still asleep, but she was thoroughly startled—reminding her to get the hell out of there.

30. Stories

icole was in such a tizzy that she stumbled and fell when she materialized and her feet hit the ground outside Keren's house.

"Oy vey, I thought something went wrong," Keren said, looking as if she had been holding her breath ever since Nicole had left with the man.

The plaque in front of the house consumed Nicole's mind. "The Divale House," she said. "I left him in front of the Divale House. What do you know about that place?"

"It's haunted," Fen said flatly.

"Is not," Asi countered. "I've told you a hundred time even objects have memories. There's nothing but dying house charms, memories, and dust in that place."

"Can we take this conversation inside please?" Keren asked. "Before any more of the Council's men or ships come along?"

The girls obliged, and Nicole sighed, anxious to know more. They filed into the house, and Keren shut the door behind them.

"The Divale House," Nicole repeated impatiently.

"It was the home of the Divale family. They were considered the greatest family of seers in the realm, made famous generations ago by the seer Althea Divale. She earned the title of oracle," Keren said with a disinterested shrug. "It's been abandoned for decades. It was empty by the time I first passed through Witch Haven more than forty years ago," she recalled casually.

Nicole's thoughts were jarred away from the Divales. "More than forty years ago? You only *look* forty," Nicole said.

"I'm ninety-four actually," Keren replied.

"Okay," Nicole answered, overwhelmed. She put her hands up to halt the conversation, rubbed her eyes, pinched the bridge of her nose, and sighed. "I'm going to take a guess and say being a floramor means you have a lifespan more like a tree than a human."

"Your guess is right, and it was strange to me too at first," she said.

"Wait, what?"

"Sweetie, like you, I wasn't born in Veil. I didn't always know what I was."

"*What?*" Nicole was spiraling into a pit of information overload. "You know?"

"Nicole, there are countless people in Veil who came from the other realm. There was a time when everyone here was from the old world, as we tend to call it. I ended up here by accident about eighty years ago. Didn't know I was a floramor until after being here about a month. I was just a girl who loved gardens before finding this place."

"Did you two know this?" Nicole asked Fen and Asi.

They nodded and shrugged.

"How did you know I was from the other realm?"

"Little things, dear. The way you talk, certain things you've said. And there's a look about clothes and stuff from the old world," she said, nodding toward Nicole's camping pack and then her hiking boots.

"Oh" was all Nicole could think to say.

"We'll have to get you some new clothes if you want to traipse through the Council's city without attracting attention, and maybe change your hair to make you look less like her," she said, picking up the wanted flyer with Nicole's face on it.

This brought Nicole back to the man who had handed that flyer to Keren, the man who had seen her face twice now. He might not remember the events of this morning, but he would recognize her, even in Veilish clothes.

"How much of his memory did you erase, Asi?" Nicole asked.

"About twenty or thirty minutes' worth," she said.

"Let's hope he doesn't hang around trying to figure out what happened during that missing time," Keren said. "You would be better off with some new clothes of the latest Atrium trends than with something borrowed from me. You would just draw attention for looking like a fruit farmer."

"Right."

"I can call on my friend in Witch Haven tomorrow and find out if the

Council's man is still around. The girls and I can take some fruit and herbs to market before we get what you need." Keren finished with a stern nod that indicated the plans were final and the conversation was concluded.

Raiden delved back into the pages of *Traversing Death,* bending over the book as though it were pulling him in to consume him as fervently as he devoured its knowledge.

The more he read, the more the room around him seemed to fade away, his peripheral vision tricking him into thinking he was surrounded by a dark, hazy eternity. Part of him felt that if he looked up, he might see his mother and other departed souls, but he couldn't look away from the page.

"The waters of death flow without beginning or end," he read silently, "but these currents are not bound by time, because time is for the living. Enter these dark waters, and if you step out, you may return to find a single heartbeat has gone by, but perhaps you'll return to some moment minutes or even days in the past or find life has moved forward without you."

Raiden's thoughts drifted from there. It seemed to him that life had already gone on without him. People like Tovar and Caeruleus liked to say his mother had saved him. But his heart had never been capable of moving forward. Only the Sight connected him to the future. Dying seemed more natural to him than his own life now. Through all his isolated years he had chosen the past over the future, each and every day. His mother had left him behind so he could live, but it felt like part of him had followed her anyway, and now he was stuck somewhere in between.

After all, here he was still consumed by the past. Gwyn came to his mind. Even given the opportunity to embrace the future he had been seeing for so long, his heart still could not let go of the past. He'd spent almost a decade preparing to confront Moira, ignoring his ability to choose freedom and leave Cantis behind him and live the life his mother had given him. Had it not been for the fera, he'd have died trying to deliver justice that night.

In all those years he'd felt abandoned, not saved. He wouldn't wish that solitary sentence on anyone. Perhaps in his heart he had always been looking for passage, that path that would allow him to follow everyone who had left him. What boy could understand that desire? A boy could understand provoking the same beast that had taken his loved ones, even if he knew he had no chance against it. Perhaps his quest to confront Moira had always been a death wish. Even this mission to dismantle the Council, something far bigger than any one man could accomplish, was arguably an elaborate way to finally get to where everyone else had gone when they'd left him behind.

What would bringing down the Council really accomplish anyway—justice for those left unsheltered by their promises of safety and unity, freedom for him and Caeruleus if they didn't die along the way in one of the Council's personal battles? Would he be satisfied? Would he suddenly feel inspired to live and love?

He didn't think so. He couldn't stop imagining his mother standing at the fringes of his vision—the only person in the world who had loved him reduced to a ghost in his mind. Although his gaze felt immovable, lost in the words on the yellowed pages, he chose to turn his head toward the darkness around him.

As soon as his eyes left the book, the room appeared again, blurred to his stinging eyes. He stood up, slamming the book shut. His blood turned hot. Anger proliferated through every cell of his being. He was angry at his mother for leaving him alone and angry at himself for being unable to change it. He hated himself, for all the years he'd wasted on Moira, running from the life his mother had given him, for wasting time still today. He felt ill for wanting death more than life, even for a moment. He didn't even want to touch the book again.

With a wave of his hand the book was thrown back into its place on the shelf so hard that the shelf wobbled and a few things tipped over. He sighed, crossing the room to the bookshelf. A long wooden box that had been resting atop the books was now sitting precariously on the edge of the shelf. Out of curiosity Raiden flipped the little brass latch and opened the lid. The box was filled with folded parchment. A word written on the edge of one of the pieces of old paper caught his eye—*Candhrid*.

Raiden brought the box over to the table and removed some of its contents. On the outside, the pieces of parchment were blank except for the names of the realm's old kingdoms on them: Nol, Meridian, Orodon, Taroth, Candhrid. Raiden unfolded the one labeled as Candhrid and verified his suspicion. They were maps.

The map of Candhrid was old. It still showed the peninsula and chain of islands that had been lost to the sea more than two decades ago, but it was recent enough to show the city of Atrium. There were marks and annotations on the map in what Raiden assumed was Tovar's handwriting, but the notes were in a language he didn't recognize. He dumped the rest of the maps out and shuffled through them, looking at all the names written on the outside.

One of the maps was marked "Atrium." He pulled that one from the pile and opened the parchment. The paper crinkled as he spread it out over the other folded maps. It was a map of the city, with every street and alleyway labeled with its name and classification—*v* for vehicle-friendly thoroughfares or *p* for pedestrian-only streets.

He scanned the map, finding the streets he knew in the southeast part of the city. Even in his wanderings he had only covered about half of Atrium. Then two words caught his eye, the names of two streets that intersected on the north end of the city: Moon and Stone.

"Moonstone," he said, dumbfounded by the simplicity of it. Then he let out a bitter laugh and smacked his hand against the map in triumph. He stumbled to get around the table and to the door.

A rumble rolled through his ears and his body, startling Caeruleus awake. He snapped bolt upright. Instinctively he reached for his gun, pulling it out and holding it at the ready before his eye even focused.

The sky above was gray, and a cold wind cut through the air. Another rumble like boulders tumbling through the clouds made the ground tremble. There was no one around. He could see several houses in the distance. Twisting around to see what lay behind him, he saw the dark manor looming over him and spotted the plaque on the fence pillar. He was outside the old Divale Manor.

How did I get to Witch Haven? he wondered. The last thing he remembered was leaving the beach and flying over the forest between the coast and Atrium. Now suddenly the storm he had seen out at sea was shaking him awake in Witch Haven? He had no doubt something wasn't right here, but the thunderheads were crawling over the village now, and he decided he was better off getting back to Atrium ahead of the storm.

In a panic he remembered his ward, and he clapped his hand to his chest, checking to see that the pendant was still there. He sighed, feeling the hard lump between his sternum and his hand. Catching the chain beneath his collar with a finger, he pulled the round pendant out.

He sighed again, releasing his wings from the spell that concealed them in his back. It was a strange sensation, his body sprouting two extra appendages. He still wasn't used to it, but he liked the freedom of flight.

Another grumble from the clouds nagged at him to get moving, so he did, breaking into a few powerful strides as he beat his massive wings. He jumped into the air, and soon he was in the sky, soaring away from the coming storm and toward Atrium.

"So much for harvesting," Keren said with a sigh as encroaching clouds shrouded the day. She placed her hand on the tree the four of them were working on, and it ceased dropping apples into their waiting hands.

"At least we got a couple baskets filled," Fen said, catching the last apple.

"True," Keren agreed.

Nicole placed an apple into the basket between her and Asi. She was still wading through her thoughts about the manor and the famous seer Althea Divale. This new information raised the question, assuming Raiden's mother had been named after her great-grandmother, which Althea had written the journal?

"Let's get these baskets to the storeroom before we get caught in the rain," Keren said.

Asi and Fen each took a handle of one basket. Nicole grabbed the second basket and heaved it up onto her shoulder, following the girls. The storeroom was a garage of sorts, attached to the back of the house. They set the two lonely baskets in the empty room, and Keren locked it up.

"Goblins like to pilfer our fruit stores," Keren said.

"Are they like shrunken men with long fingers?" Nicole asked.

"Sounds about right."

"I caught one yesterday morning," Nicole said as they returned to the shelter of the living room and shut the door behind them. "He was trying to steal Gim." She gestured toward the fireplace.

Keren nodded. "They're greedy little things."

"And fast," Nicole added as she sank into the couch.

"But you caught it?" Asi asked, perching on the arm of the couch to face Nicole.

"Oh, they don't like that," Fen said, adding a couple of logs to the fireplace. "If goblins ever offer you something or make a promise, they're compelled to abide by it, but they'll turn around and steal whatever they gave you right back if they can."

"All the fey are funny like that. They take sincerity quite seriously. It's against their nature to break promises, but some of them are more noble than others," Keren explained as she sank into the armchair.

"Kind of like dragons owing a debt to someone," Nicole said, not stopping to think about mentioning dragons.

Asi stared at her from the end of the couch, and Fen turned away from warming her hands near the fire to look at Nicole with wide eyes.

"How did you come to know about that?" Keren asked.

"My friend, the one stuck in Atrium, warned me about dragons," she said, which was true. That old pang of anger at Raiden's prejudice slipped through time to ring in her chest once more and turned into a long note of sadness. She missed Gordan. She missed Raiden.

"That's an odd thing to warn someone about when the dragons have been exiled in the Wastelands since the end of the wars," Keren mused.

"Why *are* they called the Wastelands?" Nicole asked. Since they knew she wasn't from Veil, she wasn't afraid to bare her ignorance.

"There was a point early in Veil's history when the two realms were still very much connected, and there were always more of us fleeing, looking for sanctuary from a world waging war on itself and us. But not just people and creatures arrived. There was a time when whole cities, temples, and monuments slipped away between the realms. No one wanted to live among the ruins of those lost lives. The people chose the mainland to settle, and those remnants of the old world were left behind in what they call the Wastelands."

A distant rumble shook the sky, and they could all feel it, even inside the house.

"It's a good thing we're inside," Asi said. "I wonder if that man has woken up yet."

"Don't you worry about him. If he's stuck in the rain, that's what he gets," Fen said.

Nicole tried not to laugh as Keren made a disparaging face at Fen's callous remark. The fire crackled as Gim played on the burning logs. The sky outside grew darker, and so did the living room, lit only by the glow of the fireplace. Keren stood and reached up to touch the hanging plants, stirring their inner light to brighten the room. The fire held Nicole's gaze, almost hypnotizing her.

She usually felt that thinking about a future without the Council and without Venarious, the leader of the mysterious sect that called itself Dawn, lurking in her life was bad luck somehow—like it was overconfident to assume she would win in the end and take her life back. At the same time, entertaining the possibilities felt like a pessimistic attempt to experience a life she might never have except in daydreams.

At the risk of jinxing her future, she found herself imagining a life in Veil, maybe living somewhere near Keren and the girls, seeing them often. She pictured a future where the dragons returned to the mainland and were welcome, where she and Gordan weren't outcasts.

The more she built this future in her mind, the more it seemed to crumble under the weight of disbelief, and her reverie was broken about as swiftly as it bloomed in her head.

"Are they trying to kill you?" Asi asked, moving from the arm of the couch to the cushion beside Nicole. Her question caught Nicole off guard.

"The Council?" Nicole asked, stalling.

Asi nodded.

Nicole had tried to avoid this thought directly. Since discovering their mission to apprehend her, she'd imagined that they were trying to put her in a cage, use the safety of both realms to justify taking her freedom. Faced with Asi's question, Nicole was forced to confront the knowledge that everyone believed the fera were gone, practically a myth now, and a shining example of the Council's success as protectors of the realm. Where had the fera gone if they weren't all dead? The answer was obvious.

"Yeah," she finally said. "I guess they are."

"How are you so calm about it?" Fen asked.

"I wouldn't call it calm," Nicole said with a sad attempt at a laugh. "It's more like being numb. When you're scared and angry every day, you eventually stop noticing it."

The room was silent except for the low whispering of flames in the fireplace and the occasional pop of the blackened wood. It seemed like it was night already—after everything that had happened that morning, Nicole felt drained—but it was only midday. The first few taps of rain against the window heralded the downpour.

"It took a long time for me to stop worrying," Fen confessed, "after we left Taroth. It seemed too easy. Maybe they think we left by way of the cliffs. That happened sometimes. I knew a girl who jumped when her father refused to give her to the man she loved. He gave her to an older man whose first wife was no longer bearing children."

Nicole was too slow to hide the disgust on her face. She looked to Keren, whose head was bowed with a kind of solemn respect for the story being told. Keren knew these stories.

"They brought a lot of girls to see me after that," Asi said, the cheer gone from her voice.

"To have their memories erased?" Nicole asked.

Asi nodded. "If a husband hit his wife or if a boy took a girl's body for his pleasure, their families would bring them to me." Asi glanced at Fen. "'To save them from their pain and give them happiness again,' my father would say to me."

"My family brought me to Asi," Fen said. "That's how we met."

"Father told me they all *wanted* to forget," Asi said. "And when I saw the memories I was to erase, I believed that without question. Until I met Fen."

They were smiling at each other. Nicole was astonished. Despite the story they were telling and reliving, they smiled.

"I didn't want to forget about that girl," Fen said. "I felt the tragedy of it, but to me she was the first girl I knew who had taken control of her own life. I wanted to remember her—remember that we have the ability to choose. That's what they wanted to erase from our minds—not the sadness, but the choice to leave."

"When she said that to me, I felt the same. I didn't want to spend the rest of my life collecting horrible memories. I didn't want to steal the truth from girls' minds anymore, no matter how painful or ugly it was," Asi said. "They left Fen and me alone like they always did while I did my work. That's when we snuck out the window."

"We spotted Keren's caravan on the road and hid inside," Fen said with a proud chuckle.

"And you know the rest," Keren said, lifting her head with a soft smile.

"How old were you when you started erasing girls' memories?" Nicole asked.

"Five, I think."

Nicole could only shake her head. Asi had been forced to grow up bearing witness to every horrible memory she'd erased. It occurred to Nicole that, in spite of all those horrible stolen memories, Asi seemed to smile the most out of the three of them. Nicole could hardly fathom this girl, only fourteen. She hoped to be as strong as Asi someday.

"I think that's enough of the past for one day. How about some tea?" Keren asked, standing up from her chair. "What do you say?"

"And toast," Fen said as she moved toward the kitchen.

"With jam," Asi added, popping up from her spot on the couch, her past tucked away once again.

"Sure," Nicole agreed, still trying to drag her thoughts out of Asi and Fen's story.

31. Questions

Raiden followed Stone Street, ignoring the threatening rumble from the sky as he got closer to the intersection with Moon. There were hardly any shop fronts on Stone, mostly just apartment and inn entrances.

He wasn't sure what he was looking for, but at least he knew where to look—Moon and Stone. Maybe there would be someone waiting around—no, it would be too conspicuous for the rebels to have someone there day in and day out. Perhaps there was a hidden entrance, then, but surely there would be some precaution. He tried to recall the rebel posters in his head, wondering whether there was some commonality that might hold the answer.

Just wait and see, he told himself. Thinking too much could be as much of a weakness as a strength. He tried to keep his mind from returning to the book about death and the dark thoughts it had conjured up. As much as he liked to think those ideas had come more from the mysterious pages than his own heart, he couldn't convince himself that they hadn't always been lurking behind his actions all these years. The book hadn't been there the past nine years, making him feel nothing, anchoring him to people who were gone and the idea that avenging their memories mattered more than living.

Raiden had always thought he would shake off the numbness when he left Cantis. He'd expected feelings to come back to him. He'd had brilliant visions that overwhelmed him with passion in just a few moments—and yet he felt no spark when he stood beside Gwyn in person.

It made him wonder, if he remained on this path, would that future eventually die? What did he want more, to live that embrace he had seen and felt so many times through the Sight or to ruin the Council for not protecting Cantis? The latter wouldn't bring the lost lives back. It wouldn't make his mother's absence any less painful.

He stopped in his tracks, suddenly stuck by the impasse of two desires in his mind. The sky above shuddered, and the clouds broke open. The rain came down. People around him hurried under the shelter of buildings or opened umbrellas. In seconds his hair was plastered to his forehead and temples. His body gave a convulsive shudder against his cold, wet clothes.

For a moment, standing there in the rain, he seemed to have a faint vision of himself standing in a yard of clovers as a girl threw her head back and spread her arms wide, laughing as the rain drenched her. It was brief and dull, like a faded memory, not a vision. But as swiftly as it came, it was gone, with the illusiveness of a dream after waking, washed away by the rain.

"Raiden?" a voice overhead called, nearly drowned out by the din of the rainfall.

He looked up, and raindrops hit his eyes before he could see what was happening. After blinking furiously, he finally saw Caeruleus as his feet hit the ground just a few strides away.

"Why are you standing out in the rain?" Caeruleus asked as he retracted his wings into his back.

"I—" Raiden began without an answer. "I don't know really," he admitted. "Where have you been?"

"Out searching." He paused as someone hurried past. "Well, you know. I ran into a complication. Come on; let's get out of the rain."

Raiden nodded in agreement. He put his hand on Caeruleus's shoulder, and they disappeared, dissolving into the air between the raindrops and zipping through space in a blink.

They emerged from the ether into Raiden's apartment, dripping wet. Raiden crossed the kitchen and stepped into the bathroom to grab a couple of towels. He returned to the living room and tossed one at Caeruleus, who caught the towel and rubbed it over his head, knocking his patch off his face in the process. There was only a depression of healed pink skin where his right eye used to be. Raiden felt a pang of anger at the sight, and his conviction to see the Council brought to ruin was rekindled.

"So what happened?" Raiden asked.

Caeruleus caught his patch tumbling down his chest and put it back on. "I was out at the coast. The fera is on the mainland, and it turns out she's extremely close with that dragon. It brought her here, but they split up on the beach."

"How do you know that?"

"Phantasm spell—wasn't the clearest, so it must have been a couple days ago now."

"Where'd the dragon go?" Raiden asked, worried.

"West, back to the Wastelands I hope. I followed the fera's path toward Atrium. I was flying over the forest between Atrium and the coast, and next thing I know I'm waking up on the ground on the outskirts of Witch Haven. I lost a few hours. I know because that rain out there was over the ocean when I was on the beach, but when I woke up, it was rolling into Witch Haven."

"How could you just lose several hours?" Raiden asked.

"I was planning on heading for the courts to see the healer in case he might be able to recover them," Caeruleus said, shaking his head.

Raiden knew this look. Caeruleus was berating himself, a habit he had picked up growing up with his father's near-constant disapproval. He'd learned to scold himself in the vein of his father when the man wasn't there to do it himself. Raiden frowned at seeing that look on Caeruleus's face again. He'd never liked his friend's father.

"I'm no expert on altered or lost memories," Raiden said. He was reluctant to offer to interbound Caeruleus to the courts, not wanting to poke the sore spot of Caeruleus being unable to do so himself, but he was anxious to get rid of Caeruleus so he could get back to the intersection of Moon and Stone. "I can take you to the courts, if you want."

Caeruleus chuckled. "I came to terms with my utter lack of talent for interbounding years ago. That would be great." He tossed his damp towel over the back of the dining chair in the kitchen.

"Do you want some dry clothes?" Raiden asked, hitching his thumb toward the dresser back in his bedroom.

"No, they'll have drying charms at the courts. Let's just go."

Raiden shrugged, took hold of Caeruleus's shoulder once more, and away they went, twisting and dematerializing into the space between Raiden's apartment and the designated arrival platform in the courts. Two other agents arrived alongside them, sopping wet and eager to step off the platform. The other two agents hurried through the doorway and out into the hall. The air in the doorway gave a little wiggle like a mirage as they passed through it, and they stepped into the corridor completely dry. Inside the room, an enchanted mop was dancing itself around, wiping up the puddles, drips, and dirty footprints left behind the soaked arrivals.

"Come on," Caeruleus said, heading toward the door.

Seeing no reason not to dry off before he left, Raiden followed Caeruleus through the charmed doorway. His hair, his clothes, and his shoes were dry and warm in an instant. He let out an involuntary sigh as the warm magic chased away the chill on his skin. For some reason the comfort of that wave of warmth left him with a sinking feeling, almost as though he had forgotten something.

"Hey," Caeruleus said, accompanied by a light smack on Raiden's back.

"What?"

"You have been drifting off a lot lately."

"Just a habit from those years alone, I guess," Raiden said with a shrug.

Caeruleus's frown seemed to indicate complete acceptance of the explanation.

"Well, thanks," he said. "I'm going to find that healer and report to the Council."

"Good luck." Raiden raised his hand in a halfhearted wave, his self-doubt from earlier creeping back into his mind. Taking on the Council might be an obsession with the past, but if giving up the chance of the future he'd seen in his visions meant Raiden could keep Caeruleus from being yet another sacrificed pawn, then he was willing to make that sacrifice. There would be another future for him after the Council was undone, and Raiden didn't care what it was so long as Caeruleus had a future too.

A heavy hand came down on Raiden's shoulder and gave him a start.

"Cael," a low voice said above him.

Raiden stepped away and turned to see Loak, with those striking golden eyes set in his dark face. The lights high above made white gleams on his bald scalp.

It took effort for Raiden to reply with a respectful "sir" rather than scowl at the man's inconvenient and uncanny ability to catch him in the corridors of the court building.

"I'd like a word," he said.

"Which word would you like, sir?" Raiden asked with a curt smile.

Loak's mouth twitched, but Raiden couldn't read the meaning behind it.

"The private kind," Loak answered, lowering his words to a murmur that was unsettling for such a booming voice.

Raiden couldn't avoid him this time, so he followed as Loak turned around and marched through the corridors, leading him, eventually, to the empty training hall. The rain drummed against the skylight overhead and echoed through the vast vaulted chamber. Raiden wondered whether this would be the moment Loak used the knowledge about him having the Sight for coercion.

Loak shut the tall door with a hard shove before he spoke. "Whatever you're doing, you need to stop now, Raiden."

That wasn't at all what Raiden had expected to hear. "Or what?"

"No 'or what.' Just stay away from the courts, stay away from your friend Stone, and whatever you may have learned about the rebels, pursue it no further and tell no one."

"Why?"

"Because they are looking to charge you with treason. Stone is working a sensitive and highly classified mission. They will use you being close to him as evidence of information gathering. The moment you provide any tactile connection to the rebels beyond information the Council provided you, they will be ready to arrest you. The decision has already been made; it's all just a matter of when you give them the circumstances they're waiting for."

This really wasn't what Raiden had expected. The message wasn't shocking, but the messenger was.

"I can't say that is surprising to hear," Raiden said. "But I'm not going to stop. That was always a part of the risk. It's not my neck I'm worried about."

"The more you interact with Stone, the more his failure to apprehend the fera will be attributed to you. He could go down with you for treason at this rate if he fails. I don't think you understand how desperate the Council is to capture the fera. They claim to have rid the realm of that threat decades ago. It goes beyond their desire to keep the fera out of Dawn's hands. Their reputation—the foundation of their power in Veil—is at stake."

Raiden hadn't considered that his attempts to help Caeruleus or their frequent interactions might condemn them both. His desire to keep Caeruleus away from confronting the fera might have backfired already. Raiden thought about all that had happened since he'd arrived. He'd convinced Caeruleus not to go through that portal in the Cantis forest, causing Caeruleus to miss that chance to pursue the fera, and then he had assisted in Caeruleus's second attempt, which had ended in failure. The question was, how much had Caeruleus told the Council about Raiden's contributions?

The rattling hiss of the rain against the skylight filled his ears, and the emptiness of the training hall seemed to press upon him as he tried to divine the right path to take from here. One more question added to his confusion.

"I don't understand why you're so concerned about all this, about me."

"Because I've seen what the Council will do to those they deem an enemy." The anger in Loak's voice shook like the thunder in the sky outside. "It took a long time to earn back a place in the Council's esteem after they charged my partner with treason, and he wouldn't appreciate if I let the same happen to you."

Raiden's heart lurched in his chest. "Hold on," he said, taking a deep breath as his pulse raced. His mind stumbled over what Loak had just said: his partner wouldn't appreciate ... "Your partner ..." Raiden began, pausing to push his heart back down his throat, but he couldn't find the words to finish.

"He never wanted you to end up here," Loak said.

Raiden knew. He didn't want to say it. He didn't even want to think it. It was all he could do to keep his breathing steady.

"I recognized you the moment you walked into this hall," Loak said.

Raiden shook his head, torn between wanting to hear these words and not.

"How do you think I knew about the Sight, Raiden?"

Raiden took a deep breath and forced it back out. "Stop. I don't want to hear any more."

"Fine. Just promise you'll stay away from the courts, let Caeruleus do his job, and stop looking for the rebels for a while."

"I can't promise you that," Raiden said.

"I'm not the one asking you—"

Raiden was done. He threw his hands up. The spell *aperi* erupted in his mind, and the door burst open with a bang. Without looking back to see whether Loak was following, he stormed down the corridor and back to the interbounding platform. He welcomed the scattering of his thoughts that came with the jump through the ether.

Caeruleus walked out of the medical ward with no answers as to how he'd lost several hours, let alone a remedy to restore his missing memories.

He snorted in annoyance to himself. "Your memories are just gone," he repeated. "I don't know what to tell you." He was beginning to seriously doubt that man's qualifications as a healer. Suddenly a strange force seized him by the stomach and wrenched him through space.

He was spit back out before the Council in their dimly lit hall. As he materialized, the urge to vomit crept up the back of his throat for a moment. He had never been summoned before, interbounding so unexpectedly and unwillingly. He could see his reflection sway upside down in the deep-green marble floor.

"We heard you were back in the courts with the healer," a councilwoman with a light voice said, getting right to business.

"Yes," he said, swallowing back the last of his nausea as he steadied himself. "I ran into some trouble while searching today. After finding evidence of her arrival on the beach, I was searching the forest between her arrival point and Atrium, but then I woke up in Witch Haven without any recollection of how I'd gotten there."

"That is indeed troubling," one of the councilmen said.

"With the ships scanning for magical anomalies and finding nothing in the last two days, we can only assume that the fera is capable of evading detection," another said.

"This makes her arguably more dangerous than the others of her kind," said a different Council member. Caeruleus couldn't keep up.

"We think it would be best to change our tactics."

"We know she is coming to Atrium. Instead of trying to impede her arrival, we think it best to let her come and be prepared."

"You mean set a trap for her?" Caeruleus asked.

"Precisely."

He couldn't help but wonder about the future the seers had reported of the fera bringing destruction to the courts. Were they intercepting her on the path to that future, or were they about to force her onto that path?

32. Prepared

The next morning the sky was clear. Keren and Nicole were up early and filled another few baskets with apples before the sun had even climbed above the treetops. The girls were awake by the time they returned to the house to make breakfast.

They ate in silence, everyone thinking about the fact that today they were getting Nicole ready to walk into the lion's den. Fen and Asi kept glancing at each other as though they were having a silent conversation over their eggs in a basket. Keren seemed to notice the girls' glances as much as Nicole did but said nothing as she sopped up the runny yolk on her plate with a piece of toast.

Nicole treated every bite of her own eggs and toast like a duty, eating with resolve but no appetite as her stomach twisted in anticipation of her departure. She looked into her cup of tea, wishing it was black coffee instead. The ceramic handle tingled in her hand as she brought the cup to her lips, and she almost spit her sip out in surprise when coffee met her tongue instead of tea.

"What?" Fen asked as Nicole sputtered and put her hand over her mouth.

"I accidently turned my tea into coffee," she explained with a chuckle.

"I've never had coffee," Asi said.

"Me neither."

"You're welcome to try, but I'm warning you, it will probably taste awful the first time," Nicole said, placing her cup in the middle of the table.

Fen took it first, not deterred by the warning. She took a sip, and her face twisted with disapproval. Asi laughed at her expression and took the cup to try for herself. When she took a sip, she squeezed her eyes shut and gave her head a little shake, but she didn't seem as put off as Fen. She passed the cup back to Nicole.

"Ugh, why would you want to drink that?" Fen asked.

"My dad is a coffee drinker. It sorta became something we do together every morning," Nicole explained, feeling terrible about leaving her family without answers.

"All right, you two," Keren said, standing up from the table, "I'm going to get Ferdie and the cart hitched up. Be ready to go in fifteen minutes."

"Okay," they replied in unison. They too got up from the table and disappeared from the kitchen, leaving Nicole alone with her coffee and breakfast.

With a sigh she hurried through the rest of her eggs, grabbed the hunk of bread from her plate before depositing it in the sink, and left the kitchen with toast in one hand and coffee in the other.

The girls came back down the stairs, dressed and ready to go. Nicole walked with them out the door and around the house to the barn, where the horse, the cart, and Keren's old caravan all resided. Keren had the horse hitched up and ready, the five baskets of apples already in the cart.

"What if our friend is still in Witch Haven?" Nicole asked.

"That's why you're staying here," Keren said. "He doesn't remember us."

"Right." Nicole tried to sound reassured.

"If any more of the Council's toads come round, just don't answer the door," Fen said with a smile.

"Thanks, Mom," Nicole chuckled as Fen climbed onto the bench at the front of the cart.

"What's your favorite color?" Asi asked.

"Red," Nicole answered. "Why?"

Asi just smiled at her, gave a little shrug, and climbed into the back of the cart to sit with the apples.

"We shouldn't take longer than a few hours. Fruit this early will go fast," Keren said as she climbed up to sit beside Fen.

Nicole watched them ride off down the track that led away from the barn and onto the road. She sipped her coffee and tore a bite off her bread more out of frustration than interest.

Raiden spent the whole rest of the day and night pacing his apartment. He would walk to the door, thinking about going back to the intersection of Moon and Stone, but then he would turn away, remembering what Loak had told him. Now that he knew definitively that the Council was waiting for him to gain the smallest connection to the rebels, he wasn't so sure about his conviction to find them, at least not quite yet.

Not that he hadn't expected to be arrested for treason at some point, but if it happened now, that meant he couldn't help Caeruleus, and the fera was coming. Despite what Loak had said about incriminating Caeruleus, Raiden felt there were still ways he could help. If he had to stay away from the courts, he could do that. If he had to let the Council fall in their own time, be that at the hands of the rebels or the fera, he could sit by and let it happen.

What he needed was more information, which he could have gotten from Loak if he hadn't refused to hear more indirect references to his father. He had been too afraid to know any more about what had happened, and so he'd lost the chance to know more about anything else. Did the Council have people following him, watching where he went? Did they know how much time he spent at Tovar's shop? Had he implicated someone else through association?

He knew he couldn't just hole up in his apartment. If there were agents watching him, his sudden retreat and inactivity would be immediately suspicious. His best bet would be to go about his business, even if he had no intention of making contact with the rebels. Still, there was no telling how much time he could get away with not providing some information to the Council. His lack of progress tracking down the rebellion would be noticed eventually. It all depended on the Council's patience and how badly they wanted justification to arrest him.

He spent all night grappling with his options. There was no avoiding suspicion. The Council had already made their decision to charge him with treason. After enough hours of pacing, the only conclusion he could come to was that if the Council didn't fall, he would be arrested sooner or later. What mattered was how he used that time. He could still help Caeruleus. He had the mask. He could listen in whenever he wanted.

With that resolved, there was still one issue he desperately wanted to keep out of his mind, his father. Loak said Raiden's father had been marked an enemy by the Council. It wasn't hard to believe that the Council's story about his father dying in service to the realm had been a lie in part or in whole. Knowing the Council's obsession with their honest and just reputation, they probably considered the execution of a traitor to be a service to the realm.

But that just led Raiden to more questions he hadn't had the courage to ask yesterday. What had his father done that would earn him the charge of treason? If he hadn't been loyal to the Council, what had he been doing all that time he'd been away from his family?

Stop, Raiden told himself, striking his forehead with the bottom of his palm. He couldn't keep agonizing over the past. What he needed to do was focus on doing something productive, like assisting Caeruleus in any way he could *while* he could. He would go to Tovar's and keep up with his usual patterns. There he would listen through the mask and keep track of where Caeruleus was in the city.

His mind was hazy with the smoke of an all-out war in his head that hadn't cleared yet. He supposed it could have something to do with more than two days without sleep thanks to that damn book and Loak. Still pacing the apartment, he stopped at the kitchen table, where the picture frame from home sat patiently.

He lifted the frame. It felt heavier than usual. In the black-and-white image his mother's dark-gray face was frozen in happiness beside a man still cloaked by a decade of dust. Raiden sighed and wiped the dust from the other half of the picture, revealing his father. He glanced at the man beside his mother for only a moment before setting the frame back down.

He hoped a shower would clear his head. If not, he knew where to get himself a bottle of wakefulness. Now was not the time for sleep.

Nicole occupied herself with cleaning up the kitchen, but by the end of twenty minutes she was done. Every time she thought about leaving for Atrium, her heart gave a nervous pound against her ribs, Morse code: *Don't go.*

She shook her head. She wasn't going to let fear—of what was already coming for her, whether she ran away from it or toward it—stop her from fighting. She was going to put her family back together; they would fight this together.

Gordan was waiting for her in the Wastelands. She was going to find Raiden and bring him with her to get Gordan. *They want us separated.* She shook her head. *They want me alone.* She wasn't giving her enemies what they wanted anymore.

As she left the kitchen and crossed the living room, she spotted the wanted poster on the arm of the couch. She picked it up and studied the strange likeness, vivid and also uncertain. The girl in this picture was angry, scared, desperate, and dangerous—Nicole could still feel that girl inside of her.

With a sigh she looked up the stairs and made her choice. She carried the flyer with her to the bathroom, where she set it upright behind the sink.

She stood in front of the mirror, really seeing herself for the first time in she couldn't say how long. Her long tangle of soft brown spirals hung almost to her elbows now, and it was bushier, more unruly than she remembered it. The delicate curls were usually so weighed down. She put a hand into her hair. It was still soft and fine, but it had grown several inches in a matter of two weeks. Somehow it seemed to defy gravity with a life of its own. There was a slight tingle in the strands as she moved her fingers through them.

Nicole bent down to open the drawers below the sink, rummaging through each one until she found what she was hoping for—scissors. She pulled her hair back at the nape of her neck and secured it with the hair tie she wore on her wrist. With a final deep breath, she wiggled her fingers into the scissor handles and opened the blades, secured her doomed ponytail in her left hand, and sawed through the hair just above the hair tie.

When the scissors slid shut, severing the last of the hair, and the ponytail came free from her head, Nicole looked up to see her remaining curls fall around her face. She let out a sigh, realizing she had been holding her breath while she'd cut. The picture of herself on the wanted poster watched her, and she looked back at it, then up at her reflection, nodding in approval.

Since she still had a few hours to kill, Nicole attempted to soothe her tension with a bath. She then busied herself with evening out and layering her wet hair by trimming it above her head. She cleaned up the bathroom once she was dry and dressed and then returned downstairs to check her bag. It was mostly clothes she wouldn't need to bring with her. She pulled Althea's journal out of the bag and turned it over in her hands.

Checking the pocket watch Raiden had left her, she saw that she had only whittled away an hour and a half. She let out a little groan of self-pity and sank into the couch with the journal.

"Got any advice, Althea?" she asked, opening the book. Aimlessly, she flipped one page at a time, vaguely scanning the tangle of writing. Nothing jumped out at her, so she flipped the leather book over to examine the writing that Althea had added in between the original lines, cramped and upside down. She combed through the pages again.

Something crawled up her leg and made her jump in her seat. She let out a little shriek before realizing it was Gim.

"Oh," she said as he scurried across the open journal, onto her hand, and up her arm. She looked up at the dark fireplace. "Aw, your fire went out. Sorry,

Gim." He scrambled over her shoulder and ran a lap around her bare neck, unhindered by her hair, raising goose bumps on her skin.

Leaving Gim to make himself comfortable—which meant making a few more circuits around her shoulders before taking his favored spot around her neck—she returned to the pages of Althea's thoughts and visions.

"I met a young man today, no more than twenty years old. People always want to know their futures, although most are too fearful to ask, but he was eager to know, hungry to hear what lay ahead. I didn't like the fervor in his eyes. The intensity with which he pleaded for my Sight told me that my answer would stoke a terrible fire, no matter what I told him. His future was strange. I could hardly explain it to him because it was difficult for me to understand. I hope I never see him or his future ever again."

Nicole cringed, wondering what kind of horrible future was so bad that Althea didn't even want to recount the visions. This realm had clearly not escaped the evils of humanity when its people had fled the old world. Asi and Fen's past in the royal state of Taroth was enough proof of that.

She stopped reading and flipped through more pages before stopping at another section of upside-down writing. "I gave birth to a girl today. She brings me joy twice over, because her arrival means the son I have seen is yet to come, and so I will have two great loves in my life."

Nicole smiled, glad to finally read something happy. She flipped through more pages, and another section caught her eye.

"My heart grows heavier every day. As my body grows older, I fear my womb is withering. I saw my son so clearly. My daughter, my unseen miracle, is becoming a woman, and the Sight has chosen her as it chose me. I have seen countless visions come to pass, yet this one so dear to my heart eludes me. Have I taken some misstep? Did I want that future too badly? I feel I have put too much trust in the Sight, or perhaps I have misunderstood fate. How many times have I told some poor soul that our desires do not always lead us down the paths we expect? I do not wish to see any more of the future."

That was the last of the upside-down entries. Nicole wondered how old Althea had been during that final entry. Had she ever had the son she'd seen? If not, then this Althea couldn't be Raiden's mother. Nicole's heart gave a guilty thud, as she felt hopeful knowing Althea had been wrong about her own future. She felt awful for Althea's broken heart yet relieved to know not all visions came to fruition.

By the time Raiden was walking down the street, beneath an unsurprisingly gray sky, he could feel his lack of sleep catching up with him. He stopped to purchase two belly buns and continued on to Tovar's shop.

When he walked through the propped-open door, Tovar looked up from straightening the products on his shelves.

"Good morning," Tovar said.

Raiden held out the second belly bun. "Still warm," he said. He hadn't taken a single bite of his own yet—he was too tired to chew.

"Much appreciated," Tovar said as he took the bun. "Any luck with Moon and Stone yesterday?"

"No," Raiden said.

"That's a shame," he said. "Back to the books, then?"

"Actually, I'm going to listen in on Caeruleus through the mask. It's only a matter of time before he meets the fera again. I'd rather see him succeed than end up dead."

"You want to help him apprehend someone whose only crime is existing?" Tovar asked.

"Caeruleus is my friend. That girl might not be guilty of anything, but she is dangerous to those who threaten her. Caeruleus isn't about to give up on this assignment, not after losing an eye for it."

"Have you tried convincing him this is wrong?"

"I'm afraid that wouldn't help him, even if I could. It was brought to my attention that the Council is looking for a chance to charge me with treason. That's why they sent me after the rebels, I guess," he said with a wry smile. "My association with Caeruleus alone might have already put him at risk. If he fails the Council, he could face the same charge."

"That is a predicament," Tovar agreed. "But how are you going to help him?"

"I don't know yet. All I can do is listen in and keep track of where he is through the mask. It all depends on how this business plays out. I may be able to help; I may not."

Tovar frowned and took a bite of the belly bun in his hand.

"Do you mind if I use one of your bottles of wakefulness? I noticed them yesterday. I just can't risk falling asleep right now."

"Of course—help yourself," Tovar said.

"Thanks," Raiden said, raising the belly bun in a sort of toast before finally taking a bite.

He headed toward the back room, checked that no one was coming into the store, and slipped inside. With his food still in one hand, he went to the cabinet, retrieved one of the small bottles of sky-blue liquid and downed it in one eager swig. Then he placed the empty bottle on the shelf at his shoulder.

The potion spread through him, awakening his mind and his appetite. He took a monstrous bite of the bun and pulled the handheld looking glass from his pocket with his free hand. He activated the mask's ears on the glass and listened. At first he could hear nothing over his chewing, so he leaned in closer. He then heard footsteps moving at a brisk pace and the whisper of rubbing fabric. Caeruleus was going somewhere.

"Good day, Stone." Raiden recognized Loak's voice.

"Sir," Caeruleus answered.

"Any sign of Cael today?"

"Not today, sir."

Loak's answer was a low harrumph and what Raiden thought sounded like a grumbled "Good."

Raiden paced while he ate and waited to hear anything significant, getting used to the idea that he had no plan anymore. He finished his food without tasting it, forcing down the last bite sooner than he should have. When the sound of Caeruleus's feet suddenly got louder, echoing around a great space, Raiden rushed back to the table, yanked out the chair, and sat down to bend closer to the glass.

He waited, listening, his heartbeats striking his chest almost in unison with Caeruleus's steps.

"We've just had word. The seers still place her in Atrium, but her plans are uncertain to her, and her path is obscured. Because she knows nothing of the city, there is little we can see. Other than vague glimpses of her walking the streets, there are no definitive details at this point."

"So you're saying you can't be certain she even has plans to attack?" Caeruleus asked.

"There are traces of that future, but it comes and goes," a councilman answered.

The burden of Raiden's choice to help Caeruleus pressed down on him as the certainty of the fera's threat became *less* certain. As sure as his priority was his friend's safety, Raiden would still have to live with the mounting guilt that he'd helped the Council detain an innocent person.

"Apprehending her before she gets into the city would be ideal. We have doubled the guard at all gates, as well as armed them all with detections. When she tries to sneak in, we will know."

"We have sent out the posters of her. By now everyone in the city will have seen her face."

Raiden didn't see how this girl could last long without being caught. Perhaps because the grim thought had so recently darkened his own mind, he wondered whether maybe she had a death wish. She was willing to risk her freedom and her life to come here. He knew why he would do something that stupid, but why would she?

Nicole was almost asleep on the couch—which meant she was holding her eyes shut and hoping she could force her mind into a few peaceful seconds without thinking about Atrium, the Council, and the difficulty of finding Raiden in a city she didn't know.

When she heard the clopping of Ferdie's hooves outside, her body snapped upright, and her heart wavered between relief that they were back and dread that her departure was that much closer.

Through the window she could see Asi sitting beside Keren as they rode up to the house. Before Nicole could wonder where Fen was, the older girl sat up from lying down in the back of the cart. Nicole opened the front door and went outside. The girls waved. She waved back, glad they couldn't see the sadness on her face from so far away. As the cart pulled up to the house, Fen jumped out with a bag dangling from her shoulder. Keren brought Ferdie and the cart to a stop, and Asi climbed down from the bench to chase after Fen, jogging up to Nicole.

"Wow, your hair!"

"I like it."

"We found you a great disguise," Asi declared.

"You're going to blend right in with the people of Atrium," Fen said.

"I'll be right there after I get Ferdie settled," Keren said.

"Come on," Asi insisted, hopping with excitement where she stood as Fen took Nicole by the arm and pulled her inside.

Nicole let them take her hostage.

"I picked out the cloak," Asi said as Fen set the bag down on the couch.

"We both did," Fen corrected as she pulled out a dark-burgundy garment that looked to be a poncho with a hood. She held it up for Nicole to see.

Nicole took hold of the hem. The material was thick like a wool coat. Some strands in the fabric glinted in the light. It was indeed a cloak but one that probably wouldn't hang much past her knees.

"It's reversible," Asi said, turning the hood inside out to show the interior fabric was a dark gray like a storm. "So you can change your appearance without magic, if someone's following you."

Nicole nodded.

"And it has some basic charms woven in," Fen said. "You know, to keep you dry. It has its limits, though. I don't think it can hold up in a downpour. From what we hear the city is constantly cloudy and misty."

"It's all the residual magic that builds up in the city," Asi explained. "Just hangs around causing fog and clouds and rain."

"Boots," Fen announced as she pulled them from the bag.

Nothing like Nicole's lace-up hiking boots, these black leather boots were basic pull-ons. The leather was scratched, scuffed, and faded, and the shafts looked too soft to stand up—these boots were used.

"We figured if they didn't fit right you wouldn't have a problem making them smaller," Asi said with a grin.

Nicole appreciated Asi's attempt to make her laugh and managed to give her a smile, but she was only feeling heavier with dread. She realized now that it was less about the uncertainty of finding Raiden and more about having to say goodbye to *more* people and face the prospect of never seeing them again.

The door opened, and Keren came inside. "How's it going in here? Hey, your hair," she said.

"Do I look different enough?" Nicole asked.

"Hardly recognized you," Keren said.

"Don't forget about the bag," Asi said, pointing.

"Oh, right," Fen said, handing Nicole the boots so that she could pick up the bag. "It doesn't look like much, but that's the whole point."

It was a canvas bag, similar to a moderate-sized duffel bag, with a single strap.

"It has a featherweight charm," Keren said. "Won't get heavy, and it should help cover up having that sword under you cloak."

"You three thought of everything," Nicole said.

"Well, we're hoping you'll make it back here with that friend of yours," Keren said. "Which reminds me." She reached into the large pocket of her baggy coat and pulled out a small piece of stiff paper.

"What's this?" Nicole asked as Keren handed it to her.

"It's mindgraph parchment," she explained. "It forms any image from your memory. I thought it might help if you had a picture of your friend to help you find him."

"Oh, wow. How does it work?"

"Just hold it to your forehead and picture the image you want."

Nicole placed the palm-sized parchment against her forehead and closed her eyes. It wasn't hard to picture Raiden at all—his latte-brown skin, the dark-auburn hair that he was constantly raking back with his fingers, those green-blue eyes, the half smile he'd seemed to constantly wear when they hadn't been fighting golems or arguing about rescuing dragons or hoping they would make it off a crumbling bridge alive.

She felt the paper grow warm against her skin. After five seconds, she dared to open her eyes and look at it. The clarity of the image was surprising, almost photographic but not quite.

"Let's see," Keren said.

Nicole passed her the picture and watched her expression change from curiosity to warmth.

"I want to see," Fen said, hurrying over to look.

Asi was right behind her. "What's his name?"

"Raiden," Nicole answered.

"He's handsome," Fen said.

"I hope we get to meet him," Asi said, handing Nicole the picture.

"I do too," Nicole said, setting the picture down on the arm of the couch.

"Girls, why don't you take the bag and get it packed up with some food for Nicole," Keren said.

This request seemed to remind Asi and Fen that Nicole was indeed leaving, and their expressions fell as they trudged toward the kitchen with the bag.

Nicole sat down and loosened the laces of her hiking boots so she could switch them for her new secondhand boots. The shafts of the boots did sag a little, but for the most part they looked like they would keep her dry from midcalf to her toes. She stood up.

"The rest of this will be fine?" Nicole asked, presenting herself to Keren. She had put on her plainest clothes—a pair of light-gray thermal running tights and a white long-sleeve thermal shirt under a faded black T-shirt that hung loose and covered the reflective logos at the hem of her shirt and top of her leggings.

"That will be fine," Keren said, picking up the cloak and turning out the dark-gray side. "Here."

Nicole grabbed Raiden's sword from beside the couch and adjusted the strap so that the hilt sat between her shoulder blades and didn't show from the front. Then she took the cloak from Keren and put it on. There were slits in the cloak for her to put her arms through. Nicole turned her back to Keren. "Does it show?"

"A little, but the bag should do the trick," she said with a sigh that sounded displeased.

"What's wrong?" Nicole asked, turning back around.

"I was in your position once, with the chance to run or to face the horrors coming for me," Keren said softly, low enough that her voice would not penetrate the kitchen door. "I happened upon a portal, and that's how I ended up here. I realized too late that I shouldn't have run when so many others could not. I spent decades traveling Veil, searching for another portal, until I met the girls."

Nicole stood there in grave silence.

"We all ran from our fights, Nicole, and not a day goes by that I don't see those two girls wondering, like I did, whether they could have done something that might've changed things. If it weren't for those girls in there, I would still regret my choice. Being there for them saved me."

They stood there in silence for a moment as Keren blinked back moisture in her eyes. Nicole didn't know how to respond.

"And until you came along, I wondered what would save them from that same sorrow," Keren said, keeping her voice quiet. "I think you have. You give them hope that someone can take on anything."

"You're giving me credit for winning a fight I haven't fought," Nicole said.

"It's not about who wins. It's that you have the courage to stand up," Keren insisted.

More like foolishness, Nicole thought. She didn't feel proud of the idea that she might be inspiring Fen and Asi to be like her, walking into what very well could be a losing battle. She was going to die someday, and the chances were high that it might happen soon. She didn't think she deserved an award for accepting that.

Keren placed her hands on Nicole's shoulders, forcing Nicole to look her in the eyes. "Don't believe for an instant that you're alone, you hear me?"

"I hear you," Nicole answered with a feeble smile.

"Good," Keren said, releasing her.

"We have to leave her *some* room for other stuff," Fen insisted as she and Asi came out of the kitchen with the bag.

Keren placed her hands on her hips and smiled, as if resetting to the moment before their solemn conversation.

"Here you go," Fen said, handing Nicole the bag.

"Thank you." She peeked inside to see a loaf of bread wrapped in a clean dishcloth, several apples, and a leather pouch stuffed full of something. She knelt down beside her camping pack and dug out a couple of extra pairs of her thick, long socks and stuffed them into her new bag. Then she grabbed Althea's journal and put that inside too, along with her large water bottle, which just barely fit.

She swung the bag onto her back, positioning it directly over the sword, which was now completely unnoticeable beneath the bag and the roomy cloak that hung to her shins.

"Don't forget Raiden," Asi said, picking up the picture from the arm of the couch and tucking it into the pouch sewn to the bag's strap.

Nicole took a deep breath. "I guess it's time to go, then." She forced a smile, and her heart struck an anxious chord in her chest. She crossed the room to stand before the door.

"Be safe," Keren said.

"Come back as soon as you can," Fen said.

"I will," Nicole promised, her heart pounding with something more to say. "Thank you again for everything."

They smiled back at her. She dropped her gaze to her feet as she reached for the knob and pulled the door open. It seemed far too bright and beautiful a day for this. Nicole stepped out under the clear blue sky. She had decided to throw caution to the wind; she was walking right into a death trap after all. Her first destination was the Divale Manor in Witch Haven.

Nicole took one last glance over her shoulder to see Keren, Asi, and Fen wedged into the wide doorway, their smiles failing them. She waved and closed her eyes before she slipped away into the air like smoke.

The Divale Manor filled her vision when she solidified on her feet once more. She shook off the momentary daze from the leap and regained her focus on the tall stone house with its peeling white trim, vine-shrouded chimney, and mossy roof.

"Okay," she said in an attempt to psych herself up. She'd come to Witch Haven because she needed a little time to convince herself to do what she was about to do. She hadn't told Keren and the girls her plan because she didn't want them to know how insane it was, how likely it was that she might be leaping right into the pit of snakes.

A nervous laugh escaped her as she thought of how furious Gordan and Raiden would be at the idea. Interbounding into the city wasn't a good idea to start with. Planning on popping in right at Raiden's side had a good chance of landing her precisely where she didn't want to be, in the courts with the Council, surrounded by everyone they had at their disposal.

She took a deep breath, telling herself, *Maybe he's alone somewhere safe.* Surely she had as good a chance or better that he *wouldn't* be in the courts.

If she was going to risk going to the city, if she was prepared to confront the Council, then there was no reason not to make finding Raiden easy.

"Okay," she repeated, trying to convince herself she was ready.

She took in her surroundings one last time. The quiet house, the village of Witch Haven down the slope in the distance, the vibrant sky overhead, the winter birds singing into the crisp air. Before she bounded into utter chaos, she wanted to remember this peace.

Now, she thought, *or you never will.* She closed her eyes—thinking of Raiden and only Raiden—and she let her magic surge through her and whisk her toward Atrium.

33. Atrium

Her mind was locked on Raiden as she slipped and spun through space. Then a sudden deafening ringing filled her ears as if she had been hit. The unexpected impact jarred her, throwing her backward. She hit the ground and lay on her back in the dirt. Her head spun as she sat up, patting herself to check that she had all her limbs.

There were trees around her. Although she didn't know where she was, the forest of oak trees felt familiar to her now. The sky overhead was gloomy and gray. It occurred to her that she was somewhere outside of Atrium, unable to interbound in.

"Shit," she cursed under her breath, picking herself up and brushing off the dirt. Then the sound of people talking in the distance caught her ear.

She looked around and spotted a wagon loaded with barrels. It had to be heading to the city. So she wandered in that direction until she came to the road. Straight ahead she could see the wagon well ahead of her, and in the distance was a city with a high wall around it.

The sight of it made her heart reel into a panic. She urged her legs forward, taking deep breaths and focusing on the wagon and the sound of her footsteps on the dirt road instead of the city ahead.

A terrible shrieking sound warbled through the glass, and Raiden threw himself back against the chair, covering his ears. Even with his hands over his ears, the sound rattled his head, but in a matter of seconds it stopped. Still, he almost couldn't hear Caeruleus's next words.

"What was that?" Caeruleus's voice was aghast.

"Someone has just attempted to interbound into the city," a councilwoman said. "She is outside the city."

"If she is going to get in, it will be through the gates," a councilman said.

"I will be waiting for the alert," Caeruleus said.

"Oh, and a word to the wise," a different man said. "Wear your mask. You only have one eye left."

"Of course." Caeruleus's answer was so strained that Raiden could almost feel his anger radiating through the glass.

Raiden rubbed his eyes and cringed. Then an idea occurred to him so suddenly that he stood up, knocking the chair back.

"Wear your mask," he said, striking his forehead. That was how he could help Caeruleus. He snatched the glass off the table, shoved it back into his pocket, and turned toward the door.

He stopped himself just short of charging through it without first knocking to check that it was safe to emerge into the shop. Once Tovar had knocked back twice, Raiden burst through the door with force.

Tovar jumped, seated upon his stool. "What's going on?"

"I have an idea. I know how I can help Caeruleus without them knowing I'm helping." The words rushed out of his mouth as he crossed the shop, half running.

He stepped outside, almost crashing into a couple passing by. Then he plunged into the ether and emerged in his bedroom. He ran to the corner of his room where he had unceremoniously thrown his uniform. He fumbled through the fabric until he found the mask he had taken from Caeruleus the day of the ceremony.

Thinking he ought to look the part more, he pulled off his coat and shrugged on the uniform jacket over his parchment-colored shirt. He left the jacket open and decided to forgo the waist belt and short sword. He easily plucked the decorative buttons off the jacket with a good yank, but he begrudgingly left the Council's silver emblem on the breast. Deciding to stay in his brown slacks, he put on the tall black boots that went with the uniform.

With the dress uniform stripped down to look less formal, Raiden was as ready as he was going to be. Retrieving the mask from the bed, he held it in his hands and stared into the interior, remembering how he'd once thought he would never have to wear it.

As Nicole got closer to the city, it loomed ever taller, and it became harder and harder not to look up at it and let her heart turn into a frantic mess. *Deep breaths*, she kept reminding herself. They had to know she was coming. After all, they "employed" almost every seer in the realm.

If there was anything she could rely on, it was that the Council *thought* they knew her. To them she was out of control and dangerous. They obsessed over her strength and condemned her for it. They expected her to rely on that power. She had just tried to interbound in and failed. If they were capable of keeping people from interbounding into the city, they had to know about her attempt.

She eyed the wagon on the road. It was moseying along, and she gained on it easily with her brisk, anxiety-fueled pace. By the looks of things, she had been repelled less than half a mile away from the city. She was just able to make out the gate at the end of the road when something white on a tree ahead caught her eye. Her heart went cold at the sight of her own furious expression looking back at her upon the wanted poster nailed to the tree.

There seemed to be a small buildup of traffic entering the city. She supposed security was unusually tight at the gate today. Cringing, she let out a little groan. She stepped off the road and back into the trees, where she would have more cover as she approached. All the people waiting to get in had most likely seen the poster.

She was close enough to hear the two men in the wagon of barrels talking. A third man sat in the back sleeping, his head cushioned by a folded arm upon a barrel labeled ALE.

"Atticus still asleep?" the driver asked.

"'As been for the last hour. Did 'e give you 'is entry license?"

"Got it right here. How 'bout yours, ey?" the driver asked. "Never seen entry so bloody slow."

The first man handed over what looked like a small leather billfold. Nicole stopped in her tracks and let the distance between her and the wagon increase as it arrived at the gate. The men in the ale wagon had to wait for several travelers to hand their identification to the guards.

Nicole's heart palpitated with dread at her sudden idea: switch places with Atticus. She had to time it right—too soon and the guy might wake up and come running down the road before the wagon was let through, too late and the guards might notice the switch.

The wagon was next, and the guards were still scrutinizing the papers. They didn't seem to be studying the travelers' faces all that closely. No, they were much more concerned with people's entry licenses than the people themselves. There had to be other measures in place anticipating her attempts to get inside the walls—barriers, alarms against anyone who didn't have the proper identification maybe. Since she had no way to know what those other measures might be, she resigned herself to cross that bridge if and when she came to it.

"Now or never," she muttered, flipping up her hood. "Time to trade places, Atticus."

She took one last hard look at the man asleep in the back of the wagon, imagining herself in his place and him in hers behind the tree. With her eyes closed, she tapped into the swirling power deep inside her. Her anxiety had her magic in a death grip, but as soon as she stirred her power, that death grip popped like a bubble, and a burst of hot energy rushed through her.

For a split second all she could feel was the wave of heat in every cell, and then suddenly her senses returned. There was a crate under her butt and a barrel under her arm, where she kept her face buried. Pretending to be asleep felt impossible with her heart rate skyrocketing.

"All right, go on in, then," one of the guards said. "Pull up, sir."

"Mornin'," the driver said. "That's all of 'em."

There was a pause. The horse snorted. A bustle of noise wafted through the gate behind her.

"Looks in order. Someone sleeping on the job, I see."

"Always does," the driver said.

Nicole swallowed the lump in her throat, hoping neither the driver nor his colleague would feel the need to look back at Atticus. She couldn't be sure her heart was even still beating; it was going so fast it might as well be a constant hum in her chest. *It's not gonna work*, she thought. Some magic might hear her panicked thoughts or detect her elevated heart rate as they passed through the gate.

The wagon lurched, and her heart stopped. She held her breath. As they passed, she heard one of the guards speak. "None of our detections have been tripped here at the south gate," he reported. "Nothing but our usual entries."

Nicole tensed, waiting for Atticus to shout from down the road, for the driver to turn around and expose her, for the guards to surround them. All she heard was the creaking of the wagon, the clopping of the horses' hooves, and the din of people. She dared to lift her head a little and peek out from under her hood. They were inside the wall. The gate was shrinking away behind them.

Cautiously, she straightened and looked around. The wagon was on a road that seemed to follow the wall around the city. There were carts and stands set up between the wall and the road where people from outside the city had set up shop to sell their wares. She hopped off the wagon and slipped into the foot traffic alongside the road, looking back to catch a glimpse of the wagon continuing on its way. The driver and the other man still hadn't looked behind them to check on Atticus, who might very well still be fast asleep right where she'd left him.

The farther from the gate she got, the better. She looked around at the faces in the crowd. Countless people wore their hoods up, which eased a little of her anxiety over looking suspicious. No one seemed particularly interested in making eye contact, so she went about her business taking in the city, looking for the posters with her face on them.

She walked a few blocks before it sank in that she had made it into the city. Then the dreadful *Now what?* crossed her mind. The tiny success of getting in made her reluctant to risk her initial plan to get to Raiden immediately, no matter where he might be. She was in, and she might as well be covered in black hellebore powder for as much as the people around noticed her. It certainly wouldn't be an expeditious search, but she suddenly felt she had a real chance of finding Raiden without being discovered.

Raiden materialized once again outside the shop, mask in hand. He couldn't risk putting it on—not yet anyway. Wearing it would activate many of its interworking spells. What he needed was a mask, nothing more. He didn't want to take the chance that the Council might notice what he was doing. He certainly wouldn't put it past them to track all their agents with the equipment they were issued. Raiden could have tried to alter the mask himself, but since Tovar had worked on the other mask, he knew how all the spells worked better than Raiden.

When Raiden strolled back inside, Tovar looked up.

"That was quick," Tovar said. Noticing Raiden's clothes, he added, "You changed?"

"I popped home to get this," Raiden explained, holding up the mask.

"What for?"

"To lend Caeruleus some assistance without anyone knowing it's me."

Tovar nodded and gave him an appreciative look. "Smart."

"Only one problem."

"You don't want to risk activating it," Tovar said, jumping into Raiden's train of thought easily. "I've got just the thing. Give me a moment."

Tovar went to the front of the store, shut the door and locked it, then returned to the back to open the door into the workroom. He motioned Raiden to proceed to the worktable and shut the door behind him.

"We just need one thing," he said, crossing the room to one of the cabinets. He opened one door after another, rummaging around inside each one, until he found what he was looking for—a short, fat earthen pot. "Sorcerer's herb," he said. "Or thornapple, if you prefer the more mundane name."

Tovar brought the pot to the table, plucked the lid off, and reached inside. "Oh, turn the mask facedown. The spells are all laid in the interior."

Raiden turned the mask over so the glass eyes were peering into the wood.

"Just a little will do the trick," Tovar said, removing his hand from the pot with his fingers pinched together. He held his hand over the mask and rubbed his thumb against his fingertips, sprinkling a fine powder over the mask as if he were seasoning it. The powder hissed and sparked for several seconds as it fell onto the mask.

"It breaks spells and completely strips them down," Tovar explained as the mask gave a few last feeble pops. "Done." He put the lid back on the little brown pot.

"It's that simple?"

"Of course it is. Destroying something is always simple. It's creating something that's difficult." He took the pot back to the cabinet.

Raiden picked up the mask. There wasn't a trace of the powder, and he realized it must have burned away in the reaction to the spells.

"Congratulations," Tovar said as he crossed the room. "You now have a completely useless mask."

Raiden chuckled as Tovar stepped back into the main shop.

Alone now in the workroom, Raiden resumed monitoring the efforts to find the fera. Leaving the mask on the table, he pulled his portable looking glass back out from his pocket and activated both the listening spell and the tracking spell in Caeruleus's mask.

"Holger, anything?" Caeruleus asked. By the sound of his voice coming through the glass, he was speaking through the vox channel with his fellow agents.

"None of our detections have been tripped here at the south gate," a man replied. "Nothing but our usual entries."

"Damara?"

"Nothing here at the west gate," a woman answered.

"Elyn?"

"All clear at the north gate."

Caeruleus let out a groan. "What about you, Kai?"

"Not a thing. We sure the detectors can pick up *everything?*"

"Yes," Caeruleus huffed. "*Any* spell that passes through the gate, even if someone comes through with a glamour to change their eye color."

Raiden checked the glass, which showed a shadowy outline of the city, its circular wall and the main thoroughfares that led to the courts and divided the city into eight wedges. A small dot of light showed him where Caeruleus was in the city, and judging by the dot's swift movement across the diagram of Atrium, Caeruleus had to be in the sky.

Caeruleus spoke again. "All right. Get everyone here, and I mean everyone. If you're on patrol, report to the wall."

"What is all this about?" someone asked. "Who is trying to get in?"

There was a pause.

"Someone we don't want in the city," Caeruleus answered.

Raiden sighed, relieved to hear Caeruleus abide by the Council's desire to keep the identity of the fera concealed. Although he didn't think keeping all the agents in the dark when they were facing something like the fera was right, he was more concerned about Caeruleus keeping the Council happy and preserving their faith and trust in him. Raiden couldn't help but wonder, though, if Caeruleus did everything he was told to do and still failed, would the Council take responsibility or blame Caeruleus?

At least the fera hadn't gotten in yet. Had the fera given up trying to get into the city after just one attempt? They were so focused on her using magic to get in. What if she just walked right in? *No,* he thought, dismissing the idea with a shake of his head. The Council was overly cautious. People needed merchant licenses, passports, or residential identification to get into the city.

He didn't think the fera would give up that easily. As he listened and waited, his legs yearned to move, and his feet fell into that same old rhythm of pacing.

Nicole placed her hand over the little pouch on the strap across her chest, hesitating as she considered pulling out the picture of Raiden. There had been a lot less pressure to make the right choice when she'd thought there was no right choice. Making it into the city unnoticed suddenly meant she had a chance, and that meant treading more carefully. In his letter Raiden had mentioned that it wouldn't be wise to search for him, as it would be suspicious. But she didn't plan on spreading his name around; his picture had to be safe to share, right?

The scent of manure caught her attention as she passed a large stable at least twenty stalls long where merchants could put up their horses. She walked along the road that followed the wall. It didn't seem the likely place to find Raiden, out on the very edge of the city, where the visiting merchants set up their temporary shops for the day.

Although the towering buildings of the city to her right loomed over her with an intimidating challenge, she knew she'd better delve deeper into Atrium if she wanted to find Raiden. So at the next street she turned right and headed toward the center of the city.

For a few blocks she looked around at the buildings, the countless windows, the people passing her on the street. There were no vehicles on this street, just pedestrians going about their business. Not knowing where she was going made it easy to pick the next street and veer left to avoid a dense crowd.

She passed a block where a stream of kids hurried toward the doors of a narrow gray building and got the impression she was passing a school. Another block down she came to a bustling road where vehicles drove—wagons, carts, trucks. There was even something that looked like a motorcycle, but it rushed by her before she could get a good look at it. The street she followed turned into a bridge to carry pedestrians over the traffic.

With a shrug she decided to head over the bridge. At the apex she stopped a moment to look down the street and saw that it led directly to a hill in the distance. Atop the hill was a great white building. The sight struck her colder than the gray chill of the morning. That had to be the court building.

So that's where they are, she thought. There, maybe two miles away, the Council sat thinking they had the right to decide who and what she was. Her body went hot with anger for a moment, chasing away the chill in the air. She took a deep breath and convinced herself to turn away. *Keep walking.*

One block past the vehicles' thoroughfare that led to the courts, the street ended, meeting a perpendicular street in a T. Preferring not to head closer to the enemy at the center of the city, she chose left, and before she knew it, she came to another T. She turned right this time, sinking into the dreadful realization that she was navigating a maze not a city. *What does Veil have against grids?* she thought as she headed down the long, straight street.

She tried to convince herself that knowing where she was didn't matter since she was wandering around trying to find a single person out of who knew how many. But that didn't shake the discomfort of feeling utterly lost when less than an hour ago she had been in the living room of a safe home with Keren, Fen, and Asi.

Atrium was an odd mixture of the familiar and unfamiliar. There were times when she could almost convince herself she was just walking down the street of some old European village turned metropolis. The stone streets were narrow, cramped by the tall buildings crowded to fill the space inside the city walls. People leaned out their windows and chatted with neighbors in windows across the streets and alleys.

And then there were times when she felt like she was in wonderland, like when a woman lounging on her stomach upon a flying carpet whizzed by. The more attention Nicole paid to the faces around her, the more she spotted people who certainly weren't human. A man with long grayish-brown hair, fierce yellow eyes, and pointed furry ears on top of his head passed by her, a bushy wolf tail swishing behind him.

She had to remind herself not to stare at people. Her amazed observations of the city screamed *Outsider!* loud enough without her gaze getting caught on every person with nonhuman features. What she wished she had was a map of the city, a directory with a big arrow pointing to where she was. But her enemy had seers, it was an advantage to not know where she was going. Her best bet was to just wander and cover as much of the city as she could, hoping to spot Raiden somewhere.

Following the same straight street, she came to another bridge that crossed over a perpendicular road—Zephyrus Street, according to the sign—that led to the courts at the center of the city. Again she looked toward the Council's safe haven upon the hill, clenching her teeth hard together until her ears started ringing.

The idea of interbounding right to Raiden was still tempting, but she was growing ever more attached to the hope that she could get away with sneaking into Atrium and escaping with Raiden. Then doubt crept into her mind. Was that even a viable plan if the Council could just summon him right back like they had the first time?

A groan broke past her lips as she trudged onward down the street. The road started to curve slightly to the right, and not long after that she was at yet another bridge crossing over an identical thoroughfare, where vehicles were either heading toward or away from the courts at the center of the city. There were several lanes going each direction, with the two outermost lanes used for vehicles stopped for deliveries or loading. A sign at the intersection identified the bustling road below as Circios and the curving street she walked as Solis.

She sighed, understanding now that the main roads for traffic all led to the center and divided the city up like a pizza—and the court building on the hilltop was the little plastic table stuck in the middle. Before she went on her way, she threw a dirty look toward the courts.

The sky overhead was a constant cover of clouds. The sun didn't peek through once, and she found it difficult to comprehend the passing of the day without pulling out her pocket watch repeatedly. Anxiety kept her stomach uneasy, and she didn't feel like eating at all.

Whenever the magnitude of her task to find Raiden seemed too daunting, she considered that she would be just as difficult for the Council to find as Raiden was to her. She just needed to find him before they found her. *No problem*, she thought bleakly.

34. Listen

If not for the wakefulness potion, Raiden would have fallen asleep listening to the fruitless watch for the fera at the gates for the better part of the day. There had been no second attempt to breach the city in almost four hours. He sat bent over the table, his forehead resting against the wood. Lucky for him he had a lot of practice waiting. Nine years of waiting made four hours seem like nothing.

The looking glass lay beside his head. There were books scattered around him on the table, attempts to find an answer as to how the fera could get past the detection spells. He was of the firm but unsubstantiated opinion that she was already inside the city. If they wanted to find her, they should assume she'd managed to get in unnoticed, even if it was supposed to be impossible.

He couldn't exactly go give Caeruleus his advice, but he could get out of the workroom and do his own searching. What other methods were there to find one girl in the city, unless she made herself known somehow?

He slipped the glass into his pocket, picked up the mask, and marched toward the door.

Nicole chose to walk the streets in the wedge between Zephyrus Street and Circios Street. They served as a reliable enough guide to help her systematically search the streets of Atrium. As she wandered, her body and her feet felt heavier, her anxious pace slowed, and she grew disheartened.

If she didn't focus on the din of the city, the low roar of bustling crowds, the drumming of so many footsteps, she might start listening to the voice of doubt in her head. She felt like she was arguing with the girl she had been before the portal and Raiden and magic.

What do you think you're going to accomplish? If you die young, it's going to be because you were stupid enough to do this.

I'm taking control of my life for once.

And you're going to die for it. Yeah, that's much *better than finishing high school and going to college and getting a job like everyone else.*

It's not like I can go back to a life without all this. I can't just be an ordinary nobody again—I never want to be that girl again.

At least she would have lived past eighteen.

Nicole tried to shake the nagging thoughts by focusing on her boots, adjusting her bag, checking that Gim was still curled up around her neck, and filling her senses with the city around her—the telltale tingle of magic in the air, the smell of mint and basil as she passed a stall filled to the brim with neatly tied bunches of freshly cut herbs.

You could have gone with Gordan and lived in the Wastelands. You might be happy there with all the other exiles everyone hates.

She accepted her failure with a sigh and continued her argument. *And never see my family, not to mention just leaving Raiden here while he commits treason for my sake.*

He's a grown man. It's his choice what he does.

And he's stuck here because of me, because I exist, because I opened a portal and they wanted him to do their dirty work.

He doesn't want to be saved. He told you not to come.

It's not about saving him. The Council can't just commandeer our lives. Not mine and not Raiden's.

So this is *about confronting them. You're trying to trick yourself into the fight. What, are you afraid to be that person? To attack, to be the aggressor, to embrace that violent power slumbering inside you? Come on; you know what this is all leading to. You don't have to pretend to look for Raiden while you wait for them to attack. You aren't going to find him, and what does claiming self-defense really accomplish? Will it make you feel better if you win with blood on your hands? The answer is right in front of you.*

Nicole came to Circios again and looked down the busy street at the white building in the distance. The darker voice continued, *Quit with the pretenses. You came here for them, to take your life back or die trying. Go ahead and do it.*

Nicole took a deep breath. It was tempting to just get it over with on her terms, knowing that the fight was coming either way. Then for some reason what Mitchell had said to her came to her mind. *"I just don't think you should do something stupid like go up against people who have a whole army at their disposal by yourself."* She couldn't help rolling her eyes at her brother—typical Mitchell, showing up to contradict her even when he was an entire realm away.

"We were better off together," Nicole muttered to herself. She most certainly would bring the fight to the Council, but she wouldn't do it alone.

All the other fera must have put up a fight, she realized. *They had as much power as me, and the Council still destroyed them. I would rather go out giving them one hell of a fight than rush into it alone and make it easy for them,* she thought to the nuisance in her head.

That seemed to silence the voice, at least for now. She smiled to herself with morbid self-satisfaction. She would rather die making them regret ever coming for her than live a long life in hiding.

Walking down the street wearing the mask made Raiden uncomfortable. Whenever he'd walked the streets before, he'd felt virtually invisible. People had never paid him much attention. But with the mask on, everyone he passed seemed to look at him. People eyed the mask with anxious glares, sideways glances, and discreet stares. He didn't like being so conspicuous, he didn't like the humid discomfort of his hot breath trapped against his face, and he hated the strange green-tinted world he saw through the mask's glass eyes.

The mask did have one advantage: people moved out of his way as he walked down crowded streets. He doubted this avoidance was deference, but it meant he could walk freely. Wearing the mask gave him a sense of how the people felt about the Council's agents at least, and if the people didn't care for the Council's agents, they couldn't care all that much for the Council themselves.

As expected, Raiden found one of the posters of the fera, plastered over a propaganda poster spouting unity and freedom. She looked nothing like he remembered her. The person on this poster was not the person he had encountered that night in Cantis. This image had captured a woman with darkness in her expression, a wild anger in her eyes.

For some reason he couldn't explain, as he looked into the ink-rendered gaze of the fera, his heart beat heavily, and his core flushed with heat. Having such a visceral reaction to her face seemed strange. He could only guess that knowing what this girl was capable of and seeing the danger in her expression had sparked unease in his gut. *No wonder Caeruleus lost an eye,* he thought with a guilty cringe.

Suddenly the people all around him looked remarkably different to Raiden. Instigating a fight with the fera in the streets couldn't possibly end swiftly or neatly. People might get hurt. Raiden couldn't help but feel that what he should be doing was evacuating people from Atrium. His concern made him realize how much he didn't know about what had happened to the other fera. How had the Council handled those encounters? Had it really been about keeping the people of Veil safe if they were willing to take on the last fera here in their own city full of people?

He wandered down Mat Street, where the fera's face was everywhere. People went about their business, sitting down to enjoy a meal, sharing treats with friends, chatting about food and which establishment they would visit today. Several people paused to look at the posters. They didn't even know what she was. What did they think, that this girl was some hardened criminal, unassuming and therefore strangely suited for whatever crimes she'd committed?

With as many posters as there were on the lampposts lining Mat Street, Raiden found himself facing the fera once again. He stood outside Meat Pies & Sweet Pies and spared a glance toward the pie sellers. Gwyn was at the window today, but when she looked up at him, she saw only the mask and immediately looked back down. So he turned back to the fera.

Something about her face brought the Sight to the fringes of his mind. His habit was to resist it, but if he let the impending vision into his head, maybe he could find her. But what then?

The thick layer of gray clouds choking the sky seemed to creep into Nicole's head, turning her psyche into a mirror image of the gray sky by the end of the day. After walking every street between Circios and the next main road, Boreas, and then every street between Boreas and Caicias Road, she felt drained, but she couldn't even entertain the thought of sleeping. Not only did she have no place where she could, but she knew her thoughts would not quiet enough to sleep.

A terrible growl from deep in her stomach disturbed her thoughts for a moment. Her appetite returned with a vengeance, so she looked around for a place to sit down where she could dig into her bag. Not finding one, she continued along Solis Street. She had been following the road for a while. Although she didn't have a map, she felt she had a basic understanding of the city's framework. The continuous curved road seemed to cross every main street that led to the courts, and the court building always stayed the same distance away each time it came into view at the end of the busy streets. So even without a map, she knew Solis Street was a perfect circle about halfway between the courts and the outer wall.

Instead of a bridge over Caicias Road, Solis went beneath into a dark underpass. Along the ceiling of the tunnel were glass domes containing several orbs of light, bobbing lazily and offering only a dim glow in the darkness. Voices from the other end bounced through the passage. Her footsteps sounded magnified in the enclosed space, and as she passed under the glass fixtures, the little glowing orbs went suddenly bright as tiny suns.

"—they can't even get a passport to visit."

"I heard the Council hasn't approved any new passports in years."

The couple walking toward her went silent as they drew nearer.

She kept her pace brisk and her eyes down. The lights continued to grow brighter as she passed beneath them, fading back to their usual dimness as she left them behind.

After she'd passed the couple, one of them murmured, "Don't see that every day."

Nicole's body went hot with embarrassment and anxiety from the attention. She was relieved to emerge from the tunnel back into the dull gray daylight. Her stomach still churned and gurgled at her. Not a block past the underpass a rainbow of savory and sweet aromas drifted in the breeze. Her nose latched onto the scent of food and led the way.

At the next cross street she followed the smell of frying oil and caramelizing sugars to the right, then immediately to the left. She looked up to read the street sign—Mat Street. If not for the people in this city trying to find her so they could kill her, Nicole could have loved Atrium.

Other than the wheel-spoke roads from the wall to the courts, all the streets seemed to be welcome only to pedestrians. Mat Street was wide and lined with restaurants and food vendors. Tables, chairs, and benches were scattered around. The people here seemed like a completely different sort from those she'd seen so far while wandering through the city. There were more smiles here as people enjoyed their social meals.

Nicole spotted an empty bench and sat down, careful not to let the sword on her back clank against the stone. She removed her bag and adjusted the back of her cloak and the sword to hang over the bench behind her. With the bag in her lap, she removed the cloth-wrapped bread and tore the heel off the end of the loaf.

The first bite quieted her stomach. As she ate, she looked around. People watching in Veil was even better than back home.

A mother pulled her son along by one of the ridged, curled horns on his head, scolding him, "I told you that if you couldn't behave, you were going straight home. Come on."

Across from Nicole was a noodle shop. Beside it was a skewer shop. Her gaze traveled left down the street. A figure walking toward her caught her eye, and her heart nearly stopped at the sight of the strange silver mask and what looked like a military uniform. She turned her attention back down to her bag as casually as she could, trying to act like her heart wasn't fighting to escape her chest.

Her bread still firmly in one hand, she fussed with her bag, pretending to dig one-handed through its contents in search of something. As she fought to keep her stomach from coming up her throat, the man walked by. While pulling out the leather pouch Fen and Asi had packed, she raised her eyes slightly to see his boots pass in front of her. Her lungs ached, and she reminded herself to breathe. Even as she watched the Council's agent reach the end of Mat Street and disappear around the corner, she couldn't convince her nerves to settle.

One of the Council's agents had just walked right by her, and as far as she knew, he hadn't even given her a second glance—not that she could tell where his gaze had been directed beneath that uncanny mask. Her mind went on a rampage into the future. They wouldn't go on thinking she was still outside trying to get into the city forever. Eventually all those agents would be combing the streets for her.

Mat Street no longer felt welcoming. The Council's man had stolen that moment of contentment. She sighed, stuffing the hunk of bread in her mouth to free up her left hand. The leather pouch was still in her right hand, her prop to seem preoccupied and keep her face down as the Council's agent had passed.

She moved to put the pouch back and heard its contents jingle. Curious, she unfastened the little brass clasp and opened the flap. Inside, the pouch was filled with pieces of silver and copper. The sight stunned her. Her brain went blank. Her mouth fell open in shock, and the bread came tumbling out, startling her out of her stupor. She managed to catch the bread against her chest but still couldn't wrap her head around the contents of the pouch.

As she processed the pouch of silver and copper, she grew frustrated trying to settle on an emotion. Part of her wanted to be angry that they would send her away with so much of their money, though Nicole had no real idea how much this amounted to in terms of their income. Of course she was grateful, which led her to tearful, which she then had to fight by opening her eyes wide and blinking the moisture back.

She looked inside the pouch once more and noticed a note half buried in the money:

> If you want to repay us, you will just have to come back.
> Keren, Fen & Asi

Nicole let out a laugh and a sob at the same time. She buckled the pouch shut and tucked it back into her bag. With her bread in her mouth again, she closed up the bag and put it on. Ready to be on her way, Nicole grabbed the bread from her mouth, tearing away another bite, and stood up.

When she turned to head down Mat Street—she wasn't about to go back the way she'd come after watching the man in the mask go that way—she almost ran into a lamppost, and suddenly she was standing face-to-face with herself. She had seen several of her posters in the city already, but she'd generally kept her distance so that the likeness between them wouldn't be obvious.

As quickly as she could while still acting casual, she hurried past the lamppost and down the street, realizing that *all* the lampposts had her posters attached to them. Seeing so many images of herself made her heart lurch into a panic. *It's fine*, she insisted, keeping her head down as much as she could as she made her way down the street. *No one has noticed.*

A stream of people came down Mat Street—the dinnertime rush, she supposed—so she took a path away from the crowd, veering closer to the shop fronts and weaving around tables and chairs.

Still following Mat Street, she crossed over the next wheel-spoke road, Eurus. The bridge was wide, and there were even a few treat vendors with their stands set up on either side, blocking the view of the court building. At the next block Nicole turned left and found her way back to the circular Solis Street.

With the memory of the Council agent in her mind, Nicole kept an unsettled eye out for more of the masks. She couldn't help but wonder why the government would put their law enforcers in masks. Did the Council *not* want the people to trust their agents? Whatever the reason, she just hoped they would all be wearing those masks, so she could see them coming.

35. History

Caeruleus stormed through the corridors of the courts, fuming from a day of searching for absolutely nothing. They had every precautionary spell at the gates to prevent magical entry. Every single agent in the city had spent the day patrolling the wall inside and out and combing through the forest surrounding the city.

Everyone in the corridors seemed to hear his frustration in his footsteps and see the annoyance in his eye, and they drifted out of his path.

If the fera had been trying to get in, she would have been spotted. Either that girl had given up after her first attempt, or she was already in the city. He wasn't going to waste another day being made into a fool by her.

At the very end of the north corridor there was only a stained glass window portraying the Council's crossed keys shining like the sun over an open book. "*Unum*," Caeruleus grumbled at the window, and the stone floor under the stained glass opened like a yawning mouth, the stones shifting and tumbling over themselves to reveal the stairs leading to the lower corridors.

He practically flew down the stairs, his steps echoing off the cold stone. The air grew chilly as he descended. As he reached the bottom of the stairs, the stones shifted above him, and the opening at the top of the stairs closed.

The stones of the lower level were enchanted to emit light whenever someone walked the corridors. Ahead of him the passage was dark, but the stones under his feet, in the walls beside him, and above his head all glowed with a soft white light that traveled with him as he went.

He passed the door to the arsenal chamber and the door to the court spell workers' workshop before the corridor made a left turn and he came to another set of stairs. The steps lit up under his feet, and he reached the bottom with an eager bounce in his step as he resisted the urge to get to his destination faster.

The first doorway he walked past was tall with twin doors. It was the Chamber of the Sight, where the seers joined together to strengthen the Sight as a collective. Caeruleus had never personally seen inside the chamber. Although curiosity beckoned him, he pressed on down the passage, the white light of the stones following the vigorous tempo of his feet.

His sight was set on the wide door ahead of him, the Hall of Records. Before he reached the door, the stones at the end of the hall glowed, warning someone's approach. Loak Clyson rounded the corner; his incredible stature almost filled the corridor.

"Stone," he greeted Caeruleus with an uncertain tone. "Visiting the Hall of Records?"

"Yes, sir," Caeruleus answered, his pace slowing.

"Did the Council send you down here?"

Caeruleus couldn't muster up a sliver of concern over a lack of orders. "No, sir," he said easily.

Loak raised his eyebrows and regarded Caeruleus with a slight tilt of his head. "Very well," he said. "Carry on." He continued down the hall, leaving Caeruleus standing there baffled.

Caeruleus had just told one of the highest-ranked agents in the courts that he was acting without orders, and the man had shrugged it off. Caeruleus turned to watch Loak make his way down the corridor and up the stairs. For a wary moment he just stood there, wondering why the strictest agent in the city didn't care, until he realized it didn't really matter. Bounding the last couple steps to the door, he heaved it open and stepped into the Hall of Records.

Caeruleus expected a vast, dim, and dusty hall stuffed utterly full with every shred of Veil's history, from its strange, gradual emergence from the ether, through the division of the realm into kingdoms, the centuries of conflict, the Dragon Wars, and up to today.

He certainly didn't expect the brightly lit room bustling with movement. On the wall to his left there appeared to be a small fireplace, but it was clean and empty. A rolled-up report drifted down from the chute and floated out of the opening just as a swift black shape swooped down to snatch it up. Two more reports flew out of the opening and were met by two more flapping black shadows.

They were ravens, he realized, and about that moment another of the large black birds glided down from atop the towering shelves to land on his shoulder. The sleek bird bent its head to look at him with one shining black eye. It tilted its head this way and that, as though studying his face and waiting for something.

"Uhh ... I'm looking for the records on the fera," he told the raven, which immediately clicked its beak and straightened up. Its talons dug briefly into his shoulder as it took off toward one of the shelves.

Caeruleus followed as it flew down the center aisle. As he walked, a raven with a report in its beak landed on a nearby shelf. It released the report, and the parchment unrolled itself and slipped into a file. Enchanted shelves, he noted, but the ravens still had to know which shelf to bring the reports to depending on their type.

Ravens flying overhead caught his eye, leading his gaze to the tall, narrow door at the far end of the hall. He almost lost track of the raven he was following in his interest in the others going about their business. In fact, he *had* lost it until it swooped down to skim his head and regain his attention.

The raven led him several shelves deep into the hall before swooping to the right between two rows of shelves. It landed on the floor and took a few hops to reach a certain section of a bottom shelf. Then it looked up at him, clicked its beak, and raised it feathers and around its head and neck.

"Thanks," Caeruleus said as he crouched down. He reached for a roll of several large pieces of parchment. The raven pecked his hand. "Ouch! I'm sorry—I don't have anything for you." It opened its beak wide and gave him a rude caw before departing.

He returned to gathering the information—the roll of parchment, a large leather envelope, and a stack of separate files bounded together with cord. With the records tucked under an arm, he stood up and returned to the center aisle, where several long, narrow tables divided the walkway. After dumping the contents of his arm on the table, he untied the rolled-up parchment and spread it open on the table.

What lay before him appeared to be a stack of several old posters regarding the different fera. It looked like mostly propaganda from the height of the fera panic. The posters were mostly text talking about destruction and the loss of whole villages to incidents involving the mysterious fera.

He opened the leather envelope and found it full of scraps and whole pages from newspapers, even handwritten accounts about the fera. From his scan through the flood of evidence, the fera had never been difficult to find. In fact, it seemed to him that the fera had been hardly able to contain the power within them, let alone control it. None of them had been capable of hiding for long. All accounts described them as skittish and volatile.

Caeruleus's face pinched in confusion. This fera was different. None of this information could help him find someone who *could* hide among the crowds and control her abilities. The more he read, the more troubled he was by everything the Council had not shared with him.

None of the firsthand accounts described the fera in the way the Council described them. These accounts spoke of accidents and minor interactions leading to unforeseen outbursts of power. The Council's propaganda all spoke of malicious beings that craved destruction and relished turmoil. There weren't many of the firsthand accounts, and so it would seem most of the realm knew the fera only as the Council had painted them.

With a sigh he moved on to the stack of files, removing the cord that bound them all together and opening the first folder. They were the detailed reports on each fera and the efforts to apprehend them.

He spread out the files, opening them all to work through them more efficiently. Many of the files had images on memory parchment. Some of them, however, did not—these cases had had no surviving agents to provide memories of the final encounters. Worse than the incidents with no survivors was the fact that all the images were of children no older than twelve.

A lump of apprehension formed in his throat. The flapping of wings and the occasional caw of the ravens going about their tasks was the only company he had as he faced the sobering reality of his assignment.

He read, "When we found the fera, I thought surely this was all wrong. It was just a child. But no sooner had we approached the boy than he broke down into a fit of panic, crying and pleading. It seemed to me the boy didn't even know what he doing. He turned three men to dust before succumbing to his own powers. The sight of a child tearing himself to shreds is unfathomable."

The raven that had helped him landed on the table, puffed up a little, and proceeded to bend over the information spread out before him, tilting and turning its head like it was reading.

Caeruleus turned to another file and found the agent's account of events. "A man reported that everything in his house had been floating for two days and that random objects would spontaneously combust. Thankfully he had not gone looking for the source of the disturbance himself. We evacuated the family, as we suspected a fera was hiding somewhere on their property. I searched the barn while my partner searched the house. Next thing I knew, the house was being swallowed up. There was nothing but a pit in the earth."

He understood why the Council sought out the fera. The Council didn't need to portray them as monsters to prove they were a threat to people. Unfortunately, he now understood why the Council had only fed him the propaganda. Dangerous though they were, the fera had been terrified children seeking safety and unable to tame their own powers. Not one attempt to apprehend a fera had been successful due to their unstable nature. Why then was the Council so adamant that this last fera be treated like the fera of the propaganda? She did indeed have terrible power, but she was nothing like these accounts. Surely the Council realized this fact as plainly as Caeruleus could.

He scanned the pages again, trying to understand why the Council would turn these unfortunate souls into unassuming monsters. As far as he could tell, the fera were actually a fairly small problem. There were only fifteen files, fifteen fera in the realm. Had the tales of terrible, inconspicuous monsters started as a rumor among the people?

The fera's potential for danger and propensity to cause destruction wherever they went was very real, as the firsthand accounts made clear. But he could only imagine how people might receive the news of the Council tracking down and taking care of these threats only to find out the fera were misunderstood children who needed help. He could see why the Council had stuck with the story that the fera were deceiving, manipulative, and malicious. Then, when the job was done and the threat was gone, the people of Veil could do nothing but praise the Council.

Now he wasn't sure what to think. The fera he had encountered was clearly different from these timid creatures with destructive powers. She was not fragile and unstable. She hadn't crumbled into a self-destructive fit when he'd confronted her. He had seen the fire in her eyes, and she'd harnessed the magic within her with purpose. If anything, he would argue this made her more dangerous than those children had been. She had already aligned herself with dragons, and he knew Dawn wanted to find her.

Yet something remained disturbingly unclear to Caeruleus. While he undoubtedly agreed that the fera had to be kept out of the hands of Dawn, he couldn't say he knew what the Council intended to do with the fera once she was secured. Those plans had never been explicitly discussed.

The other fera had perished, but it seemed no more than the tragic fate of their fragile yet volatile existence. What would the Council have done with them if they had not brought about their own demise, and what fate was he going to lead this last fera to when he brought her to the Council?

He couldn't deny the obvious and terrible possibility that they might put her to death. Just because they put the safety of the realm before any one individual's freedom, did that mean the Council could be so monstrous? Surely not—they'd stitched this realm back together with a deep reverence for justice.

He maintained the necessity of apprehending her. After all, even if it was forced on her, it could still be considered protective custody, not just for the good of the realm but for her too. But he couldn't deny that as long as she was something Dawn wanted to obtain, she was a liability. He felt himself sink into a dreadful realization.

The Council would want to eliminate *any* chance of Dawn acquiring the power of the fera, and the only way to definitively remove such a chance would be removal of the fera from the playing board. If that was indeed the case, could he justify sentencing her to death in order to keep her tremendous power away from Dawn? *She's formed an alliance with dragons,* he reminded himself. That alone was treason worth death. Who was he to question that?

It was tempting to pore over every shred of information there was here, but from what he had read, it all followed the same unfortunate pattern. Not wanting to risk getting caught in the records hall, he gathered up the material. As he closed all the reports, he noticed each one was labeled with the location of the incident. One in particular caught his eye: Candhrid.

He opened this folder and looked more closely at its contents. The image of this fera showed an aged face. He checked the date. This incident had occurred some ninety years after the others. The fera, who had to have been a hundred years old, had been discovered living on one of the Candhrid islands.

Caeruleus's heart struck his chest with understanding before he even read the agent's account. "The ship managed to escape, but the island crumbled into the ocean, and a hole opened up, pulling in the other islands and the peninsula. The fera and countless lives were lost." Caeruleus read the name of the agent who had written the report, Leone Cael. Raiden's father had been assigned to the last fera mission and had witnessed the destruction of the Candhrid peninsula. His partner was listed as Loak Clyson.

Caeruleus knew Raiden's father had been an agent, but that didn't dampen the surprise of seeing his name in the report. This had occurred years before Raiden had even been born. Fighting through his daze, he rolled up the propaganda, secured the files together with the cord, and piled all the material in his arm to return to the shelf.

This time the crow followed him, landing one shelf above where he would be returning his armful of records. As he returned each item to where he'd first found it, the raven clicked its beak and gave a loud caw in his ear.

He cringed away but chuckled. "What?"

The large black bird looked at him, tilting its head to blink at him. For a moment he swore the bird was giving him a look of contempt. Then it bent forward and tapped its beak against the handwritten label adhered to the edge of the shelf. It read, "FERA, 4 items—public accounts, agent reports, public announcements, Hessian journal."

"Hessian journal," Caeruleus muttered. He searched the surrounding shelves, but there were only boxes filled with envelopes and folders, baskets of scrolls, and thick historical tomes. "Where is it?" he asked the raven.

In response the bird adjusted its wings, a gesture that resembled a shrug, and tilted its head. Caeruleus sighed. He stood up. "Thanks for your help," he said. The raven fluffed its feathers and cawed once more at him as he turned to leave.

Nicole was torn over whether she should find an inn and try to sleep or just keep searching through the night. She weighed the factors. Even if she had a locked door to sleep behind, would she really be able to quiet her mind enough to sleep? She needed sleep whether she was restless or not, though, and she couldn't deny that magical impulses were always harder to control when her body and mind were exhausted.

She had no idea what the chances were that Raiden would be out and about in the middle of the night, but it was worth considering that she might draw unwanted attention being one of very few people wandering the streets during the more-unreasonable hours of the night. Part of her insisted that it would only be a matter of time before the Council's agents were out in the streets in full force. They would realize she was in the city eventually, and the time until they did was the best time for her to search.

Ultimately, she kept coming back to the idea that being on the streets through the night was more conspicuous than advantageous, and no matter how anxious she was, she had to at least try to sleep, even if it only amounted to a few hours.

She sighed, her decision made. All day she had been more concerned with scanning every face she saw for Raiden's. Suddenly she cared about the establishments around her. She was at the intersection of Pearl and Twelfth. People passed by her without interest. She had never been shy talking to a stranger in her life, but the prospect of inviting someone to acknowledge her presence and study her face made her uneasy.

Down the street a woman carrying a basket full of flowers made her way toward Nicole, holding out a sprig of heather to anyone who looked her way. Nicole pulled her bag around to her front so she could dig out the money purse. As the woman drew nearer, Nicole repositioned her bag and took a few of the copper pieces out of the purse.

The woman spotted Nicole's gaze and held up the stem of heather covered in newly opened, soft violet flowers, a cluster of unopened buds at the top.

"Heather for protection," she said, taking a cursory glance around Nicole, "for a young woman out alone."

"How much?"

"Two coppers, dear."

"Do you know," Nicole asked as she plucked two of the three coppers from her hand and placed them in the woman's palm, "is there an inn nearby?"

The woman closed her fingers around the two copper pieces and bestowed Nicole with the heather. "Go up Twelfth three blocks, then turn toward the wall. Look for the robin," she answered with a kind nod.

Nicole nodded back, hoping that was the proper gesture. "Thank you."

The woman went on her way down Pearl Street. Nicole turned left and headed up Twelfth—north, she thought. The woman had told her to head toward the wall. Apparently in Atrium directions were given based on whether you were headed toward the courts or toward the wall. She supposed for the people who lived here the courts and the wall replaced left and right.

She twirled the heather between her fingers as she walked. Twelfth Street veered slightly left past the second block, and Nicole was certain that "toward the wall" at the next street meant *go right*. Sure enough, after wandering uncertainly one block to the right, she spotted a sign for an inn hanging out over the street from a modest three-story building. On the sign, the name of the establishment, Goodfellow Inn, was painted in a circle around a picture of a robin.

Pausing to study the sign—although the paint was faded, the gray bird with orange face and breast hopped and fidgeted upon its perch—she took a sweeping glance around the street. There was minimal traffic here. Only a few people strolled by her. Still clutching the leather purse, she nodded and took a resolute step toward the inn's door.

Raiden returned to the workroom and put the looking glass on the table just as the light that marked Caeruleus's location blinked suddenly from his path away from the courts back to the very center of the building. Suspecting Caeruleus had just been summoned to the Council, Raiden touched the glass to listen.

"It would seem, despite your efforts at the wall today, Caeruleus, the fera did indeed make it into the city."

"Worry not—we expected her to come, and we remain prepared. What have you learned from your efforts today?"

"I—I—uh," Caeruleus stammered, something Raiden had only heard him do when speaking to his father after having done something he shouldn't have. "I believe the fera is relying less on magic than we expected her to. In fact, her behavior would indicate she has far more control over her abilities than we expected."

There were a few moments of silence, and Raiden wondered what had gotten into Caeruleus that he was suddenly so rational about the fera.

"Indeed," a councilman answered. "This has made her far more difficult to apprehend. Her presence in the city has remained hazy to the seers. She has been wandering and does not know the city well enough to make a clear path for them to see. However, they managed to glimpse her standing beneath a robin and walking through a blue door."

"That's all?" Caeruleus asked, and Raiden felt his frustration at having so little to go on and his irritation toward the Sight, which was not always as clear as people wished it to be.

"That is what they see. The fera's future currently resides beneath a robin and behind a blue door. Brief though it might be, the vision was clear, which would indicate that it is both near and stable. We cannot tell you how long she will remain."

A robin and a blue door, Raiden puzzled.

"I will contact the patrol leads for each district," Caeruleus said. "Do the seers continue to see the fera's destruction?"

"That future has disappeared for the time being, and we have faith that it foretells the success of your efforts. Let us hope the current path remains intact for us all."

"Yes," Caeruleus said. This time Raiden heard the guarded voice of the young, defiant boy he'd once known so well. What was Caeruleus thinking? The conversation was apparently over, because all Raiden could hear was the echoing of Caeruleus's footsteps across the Council's great hall.

Raiden pressed his face into his hands and sighed, trying to fill in the gaps between Caeruleus's manic desire to repay the fera for his eye and the odd new defiance in his voice when addressing the Council.

There came a knock from the main shop, and he crossed the workroom to open the door for Tovar.

"Any progress today?" Tovar stepped into the workroom, leaving the door open. Past Tovar, Raiden could see that the window covers had been pulled down. The shop was closed for the night.

"No," Raiden admitted. "But I have a feeling it is going to be a busy night. The fera is in the city."

"I see. Can you take another night without sleep?"

"Only with another dose of wakefulness," he said, feeling his last dose waning. His head felt light, and his vision was starting to blur. He blinked, trying to refocus his eyes as he went to the cabinet to get another bottle.

"And when do you plan on sleeping?"

"I don't," he answered with a tired chuckle before downing the mouthful of wakefulness potion. "Not until I know Caeruleus isn't going to get himself killed."

Raiden wandered back to the table to glance at the glass again and saw that Caeruleus was moving swiftly across the shadowy map of the city, directly for Raiden's apartment.

"Raiden, you have to sleep eventually. Relying on that potion will—"

"Oh! Caeruleus is at my place. I'll fill you in tomorrow." He grabbed the glass and the mask and hurried out of the workroom. The back room kept magic contained inside and prevented it from entering, but out in the shop he could interbound, slipping into the space between Tovar's shop and his apartment.

He heard tense banging at the door as he appeared in his kitchen. Tossing the mask on the table and slipping the glass into his pocket, he hurried across the living room with the vigor of wakefulness in his veins to yank the door open.

"Caeruleus," Raiden greeted.

"Ray," he answered, stepping inside. He eyed Raiden while he shut the door. "Why are you wearing your uniform?"

"Oh." Raiden looked down. "I was trying a new perspective in the hunt for the rebels," he lied.

"Any luck?"

"No."

"Good, because I need your help," Caeruleus said.

Raiden knew. "With the fera?"

"She got in."

"Oh." He tried to sound surprised.

"The Council has the seers looking for her, and they say she's 'beneath a robin and behind a blue door,' which should be easy to find once I make some calls."

"So what exactly do you want my help with?" He couldn't be sure whether his suspicion as to what Caeruleus was about to ask was an inkling from the Sight or a hunch from the past.

"Do you think you can tell me what's going to happen?"

"Caeruleus—"

"I know, I know. It's what *might* happen, not what will, but can you just give me something?"

"There's no telling how far I'll see. I'm not any better at this than I was when we were kids."

"Will you or not?"

Raiden sighed. He held out his hand, and Caeruleus did the same. They clasped each other's wrists in a firm grip. Raiden searched his mind the way people search for a memory, only he wanted to find the Sight, lurking in his head as it always did. He felt like a boy coaxing a wolf out of the woods.

Caeruleus wanted to know what was coming, but Raiden wasn't sure he did. Still, he reached for the Sight, and it emerged from the edges of his mind. It engulfed him, not unlike the magic that had whisked him between two places in space only moments ago.

The Sight was like a rope dragging him furiously through the current of time. The weight of his body, the hardwood floor beneath his feet, Caeruleus's wrist in his hand, all disappeared. He glimpsed a robin on a sign, a blue door. He saw a disjointed moment of the girl, the fera, her face like that on the posters. Then he lurched into another unsteady moment. The sounds of Caeruleus screaming in pain rattled Raiden's mind and rang in his ears.

The shock and aversion jarred him out of the current. Raiden pulled his hand away from his friend.

"What?" Caeruleus demanded.

Raiden tried to wipe the horror off his face, but he was too slow.

"That bad?"

"I think it's safe to say we can find the robin and the blue door."

"What happens after that?"

"An angry fera and … well, your eye would imply the rest."

Caeruleus seemed to relax and even look relieved.

"That can't be what you wanted to hear," Raiden said.

"No, but it's what I needed to hear."

"Are you going to tell me what's going on?"

"I needed to know more about what I was up against, so I went down to the Hall of Records. I expected to learn something about the other fera, how those missions had gone, that might give me some advantage."

"Did you?"

"Yes and no. Everything I read proved how dangerous they were but not in the ways the Council claims. No encounter ended without casualties; some didn't even have survivors to make reports, Raiden."

Raiden swallowed back the concern building in his throat as he listened, trying not to assign those events of the past to the vision of Caeruleus's future.

Caeruleus crossed the living room and sank onto the couch. "The danger, the destruction, it's all true, but they weren't the monsters the Council made them out to be."

Raiden was surprised, not to hear that the Council was less than honest, but to hear it coming from someone who had been so loyal to them just days ago.

"I'm not sure I follow you. You never doubted that before," he said.

"No, but I never knew they were children."

"Who?"

"The fera. They were just children, and the reports … It's like the fera were just afraid of themselves and the world was afraid of them. They all ended up destroying themselves. Not one of them survived being discovered."

"But this fera isn't like that," Raiden said. "She hasn't lost control, not like the others anyway."

"Which is why I'm still inclined to stick with the mission," Caeruleus said with a nod. "I'm not entirely sure what the Council wants to do with her. But I know I have to keep her power away from Dawn, keep her from putting anyone at risk. I thought maybe I should try a different tactic this time, but your vision proves that she's angry and dangerous. That could be entirely our fault, but it's too late to change that. She's a threat, and she's in this city."

"So what do you want to do?"

"I want to avoid getting any more agents involved than need to be. If you and I can bring her in together, we can prevent the Council from sending every agent in the city after her and potentially throwing away lives like they did in the past with the other fera. You and I have encountered her before; we have experience no other agent has."

"Right, and you're likely to infuriate her more than anything."

"Which is where you come in," Caeruleus said. "Your encounter was far less … hostile. You said she saved your life."

"Not because she cared at all about me. It was all just" —for a split second his mind raced through that night in the castle, and he thought he remembered her saying his name— "some kind of accident," he finished with uncertainty in his voice.

"Still, she knows your face, and you never attacked her," Caeruleus pressed. "Are you going to help me or let me die like in your vision?"

Raiden suppressed a scowl and gave him an exasperated glare instead. "Of course I'll help."

Helping Caeruleus stay alive meant they would be giving the Council what they wanted, which could even earn him some redemption and solve the problem of his impending treason charge. Or, of course, he could just get himself killed right alongside Caeruleus, in which case his problem would still be solved.

36. Robin

Nicole dropped two silver pieces into the hand of the round, sour-faced man behind the desk. He scrutinized the silver in his hand for a moment. Then he turned to the cabinet behind him, opened the door, and plucked a key off the wall.

"Room five," he said, dropping the key in her hand.

She gave him more of a scowl than a smile since he clearly wasn't the kind of person who seemed to appreciate business, let alone a thank-you. With a sigh she crossed the faded and worn lobby to the stairs. Almost every dark wooden step creaked underfoot.

On the second floor there were four rooms around the center stairwell, numbers one through four. The doors were all robin's-egg blue, and the wallpaper was so faded she couldn't make out the pattern. At the landing she did a one-eighty to make her way up the next flight of stairs to the third floor, where rooms five through eight surrounded the stairwell. Room five was straight ahead when she reached the third-floor landing.

She placed the key in the hole and turned it. The door unlocked with a click and swung inward as she turned the knob. The room was dark except for the single stream of orange light from the lampposts on the street. She stepped into the room and locked the door behind her with a satisfying metal clack. She didn't bother looking for a light switch or a lamp. She avoided even touching the beam of light as she skirted the room to get to the dark, rectangular shadow of the bed.

After removing her bag and slipping the money purse back inside, she took off her hooded cloak and Raiden's sword. Across the room there was a narrow door. When she opened it, she thought it was a closet at first, but after flipping on the light switch, she found a bathroom. There was just enough space for the toilet and, across from it, a tiny basin sink that she could barely fit both hands into.

After a cramped experience in the bathroom, she turned the light off and crossed the darkness of the room to yank the drab curtain closed and hurry through the shadows to the bed. Reluctantly, she removed her boots, placing them in precisely the right place that she could jump out of bed and put them back on.

Her stomach gave another angry growl, so she dug into her bag and pulled another thick hunk of bread off the large loaf. She sat there chewing the bread, thinking how unreal it all still seemed.

Two weeks since her life had turned into chaos, and yet it refused to sink in. Her mind refused to let go of the feeling that tomorrow she would surely wake up and the only thing she would have to do that day was go to her classes and coast to graduation.

But the bed under her was real. She forced a lump of dry bread down her throat and pulled the remaining piece apart in her hands, listening to the crust crackle. Her heart pounded anxiously in her chest when she looked at the sliver of light under the locked door. The smell of dust and rotten flowers in the room, the chill in the air that made her shiver, it was all real.

She sighed through the monotonous chewing and dug into her bag for her water bottle, which she had been too afraid to pull out in public, where people would surely realize it wasn't from Veil. *Is plastic a thing here?* she wondered as she washed down her mouthful of bread.

Realizing how thirsty she was, she downed the entire water bottle and figured her full bladder would make a decent alarm clock in case she managed to fall asleep. Once she'd finished her dinner of bread and water, she pulled back the blanket of the bed and curled up beneath it in the dark, waiting to sleep, waiting for the weight of it all to come crashing down around her.

While Caeruleus contacted everyone on patrol and in the business license office that he could through the vox channels in his mask, Raiden paced the room with no better outlet for the potion-induced energy buzzing in his head, tingling in his limbs.

Raiden's mind raced through everything Caeruleus had said about the records on the fera. If the Council hadn't purposefully killed the other fera, that might not be their intention for the girl in the city. The Council had staked much of their reputation on their accomplishment of protecting Veil from the fera's destruction, though, and their portrayal of the fera as monsters to the rest of the realm did not bode well to him. Raiden wanted to know why they were so adamant about convincing him and Caeruleus that this girl was a threat, rather than someone who needed to be protected from Dawn. Something wasn't quite right there. It occurred to him that perhaps the *Council* needed to believe she was a threat, but why? Why would they be so desperate to justify the capture and disposal of this girl? Just because Dawn wanted her?

"Sard 'em," Caeruleus grumbled through his teeth as he tossed his mask onto the couch in frustration.

"No luck, I presume," Raiden said.

"There aren't any Robin Inns or Bird Inns in the city according to the license office, and no one on patrol knows about any inns with a blue door."

"I guess that means we have to find it the hard way," Raiden said.

"Or," Caeruleus said, hoisting his index finger up into the air, "maybe you can find her."

"You overestimate my abilities, Ruleus," Raiden replied with an exacerbated sigh.

"You just saw her an hour ago."

"Yes, in *your* future."

"But if we're about to go out looking, that means she's somewhere in your future too. You might see something different about her."

Raiden couldn't argue against that logic. "Fine."

The rush of wakefulness in his head seemed to feed the Sight like lamp oil to a spark. His mind sped through what had to be hours of time spent with Caeruleus searching the city, so fast he couldn't gain any clear glimpses of where they were before he saw the faded robin again. Then suddenly there was a blue door before him. It opened, and he crashed into a screaming torrent of noise and pain that confused his senses. He watched as the familiar face of the fera contorted in agony. Her mouth opened in a torturous cry that was lost to his ears, and her body was consumed by a surge of burning energy that then washed over him.

"Raiden!" Caeruleus's voice rang in his ears, and Raiden felt his body convulse.

His eyes snapped open. Caeruleus was crouched down before him and had him by the shoulders. He was on his knees with no memory of falling onto them.

"I guess your future isn't any better than mine, is it?" Caeruleus said in a quiet, somber tone.

"It doesn't look so great for her either," Raiden muttered. "She might just end up like the others after all."

Caeruleus stood up and pulled Raiden to his feet. "Where are we going wrong here, Ray? What approach are we about to take that needs to be different?"

Raiden wondered. Maybe his mistake was in thinking the Council was wrong about all this, that what they were doing shouldn't be done.

Caeruleus let out a low groan of irritation. "I wish I knew what was in that journal."

"What journal?"

"There was something listed as the Hessian journal missing from the records on the fera. There's no telling what was in it or whether it might have helped."

"Best not to dwell on it, then," Raiden said.

"So did you get *any* more clues as to where she is?"

"No. Just the robin and the blue door," Raiden said. "I think we're in for a long night."

"Long lives, on the other hand," Caeruleus said, forcing a smile through his pessimism.

"You wanted to know," Raiden reminded him.

"I did. Might as well get started, huh?"

"Sure. Let's find that bloody robin and get our miserable lives over with." Raiden's voice dripped with dark enthusiasm.

Nicole opened her eyes in the darkness, confused before she realized her straining bladder had disturbed her sleep. With slow, groggy movements, she managed to untangle herself from the blanket and shuffled across the floor. Her shoulder hit the doorframe as she found the bathroom and clumsily pulled her pants down. She plopped onto the toilet, sagging with relief.

She could see nothing but darkness, and after a moment she realized it was because her eyes were closed again. She forced them back open to see the dark shapes of her feet. She finished in the bathroom and dragged her feet back across the room. The shushing of her socks against the wood filled the silence. She slumped back onto the bed and could have easily slipped back into unconsciousness, but once the rustling of the blanket went quiet, the sound of a short whistle outside pierced her sleepy mind.

Her heart seemed to jolt awake in her chest before she could quell the irrational response. *It's nothing,* she told herself, but she got back up with a huff to prove it. She shuffled over to the window, where the curtain glowed in a failed effort to block out the light of the lamps outside.

She moved the very edge of the curtain aside just enough to look with one eye down at the street. From her room on the third floor she could see the tops of two heads, men, one pointing up at the sign of the Goodfellow Inn, and on one man's hip she saw the uncanny metal face and glass eyes of the mask that belonged to the Council's agents.

"No, no, no," she exhaled, her heart now in an all-out panic. She bolted back to the bed, her feet slipping out from under her more than once. Her mind raced as she lunged for her shoes. She yanked her socks up, shoved her feet into the boots, and grabbed Raiden's sword. *Run or fight?* she asked herself as she looked down at the folded silver wings. If she fought now, she might throw away her only chance at finding Raiden.

Raiden pointed up at the round Goodfellow Inn sign with the faded robin painted in the center. The street was quiet, so they didn't speak. Caeruleus nodded and motioned toward the door. It wasn't blue, but this was the first robin they had found all night.

"Let's check," Raiden murmured, opening the door.

They stepped into the warm, welcoming lobby, greeted by the smell of baking bread coming from back in the kitchen. Although there hadn't been any kind of audible alert, the innkeeper popped out of the air behind the desk. The man's perturbed expression immediately turned to one of peculiar interest at the sight of Raiden and Caeruleus and their uniforms.

"Kin I help ya, gentlemen?" The innkeeper's question sounded like a formality he didn't like the taste of.

"Did a girl purchase a room here tonight?" Caeruleus asked.

The innkeeper's gaze moved toward the ceiling, then back to them. He nodded. "Room five."

"I'll go," Raiden said. "You stay here—"

"In case she blows the top floor off this place?" Caeruleus muttered with a snort. The innkeeper's eyes went wide, and he disappeared in a blink, followed by the sound of muffled voices spilling through the kitchen door.

"Well done," Raiden said, turning for the stairs.

Noting the creak of the steps, he listened carefully for any moans of the wood that didn't match his steps in case the fera tried to slip by unseen. He also purposefully took up the middle of the stairway to help physically block any potential escape attempt. His heart seemed to beat faster with every step closer to the second floor. When he reached the landing, he saw only four doors—blue doors—so he proceeded up the second flight of stairs, his heart proving it could beat even harder still.

Room five was right at the top of the stairs waiting for him. For a moment he flashed back to his vision of approaching this door. He stepped up to it, feeling unnerved by the choice he had to make—force the door open or knock.

After what he had seen in the vision, he couldn't convince himself to give up his advantage and make his presence known. He unlocked the door with a simple silent spell. Fighting past his hesitation, he closed his hand around the knob and turned it slowly.

Caeruleus drummed his fingers against the desk in a nervous beat that kept time with his pulse. He stopped when he heard a strange whine from outside. Then there was a thud from above. He hurried out the door onto the street. A figure in a gray cloak was creeping along the roof.

"Ey!" he shouted as the figure—the fera, he was sure—hopped the gap between buildings to the neighboring roof. She stumbled before breaking into a run.

Caeruleus summoned his wings from his back and took off at a run down the street in the same direction as the girl. He left the ground and strained to keep her in his sight as she made her way along the rooftops in the shadows above the lamplight.

As he gained on her and soared up beside her, she looked over her shoulder and made a hard left toward him, leaping from the roof. Her foot hit him square in the back as she used him like a stepping-stone to the roof across the street. Her weight threw off his trajectory, and he lost sight of her.

He wheeled around in the air and struggled to see her in the early-morning darkness. Then he spotted movement on the buildings ahead and charged after her as fast as his wings could take him.

Nicole couldn't outrun a birdman forever. Either he would catch her, or she would run out of buildings she could jump between even with the help of her panic-stoked magic. Chancing another glance over her shoulder, she spotted him.

"Shit. Now or never," she growled to herself, pushing herself as fast as she could run as she neared the edge of the last roof. She would not stop. She would not slow. Falling was not an option. She sprinted furiously and jumped, hurling herself into the air. Then she went from sailing to falling, and the Council's man flew right over her. Her magic erupted through her, and her drop slowed to a stop, her feet dangling well above the street. Every artery, vein and capillary burned but she floated like there was helium in her bones.

Above her the Council's agent made a wide turn. She shot into the sky, and another winged shape came at her. Their bodies collided hard, and they both let out involuntary sounds of pain. With a hard kick to somewhere soft, she tore away, and he tumbled for a moment. Her furnace of magic held her aloft, and instinct seemed to propel her. She moved like a body through water but so much faster that it was startling. The two Council angels maneuvered very differently with their wings.

She lost sight of them while trying to keep track of which way was up and which was down. One came at her from above as the other appeared beneath her, so she veered away and suddenly saw the white column-lined court building upon the hill ahead of her. Her gut pulled her in the opposite direction, but they were right behind her, like they were trying to herd her to the courts.

With only the city light from below, her two adversaries were dark, faceless shapes with wings. She would avoid one, and the other would be right there. A reservoir of anger was building in her chest, but she didn't want to let it out. She didn't want to act on it again; she didn't want to be that monster that shoved scalpels into necks or took people's eyes. Her anger was for the Council.

She plunged through the air for the city below. The agents' wings would be a disadvantage in the cramped space between buildings. The wind filled her ears, and her cloak flapped against her body in the current of air.

Before she could reach the safety of the buildings, a hand caught her by the wrist. The agent who had grabbed her turned his wings like throwing on the brakes, and her arm was yanked hard as he changed direction. She heard a pop, and agony flooded her vision. She didn't even realize that his grasp had failed and she was falling until she hit the rooftop.

Her eyes swam in blurry shadows. Her head was spinning in pain that made her stomach turn. She rolled over, trying to pick herself up before she puked. Fury roiled beneath her pain, and she had to swallow back the bile in her throat. The sound of the two men landing on the roof jarred her back to clarity as she got to her feet, swaying.

"Stop," one of them said. "Just stop running."

She tried to think of something to say. She tried to let out a laugh and keep herself steady. But the roof seemed to pitch like a boat. The edge was at her heels, and backward she went, falling again. As she fell, she suddenly felt herself slip into the air, insubstantial and scattered—a few brief seconds without the pain that went with her body.

Raiden sprinted to the edge of the roof, but the girl was gone.

"Damn," Caeruleus said behind him.

Raiden turned around and stepped away from the edge, processing a slew of mixed emotions. His toe hit something that gave a little clank and rattled against the roof as it slid away from his foot. Crouching down, he felt around until he found the object.

"What is it?" Caeruleus asked.

"A pocket watch."

"Think you can use it to find her again?"

"Maybe," he said, turning the plain brass watch over in his hands and feeling a sensation of déjà vu.

"When were you going to tell me?"

"What?"

"About the wings, Ray," Caeruleus practically shouted.

He shrugged. "Didn't seem all that important until now." He couldn't really see Caeruleus's face, but he could feel the glare in his eyes.

"Well, we're both still alive," Caeruleus said in an upbeat change of tone.

"And we accomplished nothing."

"I wouldn't say nothing," Caeruleus countered. "She got a taste of payback for taking my eye."

"Well, I'm glad you're satisfied," Raiden said, his voice dripping with sarcasm. "But what's your plan now?"

"You can both report to the courts to start," a familiar deep voice said.

Raiden cringed, realizing Loak Clyson was standing there.

37. Rebels

Nicole materialized. She knew because the pain in her shoulder hit her again as she reformed. She felt a hard, smooth floor beneath her, and when she pried her eyes open, a dark wood floor filled her vision.

"Oh, nicely done," a woman said sarcastically as she bent over Nicole.

"I got her out of there, didn't I?" a teenage boy said behind the woman.

"She's hurt," the woman said, taking Nicole's good arm and helping her to her feet. The woman had chestnut skin, and her hair was concealed by a brightly colored scarf tied into a large knot like a bun on the side of her head. "Let's get her to Andrus."

Nicole blinked back her disorientation and pain to focus her vision. They appeared to be in the front room of an apartment. There was a long entrance rug on the floor and a tufted velvet couch as deep blue as the night sky with a low coffee table in front of it and a wingback chair beside it. Through the slightly parted curtains she could see the windows looked out onto the street. The boy looked out before pulling the curtains together.

The woman had Nicole's good arm around her neck and guided her across the cozy living room toward a doorway. As the boy crossed back across the room, his leg grazed the corner of the coffee table, and what had surely been solid just a moment before suddenly swirled in the air in a cloud of thick, opaque smoke before settling back into the shape of the table.

"This way," the woman said, leading Nicole into the kitchen, or what used to be a kitchen.

Virtually the entire floor was gone, revealing a stone staircase leading underground. The sink, counters, and cupboards all clung to the walls still, hanging over the gaping rectangular hole in the floor.

"Don't forget to turn the lights out, Eban. What's your name, dear?"

"Nicole," she answered before she could think better of it. "Who are you?"

The woman chuckled. "Shani."

"Did he interbound me here?" she asked.

"Eban? He did. Quite the talent he has. He just has to be able to see you. Plenty of people find it too difficult to do it for themselves, let alone others," she said. "Careful here; some of the steps are uneven."

A few orbs of soft light hovered against the walls along the staircase.

"Where exactly are we going?"

"We've got a pretty decent healer. You wouldn't want to trust me with that shoulder, believe me."

Nicole could only wince in response.

They reached the bottom of the stairs and followed a tunnel around a few poorly lit corners before stepping into a large domed chamber. Eban popped out of the air in front of them, startling Shani, who swatted him as he jumped away.

"Andrus," Shani called, her voice echoing through the mostly empty chamber.

Nicole removed her arm from Shani and stood on her own. She looked around. To their right someone was orchestrating the duplication of posters and arranging them into neat stacks. Eban trotted over and heaved one of the stacks over his arm before his form disappeared into the air like a candle flame being blown out.

"What is this place?" Nicole asked Shani.

"It's where we meet, plan, organize, you know."

"I don't actually."

"Oh, right. Forgot—you grew up in the other realm, right?"

"How did—"

"We've got a guy in the courts."

"Oh," Nicole uttered.

"This is the home of the Veil Divided Rebellion. Our goal is to destroy the Council's illusions and expose their lies. They were supposed to unite the fallen kingdoms and erase the borders, but all they did was cater to the surviving royal families and prop up the old kingdoms as states. The realm was less divided before the Dragon Wars ended," she finished with a sigh. "Andrus," she barked.

"What do you bloody want?" a voice grumbled from behind a haphazard pile of supplies in boxes, barrels, and sacks.

"We need a healer, and you happen to be the only one we've got."

"Just because we're underground doesn't mean I don't know it's too early for you to be waking me up. And who is 'we'?"

"The fera. Eban nabbed her before the Council could. She's hurt."

A man raised his head above the stack of boxes. "Oh." His voice was much less harsh this time.

Nicole felt increasingly uncomfortable with these people knowing so much about her. Knowing they were against the Council was reassuring in a way but somehow didn't quite make her feel right.

"What's the problem?"

"Shoulder," Shani answered before Nicole could.

"Let's see," Andrus said, stepping out from behind the supplies. "You should take that off so I can get a look." He nodded at her cloak.

Nicole removed her bag and then her cloak awkwardly with one arm. When Andrus and Shani saw the sword on her back, they looked at each other with quick wide-eyed glances. Reluctantly, Nicole removed the sword too and set it on the boxes beside her with her other things.

Andrus stepped toward her. He was an inch or two taller than her and had sandy hair. His face and hands were riddled with scars both faint and pronounced—everything from scrapes and cuts to punctures and burns. Nicole couldn't help puzzling over what his life had been like.

He put his hand on her shoulder and prodded a little. "It's dislocated," he said. "Easy to fix. I just need you to lie on the floor for a minute."

"Great." Nicole tried to sound upbeat and failed. She knew what was coming. She took a deep breath and lowered herself to the ground, lying down on her back.

"Can't you just use a spell?" Shani asked as Andrus sat down and braced a foot against Nicole's rib cage.

"Spells aren't always as precise as they need to be," Andrus said. "Okay, ready?" He turned Nicole's arm palm up and carefully raised it as though positioning her to make a snow angel. With a firm grip on her hand, he slowly pulled her arm away from the shoulder. Then with a pop the bone in her arm slipped back into its socket. Shani shuddered at the sound.

"There," he said.

Nicole sat up and let out a sigh of relief to have her arm back. With her arm back in place, the tension and pain had vanished, leaving only a faint sore ache in the muscle from being pulled.

"So how'd that happen?"

"I had somewhat of a … midair altercation," Nicole said, placing her hand on her shoulder and massaging it as she rotated her arm. "With a couple of the Council's men."

Andrus scowled as he stood up. "Puppets with wings," he said, making a sound of disgust in his throat.

"They tracked me down at an inn," she went on as she got to her feet as well.

"That'll be the seers," Shani said. "They cause us a lot of trouble. It's tough to plan a revolution when they're constantly on the lookout."

"We've done all right," Andrus said. "They made us better by making our mission a challenge."

"Eulina Pendinor made us better," Shani disputed.

"*Because* of the challenges we were facing," Andrus said. "Plenty of people could have done the same."

"Who?" Nicole asked.

"The leader of the revolution," Andrus said with mock grandeur.

Shani glared at him. "She rallied us when the Council squashed our movement in the streets. They didn't take well to being called liars and bought leaders in public. Whenever we gathered, they would send in agents in disguise to get violent. Then they would send in agents in uniform. They did a thorough job of vilifying our efforts to the rest of the city. Eulina put us back together after the Council dismantled our voice. It's been a slow recovery, but we're finally getting people to listen again."

"That's true. The number of active supporters has almost doubled in the last year alone," Andrus said.

"She sounds like a real inspiration," Nicole said, trying to sound interested when she didn't really want to be there.

"You want inspiration?" Andrus said with an appreciative chuckle. "Try the fera coming back from oblivion. You've destroyed the Council's reputation just by existing."

"Which is why the posters around the city don't mention anything about the fera," Shani said. "They don't want people to know there is one of you left. They made a big deal about protecting the realm from the destruction of the fera. It's practically their platform."

"So I've heard," Nicole muttered.

"The enemy of your enemy is your friend," Andrus said. "You should stick with us, fera."

"Her name is Nicole," Shani chided.

"Well, *Nicole*, you should consider it. Even a fera would be stupid to take on that fight alone."

"I don't plan on fighting alone. I came here to find someone I know, not to go after the Council." A voice in her head reminded her that wasn't entirely true.

"How's that plan been going for you?" Andrus asked, crossing his arms.

"Andrus," Shani scolded under her breath.

"It was going just fine until the two puppets with wings showed up at the inn, actually," she said, a laugh almost audible in her voice. She picked up Raiden's sword and pulled the strap back on, moving her left arm gingerly. Then she picked up her cloak and turned it burgundy side out before pulling it on.

"This person you're looking for, you two gonna take on the Council together? That's two against … how many?" He turned to Shani as though she knew the answer, but she just gave him a look like a mother would a child. "I'm just saying she'd have a better chance with us than with one ally."

"He's not the only ally I have," Nicole said, digging the picture out of the little pocket on her bag's strap. She held the picture up to Andrus and Shani. "You haven't seen him around, have you?"

"I wouldn't know 'im unless he's one of us," he said, shaking his head at the picture. "I haven't been topside in two years."

"He was pretty prominent in the early movement," Shani explained. "The Council knows his face pretty well."

"Yeah, they should. Did a number on it, didn't they?" Andrus said, turning away and wandering back around to the other side of the supplies where they had found him.

"Lost a brother in one of the public incidents too," Shani whispered, taking the picture from Nicole to look at it more closely.

Nicole frowned. No wonder the guy was hell-bent on getting her to join their fight. It might also explain why he seemed less than fond of the new leader of the rebels. But she knew that feeling, the desire to fight, to let the hate out because keeping it inside was a slow-acting poison.

Shani handed the picture back. "You should ask Vigil—he's our propaganda watcher."

"Propaganda watcher?"

"Yes, it's how we find new members. It was one of Eulina's brilliant ways around recruiting in public."

A sound of disgust came from behind the pile of supplies.

Shani rolled her eyes and continued, "We make these posters disguised as the Council's own propaganda plastered around the city. They're enchanted with eyes so that Vigil can watch through them and see when people look at them for a long time or keep noticing ours among the Council's. When someone picks up on our subtle dissent, they start paying more attention, and so we—er, Vigil—sees them more often. When he decides someone is right, he tells them the clue to finding us."

"Wow," Nicole said. "That's complicated."

"That's what I said," Andrus grumbled.

"But it works," Shani said. "Come on. I'll take you to Vigil."

"All right. Uh ..." Nicole wanted to say something to Andrus. She wanted him to know he wasn't alone in his hatred. "Hope I'll see you topside someday, Andrus."

"Yeah, good luck, fera—er, Nicole."

"Thanks," she muttered.

Shani smiled at her. "This way," she said, waving her back toward the doorway through which they'd entered.

"Is your fabulous leader responsible for your underground hideout?" Nicole asked, taking one last look around the high domed chamber before they returned to the cramped tunnel.

"These were here before the city was built. It was a strategic base during the Dragon Wars. Candhrid fell first, and the royal family surrendered immediately. The people still wanted to fight, but it was hard to argue with the relative safety of surrender. Hence any organizing efforts against the dragons had to live underground."

"The Council doesn't know this is down here?"

"If they did, we wouldn't be here."

"I guess they knew what they were doing during the Dragon Wars if the Council didn't even know about them."

"Eulina knew about them. Rebellion was in the family apparently. Her grandfather told her about the tunnels. It took us a while to find our way in. Ended up being through my kitchen floor," she said with a hearty laugh.

"If that's really your home upstairs, why is the furniture fake?"

"I moved it all down here for those of us who can't show our faces topside anymore."

"Oh." Nicole suddenly imagined that blue velvet couch behind the pile of supplies, beneath a grumpy Andrus trying to go back to sleep.

"Here we are," Shani said, guiding Nicole into another chamber, not as large as the last one but well lit.

One wall was completely dominated by a patchwork of mirrors of countless shapes and sizes. The wingback chair Nicole had seen upstairs sat facing this wall, and there was a man sitting in the chair, leaning forward as he spoke to a woman no taller than the chair itself.

"Well, I gave the clue to someone a few days ago," the man was saying, "but they haven't shown up. Otherwise the wanted posters have covered most of the propaganda."

"The posters of the fera," the woman clarified.

"Right. Eban is taking more of our posters out now, as I understand it."

"Good."

Nicole felt like pulling her hood up as Shani cleared her throat in a delicate interruption.

"Hello, Eulina, Vigil."

"Ah, Shani!" Eulina greeted her with more enjoyment in her voice than she seemed to show in her expression. She remained right where she stood. "Who is this?"

Nicole answered before Shani could. "I'm Nicole" was all she said. She gave Shani a severe glance to ensure the woman didn't share anything more.

Vigil gave her a scrutinizing look, and she hoped her haircut and awkward smile were enough to not look like her wanted poster.

"We came to see if Vigil has seen someone she's looking for," Shani said.

"Oh, you're not here to join the rebellion?" Eulina asked.

"Uh, no," Nicole said. "Sorry."

"Then how did you get down here?"

"We brought her down to see Andrus," Shani said, fidgeting in her effort to avoid giving up everything after Nicole's warning glare.

"Why?"

Nicole could tell they weren't going to keep this secret for much longer.

"Eban helped me out of a pickle with a couple of the Council's men," she said.

"A pickle?"

Nicole sighed. "They were trying to arrest me," she clarified, trying to hide her annoyance.

"Stars in the sky, you're the fera," Vigil said.

"Unfortunately I am."

Eulina smiled. It was restrained. "We are happy to have you. I shall let you question Vigil," she said, moving toward the door. "Pleasure to meet a fellow adversary of the Council. I do hope you'll return once you find whoever it is you're looking for."

Nicole nodded, pulling the corners of her mouth back into a stiff imitation of a smile as Eulina left. The moment she was gone, Nicole's whole body sank with relief.

"She's got quite the presence for such a tiny women, ey?" Vigil said with a chuckle. "Most people have that reaction the first time they meet Eulina."

"I'm sure she's charming," Nicole said. "I just can't join your rebellion at the moment. Trust me, I get that it seems like a natural alliance, but I have to find *him*." She handed Vigil the picture of Raiden.

"Eulina's life is this rebellion. Doesn't have to be your life," he said, his mouth on the verge of a smile as he took the picture and studied it. "Yeah, I've seen him."

Nicole's heart leaped in a rush of joy, the first she had felt in what seemed like ages. "Can you tell me where?" she asked, already cringing at the answer to come.

"That's hard to say," he said, passing the picture back to her. "I think the first time I saw him he was on Mat Street. He really got around looking at our posters."

"I know Mat Street," Nicole said, her heart shooting upward with hope again.

"The southeast quadrant of the city is the best I can do. Try Mat Street this morning, but I'd be careful over there. There are lots of posters on Mat and *lots* of people in the morning."

"Right. Thank you, really."

"Thanks, Vigil," Shani added.

"No problem, Shani. Nicole, nice to meet you, and good luck."

Nicole's heart was racing faster than it had been when the agents had shown up at the inn. As she and Shani left Vigil's room of mirrors, Nicole had to hold back the urge to run through the poorly lit tunnel back to the stairs and up to the apartment above. Shani walked her all the way to the living room, past the smoke furniture, and to the front door.

"I can't thank you enough," Nicole said, feeling like her words were utterly meaningless.

"You really can come back," Shani replied. "You and your friend. You would be safe down there. The Council hasn't found us yet. We're working toward the same future after all."

Nicole's heart ached a little. She really did want to help them. Their mission seemed far more righteous than her solitary defiant revenge on the Council for daring to hijack her life. The rebels were about so much more. They had *given up* so much more. "Maybe we will," she said. "I've learned not to go making plans for the future these days, though. I can't make any promises."

"I understand. I hope you find him."

"Me too."

Shani opened the door, and Nicole stepped outside. She turned back to wave, but the door was already closing.

"Okay," she said as she moved down the trio of steps to the street. She suddenly realized she didn't know where she was starting from and looked around for a sign. She was at the corner of Moon and Stone; the two signs hung beside each other. *Moonstone*, she thought with a fleeting smile, and then she set off down Moon.

38. Paths

Caeruleus stood before the Council in the great hall, his heart repeating the same anxious rhythm as he tried to anticipate their reaction. He was caught in a strange combination of pride and shame over having found the fera and yet lost her again, but he knew he could find her again with Raiden's help.

"Caeruleus," a councilwoman began, "we are concerned about your choice to endanger this mission and all of Veil."

He wasn't expecting that. "I'm sorry, but what do you mean 'endanger this mission'? I have done everything in my power every day to—"

"You included Raiden in this most recent attempt to apprehend the fera. We thought we had made it perfectly clear that his loyalty is currently in question."

"All he has ever done is try to help me," Caeruleus argued. "I can understand *your* reservations about a man you don't know, but I know him."

"And how did he assist you this time that someone more trustworthy could not have?"

"By being someone *I* could trust" was all Caeruleus said. He wouldn't give up Raiden's secret about the Sight.

The following silence was pregnant with anger.

"Since our previous suggestion meant so little to you, we must give a direct order. You are to report to the training hall to brief a carefully selected group of agents on the mission to find the fera. Our seers are looking for her as we speak. You and your team will be notified the moment they have seen her," a councilman commanded harshly.

Caeruleus had never heard so much emotion in any of their voices before now. He took a deep breath, feeling strangely constricted in the vast space of the empty hall.

"Furthermore, we demand that you have no further contact with Raiden, as he is currently being investigated for treason against the realm."

"What?" Caeruleus's astonishment escaped him.

"He openly admitted putting himself before the safety of this realm upon his arrival, and we have reason to believe he *helped* the fera evade our search efforts. Until these suspicions are thoroughly examined and his character is evaluated, we cannot allow him to have any further involvement in the mission to find the fera."

Caeruleus's first instinct was to doubt the Council's claims about Raiden and seek out his friend to warn him, but his mind was incapable of getting past the inclination and forming a plan. Defiance swelled in his chest, but he could not convince himself that he would do anything other than report directly to the training hall once the Council dismissed him. His heart struck a dreadful warning against his ribs, which felt like they were shrinking around his lungs. Something was terribly wrong here.

"Do you understand your orders, Caeruleus?"

"Yes," he answered.

"Good. Your team is waiting for you. We wish you all success."

Caeruleus turned to leave, his body obeying before his mind had even accepted that his decision had been made for him.

Loak escorted Raiden into a small room without windows. There was a table with a pitcher of water, a glass, and a chair waiting for him.

"What were you thinking?" Loak demanded after shutting the door.

"That my friend asked for help," Raiden countered in a low voice.

"Did you hear anything I told you the other day?"

"Unfortunately, yes, and I don't need to hear it again."

"It wouldn't help you anyway." Loak let out an exasperated huff and motioned for Raiden to sit down.

"Am I officially under arrest?" Raiden guessed, almost relaxed by the thought and the relief from the anticipation.

"No. They just want to ask you some questions," he said, his quiet voice resonating with more trouble than his words suggested.

Raiden sank into the chair.

"I can't help you with this one, Raiden," Loak said as he opened the door and took a step into the corridor. He hesitated, looking as though he might say something else, but he just gave Raiden one last nod and closed the door.

Raiden sighed and dropped his head back.

Nicole eventually found her way to the main road Boreas and from there remembered how to get back to Mat Street. Every step closer made her more nervous until she thought her chest might actually burst open in her heart's attempt to escape the torture.

To quell the building anticipation, she tried to dampen her hope with a little realism—she had been to Mat Street once before and hadn't see Raiden. But the voice in her head was being insufferably hopeful. *I was only there five minutes maybe; of course I didn't see him.*

One side of her brain dreamed up the moment of spotting Raiden on Mat Street, rationalizing that spending a prolonged amount of time in one place would surely increase the likelihood of seeing someone that frequented the area. The other side of her brain prepared her for the free fall to come when those towering hopes crashed back to earth.

She hated to think that maybe Raiden had already come and gone from Mat Street, and that made her wonder what time it was. The lamps were still lit, but the sky had shifted from a black curtain hiding the stars to a dark-gray blanket, so the sun had to be rising out there somewhere. Her hand moved instinctively toward the little pocket in the waistband of her pants where she kept the pocket watch, but it was not there.

"Aw man," she murmured to herself, knowing it had fallen out somewhere between the inn and the rebel hideout.

The streets grew gradually busier as people started their days. Whenever she saw one of her posters, she shifted her gaze to the ground and let her hood hide her face. When she finally turned the corner onto Mat Street, she looked around eagerly. She wandered into the invisible cloud of mouthwatering smells and the din of customers waiting in lines and eating around tables.

Nicole found comfort in hearing the conversation and laughter of untroubled people. It was so easy to let it all wash away thoughts of what else lurked in the city—at least for a little while. Her nose led her to a stand where a man was making thin buckwheat crepes on a large, flat grill. The man next to him then threw scrambled egg and other cooked fillings onto the thin pancakes and wrapped them up into edible parcels.

When she turned away from the grill with her own square pancake burrito, she almost dropped it right onto the ground at the sight of a man strolling down the street with a mask on his hip.

With a deep breath she steadied herself and took a bite of her food, even though her appetite was suddenly smothered by panic. The Council's agents might be puppets, but they probably weren't as stupid as she would like them to be. Surely they knew she would recognize the mask, even on a belt. She looked around, forcing herself to be calm, and sat down on a bench.

The man with the mask was bait; she was sure. Rather than try to find one person in a crowd, their tactic was to get her to reveal herself. She sat on a bench that let her look down the length of Mat Street and took another bite of her food. *They want me to see a mask and run*, she supposed. The man with the mask on his hip was not there to find her; he was there to alarm her.

As she ate, she looked around, keeping her eye on the man with the mask as he wandered around the street. Soon enough she spotted a woman leaning against the wall between two restaurants, scanning the street with an intense gaze. Then she spotted a man sitting at a table without any food less than ten yards away. He too seemed to be searching the people around him as their decoy passed.

Nicole smiled to herself and kept eating. They were waiting for someone to behave strangely, to see the decoy agent and get flustered, turn the other direction, or even break into a run. Did they really think she was that stupid? Unfortunately, she had to acknowledge that her plan to hang around on Mat Street was dead.

You made plans, she scolded herself. *That's how they knew to come here.* There it was, the moment her hopes fell out of the sky. She finished her breakfast in a gloom of disappointment, not tasting a single bite as she kept her eye on the few people she had already pegged as Council drones.

She spotted a group of women at a table nearby and waited for them to leave together. Once they left their table, Nicole got up, popping her last bite in her mouth, and followed behind them close enough that she looked like a part of their group as they walked and chatted away. Nicole put on a smile as the women laughed at some remark and walked down the street with them, past the decoy agent, whose eyes passed right over their group. She took a deep, unsteady breath and stuck with her new friends until they turned off Mat Street.

She stopped outside a bookstore and watched the group of women continue on without her. With a groan of frustration, she accepted that she was back to wandering. *No plans,* she insisted. *Just walk. Don't think about where you're going. Don't even read the street signs.*

Raiden wouldn't have known how long he had been sitting in that room alone if it weren't for the pocket watch he'd found after the fera had gotten away. He flicked it open repeatedly, partly to check the time but mostly because he hoped the more he looked at it, the sooner he would figure out why it seemed familiar.

Two hours passed turning that brass watch over in his hands, flicking it open and clicking it shut, swinging it, staring at it upon the tabletop. He couldn't understand why a simple old pocket watch seemed to scratch at his mind but never provoke a tangible memory. Its ticking was the only sound in the room, aside from his frequent sighs of impatience and the drumming of his fingers against the table when he grew tired of the ticking.

He eyed the pitcher of water with suspicion and refused to drink any of the innocent-looking water despite the dryness choking his mouth. When he heard the doorknob turn, he put the watch back into his pocket. The door opened, and in walked a woman with a round, friendly face, her dark hair pulled back into a sleek, high bun. She was carrying a folder and was wearing a delicate pair of gloves that seemed a part of her entire clean and orderly look.

"Hello, Raiden," she said as she closed the door behind her. She stepped over to the other side of the table and snapped her fingers, the sound softened by the glove. A second chair popped out of the air, and she sat down. She placed the folder down and opened it, revealing a report form. She then removed a pen. Its shaft was a piece of carved amber, and its nib looked sharp and menacing.

"I'm here to ask you about the events of early this morning regarding the fera."

"You're here to collect my memories, not my answers," he said, unconcerned. What did he care about secrets anymore? The Council was going to put him away no matter how guilty or innocent he happened to be. "Why don't we skip the pretense?"

She smiled. "Very well." She leaned subtly over the form and wrote something with tense, swift strokes before turning the folder around and sliding it across the table to him. "I just need you to sign your name."

"So it's the pen," he muttered, picking up the amber instrument, which was carved with an intricate design of flourishes.

On the report she had written a single statement: "Agent has opted to forgo verbal account." At the bottom of the page was a line for his signature. He picked up the pen and signed his name, something he so rarely did. Ink flowed off the nib as he wrote but did not drip when he lifted it from the paper. When he had finished with the last loop of Cael, he placed the pen down on the report and pushed the folder back across the table to her.

"Do you confirm every report with memories?" Raiden wondered how many agents had been caught in a lie when their memories hadn't matched their sworn statements. Better yet, he wondered how many agents were aware the Council did routine memory gathering.

She smiled at him. "Only on special occasions." She tucked the pen back into the pocket of her stiff gray uniform coat.

He nodded. "Can I go home?"

"Yes," she said, closing the folder and standing up. "Thank you for your cooperation."

Once she left the room, Raiden got up and tried to keep a vigorous pace to the interbounding chamber. By the time he reached the chamber, though, he could feel his last dose of wakefulness wearing off. The distance between the doorway and the platform felt three times as far as usual.

He stepped onto the platform, his limbs heavy, head fuzzy. He didn't have another dose of the potion with him, or he would have thrown it down his throat in an instant. He could feel his mind deteriorating. What he needed was sleep. One quick interbound away from his bed—that was all he had to do.

He set his mind on his apartment and willed his body through the space between where he stood and his bedroom. His mind was so clouded with exhaustion that he thought for a moment he might just scatter to the wind and never come back together. Then he crashed, solid and defeated, against the floor, but when he picked himself up, he realized he was not in his apartment.

Nicole was so focused on keeping an eye out for anyone who might be following her or watching her that she kept forgetting she was looking for Raiden. Her mind was crowded with self-doubt, hopelessness, and paranoia. Making plans, like choosing a place to sleep, had given up her location last night. She stopped reading street signs in case the Council's seers could catch any glimpse of her choices.

She felt more lost than ever, wandering streets, looking over her shoulder, trying not to think too far ahead. As she walked around a corner, an intricate window display of little figurines enchanted to move caught her attention. One stepped through a door on one side of the display and appeared through a door on the other side. Another figurine waved from its seat upon a flying carpet that whizzed around above the others.

The corners of her mouth twitched with a fleeting attempt to smile as she continued past the window. She pulled her hood forward for the hundredth time, a new habit since seeing the Council's men out in force trying to find her. Someone stepped out of a shop not far down the street, and she was startled to see Eban with his arm full of posters.

He spotted her and gave her a little salute and a grin before disappearing into the air. Before she could even make sense of seeing him, she noticed a man across the street with an eye patch.

Nicole veered toward the first door she saw, which happened to belong to the shop Eban had just come out of. She stepped inside without even breaking her stride, but her calm shattered the moment she ducked into the aisle between two shelves and began watching the man through the shop window. He stood outside talking to a hunched woman on the street. She shrugged at him, and he nodded once before they went their separate ways. Nicole was relieved to see him head in the direction she had just come.

"Can I help you find something?" a kind voice asked.

Nicole jumped, caught peering over the top of the shop owner's shelf rather than looking at any of his products.

"Oh, uh, I don't think so," she sputtered. Her skin went hot with embarrassment and fear at being singled out and addressed.

"Are you sure?"

Nicole studied the man's face. His cheeks and eyes were lined with years of smiling, his brow with years of frowning. His gray hair was combed straight back.

"My shop has quite a lot to offer," he said, presenting the shelves with a sweep of his arm.

She wondered whether she should pull out Raiden's picture.

Then he asked, "Do I know you?"

Her heart seized—he recognized her.

"I don't think so. Sorry to waste your time." Her words rushed out of her mouth, and she stepped around him to get to the door.

"Wait," he called behind her, but she bolted out the door.

She looked over her shoulder as she pushed the limit of how fast she could walk without breaking into a run. The shop owner hadn't followed her, but she supposed he would alert authorities. Not until she was several blocks away did her panic recede enough that she could analyze what had happened. If he recognized her, he must have seen the posters, but she had just seen Eban coming out of that shop.

She came to an abrupt halt. That shop owner had to be associated with the rebels, and she knew—judging from their knowledge of her and their attempts to convince her to join them—they had been as eager to find her as the Council. A current of dread and chagrin washed through her, and she wondered whether she should go back. If the shop owner was with the rebels, he wouldn't turn her in to the Council.

She turned around, considering whether or not to return to the shop, but that would be too much of a plan. The seers would catch her. She was stuck and sinking into a pit of uncertainty, fear, hope, desperation, solitude. Shaking her head against it all, she buried her face in her hands for a moment, fighting back the surge. The street was no place to let herself fall apart. There was no place for that, not for her, not anymore.

So she lifted her head, took a long, slow breath, and continued on. Her steps fell into a numb rhythm as she went. A black dog with brown legs and muzzle and short, folded ears ran past her in springing bounds. It looked up at her as it passed, and it seemed to smile as a girl followed in an all-out sprint to keep up. Nicole's mouth didn't even twitch. She kept her gaze ahead and her pace steady.

The gray ceiling of clouds above remained steadfast. Not an inkling of sunlight could break through. She looked to the gloom above and tried not to let it in. Something about this city made her feel like the gray shroud overhead was alive, hanging above watching. It even crept through the streets. Some alleys were home to it, a fog crouching like an animal in a hiding place. She remembered what Asi had said about the remnants of old, broken charms and dying spells lingering and growing into a constant presence over Atrium.

With her own magic churning anxiously inside her, the scattered patches of fog seemed like clouds of gas waiting for a tiny spark to ignite them and set the city ablaze. She hoped that dark feeling would remain inside its strange daydream as she descended a slope into a tunnel under one of the busy roads leading to the courts.

39. Remember

Raiden fought to keep his body upright and his vision clear. He let out a huff of frustration as he fought his tired eyes to see the street signs at the corner. He knew he'd ended up somewhere between the courts and his apartment, but he wasn't going to find his way home at this rate. His eyes finally focused, and he was glad to see he recognized the street names. He was at Spindle and Underwood Streets, which meant he wasn't far from Tovar's shop, and his apartment wasn't much farther.

The thought of his bed was both motivation and torture as he trudged along Underwood. His shoulder clipped someone in passing, and he straightened up, muttered an apology, and coaxed his eyes back into focus. He couldn't be sure whether the fog around him was from inside his head or the usual magical residue lurking around the city's alleyways.

Someone whistled a tune out a window above him. The sound of his own footsteps almost lulled him into a walking sleep. He looked up at a street sign—Rood Street—and was relieved to see he was getting closer to home. In his distraction he bumped right into someone walking down Rood with their hood up and their eyes down.

"I'm sorry," he murmured as the individual in the crimson hood jerked back to look up at him in a startled sort of movement.

"Raiden," the woman said in shock.

He looked at her, his confusion spreading through his sluggish thoughts.

Then she had her arms around his waist before his mind could form questions. Who was this, why did she know his name, why did he know her voice, and why did her embrace feel so familiar?

Then she released him and looked into his face, her honey eyes mirroring his confusion, her frown mimicking his. *I know these eyes*, he thought, baffled.

"Raiden?" Her voice seemed to echo through his memory, as if he had heard her say his name a hundred times.

"I know you," he muttered. The Sight crept into his mind, and he tumbled through her future, catching only fleeting glimpses, images he knew he had seen before—her standing before a barren horizon, looking at trembling, bloodied hands, and the vision he'd had last night of the fera consumed by a darkness that washed over him. The feeling of her hands clutching his arms, stabilizing him on his feet, brought him back to reality, or what he used to think was reality.

"Are you all right?" Her voice moved through his head slower than her lips moved. "Raiden." She said his name with a force that rattled his memory again.

His mind flooded with her, with golems, her brother, her father. All the moments he had somehow lost buried him until at last he found her name.

"Nicole." Speaking her name felt like waking up. He grabbed her arms to prove to himself that she was really standing there. She was. "How did—what are you doing—where's—?"

"He's not with me," she said, shaking her head. "Are you okay?" she asked, still wearing a troubled expression.

"I'm ... tired," he said. "Come on."

He took her by the hand, and they walked together another couple of blocks down Underwood and turned left onto Lantern. Having her there beside him made his heart flutter with panic, and adrenaline pulled him halfway out of his exhaustion. They came to his apartment on the left side of the road. He dug his key out of his pocket as he pulled her to the door.

After fumbling with the key for what felt like a full minute, he finally managed to get it into the lock and open the door. Nicole stepped inside, and he followed. Once he closed the door and locked it behind them, he leaned against it, dropping his head back, and closed his eyes for a moment. He exhaled, emptying his lungs of stress. His adrenaline abandoned him.

When he gathered enough energy to lift his head back up, he blinked in astonishment at the sight of Nicole standing there in the middle of his living room. She pulled her hood back, revealing jaw-length curls. There were dark circles under her eyes. The corners of her mouth seemed to have become too heavy to smile. This was not the Nicole he remembered.

Hiding the effort required to step away from the support of the door and cross the room, he opened his arms and closed them around her, resting his cheek against her hair. Her hands slid up to his shoulder blades, and she breathed against his chest. Holding her kept him standing in more ways than one.

His mind struggled to unscramble the mess he had made of his memories. Suddenly the events of last night and this morning emerged from beneath his regained past with Nicole. His heart went cold, turning him to ice with every dreadful beat, and he cinched his arms tighter around her.

"I'm sorry," he whispered into her hair. "I'm so sorry."

"Why?" she murmured against his chest, and the warmth of that innocent question only made him feel worse.

"Forgive me," he muttered, sinking into a pit of guilt. "I'm sorry."

She pulled away and looked up at him. He couldn't even look into her eyes. He didn't deserve to. His vision kept slipping in and out of focus no matter how many times he blinked or squeezed his eyes shut tight.

"Hey," she said, ducking a little to capture his gaze. She was just a blurry shape now. "Sorry for what?"

He shook his head, trying to find the words and hating them too much to utter a single one.

"All right," she said with a sigh. "Come on."

With her arm around his waist, she supported him across the apartment to his bed. His mind was so lost in a fog of guilt and exhaustion that he was barely aware of her touch anymore or whether he was still standing or lying down.

"You can sleep now, Raiden." He felt her warm voice against his chest, and he sank into the dark, silent depths of his mind, leaving his sorrows at the surface.

Raiden was out cold, and Nicole wondered whether he hadn't slipped into a sleepwalking delirium even before they'd walked through the door of the apartment. She wondered what he was apologizing for, how long he had been awake, how long he would sleep. She lifted her head off his chest and sat up. It didn't feel right to close her eyes and sleep. It didn't even feel right to lie next to him.

For a minute she watched him sleep, realizing that at some point between the day he'd slipped through her hands and now, she had changed. Had it only been a week? She didn't feel the same in his arms. She was glad she'd found him. Her heart had nearly burst when she'd seen him. But being with him again made her painfully aware that she was not the same person he cared so much about.

She left the room and wandered back into the kitchen. It felt strange to be in a safe place, maybe because it didn't really feel safe. Part of her wondered whether anyplace would ever feel safe. She looked around the apartment, trying to assign it an appropriate designation that paranoia could not undermine. Quiet, warm, comfortable, these qualities she could acknowledge.

Not long ago she had wanted nothing more than a place she could let down her guard, but this apartment was not that place. She felt like she didn't belong here. She removed her bag and placed it on the chair at the kitchen table. She pulled off her cloak and draped it over the back of the chair. Then she pulled Raiden's sword off her body and laid it on the edge of the table.

Having shed her supplies and disguise, she looked around again, expecting to feel different about her new hiding place. She didn't, so she bent over the bag upon the chair and opened it.

"Gim," she whispered. "It's safe to come out," she cooed. The little golden dragon emerged and scrambled into her waiting hand.

Gim's running feet, like someone drumming their fingertips lightly up her arm, brought a weak smile to her face. She felt a little better having Gim back around her neck again.

The kitchen table was scattered with papers and folders. It was all information on rebel incidents, the Council's seal at the top of every page.

What now? she wondered.

She had found Raiden. They could join the rebels and attempt to put an end to her problem with the Council. The Council was just going to keep throwing their people at her, and she was going to keep fighting back. She didn't want to hurt any more people who were just following orders. She wanted to hurt the Council, unseat them, and dismantle them.

But her mind immediately returned to Gordan. As silly as it seemed to pass up an opportunity to join a force like the rebels, she didn't want to face her enemies without him. For some reason her heart was set on the three of them—herself, Raiden, and Gordan—finishing this the way they'd started it, together. She needed them both, and maybe they needed her just as much.

Her own exhaustion crept in as she crossed the small living room. She caught the heel of one boot with her toe and pulled her foot free, then repeated. All she wanted was to sleep without nightmares. She wasn't hoping for good dreams; a dreamless sleep would do just fine. With that plea in her heart, she sank onto the short couch. Sitting sideways on the couch, she pulled her legs up close and leaned her right shoulder into the cushions. After watching the door for a few minutes, she closed her eyes.

Nicole woke up, groggy but better rested than when she'd woken up at the inn early that morning. The apartment was so quiet that she could hear Raiden's breathing in the other room. The occasional soft snore told her how deeply asleep he was.

Her stomach told her it was time to eat, so she dug her loaf of bread and an apple out of her bag. She then set her bag on the floor so that she could sit in the chair. Gim left her neck and crawled down her arm onto the table. Nicole pulled a wad of bread off the loaf and put it in her mouth. As she chewed, she pulled a little piece off and tossed it in front of Gim.

Gim didn't hesitate to snatch up the piece of bread. He chomped on it repeatedly, and Nicole watched with interest—he wasn't eating it, but charring it until it was nothing but burnt black crumbs that fell back out of his mouth. This made her laugh silently, and although it was a waste of good bread, she plucked another bit off and tossed it onto the table for Gim.

After she'd eaten the better part of the bread herself and thrown the rest to Gim, the loaf was gone, and the table was littered in burnt bread bits that looked like someone had scattered black sand over everything. To pass the time, Nicole twirled the mess into a little whirlwind and watched it dance until she got tired of it and sent it into the sink.

There was a picture frame on the table turned away from her. She leaned over and grabbed it, turning it in her hands to see the photograph. She knew immediately that the two people in the picture were Raiden's parents. It was a black-and-white window to the past.

Raiden's mother was a darker shade of gray compared to her fair-skinned husband. Her hair looked almost black in the photo, and his was light gray, probably blond. There was love in the arm he held around her and such happiness in their colorless eyes that Nicole felt a pang of jealousy.

She set the picture frame back on the table and turned it away from her. She sat. She sighed, unsure what to do with herself.

Raiden woke up to the sounds of paper crinkling and fluttering in the kitchen. He sat up and looked around his room. A piece of paper folded into a slender triangular shape was sitting on the end of his bed, and another few sat across his room on the ground beneath the window.

He got up and shuffled into the bathroom, his head too clogged with sleep to form thoughts. Slowly, as his bladder emptied, his mind cleared enough to remember who was here with him. He finished in the bathroom and headed toward the kitchen just as another paper missile sailed through the doorway, hitting the ground at his feet. He found Nicole sitting at the table, folding one of the reports on the rebel rallies. She looked up at him. She didn't smile. Her lips rested in a neutral line.

"Hi," she said.

Raiden's head was clear again, his body well rested although still a little heavy with the aftereffects of the potion. He remembered everything with even more clarity than he had before going to sleep.

"Hi," he replied, heart pounding in his chest.

"Am I mistaken," she began, looking down at the paper she continued to fold, "or did you not remember me earlier?"

"You aren't mistaken. Didn't you find my letter?" She must have, since he'd found the pocket watch that he'd left with it.

"I did," she said, nodding. "Unfortunately, I didn't get to read the whole thing."

"Oh," he said. "Well, I had a friend help me create a selective memory so that I wouldn't remember everything I knew about you. It was a precaution in case the Council decided to investigate my thoughts and memories." Which, in fact, they had; however, he wasn't so sure it had been worth it after all was said and done.

She shrugged. "Makes perfect sense." She folded. "Is that why you were so sorry?"

He sighed. "Not exactly." He reached into his pocket, pulled out the pocket watch, and set it on the table. Nicole looked up from her work and studied the watch with recognition in her eyes. His heart struck his ribs as if it were lashing out to punish him. "How's your arm?"

His stomach dropped as he watched Nicole's face turn from curiosity to understanding. She closed her eyes and pressed her lips together for a moment.

"That was you outside the door at the inn."

"I was trying to keep Caeruleus alive. After what happened the first time you met—"

Nicole's eyes opened wide, and she looked at him, covering her mouth with her hands.

"—I let myself believe you could be as dangerous as the Council claimed to justify helping him go after you. I'm sorry ... Now you know what kind of man I am."

She removed her hands from her face. "Stop."

He wasn't sure what to make of her calm.

"I'm not upset about you looking out for a friend or not knowing who I was. I don't care about who you were with an altered memory—that person is gone."

Raiden thought about the man he'd been without knowing Nicole. He wasn't so sure all traces of that person were magically gone with the return of his memories.

She took a deep breath. "I had no idea that was Caeruleus," she said, shaking her head.

Raiden sighed, wishing he could think of something to say, but words were useless. There was no balm for these wounds. They could not undo all they had done. They could not erase the paths they'd traveled this past week.

"They're changing me, Raiden." She looked him in the eye, her mouth steady and straight. "I don't like who I'm becoming. I never wanted to kill, and now I'm prepared to kill every day. I tried to kill Caeruleus." Her voice didn't waver. "How do I take back my life from them without destroying who I am?"

In that moment, as her question hung in the silence and she looked at him, he saw what a mere week had done to her. He didn't have the heart to tell her that she hadn't changed, that she was still the same girl who had captivated him and brought him back to life with her brash optimism and exuberance. Lying wouldn't help Nicole find her way out of this darkness. There was no questioning that this person, seeking an answer he couldn't provide, was not the same one he had fallen for, but this familiar stranger inspired a different admiration, a new fascination and desire to discover her again.

"I don't know the answer," he said. "All I can do is promise that we will find out together."

A tiny smile transformed her mouth, and he caught a glimpse of the Nicole she thought was gone.

"For the record, I've known you were that guy since the night we found Gordan. I can't exactly blame you for being consistent." The curl of her lips was devilish.

And as if the last week had never happened, there she was in full force. He laughed. "You're not going to let me forget that," he said.

"Never. Remembering mistakes makes us better," she said, her smile strained against the sadness creeping back into her voice.

"Where's Gordan?" he asked.

Her voice turned bitter. "Safe and sound in the Wastelands."

Raiden looked down at the table where a small golden dragon lay munching on the corner of a report, the edges of which were singed and curled.

"He left you with a gift, I see."

"That's Gim," she said, her mouth flat with seriousness.

"What about his debt? Did he—?"

"Paid in full," she said and returned to folding.

"How? What happened?" He hated to think Caeruleus might have been the one to put Nicole in enough danger that—

"Nothing," she said, curtailing his worries. "Turns out there was a bit of a misunderstanding about what he actually owed me."

"Oh."

"What do we do next?" she asked, fidgeting in the chair. "How do we get out of here?"

The world outside rushed back into his mind. The walls of his apartment would only conceal them so long. The Council had Caeruleus out searching.

"I think we can convince Caeruleus to help us get out of the city," Raiden said. "His loyalty to the Council isn't quite what it used to be. There's just one problem with being a deserter."

"What's that?"

"They can still summon us, no matter where we are. It's blood magic. They take a sample from every agent."

"But you never—"

"Apparently a father's blood is enough to summon the son."

"So we have no choice but to stay and fight," Nicole said.

"Maybe not. Tovar might be able to help. I will go talk to him and then see if I can't find Caeruleus. If we can protect ourselves against being summoned, then the three of us have a chance to get out of the city and prepare for this fight."

"Do you really think he'll suddenly change his mind about me? It's not like he has any secret memories of who I am to challenge everything he knows."

"No, but he's my friend. He'll trust me."

"Yeah, or just think you've been brainwashed by a fera," she muttered.

He gave her a stern look, trying not to hear the validity of that point. "I won't be gone too long," he said, choosing to ignore the cloud of pessimism.

"I guess I'll stay here, then."

"That would probably be best," he said as he crossed the kitchen and the living room. He hesitated at the door. He had no guarantee anything would go the way he wanted, no idea whether he would walk back through this door. So he turned around and marched right back to the kitchen.

She looked up, and he caught her face in his hands, bending over to press his lips to hers, finally remembering the warmth of her mouth. That contact was better than wakefulness potion. His body hummed, and a trace of her magic tingled through his lips like static. When he let her go and straightened up, she just blinked at him.

"I will be right back," he promised.

She nodded, and he crossed the apartment once again, trying to focus on his plan instead of Nicole sitting there behind him. This time he opened the door and stepped outside into the dark-gray evening.

Nicole listened to the metal bolt slide with a clack as Raiden locked the door behind him. Her face was still hot and her heart fluttering. It was a relief to feel that giddy rush again, to escape the dark weight of the world around her for a moment.

She looked down at her most recent paper airplane, which was lopsided from her lack of attention. With a huff she threw it anyway. It veered left and crashed to the floor. Her gaze shifted from the failed flight to Gim, who stopped munching his piece of paper and looked back at her.

"Now what, Gim?"

He tilted his head and blinked.

"Good idea," she muttered.

40. Trapped

aiden yanked the door open, and the bell rang overhead. A woman looked up over one of the shelves. Tovar looked up from the book lying open on his back counter. At the sight of Raiden he straightened up.

"There you are," he said with a hint of annoyance.

"Here I am," Raiden answered.

Tovar got up from the stool behind his counter, then stopped, considering Raiden a moment. "Something is different about you."

He chuckled. "Different like the second time I met you thinking it was the first?"

Tovar's eyes lit with understanding. "You've tapped the memories. How did—"

The bell above the door rang as the woman left the shop.

"Nicole," Raiden explained.

Tovar nodded. "She was here, you know. I realized who she was, and then she ran. I had no idea what to do, what with the altered memories and you helping your friend find her."

"Well, she ran right into me, and somehow she … fixed me."

"Yes, it's hard to keep memories suppressed when you're confronted with them. Where is she?"

"Home."

"What about your friend Caeruleus? They're still out there looking for her."

"That's why I'm here. We don't have a lot of time, and I have a serious problem. The Council brought me to Atrium by summoning me. There's nowhere I can go that they can't reach me."

"You need to break the link," Tovar said.

"Exactly."

Caeruleus strode down the corridor on his way to see the Council, his body so tense with focus that his muscles would spasm at random. His team was still out in the city, scouring Mat Street and the surrounding district. There had yet to be any sign of the fera despite the Council's insistence that she planned to be on Mat Street.

He needed to know what the seers saw now. He needed to succeed. The drive to complete his mission was like a foreign entity in his body, moving his limbs, crowding his mind and shoving every other thought out of the way. How tired he felt. He wondered what had happened to Raiden in the evaluation, but the thought quickly vanished. Any thought that deviated from the fera was quiet and fleeting. He tried to understand when he had given the Council this kind of control. There had been room for nothing but his mission in his mind ever since the Council had made their commands clear.

The massive doors moaned as they swung open for him, and he crossed the great dim hall. His echoing footsteps were hypnotic in the silence. When he reached the tall crescent bench where the Council sat, he said, "The fera has eluded us. I need to know what the seers see." His voice sounded lifeless. *I don't sound like me*, he thought, but immediately his mind returned to the fera. Had she noticed his team on Mat Street? Did she have someone's help in the city?

"The seers have been keeping close watch over the fera and the courts. The fera's path has slipped into shadow once again. It would seem her quest for destruction is growing distant."

Caeruleus supposed this was a good thing, but then a different thought came barging back into his mind. The fera was dangerous, even more so than those who had come before her. Her power made her a destructive resource. She had to be located, no matter how her intentions in Atrium might change. The Council knew what was right, and they deemed the fera a threat to the safety of Veil.

But what are they planning to do with her? That wasn't his concern. He would bring her in, and the Council would deal with her accordingly. *Do they want to harness her power?* A destructive force in the hands of the Council was not a threat to Veil, but in the hands of Dawn it would be terrible.

"She must be in hiding somewhere. It may be that she has convinced someone, or even forced them, to shelter her. So long as she is undecided in her next course of action, her path remains clouded."

"What do we do?" Caeruleus asked.

"We wait."

The thought of waiting increased the tension in Caeruleus's body as he was forced to reconcile his drive to accomplish his task of finding the fera and the Council's decision to wait. As he rooted himself to their plan in compliance, the muscles in his back seized in a spasm.

Tovar held a short knife out to Raiden. "You have to be the one to spill your own blood for this spell to work. That means Caeruleus has to do the same."

"Understood." Raiden hoped Caeruleus would believe him, hoped he would be willing to sever his ties to the Council.

Before Raiden on the table lay *Blood Magic* by R. Blackheart, open to a page with a spell for dispelling the power of summoning over someone, and in front of the book was a small, shallow bowl beside a blank piece of parchment, a plain black dip pen, and a white candle, its flame flickering patiently.

"Ready?"

Raiden took the knife and held his left hand over the bowl. He pressed the cold blade against his palm and pulled the blade across with one swift, deliberate movement. Blood seeped from the parted flesh, flowed down the path of the cut, and dripped off the edge of his hand, pooling in the shallow bowl.

His head spun as the sensation of the Sight crept into his mind, coming and going, his vision flashing between now and some future. He saw the blood dripping from his hand into the bowl. Then he saw blood dripping from his hands and pooling on the floor beneath him.

"That's enough," Tovar said, his voice jarring Raiden back into the present.

For a moment Raiden couldn't be sure whether he had seen a vision of the future or some strange hallucination. He was light-headed. He hadn't eaten in he didn't know how long, and on top of that he was draining his own blood. It could have been a moment of delirium.

Tovar handed him a clean white cloth, which he held under his bleeding hand. Then Tovar uncapped a small vile of wound-sealing serum. Raiden held his hand out, and Tovar poured the clear liquid over the cut. The serum felt like salt in his wound, and it hissed as the broken skin merged together in an angry red line that gradually faded into a faint pink shadow of its former self and then a thin white scar.

Raiden opened and closed his hand a few times, wiped away the lingering blood and serum, then bent over the table to dip the sharp pen nib into the bowl. Using the blood as ink, he scratched out the spell from the open book onto the blank parchment.

> With my own blood I make this decree.
> I will not bend to the will of another.
> With this sacrifice I free myself from summoning.

As he scrawled the final word and straightened up, a drop of blood slipped off the end of the quill and fell. Time slowed and shifted. The Sight slipped in again, and he saw blood falling into a puddle at his knees—no, the drop of blood hit the table. He was in the workroom again.

"Good," Tovar said. "Now you just have to burn it."

Raiden nodded, trying to ignore the dizziness of the Sight still hanging around him. He lifted the parchment to the candle and let the flame lick the corner of the paper until the edges blackened and curled. The Sight seized his mind again, clawing at the burning paper before his eyes and twisting it into a vision of Nicole, her face ashen, her eyes filling with darkness, her skin tearing and curling like the burning paper in his hand.

As the fire licked his fingertips, the vision broke. He jerked his hand away, dropping the remaining corner of the paper. It fell to the table and writhed, shriveled and blackened from the flame.

"I've got to go," Raiden blurted out, breaking into a run for the door. He stumbled through the dizziness as his head cleared.

"What's going on?" Tovar asked.

"I don't know, but I've got to get back to—" Raiden stopped short as he yanked the door open to find that there were several people in the shop.

Tovar was right behind him. "What do you think you're doing?" he demanded.

"Not to worry," a petite woman with a cold voice said, appearing from behind a large man with a hard scowl. "We're here for him." She nodded toward Raiden.

Raiden looked around the shop, counting the company. There were four men and three women, including the petite one whose commanding voice singled her out as the leader. As discreetly as he could, he reached into his pocket to retrieve the key to his apartment. He turned to Tovar behind him and passed the key to him.

"I don't need this," he muttered. "If you need to find me, follow it."

Tovar nodded.

Raiden turned back to the intruders. The larger men glared at him with confident sneers, and the small woman smiled, her eyes narrowing. Raiden lurched forward, into the air, slipping away before any of the men could take a single step.

He stumbled forward into a dark place. This was *not* his apartment. The air was icy. There was nothing but shadow in his eyes.

"No." He put his hands out and moved forward into a wall he couldn't see. "Damn it!" he shouted, and his voice crashed around the dark stone room.

The people in the shop had been waiting for him. While he and Tovar had been in the workroom, they had prepared. They'd *wanted* him to interbound, because they'd already cast a redirection spell on the shop.

He followed the wall to his right, came to the next wall, and found the smooth wood grain of a door. His hand found the iron handle. He grabbed it and shook the door with vicious strength. When he tried to interbound out, his body felt twice as heavy as he met the resistance of containment spells. He let out a furious cry, striking the bottom of his fist against the wood with a bang, rattling the door in the doorframe.

"That couldn't have worked out any better." Though the voice was muffled through the door, Raiden recognized it as belonging to the harsh petite woman from the shop.

"What the hell do you want?" he asked.

"Word has it that the fera was looking for you. We'd really like her help, so we're giving her an incentive to come have a little chat."

Raiden heard footsteps approaching the door.

"And if she doesn't feel like chatting?" he asked.

"That's not my call," she answered.

Another voice spoke. "Eulina, he would like a word with you."

"All right," she muttered. Then she raised her voice to Raiden. "Make yourself comfortable."

The two pairs of feet walked away in almost perfect unison. Raiden struck the door again.

Nicole sat on the living room floor, her legs crossed in front of her, while her fleet of paper airplanes swooped and soared between the floor and the ceiling. The warm tingle of her magic hung in the air like a cloud that filled the apartment, and she orchestrated the paper planes with little more than a thought.

Gim scurried around the floor waging a ground war against his aerial foes. Whenever a paper plane dipped close to him, he would spit a fiercely accurate shot of fire and strike down the enemy aircraft. His kills littered the floor where they'd crashed, burned into shriveled black ghosts.

Nicole wasn't sure how much time had passed. She didn't want to look at the clock in the kitchen just to see that what had felt like hours had only been ten minutes. Instead she let her thoughts go round and round like the planes in the air, dancing in intricate, but nevertheless repetitive, patterns.

From the time Raiden had walked out the door, she had replayed the events since her arrival in Atrium at least five times with her new knowledge of the part Raiden had played in them and of the identity of the man she had despised and almost killed as his childhood friend. That latter knowledge twisted her memory of meeting Caeruleus the first time. No matter how justified she knew she had been, every time she relived that encounter, she felt worse. The worse she felt, the deeper her hatred for the Council spread like an infection, and the more her anger festered, the faster the planes in the air whipped around the room, moving erratically.

Gim grew more agitated, spitting long streams of fire to annihilate swaths of his foes that swooped too close. Nicole watched in something like a fever dream, imagining herself lashing out at the Council as Gim did at the planes, mesmerized by the flames, the graceful destruction, the rigid white paper transforming into wispy black wraiths.

A sharp, swift succession of knocks on the door made her jump. Gim gave a startled hop straight up into the air then bolted for her bag on the floor and scurrying inside. She scrambled to her feet.

"Raiden?" Nicole called, not willing to approach the door yet. Instead she found her boots and shoved her feet inside before hurriedly grabbing Raiden's sword from where it still lay on the kitchen table.

"No—my name is Tovar," the man outside the door said.

Nicole approached the door, holding the sword firmly by the scabbard with her left hand, her right hand secure on the grip.

"Raiden gave me the key, but I didn't want to let myself in," he said.

She stepped up to the door and leaned in close enough to peer through the peephole. The shop owner she had almost met that morning was on the other side of the door, holding up a key.

"Where is he?"

"He came to the shop," Tovar said. "Several people showed up. They said they were there for him. He interbounded out of there after giving me the key, but they all seemed rather pleased about it and left in a hurry. I came to verify that he made it back home, but seeing as the door hasn't opened and I haven't heard Raiden answer, I'm inclined to think he's not in there."

"No," she answered, barely able to eke out enough volume to hear above her heart pounding in her head. She swallowed back the panic and fury in her throat and tried again. "He's not." It sank in. It filled her chest and closed around her lungs until she couldn't breathe.

"Can I come in?" He paused, waiting. "Nicole?"

She didn't answer. Her mind was swimming. *What do I do?* Who had taken him? The Council, it had to be the Council. It occurred to her suddenly that Raiden had made the same mistake she had made—planning too far ahead. He had gone to Tovar's with plans to free himself and Caeruleus from the Council's grasp. The Council's seers would have seen where he was going.

She closed her eyes and tried to slip through the space between where she stood and wherever he was, focusing solely on him. For a moment she felt herself become a shadow in the air, but her momentum reversed, and she emerged precisely where she had been standing—some magic had forced her back to her point of origin.

Fine, she thought. *I know where he is anyway.* It wasn't supposed to be like this, her going in alone, but if Raiden was there, she wouldn't be alone. She just had to find him.

"Hello?"

She didn't reply. She left Tovar outside the door waiting for an answer. Her anger bubbled up inside her, and she sliced through the air, bursting out of the ether on the steps outside the court building, sword still in her hands.

The frigid evening air enveloped her as she started up the slope of white steps. With every step her temperature rose. The great white building lined with pillars loomed above her. The closer she got to the doors, the fiercer her heart beat against its cage. Her reservoir of magic roiled inside her, and for a moment she thought it might shed her body like a husk and charge ahead.

The doors into the courts were standing open, and she stormed right inside. There was no one in sight. The wide main corridor led straight ahead to a pair of towering gilded doors. In a blur she was standing at the doors, unsure whether she had rushed through the air like wind or moved the whole world to pull the doors to her.

The ornate barrier in front of her only infuriated her more. They'd let a whole city turn into a graveyard and had sent men to die based on lies while they sat in safety behind lavish golden doors. Her body tensed, and the doors burst open with a deafening bang.

She looked into a dark hall. In the distance, at the far end of the hall in a modest pool of light, sat a row of people at a high bench. Nicole yanked the sword and the sheath apart. The scraping of the metal rang through the silence, the long note of a song. But was this the start of a ballad of the final coda? She marched forward. Her heavy footsteps filled the hall.

As she drew nearer, she could see that each member of the Council was almost indistinguishable from the next. They had shaved heads and wore high-collared robes of the same dark, heavy material.

Then, below the crescent bench, somebody stepped out of the shadows at the fringes of the hall and into the light surrounding the Council. He walked directly into her path and turned to face her, standing square between her and her enemy. His hair was black, and the patch he wore was virtually hidden by his hair falling over his brow and cheek. One blue eye stared her down. Caeruleus.

Her anger calmed at the sight of him, like the eye of a storm passing overhead.

"They have him, Caeruleus. They have Raiden. This has to end. They can't rule our lives like this." Her voice shook in outrage and desperation. "Don't defend them anymore. They'll throw you to the wolves like they did to everyone in Cantis. Please. Don't defend them anymore. Help me find Raiden."

The tension in Caeruleus's body built as the fera spoke. His mind struggled to process it. *That sword, it—how does she know my—she's here looking for—I don't think I have a choice ...*

He shook his head, and the hope in her eyes went dark.

"I'm sorry," she said, and he heard heavy sincerity in her voice.

His neck and shoulders tensed in another spasm. He wanted to speak to her. He wanted to turn to the Council and question them, but he saw the rage return to her eyes. Yes, this was the fera he knew, the violent girl he remembered, here to prove why she didn't deserve her freedom.

He lurched forward into a sprint, closing the gap between them and latching his grip onto her wrist before she could swing it. She drove her knee upward into his groin, and he buckled, his stomach on the verge of turning itself inside out. Then the nettle-ward amulet against his chest went hot, and the fera was knocked back off her feet, sliding against the polished floor. She had taken the blow she'd meant for him.

As she got to her feet, she left the sword and sheath on the floor—not her weapon of choice apparently. Her hand glowed with an intense blue light as she took a long step forward. She extended her charged arm behind her and then hurled a crackling bolt of power from her hand.

It moved like lightning, too fast to see. All Caeruleus saw was the throw and the flash. The amulet became hot again, searing his chest like a brand, and the bolt reversed course, returning to her a split second after leaving her fingertips. The strike threw her head back, and she toppled to the floor.

"Well done, Caeruleus," the Council members said in unison behind him, and a chill moved down his spine. The tension was gone, the fera subdued, his mission complete.

His body was his again, wholly his. He hurried to the fera's side. She was out cold, her face turned away from him. There were red marks on her hand, extending from her fingers up to her wrist before disappearing under the sleeve of her shirt. The same marks appeared again at her neck and up her jaw—a pattern of lightning spiderwebbing a strange path from her fingertips, up her arm, to her neck with its erratic branches. The sword lay on the floor just out of her unconscious reach. He knew this sword. It belonged to Raiden's father. He gathered the blade and returned it to the sheath.

Two agents, a man and a woman, appeared. He knew them; they'd trained together—Loudain and Tolmack. Loudain scooped the fera up like a life sized doll. Tolmack, the female agent with copper hair and a love for scars, approached the fera with a slender bottle of some black potion. She dipped a long needle into the potion and then pricked the fera on the arm. Without a word or even a nod to him, the two of them left with the fera.

Caeruleus turned back to the Council. "What was that?" he asked.

"A potion used in necromancy. A full dose severs the soul's connection to the body. The tiniest amount, however, acts as a powerful sedative. Merely a precaution—we wouldn't want her waking up before we are ready."

"Ready for what, exactly?"

"For her execution."

"Of course," Caeruleus said in a daze, trying not to show his shock. "I— uh, is there anything else you need from me?"

"No, Caeruleus," a councilwoman said with such kindness he couldn't stomach it after what they'd just said about the fera. "You have done your job well, and you have more than earned some rest. You may leave."

He nodded and turned away, forcing himself to move slower than he wanted to as he crossed the dark hall. Once he was outside the Council's massive chamber, he broke into a run. Holding firm to the sword, he sprinted through the corridors to the detainment rooms. The doors were made of bewitched glass. Anyone on the outside could see through, but anyone being held within would only see a black door.

Caeruleus ran the length of the detention corridor, peering through every door. Most of the cells were empty. Those that weren't did not contain Raiden. When he reached the end of the corridor, he bent over, gasping for air. If Raiden wasn't here, either the fera had lied, or the Council had someplace else to hold people.

The fera, he realized. They hadn't brought her to one of these rooms. If the Council had Raiden somewhere, maybe it was the same place they'd taken the fera. *Where though?*

41. Escape

aiden stood in the darkness of the cell, his forehead resting against the door he couldn't open. What had begun as a posture of defeat was now his stubborn determination. He kicked the door lightly, paying close attention to what he felt in the wood. His first several kicks had been senseless and angry, but now they had a purpose. With each kick he could feel the force of the blow ripple through the spells in the door, spells that kept it locked and warded against any magic that would unlock it or just plain turn it to ash to bypass the formality of opening it.

"How long are you going to do that?" a voice asked from the far corner.

Raiden snapped his head up and took a futile look around the darkness.

"Until everyone else in this cell announces themselves, I suppose," he said, turning back to the door.

"I'm the only one in here, besides you." The voice sounded young.

"And why are you in here exactly? They want your help with the fera too?" Raiden asked, his voice dripping with doubt.

"Yes."

Raiden's spine straightened in disbelief, and he turned back around, immediately frustrated that he could not see the person in the cell with him. He tried to cast a light charm a few times, and when it failed, he spoke the spell out loud. *"Ilumina."*

"Won't work. Wards against magic."

Raiden let out a groan. "How can you help the rebels with the fera?"

The voice chuckled. "Not the rebels."

"What?"

"It's not the rebels that want my help, and more specifically, I was brought here to read an alchemist's journal."

"Why you?"

"Because the alchemist who wrote it was my teacher's teacher. He used his own unique shorthand to write his notes, and he passed it down like anything else an alchemist teaches his apprentices."

"Who wants you to decipher an alchemist's journal? And what does that even have to do with—oh no. Not Venarius."

"There you go."

"He's here?"

"Well, he was here yesterday and the day before that."

"Why does he want you to translate the journal?" Raiden pressed.

"You've heard of the alchemist Hessian?"

"I've read about him, the youngest man to master alchemy in a millennia."

"Well, the journal is his, and it has all his notes on the creation of the fera," the voice said.

Raiden felt dizzy. He backed into the door to stop the sensation of spinning.

"He worked with Venarius, a necromancer, before they outlawed the practice."

"Venarius, but he'd have to be—"

The apprentice interrupted before Raiden could even attempt the math. "Around two hundred fifty I'd guess, if he was still alive. The Venarius we're dealing with is a great-great-grandson. I guess he was inspired by his dear great-great-grandfather's legacy, and that's why he resurrected Dawn."

"And why he's trying to find the fera."

"Right. Hessian was an alchemist, a scientist, and something of a philosopher as well. He was fascinated by the soul and devoted his work to understanding it. I guess it's easy to see why he formed a friendship with Venarius in the beginning. Necromancers are the go-to source if you want to know more about death. Life is only half the story after all. I guess somewhere along the way Hessian got the idea that he might be able to create a soul himself."

"Why?"

"Ego, I'm sure. As far as he was concerned, mastering things other people had mastered before him wasn't noteworthy enough—even if he managed to do it younger than anyone else. He wanted to accomplish something no other alchemist had. If Hessian hadn't been so obsessed with that idea, we wouldn't be in this room today. According to my teacher, Hessian sought out Venarius to learn what he could about what happens to souls in death, reincarnation, everything he could."

"But Venarius was the founder of Dawn," Raiden said.

"Venarius took an interest in Hessian's ideas, and they started working together on the project. They combined their ambition and their practices of alchemy and necromancy to create man-made souls. The way my teacher tells the story, Hessian was only interested in his success of creating a stable soul strong enough to complete the natural cycle of rebirth. Venarius was the one with the idea that they could create something better, something stronger. Venarius kept pushing Hessian to make them more powerful, but this made them unstable, and Hessian started to have reservations about pushing the limits of these man-made souls.

"Since they were so powerful, the souls had to be attached to bodies that could handle the strain. Infants succumbed to the power, but adolescents bodies withstood the new souls. Unfortunately, to have a vessel for the new souls, they had to strip the vessels of their natural souls first. According to what he wrote and shared with my master, this practice deeply troubled Hessian, but apparently he still cared more about his glory than his conscience. Until, that is, he saw what that glory really meant. Venarius had pushed and pushed until they had created fifteen fera. Once they had finished, though, Hessian realized that Venarius had no intention of letting the fera live any semblance of a life. Venarius had created the fera to be kept in cages until he was ready to use them for his own purposes. Maybe Hessian really did see them as his children in a way. In any case, he released them and disappeared."

Raiden couldn't feel his body. His mind was drowning in the apprentice's story.

"The rest of the story is more or less common knowledge. The fera were too powerful for their own good. Combine too much raw power with a fragile newborn soul without the resilience naturally gained over lifetimes, and you get a volatile accident waiting to happen."

"You said there were fifteen originally."

"That's right."

"But the Council missed one somehow."

"And *that's* why you're Venarius's new guest."

"But why does Venarius need you to decipher the journal? Surely he knows this whole story."

"I'm guessing he wants to create new fera, and he would need Hessian's notes to do it."

"But you haven't deciphered them for him, have you?"

"I couldn't give him a complete translation if I wanted to. I've only been an apprentice for four years, one of them spent in this cell. I can understand maybe half of that journal. Venarius is convinced I'm just lying, so here I am, waiting while he waits for me to change my mind." The apprentice laughed.

A sudden connection in Raiden's mind hit him. Caeruleus had mentioned a Hessian journal listed in the Council's records, but it had been missing. The Council had once been in possession of this journal, so someone in the courts had to have taken it and delivered it to Venarius.

He had heard enough. He had been still long enough. He turned back to the door, placed his forehead against the wood, and kicked.

"Not again," the apprentice muttered.

"What have you tried to get out of here?" Raiden asked.

"I've tried everything. So if transmuting the door into water isn't going work, what makes you think kicking it will?"

"I'm not trying to get through the door. I'm listening to it."

The apprentice made a sound between disgust and amusement.

"Being an apprentice, I would think you'd know the value of listening," Raiden said, smiling to himself after one last kick. "You might learn something you hadn't thought about."

He reached for his belt and took the knife out. He searched for the door's hinges in the dark and found them on the right side. Then he felt out the pin of the bottom hinge and guided the edge of the knife under the head.

"What are you doing?" the apprentice asked as the sound of metal tapping and scraping on metal filled the silence.

"You're listening now?" He chuckled as he freed the bottom pin and stood to work the middle hinge. "Sometimes people can't help but consider all the hardest solutions before the simplest. They guarded this room and this door against every kind of spell they could think of, but they never stopped to think someone might not use magic at all."

The shuffling of shoes against the floor told him the apprentice had gotten up. Raiden freed the second pin and moved to the final pin at the top of the door. The pin came free, and the door shifted. He threw himself against it to keep it from falling. Tossing the knife aside, he braced the door and lowered it down slowly and quietly.

The dim light of a couple of sad *ilumina* charms hovered in the tunnel outside the door. "Good luck," he said over his shoulder as he walked over the door and ran into the tunnel.

Caeruleus waited in the inlet of a doorway as Loudain and Tolmack walked down the north corridor, leaving the entrance to the lower levels behind them. Caeruleus watched from the perpendicular corridor, leaning out of the doorway to be sure they were well on their way.

As he stepped out of his hiding place, a large, heavy hand dropped onto his shoulder. He jumped and whirled around all in one startled movement.

"Clyson—er, sir," he stammered.

Loak looked down at him from his superior height, his golden eyes piercing. "What are you doing here?"

"What are *you* doing here?" Caeruleus blurted out. "Why are you always somewhere when I shouldn't be there?"

Loak leaned back a little, and a fraction of a smile shifted his mouth. "A little flustered, are we, Stone?"

"I'm looking for Raiden," he confessed.

"Why? Is he snooping around here too?"

"No, uh, I have reason to suspect the Council may be detaining him."

Loak's eyebrows shot up. "You think they have him in the lower levels?"

"I already checked the detention hall, all the cells, and he wasn't there."

"What makes you think he's down there?" Loak nodded toward the concealed entrance to the lower levels around the corner.

"The fera came blasting into the great hall *looking for Raiden*. And she had this with her," he said, holding up the sword.

Loak's eyes widened with more recognition than Caeruleus would have expected. "All right," he said, stepping around Caeruleus to walk around the corner.

"What?" Caeruleus trotted after him.

"We're goin' to check if he's down there."

"Oh." Caeruleus nodded. "Right." He stepped up to the entrance to the lower levels, holding the sword in a tense grip.

As the floor opened and revealed the stairway down, Loak looked at Caeruleus. "You know, the Council doesn't keep dragons down there. You don't have to hold that like something might jump out at you," Loak said.

Caeruleus realized that his arms were tense and that he was holding the sword ready to pull the blade out, one hand on the hilt and the other on the sheath.

"Right." He laughed and pulled the strap on, positioning the sword onto his back. "I've wanted to put this on since we were kids," he murmured.

"Come on, Stone." Loak's voice came up from the stairs, where he was already on his way down.

Nicole jerked upright and looked around, alarmed by the last memory seared into her mind and confused that she was sitting in an empty room. A dim light seemed to come from everywhere, like the walls themselves were the source. The room looked gray and cold although she didn't shiver or even notice the temperature of the air. In fact, she didn't notice any sensation, now that she thought about it. Much like a dream, she felt like only her mind was here.

She looked down and saw her legs. She was sitting upright on some kind of bed/table. Then she noticed a strap on each ankle. That seemed odd, to strap down her ankles but not her wrists. When she turned to look down at the table behind her, the sight shocked her, and she suddenly understood why she didn't *feel* anything.

Her body was lying there, wrists strapped down, and she was apparently having half an out-of-body experience. Curious, she swung her legs off the table, and sure enough, she was as free as could be—except for the fact that her body was strapped to a table and she couldn't be sure what she even *was* at this point.

Am I dead? She leaned over her body and watched closely. Her chest rose and fell in steady, shallow breaths. *Only mostly dead, then,* she figured. All things considered, it was only a matter of time now. Then she leaned closer still, lowering her ear down to her face, and determined that she could at least hear the movement of air through her nose.

Still curious, she reached out and touched her face. Her faint hand passed right through her own head, and on top of that she didn't feel anything. Whatever she was, she couldn't do anything to help her situation if she couldn't *do* anything. She let out a cry of frustration, which turned out to be far less satisfying than it should have been without the air in her lungs or the force of her exhalation or vocal cords to vibrate with anger. To her horror not even her voice existed in this strange state.

Maybe this was a dream. It had to be, but she walked around her unconscious body and noticed something far too vivid to be part of a dream, even without the rest of her senses. There was an odd branching pattern on her neck, irregular red tendrils. The same pattern looked to be present on her hand, and she supposed it went all the way up her arm. The last thing she remembered before waking up was attacking the Council. It was obvious who had won that confrontation.

I'm screwed anyway—why stand around here waiting? If she could pass through her own body, maybe she could pass through the door to this room. She turned around and walked toward the door and then right through it.

Somehow she had the impression that she was walking, yet she was uncomfortably aware that her forward movement didn't match her imagined steps, nor did she feel the ground under her feet or the synchronized firing of her muscles. She just sort of *went* forward. The lack of physical feedback bothered her, but she couldn't *feel* any of the visceral effects of her distress, which only bothered her more.

To escape that eerie, spiraling conundrum, she turned her dreamlike presence around to see where she was, shifting her focus to the only sense she seemed to have. She was in a cramped hall, and the very stones all around her emitted a faint glow. As she chose the way to the right, the glow followed her. *At least the walls know I'm here*, she thought with pitiful optimism. It proved she still existed in some way she supposed.

A short way down the hall she came to another door, so she stepped—or drifted, rather—through it. This room was like hers, except it wasn't as dark and dreary. The stone floor and walls were brighter here, and the occupant inside lay upon a simple cot. There was a pot in the corner and a mostly empty plate on the floor. This room wasn't merely occupied; it was inhabited. The person on the cot lived down here.

As she was just some dreamy, quasi ghost, she didn't think anything she did could really count as invading someone's privacy. Her curiosity pulled her forward, without so much as a single pretend step for formality's sake. The person on the cot lay supine, blinking up at the ceiling with an interest that would suggest he had memorized every pattern in the stones, every crack and joint, ages ago.

His eyes were brown, and his long hair was dark blond. His skin was white from years away from the sun and lined from years of frowning. Something about his face made her think she was hallucinating, or maybe it was just the strange effects of being no better than a hallucination herself that caused her mind to not quite work properly outside of its squishy gray domicile. Whatever the case, the man's face was somehow Raiden's face through a strange inverted lens. Light skin instead of dark, dark eyes instead of light, weathered instead of youthful.

The man turned his head and looked at her—through her, at least. She backed away from his gaze, whether he saw her or not. This man couldn't be … but the resemblance to the photograph of Raiden's parents *had* to mean … Her mind was spinning, but she had no physical outlet to react. How did she know *what* she was feeling if she couldn't *feel* anything without her body? Wasn't her heart supposed to be racing, her skin growing cold with sudden anxiety?

She slipped back through the door and into the hall before the desire to leave the chamber was even an articulate thought. The halls unfolded before her, and she drifted, trying not to think anything, but that was all she had—no body, just a maze of thoughts and emotions wandering aimlessly through a world she would soon leave. At least, she assumed that when the body she'd left behind was gone, this part of her, this form, would be gone too. It wasn't a troubling thought in the least. Strangely enough, the idea of being stuck like this for an eternity was a more unsettling thought. She couldn't even process her overwhelming desire to escape this state—a consciousness without substance to experience and interact with the world around her.

She wondered what would happen if she could manage to stop thinking. Would her consciousness just disperse and diffuse through the air until she was gone, free? Her drifting became so thoughtless that she was no longer following the passages. She drifted ahead through walls and halls until her surroundings were suddenly vast and bright.

The room around her was a high chamber filled with towering shelves. A blurred black shape swooped in front of her. She looked around, searching for it, and realized it was a raven as it flew past her again. There was a small army of ravens, some gliding here and there, others perched atop the shelves. She followed the natural path across the center of the hall. The long aisle, flanked by tables for sitting and reading, divided the hall in two and led to another door at the far end.

The ravens seemed to watch her. She was sure this wasn't her imagination. As she looked up at them, they looked back down at her, following her progress across the large chamber. One raven even landed on one of tables and tilted its head in curious observation of her.

I don't know what I am either, she thought at the bird, seeing the question in the raven's blinking eyes.

She turned her eyes back to the door at the end of the aisle. It seemed to rush toward her, and she passed through it abruptly. Her pace and progress seemed directly tethered to her thoughts, and she found herself in a room that was a stark contrast to the chamber behind her. This room was filled to the ceiling with absolute darkness. In fact, she couldn't make out a wall or ceiling or even a floor. The room might have been an infinite void for all she could tell.

Ahead of her a stone pedestal stood glowing with its own light like the walls and floor of the passages. It chased back the shadows and revealed a circle of stone floor around it, an island of light and matter in a sea of dark, empty space. There was a large book atop the pedestal.

Before she could raise her hand—or even stop to realize how useless that instinctual tactile curiosity was to her now—the book flipped open with a bang like its cover was made of stone and with such force it might have spilt down its spine. The pages fluttered, pure light without words, and then stopped, open to the middle of the book.

A voice erupted from the tome. She had no delicate eardrums to protect, but the sound shook the room, and Nicole's very consciousness was rattled. The voice was distorted either by its sheer volume or the fact that it seemed to scramble her—whatever she was.

"Those who seek to save us will set loose children of discord and destruction. Among them they have but one fate and will break down the walls that seclude us. The pillars upon the hill will fall before dawn when chaos finds peace and peace embraces chaos. Two opposed in harmony will forge the key and unlock our chains."

The voice seemed to duplicate, speaking in rounds, overwhelming her consciousness, shaking her presence. She knew these words, and she fought to comprehend them deeper than mere recognition. She willed her thoughts into focus, and consequently her presence seemed to steady. The room's violent shaking—or perhaps it was her that was shaking—shrank into a tremble. The voice kept repeating, now split into three, and Nicole struggled to grasp the words again, losing them in their overlapping repetition.

Then she heard a different voice in her head. It sounded both distant and near.

"This is the last one. Looks like he's not here."

"That's her."

"The fera? Sure doesn't look like she could hurt anyone."

The voices came with an odd sensation, a fuzzy perception of weight and pressure against the back of her body. Suddenly she was being pulled backward, away from the book and the voice speaking in rounds, out of the dark room, across the chamber of ravens and their shelves full of books and records, through the walls and passages, until she composed herself in the room where she'd started, standing beside her body on the table. There were two people standing on either side of her imperceptible form, not noticing her standing there between them as they looked down at her physical form strapped down and unconscious before them.

"You haven't seen what she can do." It was Caeruleus.

She felt a bizarre voyeuristic discomfort as she watched the two men watching her body and looked at her own body, lying there oblivious to it all. In her head she groaned, and to her surprise her body took a deep breath and sighed. *I'd rather be completely unconscious right now*, she thought, shaking her imaginary head. Her real head did not move.

"What do you think is going on here, exactly?" asked a man she did not know.

As she turned to get a better look at the large stranger on her right, her presence shifted to the other side of the table so that she was looking over her body at the two men standing over her. The man she didn't recognize was a veritable giant compared to her supine body and Caeruleus standing beside him.

"I don't know. She knew my name. She begged to stop helping the Council. She insisted that they had Raiden."

"When was the last time you saw him?"

"When we came in this morning. I reported to the Council, and Raiden went with you."

"I had to leave him for evaluation. That's the last time I saw him," the massive dark man said.

"That's when things got strange. The Council told me he was under investigation, that they didn't trust him. They ordered me to focus on the fera and leave Raiden out of it."

"You never saw him after that?"

"No. We were out looking for her." Caeruleus nodded at Nicole's body. "She managed to evade us, and I returned to the courts for anything the seers could tell me. The Council decided it was time to wait."

"And then she showed up all on her own."

"She came into the hall looking ready to spill blood, but she tried reasoning with me. It all happened so fast, and I couldn't even react to what she said. It was like I was ... overpowered by my orders."

"Yes, well, you took an oath when you got those wings, Stone. You vowed to heed orders, and you signed your blood to it."

"I knew something was wrong, but I didn't make the connection at the time. There was something in my head, making me focus on what they wanted. It wasn't like being a puppet along for the ride—it was worse. Something hijacked my mind, steering and correcting my thoughts. I heard what she had to say, but I focused on how dangerous she was, convincing myself the Council was right."

"And now what do you think, now that your mind is free and clear?"

"I think she was sincere. If she came to Atrium for the Council, she could have come to the courts right away. I don't think she would have risked ending up like *this* to find Raiden if he wasn't important to her."

"He never mentioned knowing her?"

"No. But can you blame him? He's been protecting her since he got here," Caeruleus said. "I believed in the Council's motives. I sure didn't give him any reason to trust me with this."

"Well, now what? He isn't here, Stone. We checked every room. She was wrong."

"All right, she was wrong, but why did she think he was here?" Caeruleus asked, peering into her face as though she might wake up and explain.

"How should I know?"

"I think something happened to him. He's gone, and she just came looking in the wrong place."

"If this has anything to do with her"—the dark man nodded at her body—"I can tell you who has Raiden—Dawn."

"What makes you so sure?"

"They've been after this girl longer than she's been alive. If Raiden got involved with her, then he's gotten himself mixed up with them; I guarantee it."

"All right," Caeruleus said, bending over Nicole to reach the other side of the table and unfasten her wrist.

"What do you think you're doing?"

"What Raiden would be doing if he was here," he answered, fumbling with the restraint on her other hand closest to him.

Nicole watched, surprised both at what she was seeing and that she could feel the tugs on the strap. Her heart in her chest fluttered anxiously and the sensation made her giddy with relief. *It's still beating*, she savored the glorious thought.

"You might want to stop and consider what you're doing. You made a vow to serve the Council."

"They're preparing for her execution. I can't allow that knowing—" Caeruleus jerked and let out a sudden cry, arching his back in pain.

"Stone!"

Nicole's elation at the return of her senses turned to horror as Caeruleus crumpled to the floor, screaming in agony, his hand still clinging to the strap on her wrist. Two twisting shadows sprouted out of his back into wings. The feathers disintegrated into dust. The bare appendages jerked and writhed, the bones popping and snapping beneath the shriveling flesh. She could feel his grip tighten on the strap, shaking furiously.

Wake up! Do something! She attempted to scream at her body, willing it to move, to help him. He tried to pull himself up, fighting. His hand moved, taking hold of her arm as he sagged beneath the torture again. Not even the crushing force of his hand on her forearm could stir her stillness. She felt it, but she could not make her body move.

The other man broke free from his horror and lunged forward, pulling the sword free from the sheath on Caeruleus's back. One swift swing cut through the air with a flash of light, and the writhing, cancerous wings fell away from Caeruleus. The sword's sheath clattered against the stone floor, the strap severed. Caeruleus's grip on her arm went slack, and he sank to the ground. The disfigured wings continued to twitch and shrivel where they'd dropped.

The large man muttered something under his breath and suddenly his hands were glowing white and Nicole could feel the heat radiating off them against the side of her sleeping face. Without hesitation or warning the man laid his blindingly hot hands against two bleeding wounds on Caeruleus's back. Caeruleus cried out again, his voice hoarse now from screaming. His partner removed his hands, cooling as the spell wore off, and silence fell over the room. Caeruleus's shuddering breaths were the only sound. Then he grabbed the edge of the table and pulled himself onto his feet, hunching over Nicole as he fought to straighten his spine.

"Get the straps at her ankles," Caeruleus strained to say as he returned to the restraint on her wrist and unfastened it.

"You're sure you want to do this?" the massive man asked, breaking the straps from the table with a quick yank.

"Well, I already went back on my oath, didn't I? They can't make me follow orders anymore."

"They can still kill you."

"What option doesn't present that risk at this point?" Caeruleus slipped his arm under Nicole's knees, but the other man stepped forward.

"Don't be foolish. Here," he said, pushing the sword into Caeruleus's arms and forcing him away from Nicole. He scooped Nicole's body up like a sleeping child. Seeing herself in his arms, she marveled at his size again. Feeling her body move, even limp and useless, was somewhat of a relief. She rejoiced in the tactile feedback.

Who is this guy? Nicole wondered now that the complete stranger was holding her against his chest. Caeruleus winced as he bent forward to pick up the sheath. She felt like an imaginary friend as she hovered over Caeruleus's shoulder while he straightened up and returned the sword to its scabbard.

"Now let's get out of here," Caeruleus said.

"We have one stop to make on the way," the other man said.

"For what?"

"A friend."

Nicole followed their exchange with confused interest as her heart was swept up in a surge of hope. Knowing she had a chance of escaping her execution was more torturous than the thought of that fate had been an hour ago.

42. Siege

Raiden moved quickly down the tunnel. He tried not to run, tried to look like he belonged in the passageway. There were only seven people who knew his face and that he was supposed to be in a cell. All he could do was find his way out of these tunnels and hope none of those people would come along.

He came to a fork in the passage and a choice between continuing straight ahead and going right. The tunnel to the right was darker than the one ahead, but he could see light spilling from an open door not far down. His gut decided to go right, where someone passing in the tunnel wouldn't be able to see his face clearly.

As he neared the open door, he heard voices. He slowed down and pressed his back against the rough wall.

"Sir, we've received word that the fera was captured and is currently being held in the courts awaiting execution," a timid voice said.

"What?" The shocked female voice sounded like the petite woman from Tovar's shop.

"That does present a problem," a calm, quiet voice said so smoothly Raiden thought perhaps the man hadn't actually heard the news.

"I was counting on her turning the tides in our favor," the woman grumbled. "We don't have the numbers to go up against the Council's forces, not without massive casualties. It would be different if we had the whole city behind us."

"Unfortunately for those unlucky casualties, that is exactly what we will have to do," the man said with a gentle tone that did not match his words.

"I beg your pardon?"

"I can't allow the last fera to be destroyed. You will tell your loyal followers that tonight we move on the courts. This is the spontaneous attack they have been preparing for."

"This is doomed to fail. You promised me victory—"

"No, I promised you the admiration and respect of leading the rebel movement. I promised you that these people would rally behind you, that they would believe in you. And in return you promised to follow my every instruction. I have provided your infamy. I made no guarantee of your rebellion's success."

There was no reply from the woman.

"Now, you will send your people to the courts. We are going to retrieve the fera, even if it costs every life."

"I am not going to be remembered as the leader who sent her people into a bloodbath," she said, the moan of a chair sliding across the floor punctuating her words. "You can go get the fera on your own." Her voice drew nearer, and Raiden tensed as her shadow moved across the light spilling from the room.

But she didn't step through the doorway. Her body fell to the floor with a thud, her head and shoulders in the passageway, a knife protruding from the back of her skull. Raiden jumped away as her head lolled to the side and her blank eyes pointed at him. He stood frozen in shock and then curiosity, as no blood pooled around her head.

The man spoke once again. "Get up, Eulina."

The woman dragged her hands forward and planted them against the floor. She picked herself up, letting her head roll this way and that until she straightened her spine. Then she reached back and yanked the knife out of her head. The blade was black with markings that glowed red. It flicked out of her hand, pulled back into the room.

"Now be a good girl and send your people to the courts. Tell them half the Council's men have left the city in pursuit of the fera."

Eulina turned away from the doorway, toward Raiden. Her dead eyes moved right over him, but she did not react to his presence. She walked down the passage the way he had come. Realizing she could guide him through the tunnels, he followed behind her, cautious not to make much noise or get too close, but she either didn't hear him or didn't care that she heard him.

After several turns through the tunnels, which Raiden would have failed miserably to navigate, Eulina turned through a doorway into a large domed chamber teeming with people. He slipped into the crowd as Eulina stepped up a short set of wood steps to a raised platform.

When Eulina appeared above everyone, a self-induced hush crept through the chamber without her having to call for silence.

"Good evening." She raised her voice and filled the dome with her words. "Our opportunity has come. Half the Council's men have left the city in pursuit of the fera. Tonight we will march on the courts. Take to the streets. Raise your voices. Our numbers have grown. Our message has spread. Trust in what we fight for, and others will join us."

Everyone around him nodded in agreement to Eulina's flat speech. Maybe it wasn't all that different from her usual performance. They all erupted in cheers, throwing fists in the air as countless people disappeared like wisps of smoke. The crowd dwindled, with those who could not interbound filing toward the exits.

After his last attempt to interbound had gone so wrong, Raiden hesitated. But with hundreds disappearing around him, he felt safe to make the jump.

His feet hit the floor of his living room with a thud, and Tovar let out a startled sound that in turn startled Raiden.

"Tovar."

"What happened? Where have you been?" Tovar asked, wringing his hands.

"I got held up with the rebels. They're setting out to march against the courts as we speak. I overheard that Nicole was there. I just couldn't believe—"

"Oh stars. The rebels. I'm sorry, Raiden. I came here to find out if you were all right, and I told her what had happened in the shop, but since you weren't here—"

"She confronted the Council because they were the most likely culprit," he said, sinking into the reality. She really was in the courts.

"I didn't know. I've helped the rebels for months, but I only ever met the boy who brought the posters. I never thought they would do something like that. I'm so sorry." Tovar shook his head.

"It's not your fault. Right now I have to go." Raiden didn't hesitate this time. He stepped into the ether, cutting through space, aiming for the platform inside the courts, but instead he was thrown to the ground outside at the bottom of the steps. The courts were barred from magical entry, and at the top of the steps every last man and woman who answered to the Council stood shoulder to shoulder awaiting the rebels.

Nicole waited beside her body and the man carrying it as Caeruleus unlocked the door she had drifted through in her earlier wandering. When he opened the door, the middle-aged blond man was standing there waiting with a grin on his face.

"Loak," he said.

"Leone."

Although she drifted along separate from herself being carried against Loak's chest, Nicole could feel the rumble of Loak's deep voice against her unconscious body before he released a hearty chuckle.

"Caeruleus," Leone said. "You're taller than I remember."

Caeruleus had a stunned look on his face, and Nicole's heart swelled with certainty in her chest. The resemblance was not just a coincidence. This man was Raiden's father—very much alive.

"Who is this, Loak?" Leone's tone was suddenly serious.

"The fera," Caeruleus said, finding his voice.

"She's a friend of Raiden's as I understand it. Like father, like son, ay, Lion?" Loak said, his mouth twisting in something between a smile and a frown. Leone looked at Nicole's unconscious form and sighed.

"Where is he?"

"At the moment we don't know," Loak said. "First we've got to get out."

"Right. Lead the way."

Nicole was still marveling at the confirmation of Leone's identity. Caeruleus turned to continue down the hall.

"Is that my sword?" Leone asked.

"Er, yes, sir. I believe it is."

They hurried down the halls, Nicole's detached consciousness being dragged along. She seemed to be anchored to her body now, and the chain between her mind and her body was continually getting shorter. The more aware of her body's physical senses she became, the harder it was to remain separated from it. She had taken to resisting this return because she didn't want to be trapped in there, unable to see what was going on around her.

As the three of them ascended a flight of stairs, the jostling of her body dragged her consciousness back. Every time her cheekbone bumped against Loak's chest, every time his arms tightened even slightly around her, the cacophony of now three pairs of heavy feet filling the corridors and her ears—all this seized her mind and reeled it back into her body where it belonged.

She was in darkness, trapped inside a cage of unresponsive flesh and bone.

All she could do now was listen to their footsteps and study the sensations of her body as she was carried—hopefully to safety.

Raiden turned away from the court building to see the road filling with people. Many flickered out of the air; others poured in from the surrounding streets on foot in swelling crowds. There were far more than he had seen in the domed chamber.

The flood of people surged in so quickly that the rumbling of their collective footfalls and the roar of their chorused cries stunned him. When they broke into a fervent charge up the courts' steps, the line of the Council's agents readied their guns. These people were fighting for something completely different from what they believed. He pitied them for the exploitation of their fears and dreams, but what mattered most to Raiden was getting inside. He forced his way into the current of people.

All the spells he had memorized throughout his years of preparation to face a single murderer flooded his mind. He had obsessed over adversarial spells for a decade. Now at least it would pay off.

The noise rose up around him, sweeping him back to that day in Cantis the same way the Sight swept him into the future. He focused on his heartbeat, pounding in his chest and in his head, drowning out the din of chaos, and shut that door to the past. He could not go back to that place now. He forced his mind and his senses to root themselves to the present.

The agents above fired into the wave of people that came rushing up the steps. Several people fell and took down even more just by obstructing the path. Raiden sprinted, weaving through people to get to the top of the steps. He knew what was coming. Hundreds made it to the top before the steps went flat and the stairs became a smooth slope. The wave of people making their way up suddenly toppled and slid backward. Some managed to scramble on all fours and still reach the level ground at the top of the hill.

Raiden peered through the throng of citizens fighting the Council's agents, swarming them to pull the protective masks off their faces. The entrance doors were shut tight. On either side of the doors, the walls were solid stone, as if the many windows had never been there at all.

"I know you," a voice said.

Raiden's eyes refocused to see a man toss one of the court agents down the slope. As the agent slid to the bottom, the man, skin riddled with scars, nodded at Raiden. "The fera—Nicole—was looking for you," he said.

"Now I'm looking for her," Raiden said. "I need to get through those doors."

"In there? Eulina—that lying pile of—she said—never mind," he cut himself off. "Fine. I like a challenge. Let's do it," he said, drawing a gun with a great gap between the handle and the wide barrel. He slapped a cylindrical chamber filled with spell cartridges into the gun.

They pushed into the fray. Spells jumped from Raiden's mind with a life of their own as he navigated the turmoil. A trio of court agents still in their masks cut a swath through the fight. One had a short sword in each hand; another had a gun in each hand firing rounds into the crowd. They flanked the third, who cast spells at anyone who got past the other two.

Raiden knew he couldn't cast anything at them, as they had too many protections in their masks alone. So he targeted the floor beneath them, turning it to a liquid pool of sand that swallowed up the three masked agents in a blink. His impromptu ally beside him laughed, then pulled a hilt from the sheath on his hip, revealing a long, straight broadsword that he wielded with just one hand.

"No, ma'am," he said, swinging it in an arc over his head. He brought the blade down on the wrist of a woman without her mask pointing her gun at the back of a rebel woman. Her hand fell away, still clutching the gun, and she crumpled, clutching her bloody wrist.

They pushed on toward the door. The man with the broadsword fired his gun, taking aim at the masks still in the crowd. The shots left the gun with a deep ringing vibration that rippled through the air. Short yellow spears of light struck the agents right in their masks and at first appeared to do nothing. But when rebels' spells suddenly took effect, the purpose was clear. The shots had unraveled the defensive wards in the masks.

"Levels the playing field," he said with a dangerous grin. He fired several more successive rounds as they approached the last line of the Council's defense. His shots hit every single mask in the line of five.

Raiden cast an eternal darkness, and the agents all pulled their masks off in an attempt to escape their sudden blindness. Then Raiden swept them all aside with a wave of his hand.

The man with the broadsword gave him a nod of approval. As they reached the doors, someone hooked an arm around Raiden's neck from behind him and pressed a gun against the side of his head. He cringed, casting a rebounding ward as the agent pulled the trigger. The gun erupted from the force of the spell reversing back into the chamber. Raiden managed to pull his head away, but the small explosion knocked him over. His assailant jerked back screaming, bending over his hand, which was riddled with shreds of metal.

"Hold my sword," Raiden's ally said as he plunged his broadsword through the shoulder of the injured agent, who cried out again. He then flicked his gun, and the spent cylinder of cartridges fell out. His left hand, free of the sword, moved to his belt and retrieved a cylinder that appeared to have one massive round in it. He shoved it into the gun and yanked his sword back out. The wounded man to toppled over, squirming in pain.

Raiden picked himself up, trying to shake the ringing from his ears.

"Brace yourself," his partner said as he aimed the gun at the doors.

Caeruleus heard the commotion long before the entrance to the courts was even in sight. They rounded another corner on their way to the central corridor.

"You hear that?" he asked.

"Guess we know where everybody went," Loak said.

They hadn't seen a single person in the corridors.

"That's going to be a problem," Leone said as they reached the central corridor. The massive doors were shut and enforced with three crossbars that nearly covered the doors completely.

With the doors to the Council's great hall behind them and the sealed doors preventing their exit ahead of them, they all froze.

"What do we do?" Caeruleus asked.

The answer came in a sudden earthshaking bang as the doors exploded into a cloud of fire and kindling. They turned away, and the eruption of splinters pelted their backs. Caeruleus winced as wood fragments slapped against his shoulder blades.

The roar of fighting poured into the corridor. When they turned around, Caeruleus couldn't believe what he saw. Raiden sprinted through the doorway and stopped, spotting them in the corridor immediately.

"Caeruleus!" he called, leaning into a run.

As he neared, Caeruleus saw his eyes fall on the fera in Loak's arms. His relief was clear in his eyes and his shoulders sagged forward, causing him to stumble for a stride. Raiden ran right into Caeruleus, stopping and steadying himself with a firm grip on Caeruleus's arms.

"Stars, Raiden, what happened? What's going on out there?"

"Rebels," he said breathlessly. "Following Dawn's orders, but they don't know it. Venarius is coming for Nicole. He—" Raiden's voice got caught in his throat, and Caeruleus realized he had just spotted Leone standing behind Loak.

Raiden's posture went rigid, and he blinked back the same astonishment Caeruleus had felt when he'd laid eyes on Raiden's father in the cell downstairs. Leone attempted a smile at Raiden's stunned reaction. Then Raiden shot an accusatory look up at Loak, whose mouth twisted in an uncomfortable grimace.

Raiden shifted his attention to the girl in Loak's arms again. "Is she all right? What happened?" Raiden examined her, touching the branching red marks on her jaw.

"The Council dosed her with some potion," Caeruleus explained. "They've been preparing—"

"I know. Dawn has someone in the courts. We need to get her out of here." He paused, looking concerned. His jaw clenched. "Did you notice this?" Raiden asked, pointing out a small bloodstain on her white sleeve in the crook of her elbow.

Loak and Leone exchanged wide-eyed looks.

"They took blood," Loak said.

"No." Raiden's words barely made it past his lips.

Before Caeruleus could even wonder what they could do, Nicole slipped away into the air. Her body turned to smoke in the wind, leaving Loak's arms empty.

"It's like they were listening," Caeruleus muttered.

"They were," Loak said. "They like flaunting their power."

"I need that, Ruleus," Raiden said, holding his hand out for the sword.

Caeruleus obliged. Raiden's knuckles went pale as he gripped the scabbard. He pushed past Caeruleus and Loak, his sights set on the doors to the Council's chamber.

"Raiden," Leone said as he passed. Raiden stopped, and they looked each other in the eye, but Leone didn't say anything more. Caeruleus wondered what Leone had been about to say and whether he had changed his mind or had just needed to say Raiden's name.

Loak, Caeruleus, and Leone exchanged glances and all nodded in agreement. They fell into step behind Raiden as he strode toward the Council's doors.

48. Darkest

ait, what happened?! Still trapped in the darkness of an inert body, Nicole didn't understand who had taken blood until she'd felt like she was falling, the arms around her gone.

The sudden shock of the cold, hard floor beneath her made her eyes snap open. Her heart pounded with joy over this accomplishment, but the view above her was not much different than the view behind her eyelids. There was a lot of darkness, and through the shadows she could barely make out a high, ornate ceiling.

She understood where she was—the great hall from before. Since she couldn't move her head, she could only imagine the Council sitting at their crescent bench looking down at her. Her body went cold and rigid with dread, like she was merging with the icy marble beneath her. The dark ceiling above her blurred as her eyes stung, and her heart broke into a frantic rhythm as fear welled up in her eyes.

Why? A sob slipped from her lungs. *Why are you doing this?* She didn't expect an answer, but somehow her question was heard.

"Your kind was created for one purpose: to dismantle the sanctuary of Veil. We are freeing you from that fate, like the rest of the fera were set free, in order to protect this realm," a voice overhead said.

Nicole remembered the terrible voice from the book in the dark room, the words scrawled in Althea's journal. *This is about some prophecy?* Her disgust churned in her stomach.

"We have done everything we could to ensure the safety of this realm. Veil is a haven from the old world and its vile beliefs that turned us into devils and demons to control weak-minded men. We learned long ago that there was no place for us in that world, and we will not allow Dawn to send the people of this realm back there, to be the victims and scapegoats of those backward beliefs."

Their words spun around Nicole's mind, colliding with the prophecy in her memory. *Those who seek to save us will set loose children of discord and destruction.* Dawn wanted her for some scheme to return Veil to the other realm. *They have but one fate and will break down the walls that seclude us.*

"You understand, then."

No. No! She screamed her will to move into her limbs, but she couldn't even shake her head.

"We had to deliberate over how to do this," one of them said.

"You have proven to be far more resilient than the others. They required only a little fear and the slightest agitation to push them over the edge and lose control of themselves."

"That's the key, you see. The first incident was an accident, but with the help of your creator we understood how the volatile souls of your kind could be provoked to destroy themselves beyond repair, unable to return to this world."

Another voice spoke. "It may not be as easy to push you to that catastrophic state, but we have an idea of how to do it. First, we'll help you up."

Nicole's panicked heart went hot and tingled with magic that spread through every artery and vein, surged through every muscle, until her whole body hummed, raging with an ominous fever.

Her body moved. Her head lifted off the floor. Her arms pushed her upright. Her legs folded underneath her and stood. But none of these movements were hers. She was a passenger, her mind still disconnected from flesh and bone, along for the ride and stuck watching through her own eyes. Her body turned to face them as they spoke.

"Blood can be dangerous in the wrong hands, you know. Just a few drops and we can summon you from any corner of the realm. A few more drops and we can command the very blood in your veins."

Nicole screamed inside her head, anger burning her eyes. Then the low moan of massive hinges flexing chilled her.

"We believe you were looking for him," a voice among the Council said, and her legs turned her around.

There were four figures in the doorway across the hall, just black human shapes with the light from the corridor behind them, one standing a head and shoulders taller than the others, but she knew their names.

A sickening epiphany stopped her heart as the Council spoke again.

"We only require Raiden's presence tonight."

"The rest of you can wait outside."

Three of the four were thrown back like leaves in a sudden gale that slammed the door shut behind Raiden. His shape was lost in the darkness, but as the echo of the bang died away, she could hear his footsteps crossing the hall in a calm, steady approach.

Turn around, Raiden, she thought. *Don't do this,* she pleaded to the hands pulling her strings.

"Welcome, Raiden."

He appeared, stepping out of the shadows into the pool of light around the Council. Nicole's heart clenched. Her lungs strained as she inhaled to their limit and exhaled at her own command, but she could not yet claim her voice.

Shit. No. Damn it! The floor rumbled. All she had were her burning eyes and her lungs shuddering with every breath. A frantic pounding against the doors across the hall mimicked the heart in her chest. The Council's control was a fiery grip that until now had drowned out the heat of her own magic churning inside her, bubbling up to the surface.

"Will you show her mercy? A quick end would be much easier for her."

Her heart felt like it was tearing in two. This was how they would do it, tormenting her to the limit of her sanity. The building trembled around them. *Oh no.*

Raiden never took his eyes off Nicole's. His response to the Council's sick invitation was to drop his sword in front of him in defiance. They moved her. Her body bent down, reaching for the sword. Her desperate resistance had little effect, only halting her muscles for a split second at a time. When her body straightened up, her right hand had the hilt. Her left hand pulled the scabbard off the blade and dropped it. The blade rang through the silence as the scabbard clattered against the floor.

Her grip trembled with the tension between the Council's control and her effort to release it. *I will not,* she glowered, and the polished floor fractured around her feet.

"Let's begin."

No, no, no! Nicole's whole arm trembled, but it still moved at the Council's command. The sword sliced through the air. Its sharp tip tore through Raiden's clothes and opened a red gash on his shoulder. He winced.

Her heart clenched in agony. They swung the sword again, and she watched the blade part the fabric and skin on Raiden's thigh, then his abdomen, his chest, each time cutting just deep enough to make another smiling red mouth that laughed at her, dripping blood.

Stop. Stop! Raiden stood there and took every strike, cringing, wincing, maintaining his gaze. Did he see her struggle to resist in every swing? The next swing was aimed at his face, and he leaned away only slightly. The blade caught his cheek.

"Can you hold out longer than she can, Raiden? No one can bleed forever."

Nicole clenched her jaw, and her fury shuddered through her. She could feel her magic swelling like a trapped storm, threatening to tear its way free.

"Whose misery do we end first?"

Nicole's arm raised the sword, and her body took a step forward to land a blow that would cut him down. A scream expanded in her lungs, and her arm shook with the war between the Council's control and her own.

The tension snapped, and her rage ripped through her vocal cords as she jerked her body around, hurling the sword at them. The blade flashed through the air and pierced one of the councilmen through his mouth, pinning his head to the high chair behind him. His last breath rattled through the blood in his airway. Those on either side of him jumped out of their seats, their confidence suddenly gone.

She lost herself, screaming at the top of her lungs, relishing the pain of that hoarse anger clawing up her throat. They tried to subdue her, locking her body down. A savage force crashed through her, igniting the Council's magic like fire traveling along the strings to their source, revealing who was at the other end. A councilwoman arched backward with a shriek of pain, dropping a crystal stained red with blood as her body blackened and curled like a piece of paper.

The blood magic that held her broke, and Nicole rolled her head and shoulders, releasing the tension from her neck and back. They were all out of their seats now, stumbling over themselves, tripping on their robes. That rage rolled up her throat in another scream. Her whole body shook. There was a kind of ecstasy in the pain, the bliss of owning her body once more and letting her fire crash through it, even if it threatened to consume her.

Raiden jumped away from an opening rift in the stone floor. He shouted Nicole's name, but she didn't seem to hear him. The pillars lining the hall shuddered. The walls trembled. The earth rumbled. The ceiling cracked.

Nicole's scream echoed through the hall, warbling through the waves of magic rolling off her. Each one hit him with a heat he felt could cauterize his wounds. It didn't just wash over him; it crashed *through* him, scrambling his thoughts, distorting his vision, burning down to his bones.

He picked himself up, squinting to correct his focus. The Council's practiced calm was nowhere to be found. They fell over themselves with expressions of terror twisting their faces. Two tried to flicker away, but their bodies fell dead to the floor only feet from the bench, one slipping into a growing crevice that split the crescent bench in two.

Nicole's hands were balled into fists, blood seeping through her fingers and dripping to the floor. An unseen force seized the remaining figures trembling upon the high bench. Their bodies all twisted with a violent jerk. The sound of snapping spines and breaking bones made him cringe as he watched the Council receive justice for their actions—swift deaths far better than they deserved after what the people of Cantis and all the fera had suffered.

The last councilman's body fell limp, but Nicole's rage did not die with them.

"Nicole!" he cried through the rumbling of marble around them.

Her arms folded up against her chest as her back contracted, bending her spine backward to its limit. The floor continued to fracture and rip apart. The Council's crescent bench buckled and split, tumbling down to the pit below. The ceiling began to crumble, great pieces falling down around them.

The ground opened up beneath Nicole, but she did not fall. She remained suspended there, lost in the storm. He stumbled forward between the growing rifts in the floor that spread out from Nicole like a starburst. The floor beneath him shuddered and fractured. He jumped across the gap as it crumbled and landed hard on the narrow bridge across the expanding darkness below.

He crept closer, resisting the current of energy swirling around her. The floor grew narrower as he went, and at the end of the broken floor he had to reach for her, leaning out over the abyss to take her hand. The contact sent a shock of energy through him, but he did not release her. The expression on her face was a grimace of pain, anger, sorrow, and solitude. He would not leave her to that.

He pulled her into his arms, away from the gaping black mouth below her, prepared for whatever came next.

"Nicole, are you still with me?"

Through the torrent of anguish in her body, she thought she felt the secure embrace of arms around her, and through the ringing in her ears, she thought she heard a familiar voice. In the back of her mind, she realized Raiden was still there, that she wasn't alone. In the midst of her berserk fit of rage, after seeing the person he had loved change into something monstrous, he was willing to stay.

It was a rope dropped into her abyss. If she took it, if she climbed out, she would have to face the reality of what she had done. She would have to decide *what* she was and *who* she was after all this. She would have to face a world where there were more enemies coming for her.

If she pulled herself out, she would have another fight coming, more pain and anger, more sorrow and fear. She could emerge from this darkness if she chose, but did she deserve to return to the family and friends who believed she wasn't a monster—her dad, Mitchell, Anthony, Frances, Ryleigh and Ashley, Roxanne, Raiden, Gordan, Keren, Fen and Asi? This agony, this black abyss around her, this was what a monster deserved.

She couldn't take back what she had done, and she didn't regret it. But was there a way back from this place? She didn't know whether she deserved them, but she knew she wanted to see them all. Her father, her brothers, her friends—if she didn't climb out of this darkness, she would never see them again, never get to thank them for believing she *was* the person she wanted to be. Maybe she could still be that person.

Raiden braced himself, clinging to Nicole in anticipation of the fate he had seen in more than one vision, but her tense body relaxed against him. The floor ceased quaking. After the ceiling finished crumbling and crashing to the remnants of the floor, silence fell.

He realized his lungs were frozen around his last breath of air, and he let it go with a sigh. A gentle, warm hum of magic spread through him like a balm, and he felt his wounds close.

"Nicole?" he murmured in her ear.

She nodded her head against him.

He sighed again, his body sagging with relief as he squeezed her a little harder, not ready to let go. Against his wishes he set her down on her feet and released her.

She straightened up and looked around. Her eyes filled with terrible awe at the sight of the destruction. "Jeez," she murmured.

At the other end of what remained of the hall, the doors burst open with a deafening bang, erupting into a rain of glittering, gilded splinters. In the doorway the man who had helped Raiden get through the court entrance flicked his gun and let the single massive cartridge fall from the chamber to the floor.

"You're welcome," he said to Caeruleus, Loak, and Leone, who were all standing around him in amazement.

"Let's get the hell out of here," Nicole said, taking Raiden by the hand and leading the way across the wedge of floor left between two crevices.

Everyone in the doorway gaped at the sight of the hall as the pair walked toward them. Raiden glanced down at Nicole, who cringed at their expressions.

"Well done," said the man with the gun with boisterous approval.

"Thanks, Andrus," Nicole answered with no enthusiasm at all. She sounded more ashamed than anything.

Caeruleus, Loak, and Leone still wore expressions of disbelief. Raiden's gaze lingered on his father, who stepped forward and, to his surprise, caught *Nicole* in his arms.

"Thank you for bringing him back," he said as he let her go.

Nicole answered with a visibly strained smile. Her gaze shifted to Raiden, and he tried to smile back.

They all turned their backs on the shredded remains of the Council's great hall and wandered across the central corridor to the court entrance. Beyond the arch of the entrance there wasn't much left of the court building. Outside, every column had toppled, every wall crumbled. The slope of marble around the hill had been fractured and broken, some pieces now lying at the bottom of the hill.

The bodies of casualties from the rebels' attack lay around them, rebels and court agents alike, but it was clear from the silence that everyone had fled the fight when the courts had begun to collapse. Except for one man who stood looking up at them from atop a pile of broken marble at the bottom of the slope.

Raiden's heart seized and lurched into a furious cadence of warning. He knew precisely who the man was. Venarius.

"Uh, is everyone else seeing that?" Andrus asked, gawking up a column of white light slicing upward through the sky from the land to the stars.

"Yeah," Nicole answered, looking up at the sky with the same expression of curious awe as the rest of them.

Raiden looked as well, noting that the beacon stood to the northeast. A pulse of light rolled out from the origin of the column, rushing over the city and washing over them where they stood in a flash. Seconds later a warm, tingling breeze followed.

"What was that?" Nicole asked, turning to him.

"I—uh …" His thoughts lurched back to Venarius, but Raiden could not find him where he had been standing only moments ago. "I don't know," he said, bringing his gaze back to her and noticing a key hanging from her neck.

Then he realized she was looking at his chest with a curious expression. She raised her hand and lifted a key that was hanging against his chest, turning it between her fingers with quizzical eyes. He lifted the key that hung from her neck as well, and she looked down, seeing it for the first time.

Then she looked up at him, her eyes wide with dreadful realization.

"Oh no," she murmured.

Raiden swallowed the lump in his throat, and they looked to the column of light in the night, beckoning them toward the heart of Veil.

CPSIA information can be obtained
at www.ICGtesting.com
Printed in the USA
FSOW01n1348160218
44677FS